PT

Praise for *New York Times* bestselling author Diana Palmer

"Palmer proves that love and passion can be found even in the most dangerous situations."
—*Publishers Weekly* on *Untamed*

"You just can't do better than a Diana Palmer story to make your heart lighter and smile brighter."
—*Fresh Fiction* on *Wyoming Rugged*

"Diana Palmer is a mesmerizing storyteller who captures the essence of what a romance should be."
—*Affaire de Coeur*

"The popular Palmer has penned another winning novel, a perfect blend of romance and suspense."
—*Booklist* on *Lawman*

"Diana Palmer's characters leap off the page. She captures their emotions and scars beautifully and makes them come alive for readers."
—*RT Book Reviews* on *Lawless*

NEW YORK TIMES BESTSELLING AUTHOR

DIANA PALMER

MONTANA PROTECTOR

Previously published as *Diamond in the Rough* and *Will of Steel*

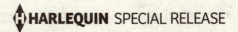

HARLEQUIN SPECIAL RELEASE

HARLEQUIN® SPECIAL RELEASE

ISBN-13: 978-1-335-47693-7

Montana Protector

Copyright © 2021 by Harlequin Books S.A.

Diamond in the Rough
First published in 2009. This edition published in 2021.
Copyright © 2009 by Diana Palmer

Will of Steel
First published in 2010. This edition published in 2021.
Copyright © 2010 by Diana Palmer

For questions and comments about the quality of this book, please contact us at CustomerService@Harlequin.com.

Harlequin Enterprises ULC
22 Adelaide St. West, 40th Floor
Toronto, Ontario M5H 4E3, Canada
www.Harlequin.com

Printed in Lithuania

MIX
Paper from responsible sources
FSC® C021394

CONTENTS

A prolific author of more than one hundred books, **Diana Palmer** got her start as a newspaper reporter. A *New York Times* bestselling author and voted one of the top ten romance writers in America, she has a gift for telling the most sensual tales with charm and humor. Diana lives with her family in Cornelia, Georgia. Visit her website at dianapalmer.com.

Books by Diana Palmer

Long, Tall Texans

Fearless
Heartless
Dangerous
Merciless
Courageous
Protector
Invincible
Untamed
Defender
Undaunted

The Wyoming Men

Wyoming Tough
Wyoming Fierce
Wyoming Bold
Wyoming Strong
Wyoming Rugged
Wyoming Brave

Visit the Author Profile page
at Harlequin.com for more titles.

DIAMOND IN THE ROUGH

For my friend Nancy C.,
who came all the way from Indiana just to meet me.
Thanks for the beautiful cowboy quilt, Nancy—
I'll never forget you!

And thanks to all of you on my bulletin board
at my website, including Nancy and Amy,
who spent hours of their precious free time making me
a compendium of all the families in Jacobsville, Texas!
Now, guys, maybe I can make fewer mistakes
when I write about them! Love you all.

CHAPTER ONE

THE LITTLE TOWN, Hollister, wasn't much bigger than Medicine Ridge, Montana, where John Callister and his brother Gil had a huge ranch. But they'd decided that it wasn't wise to confine their whole livelihood to one area. They needed to branch out a little, maybe try something different. On the main ranch, they ran a purebred bull and breeding operation with state-of-the-art science. John and Gil had decided to try something new here in Hollister, Montana; a ranch which would deal specifically in young purebred sale bulls, using the latest technology to breed for specific traits like low calving weight, lean conformation, and high weight gain ratio, among others. In addition, they were going to try new growth programs that combined specific organic grasses with mixed protein and grains to improve their production.

In the depressed economy, tailor-made beef cattle would cater to the discerning organic beef consumer. Gil and John didn't run beef cattle, but their champion bulls were bred to appeal to ranchers who did. It was a highly competitive field, especially with production costs going sky-high. Cattlemen could no longer depend on random breeding programs left up to nature. These days, progeny resulted from tailored genetics. It was a high-tech sort of agriculture. Gil and John had pioneered some of the newer computer-based programs that yielded high profits coupled with less waste-ful producer strategies.

For example, Gil had heard about a program that used methane gas from cattle waste to produce energy to run ranch equipment. The initial expense for the hardware had been high, but it was already producing results. Much of the electricity used to light the barns and power the ranch equipment was due to the new technology. Any surplus energy could be sold back to the electric company. The brothers had also installed solar panels to heat water in the main house and run hydraulic equipment in the breed-ing barn and the stockyard. One of the larger agricultural magazines had featured an article about their latest inno-vations. Gil's photo, and that of his daughters and his new wife, had graced the pages of the trade publication. John had been at a cattle show and missed the photo shoot. He didn't mind. He'd never been one to court publicity. Nor was Gil. But they wouldn't miss a chance to advertise their genetically superior cattle.

John usually traveled to show the cattle. But he was get-ting tired of spending his life on the road. Now that Gil had married Kasie, the brothers' former assistant, and the small girls from Gil's first marriage, Bess and Jenny, were in school, John was feeling lonelier than ever, and more rest-less. Not that he'd had a yen for Kasie, but Gil's remarriage made him aware of the passing of time. He wasn't getting any younger; he was in his thirties. The traveling was be-ginning to wear on him. Although he dated infrequently, he'd never found a woman he wanted to keep. He was also feeling like a fifth wheel at the family ranch.

So he'd volunteered to come up to Hollister to rebuild this small, dilapidated cattle ranch that he and Gil had pur-chased and see if an injection of capital and new blood stock and high-tech innovation could bring it from bankruptcy to a higher status in the world of purebred cattle.

The house, which John had only seen from aerial photos, was a wreck. No maintenance had been done on it for years by its elderly owner. He'd had to let most of his full-time cowboys go when the market fell, and he wasn't able to keep up with the demands of the job with the part-timers he retained. Fences got broken, cattle escaped, the well went dry, the barn burned down and, finally, the owner decided to cut his losses. He'd offered the ranch for sale, as-is, and the Callister brothers had bought it from him. The old man had gone back East to live with a daughter.

Now John had a firsthand look at the monumental task facing him. He'd have to hire new cowboys, build a barn as well as a stable, spend a few thousand making the house livable, sink a well, restring the fences, buy equipment, set up the methane-based power production plant... He groaned at the thought of it. The ranch in Medicine Ridge was state-of-the-art. This was medieval, by comparison. It was going to take longer than a month or two. This was a job that would take many months. And all that work had to be done before any cattle could be brought onto the place. What had seemed like a pleasant hobby in the beginning now looked like it would become a career.

There were two horses in a corral with a lean-to for protection from the weather, all that remained of the old man's Appaloosas. The remuda, or string of working ranch horses, had been sold off long ago. The remaining part-time cowboys told John that they'd brought their own mounts with them to work, while there was still a herd of cattle on the place. But the old man had sold off all his stock and let the part-timers go before he sold the ranch. Lucky, John thought, that he'd been able to track them down and offer them full-time jobs again. They were eager for the work. The men all lived within a radius of a few miles. If John had to wait on replacing the ranch's horses, the men could bring their own to work temporarily while John restocked the place.

He planned to rebuild and restock quickly. Something would have to be done about a barn. A place for newborn calves and sick cattle was his first priority. That, and the house. He was sleeping on the floor in a sleeping bag, heating water on a camp stove for shaving and bathing in the creek. Thank God, he thought, that it was spring and not winter. Food was purchased in the town's only café, where he had two meals a day. He ate sandwiches for lunch, purchased from a cooler in the convenience store/gas station at the edge of town. It was rough living for a man who was used to five-star hotels and the best food money could buy. But it was his choice, he reminded himself.

He drove into town in a mid-level priced pickup truck. No use advertising that he was wealthy. Prices would skyrocket, since he wasn't on friendly terms with anyone here. He'd only met the cowboys. The people in town didn't even know his name yet.

The obvious place to start, he reasoned, was the feed store. It sold ranch supplies including tack. The owner might know where he could find a reputable builder.

He pulled up at the front door and strode in. The place was dusty and not well-kept. There seemed to be only one employee, a slight woman with short, wavy dark hair and a pert figure, wearing a knit pullover with worn jeans and boots.

She was sorting bridles but she looked up when he approached. Like many old-time cowboys, he was sporting boots with spurs that jingled when he walked. He was also wearing an old Colt .45 in a holster slung low on his hip under the open denim shirt he was wearing with jeans and a black T-shirt. It was wild country, this part of Montana, and he wasn't going out on the range without some way of protecting himself from potential predators.

The young woman stared at him in an odd, fixed way. He didn't realize that he had the looks that would have been expected in a motion picture star. His blond hair, under the wide-brimmed cowboy hat, had a sheen like gold, and his handsome face was very attractive. He had the tall, elegant body of a rider, lean and fit and muscular without exaggerated lines.

"What the hell are you doing?" came a gruff, angry voice from the back. "I told you to go bring in those new sacks of feed before the rain ruins them, not play with the tack! Get your lazy butt moving, girl!"

The woman flushed, looking frightened. "Yes, sir," she said at once, and jumped up to do what he'd told her to.

John didn't like the way the man spoke to her and approached the man with a deadpan expression, only his blue eyes sparkling with temper.

The man, overweight and half-bald, older than John, turned as he approached. "Something I can do for you?" he asked in a bored tone, as if he didn't care whether he got the business or not.

"You the owner?" John asked him.

The man glared. "The manager. Tarleton. Bill Tarleton."

John tilted his hat back. "I need to find someone who can build a barn."

The manager's eyebrows arched. His eyes slid over John's worn jeans and boots and inexpensive clothing. He laughed. His expression was an insult. "You own a ranch around here?" he asked in disbelief.

John fought back his temper. "My boss does," he said, in an impulsive moment. "He's hiring. He just bought the Bradbury place out on Chambers Road."

"That old place?" Tarleton made a face. "Hell, it's a wreck! Bradbury just sat on his butt and let the place go to hell. Nobody understood why. He had some good cattle years ago, cattlemen came from as far away as Oklahoma and Kansas to buy his stock."

"He got old," John said.

"I guess. A barn, you say." He pursed his lips. "Well, Jackson Hewett has a construction business. He builds houses. Fancy houses, some of them. I reckon he could build a barn. He lives just outside town, over by the old train station. He's in the local telephone directory."

"I'm obliged," John said.

"Your boss...he'll be needing feed and tack, I guess?" Tarleton added.

John nodded.

"If I don't have it on hand, I can order it."

"I'll keep that in mind. I need something right now, though—a good tool kit."

"Sassy!" he yelled. "The man wants a tool kit! Bring one of the boxes from that new line we started stocking!"

"Yes, sir!" There was the sound of scrambling boots.

"She ain't much help," the manager grumbled. "Misses work sometimes. Got a mother with cancer and a little sister, six, that the mother adopted. I guess she'll end up alone, just her and the kid."

"Does the mother get government help?" John asked, curious.

"Not much," Tarleton scoffed. "They say she never did much except sit with sick folk, even before she got the cancer. Sassy's bringing in the only money they got. The old man took off years ago with another woman. Just left. At least they got a house. Ain't much of one, but it's a roof over their heads. The mother got it in the divorce settlement."

John felt a pang when he noticed the girl tugging a heavy toolbox. She looked as if she was barely able to lift a bridle.

"Here, I'll take that," John said, trying to sound nonchalant. He took it from her hands and set it on the counter, popping it open. His eyebrows lifted as he examined the tools. "Nice."

"Expensive, too, but it's worth it," Tarleton told him.

"Boss wants to set up an account in his own name, but I'll pay cash for this," John said, pulling out his wallet. "He gave me pocket money for essentials."

Tarleton's eyes got bigger as John started peeling off twenty-dollar bills. "Okay. What name do I put on the account?"

"Callister," John told him without batting an eyelash. "Gil Callister."

"Hey, I've heard of him," Tartleton said at once, giving John a bad moment. "He's got a huge ranch down in Medicine Ridge."

"That's the one," John said. "Ever seen him?"

"Who, me?" The older man laughed. "I don't run in those circles, no, sir. We're just country folk here, not millionaires."

John felt a little less worried. It would be to his advantage if the locals didn't know who he really was. Not yet, anyway. Since he was having to give up cattle shows for the foreseeable future, there wasn't much chance that his face would be gracing any trade papers. It might be nice, he pondered, to be accepted as an ordinary man for once. His wealth seemed to draw opportunists, especially feminine ones. He could enjoy playing the part of a cowboy for a change.

"No problem with opening an account here, then, if we put some money down first as a credit?" John asked.

"No problem at all." Tarleton grinned. "I'll start that account right now. You tell Mr. Callister anything he needs, I can get for him!"

"I'll tell him."

"And your name…?" the manager asked.

"John," he replied. "John Taggert."

Taggert was his middle name. His maternal grandfather, a pioneer in South Dakota, had that name.

"Taggert." The manager shook his head. "Never heard that one."

John smiled. "It's not famous."

The young woman was still standing beside the counter. John handed her the bills to pay for the toolbox. She worked the cash register and counted out his change.

"Thanks," John said, smiling at her.

She smiled back at him, shyly. Her green eyes were warm and soft. "You're welcome."

"Get back to work," Tarleton told her.

"Yes, sir." She turned and went back to the bags on the loading platform.

John frowned. "Isn't she too slight to be hefting bags that size?"

"It goes with the job," Tarleton said defensively. "I had a strong teenage boy working for me, but his parents moved to Billings and he had to go along. She was all I could get. She swore she could do the job. So I'm letting her."

"I guess she's stronger than she looks," John remarked, but he didn't like it.

Tarleton nodded absently. He was putting Gil Callister's name in his ledger.

"I'll be back," John told him as he picked up the toolbox.

Tarleton nodded again.

John glanced at the young woman, who was straining over a heavy bag, and walked out of the store with a scowl on his face.

He paused. He didn't know why. He glanced back into the store and saw the manager standing on the loading platform, watching the girl lift the feed sacks. It wasn't the look a manager should be giving an employee. John's eyes narrowed. He was going to do something about that.

ONE OF THE older cowboys, Chad Dean by name, was waiting for him at the house when he brought in the toolbox.

"Say, that's a nice one," he told the other man. "Your boss must be stinking rich."

"He is," John mused. "Pays good, too."

The cowboy chuckled. "That would be nice, getting a paycheck that I could feed my kids on. I couldn't move my family to another town without giving up land that belonged to my grandfather, so I toughed it out. It's been rough, what with food prices and gas going through the roof."

"You'll get your regular check plus travel expenses," John told him. "We'll pay for the gas if we have to send you anywhere to pick up things."

"That's damned considerate."

"If you work hard, your wages will go up."

"We'll all work hard," Dean promised solemnly. "We're just happy to have jobs."

John pursed his lips. "Do you know a girl named Sassy? Works for Tarleton in the feed store?"

"Yeah," Dean replied tersely. "He's married, and he

makes passes at Sassy. She needs that job. Her mama's dying. There's a six-year-old kid lives with them, too, and Sassy has to take care of her. I don't know how in hell she manages on what she gets paid. All that, and having to put up with Tarleton's harassment, too. My wife told her she should call the law and report him. She won't. She says she can't afford to lose the position. Town's so small, she'd never get hired again. Tarleton would make sure of it, just for spite, if she quit."

John nodded. His eyes narrowed thoughtfully. "I expect things will get easier for her," he predicted.

"Do you? Wish I did. She's a sweet kid. Always doing things for other people." He smiled. "My son had his appendix out. It was Sassy who saw what it was, long before we did. He was in the feed store when he got sick. She called the doctor. He looked over my Mark and agreed it was appendicitis. Doc drove the boy over to Billings to the hospital. Sassy went to see him. God knows how she got there. Her old beat-up vehicle would never make it as far as Billings. Hitched a ride with Carl Parks, I expect. He's in his seventies, but he watches out for Sassy and her mother. Good old fellow."

John nodded. "Sounds like it." He hesitated. "How old is the girl?"

"Eighteen or nineteen, I guess. Just out of high school."

"I figured that." John was disappointed. He didn't understand why. "Okay, here's what we're going to do about those fences temporarily…"

IN THE NEXT two days, John did some amateur detective work. He phoned a private detective who worked for the Callisters on business deals and put him on the Tarleton man. It didn't take him long to report back.

The feed store manager had been allowed to resign from a job in Billings for unknown reasons, but the detective found one other employee who said it was sexual harassment of an employee. He wasn't charged with anything. He'd moved here, to Hollister, with his family when the owner of the feed store, a man named Jake McGuire, advertised in a trade paper for someone to manage it for him. Apparently Tarleton had been the only applicant and McGuire was desperate. Tarleton got the job.

"This McGuire," John asked over his cell phone, "how old is he?"

"In his thirties," came the reply. "Everyone I spoke to about him said that he's a decent sort."

"In other words, he doesn't have a clue that Tarleton's hassling the girl."

"That would be my guess."

John's eyes twinkled. "Do you suppose McGuire would like to sell that business?"

There was a chuckle. "He's losing money hand over fist on that place. Two of the people I spoke to said he'd almost give it away to get rid of it."

"Thanks," John said. "That answers my question. Can you get me McGuire's telephone number?"

"Already did. Here it is."

John wrote it down. The next morning, he put in a call to McGuire Enterprises in Billings.

"I'm looking to buy a business in a town called Hollister," John said after he'd introduced himself. "Someone said you might know the owner of the local feed store."

"The feed store?" McGuire replied. "You want to buy it?" He sounded astonished.

"I might," John said. "If the price is right."

There was a pause. "Okay, here's the deal. That business

was started by my father over forty years ago. I inherited it when he died. I don't really want to sell it."

"It's going bankrupt," John replied.

There was another pause. "Yeah, I know," came the disgusted reply. "I had to put in a new manager there, and he didn't come cheap. I had to move him and his wife from Billings down here." He sighed. "I'm between a rock and a hard place. I own several businesses, and I don't have the time to manage them myself. That particular one has sentimental value. The manager just went to work. There's a chance he can pull it out of the red."

"There's a better chance that he's going to get you involved in a major lawsuit."

"What? What for?"

"For one thing, he was let go from his last job for sexual harassment, or that's what we turned up on a background check. He's up to his old tricks in Hollister, this time with a young girl just out of high school that he hired to work for him."

"Good Lord! He came with excellent references!"

"He might have them," John said. "But it wouldn't surprise me if that wasn't the first time he lost a job for the same reason. He was giving the girl the eye when I was in there. There's local gossip that the woman may sue if your manager doesn't lay off her. There goes your bottom line," he added dryly.

"Well, that's what you get when you're desperate for personnel," McGuire said wearily. "I couldn't find anybody else who'd take the job. I can't fire him without proper cause, and I just paid to move him there! What a hell of a mess!"

"You don't want to sell the business. Okay. How about leasing it to us? We'll fire Tarleton on the grounds that we're leasing the business, put in a manager of our own, and you'll make money. We'll have you in the black in two months."

"And just who is 'we'?" McGuire wanted to know.

"My brother and I. We're ranchers."

"But why would you want to lease a feed store in the middle of nowhere?"

"Because we just bought the Bradbury place. We're going to rebuild the house, add a stable and a barn, and we're going to raise purebred young bulls on the place. The feed store is going to do a lot of business when we start adding personnel to the outfit."

"Old man Bradbury and my father were best friends," McGuire reminisced. "He was a fine rancher, a nice gentleman. His health failed and the business failed with him. It's nice to know it will be a working ranch again."

"It's good land. We'll make it pay."

"What did you say your name was?"

"Callister," John told him. "My brother and I have a sizable spread over in Medicine Ridge."

"Those Callisters? My God, your holdings are worth millions!"

"At least." John chuckled.

There was a soft whistle. "Well, if you're going to keep me in orders, I suppose I'd be willing to lease the place to you."

"And the manager?"

"I just moved him there." McGuire groaned again.

"We'll pay to move him back to Billings and give him two weeks' severance pay," John said. "I will not agree to let him stay on," he added firmly.

"He may sue."

"Let him," John replied tersely. "If he tries it, I'll make it my life's work to see that any skeleton in his past is brought into the light of day. You can tell him that."

"I'll tell him."

"If you'll give me your attorney's name and number, I'll have our legal department contact him," John said. "I think we'll get along."

There was a deep chuckle. "So do I."

"There's one other matter."

"Yes?"

John hesitated. "I'm going to be working on the place myself, but I don't want anyone local to know who I am. I'll be known as the ranch foreman—Taggert by name. Got that?"

There was a chuckle. "Keeping it low-key, I see. Sure. I won't blow your cover."

"Especially to Tarleton and his employee," John emphasized.

"No problem. I'll tell him your boss phoned me."

"I'm much obliged."

"Before we settle this deal, do you have someone in mind who can take over the business in two weeks if I put Tarleton on notice?"

"Indeed I do," John replied. "He's a retired corporate executive who's bored stiff with retirement. Mind like a steel trap. He could make money in the desert."

"Sounds like just the man for the job."

"I'll have him up here in two weeks."

"That's a deal, then."

"We'll talk again when the paperwork goes through."

"Yes."

John hung up. He felt better about the girl. Not that he expected Tarleton to quit the job without a fight. He hoped the threat of uncovering any past sins would work the magic. The thought of Sassy being bothered by that would-be Casanova was disturbing.

HE PHONED THE architect and asked him to come over to the ranch the following day to discuss drawing up plans for a stable and a barn. He hired an electrician to rewire the house and do the work in the new construction. He employed six new cowboys and an engineer. He set up payroll for everyone he'd hired through the corporation's main offices in Medicine Ridge, and went about getting fences repaired and wells drilled. He also phoned Gil and had him send down a team of engineers to start construction on solar panels to help provide electricity for the operation.

Once those plans were underway, he made a trip into Hollister to see how things were going at the feed store. His detective had managed to dig up three other harassment charges against Tarleton from places he'd lived before he moved to Montana in the first place. There were no convictions, sadly. But the charges might be enough. Armed with that information, he wasn't uncomfortable having words with the man, if it was necessary.

And it seemed that it would be. The minute he walked in the door, he knew there was going to be trouble. Tarleton was talking to a customer, but he gave John a glare that spoke volumes. He finished his business with the customer and waited until he left. Then he walked up to John belligerently.

"What the hell did your employer tell my boss?" he demanded furiously. "He said he was leasing the store, but only on the condition that I didn't go with the deal!"

"Not my problem," John said, and his pale eyes glittered. "It was my boss's decision."

"Well, he's got no reason to fire me!" Tarleton said, his

round face flushing. "I'll sue the hell out of him, and your damned boss, too!"

John stepped closer to the man and leaned down, emphasizing his advantage in height. "You're welcome. My boss will go to the local district attorney in Billings and turn over the court documents from your last sexual harassment charge."

Tarleton's face went from red to white in seconds. He froze in place. "He'll...what?" he asked weakly.

John's chiseled lips pulled up into a cold smile. "And I'll encourage your hired girl over there—" he indicated her with a jerk of his head "—to come clean about the way you've treated her as well. I think she could be persuaded to bring charges."

Tarleton's arrogance vanished. He looked hunted.

"Take my advice," John said quietly. "Get out while you still have time. My boss won't hesitate a second. He has two daughters of his own." His eyes narrowed menacingly. "One of our ranch hands back home tried to wrestle a temporary maid down in the hay out in our barn. He's serving three to five for sexual assault." John smiled. "We have a firm of attorneys on retainer."

"We?" Tarleton stammered.

"I'm a managerial employee of the ranch. The ranch is a corporation," John replied smoothly.

Tarleton's teeth clenched. "So I guess I'm fired."

"I guess you volunteered to resign," John corrected. "That gets you moved back to Billings at the ranch's expense, and gives you severance pay. It also spares you lawsuits and other...difficulties."

The older man weighed his options. John could see his mind working. Tarleton gave John an arrogant look.

"What the hell," he said coldly. "I didn't want to live in this damned fly trap anyway!"

He turned on his heel and walked away. The girl, Sassy, was watching the byplay with open curiosity. John raised an eyebrow. She flushed and went back to work at once.

CHAPTER TWO

CASSANDRA PEALE TOLD herself that the intense conversation the new foreman of the Bradbury place was having with her boss didn't concern her. The foreman had made that clear with a lifted eyebrow and a haughty look. But there had been an obvious argument and both men had glanced at her while they were having it. She was worried. She couldn't afford to lose her job. Not when her mother, dying of lung cancer, and her mother's ward, Selene, who was only six, depended on what she brought home so desperately.

She gnawed on a fingernail. They were mostly all chewed off. Her mother was sixty-three, Cassandra, who everyone called Sassy, having been born very late in life. They'd had a ranch until her father had become infatuated with a young waitress at the local cafeteria. He'd left his family and run away with the woman, taking most of their savings with him. Without money to pay bills, Sassy's mother had been forced to sell the cattle and most of the land and let the cowboys go. One of them, little Selene's father, had gotten drunk out of desperation and ran his truck off into the river. They'd found him the next morning, dead, leaving Selene completely alone in the world.

My life, Sassy thought, *is a soap opera. It even has a villain.* She glanced covertly at Mr. Tarleton. All he needed was a black mustache and a gun. He'd made her working life hell. He knew she couldn't afford to quit. He was always bumping into her "accidentally," trying to handle her. She was sickened by his advances. She'd never even had a boyfriend. The school she'd gone to, in this tiny town, had been a one-room schoolhouse with all ages included and one teacher. There had only been two boys her own age and three girls including Sassy. The other girls were pretty. So Sassy had never been asked out at all. Once, when she was in her senior year of high school, a teacher's visiting nephew had been kind to her, but her mother had been violently opposed to letting her go on a date with a man she didn't know well. It hadn't mattered. Sassy had never felt those things her romance novels spoke of in such enticing and heart-pattering terms. She'd never even been kissed in a grown-up way. Her only sexual experience—if you could call it that—was being physically harassed by that repulsive would-be Romeo standing behind the counter.

She finished dusting the shelves and wished fate would present her with a nice, handsome boss who was single and found her fascinating. She'd have gladly settled for the Bradbury place's new ramrod. But he didn't look as if he found anything about her that attracted him. In fact, he was ignoring her. Story of my life, she thought as she put aside the dust cloth. It was just as well. She had two dependents and no spare time. Where would she fit a man into her desperate life?

"Missed a spot."

She whirled. She flushed as she looked way up into dancing blue eyes. "W...what?"

John chuckled. The women in his world were sophisticated and full of easy wisdom. This little violet was as unaffected by the modern world as the store she worked in. He was entranced by her.

"I said you missed a spot." He leaned closer. "It was a joke."

"Oh." She laughed shyly, glancing at the shelf. "I might have missed several, I guess. I can't reach high and there's no ladder."

He smiled. "There's always a soapbox."

"No, no," she returned with a smile. "If I get on one of those, I have to give a political speech."

He groaned. "Don't say those words," he said. "If I have to hear one more speech about the economy, I'm having my ears plugged."

"It does get a little irritating, doesn't it?" she asked. "We don't watch the news as much since the television got hit by lightning. The color's gone whacky. I have to think it's a happy benefit of a sad accident."

His eyebrows arched. "Why don't you get a new TV?"

She glowered at him. "Because the hardware store doesn't have a fifty-cent one," she said.

It took a minute for that to sink in. John, who thought nothing of laying down his gold card for the newest wide-screened TV, hadn't realized that even a small set was beyond the means of many lower-income people.

He grimaced. "Sorry," he said. "I guess I've gotten too used to just picking up anything I like in stores."

"They don't arrest you for that?" she asked with a straight face, but her twinkling eyes gave her away.

He laughed. "Not so far. I meant," he added, thinking fast, "that my boss pays me a princely salary for my organizational skills."

"He must, if you can afford a new TV." She sighed. "I don't suppose he needs a professional duster?"

"We could ask him."

She shook her head. "I'd rather work here, in a job I do

know." She glanced with apprehension at her boss, who was glaring toward the two of them. "I'd better get back to work before he fires me."

"He can't."

She blinked. "He can't what?"

"Fire you," he said quietly. "He's being replaced in two weeks by a new manager."

Her heart stopped. She felt sick. "Oh, dear."

"You won't convince me that you'll miss him," John said curtly.

She bit a fingernail that was already almost gone. "It's not that. A new manager might not want me to work here anymore…"

"He will."

She frowned. "How can you know that?"

He pursed his lips. "Because the new manager works for my boss, and my boss said not to change employees."

Her face started to relax. "Really?"

"Really."

She glanced again at Tarleton and felt uncomfortable at the furious glare he gave her. "Oh, dear, did somebody say something to your boss about him…about him being forward with me?" she asked worriedly.

"They might have," he said noncommittally.

"He'll get even," she said under her breath. "He's that sort. He told a lie on a customer who was rude to him, about the man's wife. She almost lost her job over it."

John felt his blood rise. "All you have to do is get through the next two weeks," he told her. "If you have a problem with him, any problem, you can call me. I don't care when or what time." He started to pull out his wallet and give her his business card, until he realized that she thought he was pretending to be hired help, not the big boss. "Have you got a pen and paper?" he asked instead.

"In fact, I do," she replied. She moved behind the counter, tore a piece of brown paper off a roll, and picked up a marking pencil. She handed them to him.

He wrote down the number and handed it back to her. "Don't be afraid of him," he added curtly. "He's in enough trouble without making more for himself with you."

"What sort of trouble is he in?" she wanted to know.

"I can't tell you. It's confidential. Let's just say that he'd better keep his nose clean. Now. I need a few more things." He brought out a list and handed it to her. She smiled and went off to fill the order for him.

He took the opportunity to have a last word with Tarleton.

"I hear you have a penchant for getting even with people who cross you," John said. His eyes narrowed and began to glitter. "For the record, if you touch that girl, or if you even try to cause problems for her of any sort, you'll have to deal with me. I don't threaten people with lawsuits. I get even." The way he said it, added to his even, unblinking glare, had backed down braver men than this middle-aged molester.

Tarleton tried to put on a brave front, but the man's demeanor was unsettling. Taggert was younger than Tarleton and powerfully muscled for all his slimness. He didn't look like a man who ever walked away from a fight.

"I wouldn't touch her in a blind fit," the older man said haughtily. "I just want to work out my notice and get the hell back to Billings, where people are more civilized."

"Good idea," John replied. "Follow it."

He turned on his heel and went back to Sassy.

She looked even more nervous now. "What did you say to him?" she asked uneasily, because Tarleton looked at her as if he'd like her served up on a spit.

"Nothing of any consequence," he said easily, and he gave her a tender smile. "Got my order ready?"

"Most of it," she said, obviously trying to get her mind back to business. "But we don't carry any of this grass seed you want. It would be special order." She leaned forward. "The hardware store can get it for you at a lower price, but I think we will be faster."

He grinned. "The price won't matter to my boss," he assured her. "But speed will. He's experimenting with all sorts of forage grasses. He's looking for better ways to increase weight without resorting to artificial means. He thinks the older grasses have more nutritional benefit than the hybrids being sowed today."

"He's likely right," she replied. "Organic methods are gaining in popularity. You wouldn't believe how many organic gardeners we have locally."

"That reminds me. I need some insecticidal soap for the beans we're planting."

She hesitated.

He cocked his head. His eyes twinkled. "You want to tell me something, but you're not sure that you should."

She laughed. "I guess so. One of our organic gardeners gave up on it for beans. She says it works nicely for tomatoes and cucumbers, but you need something with a little more kick for beans and corn. She learned that the hard way." She grimaced. "So did I. I lost my first corn planting to corn borers and my beans to bean beetles. I was determined not to go the harsh pesticide route."

"Okay. Sell me something harsh, then." He chuckled.

She blushed faintly before she pulled a sack of powerful but environmentally safe insecticide off the shelf and put it on the counter.

Tarleton was watching the byplay with cold, angry eyes.

So she liked that interfering cowboy, did she? It made him furious. He was certain that the new foreman of the Bradbury ranch had talked to someone about him and passed the information on to McGuire, who owned this feed store. The cowboy was arrogant for a man who worked for wages, even for a big outfit like the Callisters'. He was losing his job for the second time in six months and it would look bad on his record. His wife was already sick of the moving. She might leave him. It was a bad day for him when John Taggert walked into his store. He hoped the man fell in a well and drowned, he really did.

His small eyes lingered on Sassy's trim figure. She really made him hot. She wasn't the sort to put up much of a fight, and that man Taggert couldn't watch her day and night. Tarleton smiled coldly to himself. If he was losing his job anyway, he didn't have much to lose. Might as well get something out of the experience. Something sweet.

SASSY WENT HOME worn-out at the end of the week. Tarleton had found more work than ever before for her to do, mostly involving physical labor. He was rearranging all the shelves with the heaviest items like chicken mash and hog feed and horse feed and dog food in twenty-five and fifty-pound bags. Sassy could press fifty pounds, but she was slight and not overly muscular. It was uncomfortable. She wished she could complain to someone, but if she did, it would only make things worse. Tarleton was getting even because he'd been fired. He watched her even more than he had before, and it was in a way that made her very uncomfortable.

Her mother was lying on the sofa watching television when Sassy got home. Little Selene was playing with some cut-outs. Her soft gray eyes lit up and she jumped up and ran to Sassy, to be picked up and kissed.

"How's my girl?" Sassy asked, kissing the soft little cheek.

"I been playing with Dora the Explorer, Sassy!" the little blonde girl told her. "Pippa gave them to me at school!"

Pippa was the daughter of a teacher and her husband, a sweet child who always shared her playthings with Selene. It wasn't a local secret that Sassy could barely afford to dress the child out of the local thrift shop, much less buy her toys.

"That was sweet of her," Sassy said with genuine delight.

"She says I can keep these ones," the child added.

Sassy put her down. "Show them to me."

Her mother smiled wearily up at her. "Pippa's mother is a darling."

Sassy bent and kissed her mother's brow. "So is mine."

Mrs. Peale patted her cheek. "Bad day?" she added.

Sassy only smiled. She didn't trouble her parent with her daily woes. The older woman had enough worries of her own. The cancer was temporarily in remission, but the doctor had warned that it wouldn't last. Despite all the hype about new treatments and cures, cancer was a formidable adversary. Especially when the victim was Mrs. Peale's age.

"I've had worse," Sassy told her. "What about pancakes and bacon for supper?" she asked.

"Sassy, we had pancakes last night," Selene complained as she showed her cut-outs to the woman.

"I know, baby," Sassy said, bending to kiss her gently. "We have what we can afford. It isn't much."

Selene grimaced. "I'm sorry. I like pancakes," she added apologetically.

"I wish we could have something better," Sassy said. "If there was a better-paying job going, you can bet I'd be applying for it."

Mrs. Peale looked sad. "I'd hoped we could send you to college. At least to a vocational school. Instead we've caused you to land in a dead-end job."

Sassy struck a pose. "I'll have you know I'm expecting a prince any day," she informed them. "He'll come riding up on a white horse with an enormous bouquet of orchids, brandishing a wedding ring."

"If ever a girl deserved one," Mrs. Peale said softly, "it's you, my baby."

Sassy grinned. "When I find him, we'll get you one of those super hospital beds with a dozen controls so you can sit up properly when you want to. And we'll get Selene the prettiest dresses and shoes in the world. And then, we'll buy a new television set, one that doesn't have green people," she added, wincing at the color on the old console TV.

Pipe dreams. But dreams were all she had. She looked at her companions, her family, and decided that she'd much rather have them than a lot of money. But a little money, she sighed mentally, certainly would help their situation. Prince Charming existed, sadly, only in fairy tales.

THE ARCHITECT HAD his plans ready for the big barn. John approved them and told the man to get to work. Within a few days, building materials started arriving, carried in by enormous trucks: lumber, steel, sand, concrete blocks, bricks, and mortar and other construction equipment. The project was worth several million dollars, and it created a stir locally, because it meant jobs for many people who were having to commute to Billings to get work. They piled onto the old Bradbury place to fill out job applications.

John grinned at the enthusiasm of the new workers. He'd started the job with misgivings, wondering if it was sane to expect to find dozens of laborers in such a small, economically depressed area. But he'd been pleasantly surprised. He had new men from surrounding counties lining up for available jobs, experienced workers at that. He began to be optimistic.

He was doing a lot of business with the local feed store, but his presence was required on-site while the construction was in the early stages. He'd learned the hard way that it wasn't wise to leave someone in charge without making sure they understood what was required during every step.

He felt a little guilty that he hadn't been back to check that Sassy hadn't had problems with Tarleton, who only had two days left before he was being replaced. The new manager, Buck Mannheim, was already in town, renting a room from a local widow while he familiarized himself with the business. Tarleton, he told John, wasn't making it easy for him to do that. The man was resentful, surly, and he was making Sassy do some incredibly hard and unnecessary tasks at the store. Buck would have put a stop to it, but he felt he had no real authority until Tartleton's two weeks were officially up. He didn't want them to get sued.

As if that weasel would dare sue them, John thought angrily. But he didn't feel right putting Buck in the line of fire. The older man had come up here as a favor to Gil to run the business, not to go toe-to-toe with a belligerent soon-to-be-ex-employee.

"I'll handle this," John told the older man. "I need to stop by the post office anyway and get some more stamps."

"I don't understand why any man would treat a child so brutally," Buck said. "She's such a nice girl."

"She's not a girl, Buck," John replied.

"She's just nineteen," Buck replied, smiling. "I have a granddaughter that age."

John felt uncomfortable. "She seems older."

"She's got some mileage on her. A lot of responsibility. She needs help. That child her mother adopted goes to school in pitiful clothes. I know that most of the money they have is spent for utilities." He shook his head. "Hell of a shame. Her mother's little check is all used up for medicine that she has to take to stay alive."

John felt guilty that he hadn't looked into that situation. He hadn't planned to get himself involved with his employees' problems, and Sassy wasn't technically even that, but it seemed there was nobody else in a position to help. He frowned. "You said Sassy's mother was divorced? Where's her husband? Couldn't he help? Even if Sassy's not young enough for child support, she's still his child. She shouldn't have to be the breadwinner."

"He ran off with a young woman. Just walked out the door and left. He's never so much as called or written in the years he's been gone, since the divorce," Buck said knowledgeably. "From what I hear, he was a good husband and father. He couldn't fight his infatuation for the waitress." He shrugged. "That's life."

"I hope the waitress hangs him out to dry," John muttered darkly. "Sassy should never have been landed with so much responsibility at her age."

"She handles it well, though," Buck said admiringly. "She's the nicest young woman I've met in a long time. She earns her paycheck."

"She shouldn't be having to press weights to do that," John replied. "I got too wrapped up in my barn to keep an eye on her. I'll make up for it today."

"Good for you. She could use a friend."

JOHN WALKED IN and noticed immediately how quiet it was. The front of the store was deserted. It was midmorning and there were no customers. He scowled, wondering why Sassy wasn't at the counter.

He heard odd sounds coming from the tack room. He walked toward it until he heard a muffled scream. Then he ran.

The door was locked from the inside. John didn't need ESP to know why. He stood back, shot a hard kick with his heavy work boots right at the door handle, and the door almost splintered as it flew open.

Tarleton had backed Sassy into an aisle of cattle feed sacks. He had her in a tight embrace and he was trying his best to kiss her. His hands were on her body. She was fighting for her life, panting and struggling against the fat man's body.

"You sorry, son of a…!" John muttered as he caught the man by his collar and literally threw him off Sassy.

She was gasping for air. Her blouse was torn and her shoulders ached. The stupid man had probably meant to do a lot more than just kiss her, if he'd locked the door, but thanks to John he'd barely gotten to first base. She almost gagged at the memory of his fat, wet mouth on her lips. She dragged her hand over it.

"You okay?" John asked her curtly.

"Yes, thanks to you," she said heavily. She glared at the man behind him.

He turned back toward Tarleton, who was flushed at being caught red-handed. He backed away from the homicidal maniac who started toward him with an expression that could have stopped traffic.

"Don't you…touch me…!" Tarleton protested.

John caught him by the shirtfront, drew back his huge fist, and knocked the man backward out into the feed store.

He went after him, blue eyes sparking like live electricity, his big fists clenched, his jaw set rigidly.

"What the...?" came a shocked exclamation from the front of the store.

A man in a business suit was standing there, eyebrows arching.

"Mr....McGuire!" Tarleton exclaimed as he sat up on the floor holding his jaw. "He attacked me! Call the police!"

John glanced at McGuire with blazing eyes. "There's a nineteen-year-old girl in the tack room with her shirt torn off. Do you need me to draw you a picture?" he demanded.

McGuire's gray eyes suddenly took on the same sheen as John's. He moved forward with an odd, gliding step and stopped just in front of Tarleton. He whipped out his cell phone and pressed in a number.

"Get over here," he said into the receiver. "Tarleton just assaulted Sassy! That's right. No, I won't let him leave!" He hung up. "You should have cut your losses and gone back to Billings," he told the white-faced man on the floor, nursing his jaw. "Now, you're going to jail."

"She teased me into doing it!" Tarleton cried. "It's her fault."

John glanced at McGuire. "And I'm a green elf." He turned on his heel and went back to the tack room to see about Sassy.

She was crying, leaning against an expensive saddle, trying to pull the ripped bits of her blouse closed. Her ratty little faded bra was visible where it was torn. It was embarrassing for her to have John see it.

John stripped off the cotton shirt he was wearing over his black undershirt. He eased her hands away from her tattered blouse and guided her arms into the shirt, still warm from his body. He buttoned it up to the very top. Then he framed her wet face in his big hands and lifted it to his eyes. He winced. Her pretty little mouth was bruised. Her hair was mussed. Her eyes were red and swollen.

"Me and my damned barn," he muttered. "I'm sorry."

"For…what?" she sobbed. "It's not your fault."

"It is. I should have expected something like this."

The bell on the door jangled and heavy footsteps echoed on wood. There was conversation, punctuated by Tarleton's protests.

A tall, lean man in a police uniform and a cowboy hat knocked at the tack door and walked in. John turned, letting him see Sassy's condition.

The newcomer's thin mouth set in hard lines and his black eyes flashed fire. "You all right, Sassy?" he asked in a deep, bass voice.

"Yes, sir, Chief Graves," she said brokenly. "He assaulted me!" she accused, glaring at Tarleton. "He came up behind me while I was putting up stock and grabbed me. He kissed me and tore my blouse…" Her voice broke. "He tried to… to…!" She couldn't choke the word out.

Graves looked as formidable as John. "He won't ever touch you again. I promise. I need you to come down to my office when you feel a little better and give me a statement. Will you do that?"

"Yes, sir."

He glanced at John. "You hit him?" he asked, jerking his head toward the man still sitting on the floor outside the room.

"Damned straight I did," John returned belligerently. His blue eyes were still flashing with bad temper.

Chief Graves glanced at Sassy and winced.

The police chief turned and went back out into the other

room. He caught Tarleton by his arm, jerked him to his feet, and handcuffed him while he read him his rights.

"You let me go!" Tarleton shouted. "I'm going back to Billings in two days. She lied! I never touched her that way! I just kissed her! She teased me! She set me up! She lured me into the back! And I want that damned cowboy arrested for assault! He hit me!"

Nobody was paying him the least bit of attention. In fact, the police chief looked as if he'd like to hit Tarleton himself. The would-be Romeo shut up.

"I'm never hiring anybody else as long as I live," McGuire told the police chief. "Not after this."

"Sometimes snakes don't look like snakes," Graves told him. "We all make mistakes. Come along, Mr. Tarleton. We've got a nice new jail cell for you to live in while we get ready to put you on trial."

"She's lying!" Tarleton raged, red-faced.

Sassy came out with John just behind her. The ordeal she'd endured was so evident that the men in the room grimaced at just the sight of her. Tarleton stopped shouting. He looked sick.

"Do you mind if I say something to him, Chief Graves?" Sassy asked in a hoarse tone.

"Not at all," the lawman replied.

She walked right up to Tarleton, with her green eyes glittering with fury, drew back her hand, and slapped him across the mouth as hard as she could. Then she turned on her heel and walked right back to the counter, picked up a sack of seed corn that she'd left there when the assault began, and went back to work.

The three men glanced from her to Tarleton. Their faces wore identical expressions.

"I'll get a good lawyer!" Tarleton said belligerently.

"You'll need one," John promised him, in a tone so full of menace that the man backed up a step.

"I'll sue you for assault!" he said from a safe distance.

"The corporation's attorneys will enjoy the exercise," John told him coolly. "One of them graduated from Harvard and spent ten years as a prosecutor specializing in sexual assault cases."

Tarleton looked sick.

Graves took him outside. John turned to McGuire.

The man in the suit rammed his hands into his pockets and grimaced. "I'll never be able to make that up to her," he said heavily.

"You might tell her that you recommended raising her salary," John replied.

"It's the least I can do," he agreed. "That new employee of yours—Buck Mannheim. He's sharp. I learned things I didn't know just from spending a half hour talking to him. He'll be an asset."

John nodded. "He retired too soon. Sixty-five is no great age these days." He glanced toward the back, where Sassy was moving things around. "She needs to see a doctor."

"Did Tarleton…?" McGuire asked with real concern.

John shook his head. "But he would have. If I'd walked in just ten minutes later…" His face paled as he considered what would have happened. "Damn that man! And damn me! I should have realized he'd do something stupid to get even with her!"

"I should have realized, too," McGuire added. "Don't beat yourself to death. There's enough guilt to share. Dr. Bates is next to the post office. He has a clinic. He'll see her. He's been her family physician since she was a child."

"I'll take her right over there."

Sassy looked up when John approached her. She looked

terrible, but she wasn't crying anymore. "Is he going to fire me?" she asked John.

"What in hell for? Almost getting raped?" he exclaimed. "Of course not. In fact, he's mentioned getting you a raise. But right now, he wants you to go to the doctor and get checked out."

"I'm okay," she protested. "And I have a lot of work to do."

"It can wait."

"I don't want to see Dr. Bates," she said.

He shrugged. "We're both pretty determined about this. I don't really think you'd like the way I deal with mutiny."

She stuck her hands on her slender hips. "Oh, yeah? Let's see how you deal with it."

He smiled gently. Before she could say another word, he picked her up very carefully in his arms and walked out the front door with her.

CHAPTER THREE

"YOU CAN'T DO THIS!" Sassy raged as he walked across the street with her, to the amusement of an early morning shopper in front of the small grocery store there.

"You won't go voluntarily," he said philosophically. He looked down at her and smiled gently. "You're very pretty."

She stopped arguing. "W…what?"

"Pretty," he repeated. "You've got grit, too." He chuckled. "I wish you'd half-closed that hand you hit Tarleton with, though." The smile faded. "That piece of work should be thrown into the county detention center wearing a sign telling what he tried to do. They'd pick him up in a shoebox."

Her small hands clung to his neck. "I didn't see it coming," she said, still in shock. "He pushed me into the tack room and locked the door. Before I could save myself, he pushed me back into the feed sacks and started kissing me and trying to get inside my blouse. I never thought I'd get away. I was fighting for all I was worth…" She swallowed hard. "Men are so strong. Even pudgy men like him."

"*I* should have seen it coming," he said, staring ahead with a set face. "A man like that doesn't go quietly. This could have been a worse tragedy than it already is."

"You saved me."

He looked down into her wide, green eyes. "Yes. I saved you."

She managed a wan smile. "Funny. I was just talking to Selene—my mother's little ward—about how Prince Charming would come and rescue me one day." She studied his handsome face. "You do look a little like a prince."

His eyebrow jerked. "I'm too tall. Princes are short and stubby, mostly."

"Not in movies."

"Ah, but that's not real life."

"I'll bet you don't know a single prince."

She'd have been amazed. He and his brother had rubbed elbows with crowned heads of Europe any number of times. But he couldn't admit that, of course.

"You could be right," he agreed easily.

He paused to open the door with one hand with Sassy propped on his knee. He walked into the doctor's waiting room with Sassy still in his arms and went up to the receptionist behind her glass panel. "We have something of an emergency," he said in a low tone. "She's been the victim of an assault."

"Sassy?" the receptionist, a girl Sassy had gone to school with, exclaimed. She took one look at the other girl's face and went running to open the door for John. "Bring her right in here. I'll get Dr. Bates!"

THE DOCTOR WAS a crusty old fellow, but he had a kind heart and it showed. He asked John to wait outside while he examined his patient. John stood in the hall, staring at anatomy charts that lined the painted concrete block wall. In no time the sliding door opened and he motioned John back into the cubicle.

"Except for some understandable emotional upset, and a few light bruises, she's not too hurt." The doctor glowered. "I would like to see her assailant spend a few months or, better yet, a few years, in jail, however."

"So would I," John told him, looking glittery and full of outrage. "In fact, I'm going to work on that."

The doctor nodded. "Good man." He turned to Sassy, who was quiet and pale now that her ordeal was over and reaction was starting to set in. "I'm going to inject you with a tranquilizer. I want you to go home and lie down for the rest of the day." He held up a hand when she protested. "Selene's in school and your mother will cope. It's not a choice, Sassy," he added as he leaned out of the cubicle and motioned to a nurse.

While he was giving the nurse orders, John stuck his hands in his jeans pockets and looked down at Sassy. She had grit and style, for a woman raised in the back of beyond. He admired her. She was pretty, too, although she didn't seem to realize it. The only real obstacle was her age. His face closed up as he faced the fact that she was years too young for him, even without their social separation. It was a pity. He'd been looking all his adult life for a woman he could like as well as desire. This sweet little firecracker was unique in his female acquaintances. He admired her.

His pale eyes narrowed on Sassy's petite form. She had a very sexy body. He loved those small, pert breasts under the cotton shirt. He thought how bruised they probably were from Tarleton's fingers and he wanted to hurt the man all over again. He knew she was untouched. Tarleton had stolen her first intimacy from her, soiled it, demeaned it. He wished he'd wiped the floor with the man before the police chief came.

Sassy saw his expression and felt uneasy. Did he think she was responsible for the attack? She winced. He didn't know her at all. Maybe he thought she had led Tarleton on. Maybe he thought she'd deserved what happened to her.

She lowered her eyes in shame. The doctor came back in with a syringe, rolled up her sleeve, swiped her upper arm with alcohol on a cotton ball, and injected her. Sassy didn't even flinch. She rolled down her sleeve.

"Go home before that takes effect, or you'll be lying down in the road." The doctor chuckled. He glanced at John. "Can you…?"

"Of course," John said. He smiled at Sassy, allaying her fears about his attitude. "Come on, sprout. I'll drive you."

"There's new stock that has to be put up in the store," she began to protest.

"It will still be waiting for you in the morning. If Buck needs help, I'll send some of my men into town to help him."

"But it's not your responsibility…"

"My boss has leased the feed store," he reminded her. "That makes it my responsibility."

"All right, then." She turned her head and smiled at the doctor. "Thanks."

He smiled back. "Don't you let this take over your life," he lectured her. "If you have any problems, you come back. I know a psychologist who works for the school system. She also takes private patients. I'll send you to her."

"I'll be okay."

John nodded at the doctor and followed Sassy out the door.

ON THE WAY HOME, Sassy sat beside him in the cab of the big pickup truck, fascinated by all the high-tech gadgets. "This is really nice," she remarked, smoothing over the leather dash. "I've never seen so many buttons and switches in a truck before."

He smiled lazily, steering with his left hand while he toyed with a loaded key ring in one of the big cup holders. "We use computers for roundup and GPS to move cattle and men around."

"What about your phone?" she asked, looking for it.

He indicated the second cup holder, where his cell phone was sitting. "The car is Bluetooth enabled," he explained. "So the phone is hands free. I can shorthand the call by saying the first or last name of the person I want to call. The phone does the rest. I can access the internet and my email through it, as well."

"Wow," she said softly. "It's like the *Starship Enterprise*, isn't it?"

He could have told her that his brand-new Jaguar XF was more in that line, with controls that rose out of the console when the push-button ignition was activated, backup cameras, heated seats and steering wheel, and a supercharged V8 engine. But he wasn't supposed to be able to afford that sort of luxury, so he kept his mouth shut.

"This must be a very expensive truck," she murmured.

He grinned. "Just mid-range. Our bosses don't skimp on tools," he told her. "That includes working equipment for assistant feed store managers as well."

She looked at him through green eyes that were becoming drowsy. "Are we getting a new assistant manager to go with Mr. Mannheim?" she asked.

"Sure. You," he added, glancing at her warmly. "That goes with a rise in salary, by the way."

Her breath caught. "Do you mean it?"

"Of course."

"Wow," she said softly, foreseeing better used appli-

ances for the little house and some new clothes for Selene.
"I can't believe it!"

"You will." He frowned. "Don't fall over in your seat."

She laughed breathily. "I think the shot's taking effect." She moved and grimaced, absently touching her
small breasts. "A few bruises are coming out, too. He really was rough."

His face hardened. "I hate knowing he manhandled
you," he said through his teeth. "I wish I'd come to the
store sooner."

"You saved me, just the same," she replied. She smiled.
"My hero."

He chuckled. "Not me, lady," he mused. "I'm just a
working cowboy."

"There's nothing wrong with honest labor and hard
work," she told him. "I could never wrap my mind around
some rich, fancy man with a string of women following
him around. I like cowboys just fine."

The words stung. He was living a lie, and he shouldn't
have started out with her on the wrong foot. She was an
honest person. She'd never trust him again if she realized
how he was fooling her. He should tell her who he really
was. He glanced in her direction. She was asleep. Her head
was resting against the glass, her chest softly pulsing as
she breathed.

Well, there would be another time, he assured himself.
She'd had enough shocks for one day.

HE PULLED UP in her driveway, went around and lifted her
out of the truck in his arms. He paused at the foot of the
steps to look down at her sleeping face. He curled her close
against his chest, loving her soft weight, loving the sweet
face pressed against his shirt pocket. He carried her up

the steps easily, knocked perfunctorily at the door, and opened it.

Her mother, Mrs. Peale, was sitting in a chair in her bathrobe, watching the news. She cried out when she saw her daughter.

"What happened to her?" she exclaimed, starting to rise.

"She's all right," he said at once. "The doctor sedated her. Can I put her down somewhere, and I'll explain."

"Yes. Her bedroom…is this way." She got to her feet, panting with the effort.

"Mrs. Peale, you just point the way and sit back down," he said gently. "You don't need to strain yourself."

Her kind face beamed in a smile. "You're a nice young man. It's the first door on the left. Her bedroom."

"I'll be right back."

He carried Sassy into the bare little room and pulled back the worn blue chenille coverlet that was on the twin bed where she slept. Everything was spotless, if old. He lifted Sassy's head onto the pillow, tugged off her boots, and drew the coverlet over her, patting it down at her waist.

She breathed regularly. His eyes went from her disheveled, wavy dark hair to the slight rise of her firm breasts under the shirt he'd loaned her, down her narrow waist and slender hips and long legs. She was attractive. But it was more than a physical attractiveness. She was like a warm fireplace on a cold day. He smiled at his own imagery, took one last look at her pretty, sleeping face, went out, and pulled the door gently closed behind him.

Mrs. Peale was watching for him, worried. "What happened to her?" she asked at once.

He sat down on the sofa next to her chair. "Yes. She's had a rough day…"

"That Tarleton man!" Mrs. Peale exclaimed furiously. "It was him, wasn't it?"

His eyebrows arched at her unexpected perception. "Yes," he agreed slowly. "But how would you know...?"

"He's been creeping around her ever since McGuire hired him," she said in her soft, raspy voice. She paused to get her breath. Her green eyes, so much like Sassy's, were sparking with temper. "She came home crying one day because he touched her in a way he shouldn't have, and she couldn't stop him. He thought it was funny."

John's usually placid face was drawn with anger as he listened.

Mrs. Peale noticed that, and the caring way he'd brought her daughter home. "Forgive me for being blunt, but who are you?" she asked gently.

He smiled. "Sorry. I'm John... Taggert," he added, almost caught off guard enough to tell the truth. "My boss bought the old Bradbury place, and I'm his foreman."

"That place." She seemed surprised. "You know, it's haunted."

His eyebrows arched. "Excuse me?"

"I'm sorry. I shouldn't have said that...!" she began quickly.

"No. Please. I'd like to know," he said, reassuring her. "I collect folk tales."

She laughed breathily. "I guess it could be called that. You see, it began a long time ago when Hart Bradbury married his second cousin, Miss Blanche Henley. Her father hated the Bradburys and opposed the marriage, but Blanche ran away with Hart and got married to him anyway. Her father swore vengeance. One day, not long afterward, Hart came home from a long day gathering in strays, and found Blanche apparently in the arms of another man.

He threw her out of his house and made her go back home to her father."

"Don't tell me," John interrupted with a smile. "Her father set her up."

"That's exactly what he did, with one of his men. Blanche was inconsolable. She sat in her room and cried. She did no cooking and no housework and she stopped going anywhere. Her father was surprised, because he thought she'd take up her old responsibilities with no hesitation. When she didn't, he was stuck with no help in the house and a daughter who embarrassed him in front of his friends. He told her to go back to her husband if he'd have her.

"So she did. But Hart met her at the door and told her he'd never live with her again. She'd gone from him to another man, or so he thought. Blanche gave up. She walked right out the side porch onto that bridge beside the old barn, and threw herself off the top. Hart heard her scream and ran after her, but she hit her head on a boulder when she went down, and her body washed up on the shore. Hart knew then that she was innocent. He sent word to her father that she'd killed herself. Her father went rushing over to Hart's place. Hart was waiting for him, with a double-barreled shotgun. He gave the old man one barrel and saved the other for himself." She grimaced. "It was almost ninety years ago, but nobody's forgotten."

"But they call the ranch the Bradbury place, don't they?" John asked, puzzled.

Mrs. Peale smiled. "Hart had three brothers. One of them took over the property. That was the great-uncle of the Bradbury you bought the ranch from."

"Talk about tragedies that stick in the mind," John mused. "I'm glad I'm not superstitious."

"How is it that you ended up bringing my daughter home?" she wondered aloud.

"I walked into the tack room in time to save her from Tarleton," he replied simply. "She didn't want to go to the doctor, so I carried her across the street and into his office." He sighed. "I suppose gossips will feed on that story for a week."

Mrs. Peale laughed. She had to stop suddenly, because her weak lungs wouldn't permit much of it. "Sassy is very stubborn."

He nodded. "I noticed." He smiled. "But she's got grit."

"Will she be all right?" she asked, worried.

"The doctor said that, apart from some bruises, she will. Of course there's the trauma of the attack itself."

"We'll deal with that…if we have to," the old woman said quietly. She bit her lower lip. "Do you know about me?" she asked suddenly.

"Yes, I do," he replied.

Her thin face was drawn. "Sassy has nobody. My husband ran off and left me with Sassy still in school. I took in Selene when her father died while he was working for us, just after Sassy's father left. We have no living family. When I'm gone," she added slowly, "she won't have anybody at all."

"She'll be all right," John assured her quietly. "We've promoted her to assistant manager of the feed store. It comes with a raise in salary. And if she ever needs help, she'll get it. I promise."

She turned her head like a bird watching him. "You have an honest face," she said after a minute. "Thank you, Mr. Taggert."

He smiled. "She's sweet."

"Sweet and unworldly," she said heavily. "This is a good

place to raise children, but it doesn't give them much sense of modern society. She's a babe in the woods, in some ways."

"She'll be fine," he assured her. "Sassy may be naïve, but she has an excellent self-image and she's a strong woman. If you could have seen her swinging on Tarleton," he added on a chuckle, with admiration in his pale eyes.

"She hit him?" she exclaimed.

"She did," he replied. "I wish they'd given her five minutes alone with him. It might have cured him of ever wanting to force himself on another woman. Not," he added darkly, "that he's going to have the opportunity for a very long time. The police chief has him in jail pending arraignment. He'll be brought up on assault charges and, I assure you, he won't be running around town again."

"Mr. McGuire should never have hired him," she muttered.

"I can assure you that he knows that."

She bit her lip. "What if he gets a good lawyer and they turn him loose?"

"In that case," John chuckled, "we'll search and find enough evidence on crimes in his past to hang him out to dry. Whatever happens, he won't be a threat to Sassy ever again."

Mrs. Peale beamed. "Thank you for bringing her home."

"Do you have a telephone here?" he asked suddenly.

She hesitated. "Yes, of course."

He wondered at the hesitation, but not just then. "If you need anything, anything at all, you can call me." He pulled a pencil and pad out of his pocket, one he'd bought in town to list supplies, and wrote the ranch number on it. He handed it to Mrs. Peale. "Somebody will be around all the time."

"That's very kind of you," she said quietly.

"We help each other out back home," he told her. "That's what neighbors are for."

"Where is back home, Mr. Taggert?" she asked curiously.

"The Callisters we work for live at Medicine Ridge," he told her.

"Those people!" She caught her breath. "My goodness, everybody knows who they are. In fact, we had a man who used to work for them here in town."

John held his breath. "You did?"

"Of course, he moved on about a year ago," she added, and didn't see John relax. "He said they were the best bosses on earth and that he'd never have left if his wife hadn't insisted she had to be near her mother. Her mother was like me," she added sadly, "going downhill by the day. You can't blame a woman for feeling like that. I stayed with my own mother when she was dying." She looked up. "Are your parents still living?"

He smiled. "Yes, they are. I don't know them very well yet, but all of us are just beginning to get comfortable with each other."

"You were estranged?"

He nodded. "But not anymore. Can I do anything for you before I leave?"

"No, but thank you."

"I'll lock the door on my way out."

She smiled at him.

"I'll be out this way again," he said. "Tell Sassy she doesn't have to come in tomorrow unless she just wants to."

"She'll want to," Mrs. Peale said confidently. "In spite of that terrible man, she really likes her work."

"I like mine, too," John told her. He winked. "Good night."

"Good night, Mr. Taggert."

He drove back to the Bradbury place deep in thought. He wished he could make sure that Tarleton didn't get out of jail anytime soon. He was still worried. The man was vindictive. He'd assaulted Sassy for reporting his behavior. God knew what he'd do to her if he managed to get out of that jail. He'd have to talk to Chief Graves and see if there was some way to get his bond set sky-high.

THE WORK AT the ranch was coming along quickly. The framework for the barn was already up. Wiring and plumbing were in the early stages. A crew was starting to remodel the house. John had one bedroom as a priority. He was sick of using a sleeping bag on the floor.

He phoned Gil that night. "How are things going at home?" he asked.

Gil chuckled. "Bess brought a snake to the dinner table. You've never seen women run so fast!"

"I'll bet Kasie didn't run," he mused.

"Kasie ticked it under the chin and told Bess it was the prettiest garter snake she'd ever seen."

"Your new wife is a delight," John murmured.

"And you can stop right there," Gil muttered. "She's my wife. Don't you forget that."

John burst out laughing. "You can't possibly still be jealous of her now!"

"I can, too."

"I could bring her truckloads of flowers and hands full of diamonds, and she'd still pick you," John pointed out. "Love trumps material possessions. I'm just her brother-in-law now."

"Well, okay," Gil said after a minute. "How are the improvements coming along?"

"Slowly." John sighed. "I'm still using a sleeping bag on the hard floor. I've given them orders to finish my bedroom first. Meanwhile, I'm getting the barn put up. Oh, and I've leased us a feed store."

There was a pause. "Should I ask why?"

"The manager tried to assault a young woman who's working for the store. He's in jail."

"And you leased the store because…?"

John sighed. "The girl's mother is dying of lung cancer," he said heavily. "There's a young girl they took in when her father died…she's six. Sassy is the only one bringing in any money. I thought if she could be promoted to assistant manager, she might be able to pay her bills and buy a few new clothes for the little girl."

"Sassy, hmmm?"

John flushed at that knowing tone. "Listen, she's just a girl who works there."

"What does she look like?"

"She's slight. She has wavy, dark hair and green eyes and she's pretty when she smiles. When I pulled Tarleton off her, she walked up and slapped him as hard as she could. She's got grit."

"Tarleton would be the manager?"

"Yes," John said through his teeth. "The owner of the store, McGuire, hired him long distance and moved him here with his wife. Tarleton's lost at least one job for sexual harassment."

"Then why the hell did McGuire hire him?"

"He didn't know about the charges—there was never a conviction. He said he was desperate. Nobody wanted to work in this outback town."

"So who are we going to get to replace him?"

"Buck Mannheim."

"Good choice," Gil said. "Buck was dying of boredom after he retired. The store will be a challenge for him."

"He's a good manager. Sassy likes him already, and she knows every piece of merchandise on the place and the ordering system like the back of her hand. She keeps the place stocked."

"Is she all right?"

"A little bruised," John said. "I took her to the doctor and then drove her home. She slept all the way there."

"She didn't fuss about having the big boss carting her around?" Gil asked amusedly.

"Well, she doesn't know that I am the big boss," John returned.

"She what?"

John scowled. "Why does she have to know who I am?"

"You'll get in trouble if you start playing with the truth."

"I'm not playing with it. I'm just sidestepping it for a little while. I like having people take me at face value for a change. It's nice to be something more than a walking checkbook."

Gil cleared his throat. "Okay. It's your life. Let's just hope your decision doesn't come back to bite you down the line."

"It won't," John said confidently. "I mean, it isn't as if I'm planning anything permanent here. By the time I'm ready to come back to Medicine Ridge, it won't matter, anyway."

Gil changed the subject. But John wondered if there might not be some truth in what his big brother was saying. He hoped there wasn't. Surely it wasn't a bad thing to try to live a normal life for once. After all, he asked himself, how could it hurt?

CHAPTER FOUR

SASSY SETTLED IN as assistant manager of the feed store. Buck picked at her gently, teased her, and made her feel so much at home that it was like belonging to a family. During her second week back at work, she asked permission to bring Selene with her to work on the regular Saturday morning shift. Her mother had had a bad couple of days, she explained, and she wasn't well enough to watch Selene. Buck said it was all right.

But when John walked into the store and found a six-year-old child putting up stock, he wasn't pleased.

"This is a dangerous place for a kid," he told Sassy gently. "Even a bridle bit falling from the wall could injure her."

Sassy stopped and stared at him. "I hadn't thought about that."

"And there are the pesticides," he added. "Not that I think she'd put any in her mouth, but if she dropped one of those bags, it could fly up in her face." He frowned. "We had a little girl on the ranch back in Medicine Ridge who had to be transported to the emergency room when a bag of garden insecticide tore and she inhaled some of it."

"Oh, dear," Sassy said, worried.

"I don't mind her being here," John assured her. "But find her something to do at the counter. Don't let her wander around. Okay?"

She cocked her head at him. "You know a lot about kids."

He smiled. "I have nieces about Selene's age," he told her. "They can be a handful."

"You love them."

"Indeed I do," he replied, his eyes following Selene as she climbed up into a chair at the counter, wearing old but clean jeans and a T-shirt. "I've missed out on a family," he added quietly. "I never seemed to have time to slow down and think about permanent things."

"Why not?" she asked curiously.

His pale eyes searched hers quietly. "Pressure of work, I suppose," he said vaguely. "I wanted to make my mark in the world. Ambition and family life don't exactly mesh."

"Oh, I get it," she said, and smiled up at him. "You wanted to be something more than just a working cowboy."

His eyebrow jerked. "Something like that," he lied. The mark he meant was to have, with his brother, a purebred breeding herd that was known all over the world—a true benchmark of beef production that had its roots in Montana. The Callisters had attained that reputation, but John had sacrificed for it, spending his life on the move, going from one cattle show to another with the ranch's prize animals. The more awards their breeding bulls won, the more they could charge for their progeny.

"You're a foreman now," she said. "Could you get higher up than that?"

"Sure," he said, warming to the subject. He grinned. "We have several foremen, who handle everything from grain production to cattle production to AI," he added. "Above that, there's ranch management."

Her eyebrows drew together. "AI?" she queried. "What's that?"

If she'd been older and more sophisticated, he might have

teased her with the answer. As it was, he took the question at face value. "It's artificial breeding," he said gently. "We hire a man who comes out with the product and inseminates our cows and heifers."

She looked uncomfortable. "Oh."

He smiled. "It's part of ranch protocol," he said, his tone soft. "The old-fashioned way is hit or miss. In these hard times, we have to have a more reliable way of insuring progeny."

She smiled back shyly. "Thanks for not explaining it in a crude way," she said. "We had a rancher come in here a month ago who wanted a diaper for his female dog, who was in heat." She flushed a little. "He thought it was funny when I got uncomfortable at the way he talked about it."

His thumb hooked into his belt as he studied her. The comment made him want to find the rancher and have a long talk with him. "That sort of thing isn't tolerated on our spread," he said shortly. "We even have dress requirements for men and women. There's no sexual harassment, even in language."

She looked fascinated. "Really?"

"Really." He searched her eyes. "Sassy, you don't have to put up with any man talking to you in a way that embarrasses you. If a customer uses crude language, you go get Buck. If you can't find him, you call me."

"I never thought... I mean, it seemed to go with the job," she stammered. "Mr. Tarleton was worse than some of the customers. He used to try to guess the size of my...of my... well—" she shrugged, averting her eyes "—you know."

"Sadly, I do," he replied tersely. "Listen, you have to start standing up for yourself more. I know you're young, but you don't have to take being talked down to by men. Not in this job."

She rubbed an elbow and looked up at him like a curious little cat. "I was going to quit," she recalled, and laughed a little nervously. "I'd already talked to Mama about it. I thought even if I had to drive to Billings and back every day, I'd do it." She grimaced. "That was just before gas hit over four dollars a gallon." She sighed. "You'd have to be a millionaire to make that drive daily, now."

"I know," he said with heartfelt emotion. He and Gil had started giving their personnel a gas ration allowance in addition to their wages. "Which reminds me," he added with a smile, "we're adding gas mileage to the checks now. You won't have to worry about going bankrupt at the pump."

"That's so nice of you!"

He pursed his lips. "Of course. I am nice. It's one of my more sterling qualities. I mean, along with being debonair, a great conversationalist, and good at poker." He watched her reaction, smiling wickedly when she didn't quite get it. "Did I mention that dogs love me, too?"

She did get it then, and laughed shyly. "You're joking."

"Trying to."

She grinned at him. It made her green eyes light up, her face radiant. "You must have a lot of responsibility, considering how much work they're doing out at your ranch."

"Yes, I do," he admitted. "Most of it involves organization."

"That sounds very stressful," she replied, frowning. "I mean, a big ranch would have an awful lot of people to organize. I would think that you'd have almost no free time at all."

He didn't have much free time. But he couldn't tell her why. Actually the little bit of time he'd already spent here, even working, was something like a holiday, considering the load he carried when he was at home. He and Gil between them were overworked. They delegated responsibility where they could, but some decisions could only be made by the boss. "Well, it's still sort of a goal of mine," he hedged. "A man has to have a little ambition to be interesting." He studied her with pursed lips. "What sort of job goals do you have?"

She blinked, thinking. "I don't have any, really. I mean, I want to take care of Mama as long as I can. And I want to raise Selene and make sure she has a good education, and to save enough to help her go to college."

He frowned. Her goals were peripheral. They involved helping other people, not in advancing herself. He'd never considered the future welfare of anyone except himself—well, himself and Gil and the girls and, now, Kasie. But Sassy was very young to be so generous, even in her thoughts.

Young. She was nineteen. His frown deepened as he studied her youthful, faintly flushed little face. He found her very attractive. She had a big heart, a nice smile, a pretty figure, and she was smart, in a common-sense sort of way. But that age hit him right in the gut every time he considered her part in his life. He didn't dare become involved with her.

"What's wrong?" she asked perceptively.

He shifted from one big, booted foot to the other. "I just had a stray thought," he told her. He glanced at Selene. "You've got a lot of responsibilities for a woman your age," he added quietly.

She laughed softly. "Don't I know it!"

His eyes narrowed. "I guess it cramps your social life. With men, I mean," he added, hating himself because he was curious about the men in her life.

She laughed. "There are only a couple of men around

town who don't have wives or girlfriends, and I turn them off. One of them came right out and said I had too much baggage, even for a date."

His eyebrows arched. "And what did you say to that?"

"That I loved my mother and Selene and any man who got interested in me would have to take them on as well. That didn't go over big," she added with twinkling eyes. "So I've decided that I'm going to be like the Lone Ranger."

He blinked. "Masked and mysterious?"

"No!" she chuckled. "I mean, just me. Well, just me and my so-called dependents." She glanced toward Selene, who was quietly matching up seed packages from a box that had just arrived. Her eyes softened. "She's very smart. I can never sort things the way she can. She's patient and quiet, she never makes a fuss. I think she might grow up to be a scientist. She already has that sort of introspective personality, and she's careful in what she does."

"She thinks before she acts," he translated.

"Exactly. I tend to go rushing in without thinking about the consequences," she added with a laugh. "Not Selene. She's more analytical."

"Being impulsive isn't necessarily a bad thing," he remarked.

"It can be," she said. "But I'm working on that. Maybe in a few years, I'll learn to look before I leap." She glanced up at him. "How are things going out at the Bradbury place?"

"We've got the barn well underway already," he said. "The framework's done. Now we're up to our ears in roofers and plumbers and electricians."

"We only have a couple of each of those here in town," she pointed out, "and they're generally booked a week or two ahead except for emergencies."

He smiled. "We had to import some construction people

from Billings," he told her. "It's a big job. Simultaneously, they're trying to make improvements to the house and plan a stable. We've got fencing to replace, wells to bore, agricultural equipment to buy…it's a monumental job."

"Your boss," she said slowly, "must be filthy rich, if he can afford to do all that right now when we've got gas prices through the roof!"

"He is," he confided. "But the ranch will be self-sufficient when we're through. We're using solar panels and windmills for part of our power generation."

"We had a city lawyer buy land here about six years ago," she recalled. "He put in solar panels to heat his house and all sorts of fancy, energy-saving devices." She winced. "Poor guy."

"Poor guy?" he prompted when she didn't continue.

"He saw all these nature specials and thought grizzly bears were cute and cuddly," she said. "One came up into his backyard and he went out with a bag full of bread to feed to it."

"Oh, boy," he said slowly.

She nodded. "The bear ate all the bread and when he ran out, it started eating him. He did manage to get away finally by playing dead, but he lost the use of an arm and one eye." She shook her head. "He was a sad sight."

"Don't tell me," he said. "He was from back East."

She nodded. "Some big city. He'd never seen a real bear before, except in zoos and nature specials. He saw an old documentary on this guy who lived with bears and he thought anybody could make friends with them."

"Reminds me of a story I heard about a lady from D.C. who moved to Arizona. She saw a rattlesnake crawling across the road, so the story goes, and thought it was fascinating. She got out of her car and walked over to pet it."

"What happened to her?"

"An uncountable number of shots of antivenin," he said, "and two weeks in the hospital."

"Ouch."

"You know all those warning labels they have on food these days? They ought to put warning labels on animals." He held both hands up, as if holding a sign. "Warning: Most wild reptiles are not cute and cuddly and they will bite and can kill you. Or: Grizzly bears will eat bread, fruit, and some people."

She laughed at his expression. "I ran from a grizzly bear once and managed to get away."

"Fast, are you?"

"He was old and slow, and I was close to town. But I had great incentive," she agreed.

"I've never had to outrun anything," he recalled. "I did once pet a moose who came up to serenade one of our milk cows. He was friendly."

"Isn't that unusual?"

"It is. Most wild animals that will let you close enough to pet them are rabid. But this moose wasn't sick. He just had no fear of humans. I think maybe he was raised as a pet by people who were smart enough not to tell anybody."

"Because...?" she prompted.

"Well, it's against the law to make a pet of a wild animal in most places in the country," he explained. He smiled. "That moose loved corn."

"What happened to him?"

"He started charging other cattle to keep his favorite cow to himself, so we had to move him up farther into the mountains. He hasn't come back so far."

She grinned. "What if he does? Will you let him stay?"

He pursed his lips. "Sure! I plan to spray-paint him red, cut off his antlers, and tell people he's a French bull."

She burst out laughing at the absurd comment.

Selene came running up with a pad and pencil. "'Scuse me," she said politely to John. She turned to her sister. "There's a man on the telephone who wants you to order something for him."

Sassy chuckled. "I'll go right now and take it down. Selene, this is John Taggert. He's a ranch foreman."

Selene looked up at him and grinned. She was missing one front tooth, but she was cute. "When I grow up, I'm going to be a fighter pilot!"

His eyebrows arched. "You are?"

"Yup! This lady came by to see my mama. She's a nurse. Her daughter was a fighter pilot and now she flies big airplanes overseas!"

"Some role model," John remarked to Sassy, awed.

She laughed. "It's a brave new world."

"It is." He went down on one knee in front of Selene, so that her eyes could look into his. "And what sort of plane would you like to fly?" he teased, not taking her seriously.

She put a small hand on his broad shoulder. Her blue eyes were very wide and intent. "I like those F-22 Raptors," she said breathlessly. "Did you know they can supercruise?"

He was fascinated. He wasn't sure he even knew what sort of military airplane that was. His breath exhaled. "No," he confessed. "I didn't."

"There was this program on TV about how they're built. I think Raptors are just beautiful," she said with a dreamy expression.

"I hope you get to fly one," he told her.

She smiled. "I got to grow up, first, though," she told

him. She gasped. "Sassy!" she exclaimed. "That man's still on the phone!"

Sassy made a face. "I'm going, I'm going!"

"You coming back to see us again?" Selene asked John when he stood up.

He chuckled. "Thought I might."

"Okay!" She grinned and ran back to the counter, where Sassy was just picking up the phone.

John went to find Buck. It was a new world, indeed.

TARLETON WAS TAKEN before the circuit judge for his arraignment and formally charged with the assault on Sassy. He pleaded not guilty. He had a city lawyer who gave the local district attorney a haughty glance and requested that his client, who was blameless, be let out on his own recognizance in lieu of bail. The prosecutor argued that Tarleton was a flight risk.

The judge, after reviewing the charges, did agree to set bail. But he set it at fifty thousand dollars, drawing furious protests from the attorney and his client. With no ability to raise such an amount, even using a bail bondsman, Tarleton would have to wait it out in the county detention facility. It wasn't a prospect he viewed with pleasure.

Sassy heard about it and felt guilty. Mr. Tarleton, for all his flaws, had a wife who was surely not guilty of anything more than bad judgment in her choice of a husband. It seemed unfair that she would have to suffer along with the defendant.

She said so, to John, when he turned up at the store the end of the next week.

"His poor wife." She sighed. "It's so unkind to make her go through it with him."

"Would you rather let him walk?" he asked quietly. "Set

him free, so that he could do it to another young woman—
perhaps with more tragic results?"

She flushed. "No. Of course not."

He reached out and touched her cheek with the tips of
his fingers. "You have a big heart, Sassy," he said, his voice
very deep and soft. "Plenty of other people don't, and they
will use your own compassion against you."

She looked up curiously, tingling and breathless from
just the faint contact of his fingers with her skin. "I guess
some people are like that," she conceded. "But most people
are kind and don't want to hurt others."

He laughed coldly. "Do you think so?"

His expression was saying things that she could read
quite accurately. "Somebody hurt *you*," she guessed. Her
eyes held his. They had an odd, blank look in them. "A
woman. It was a long time ago. You never talk about it.
But you hold it inside, deep inside, and use it to keep the
world at a distance."

He scowled. "You don't know me," he said, defensive.

"I shouldn't," she agreed. Her green eyes seemed darker,
more piercing. "But I do."

"Don't tell me," he murmured with faint sarcasm, "you
can read minds."

She shook her head. "I can read wrinkles."

"Excuse me?"

"Your frown lines are deeper than your smile lines,"
she told him, not wanting to confess that her family had
the "second sight," in case he thought she was peculiar.
"It's a public smile. You leave it at the front door when
you go home."

His eyes narrowed on her face. He didn't speak. She was
incredibly perceptive for a woman her age.

She drew in a long breath. "Go ahead, say it. I need to

mind my own business. I do try to, but it bothers me to see other people so unhappy."

"I am not unhappy," he said belligerently. "I'm very happy!"

"If you say so."

He glowered at her. "Just because a woman threw me over, I'm not damaged goods."

"How did she throw you over?"

He hadn't talked about it for years, not even to Gil. In one sense he resented this young woman, this stranger, prying into his life. In another, it made him want to talk about it, to stop the festering wound of it from growing even larger inside him.

"She got engaged to me while she was living with a man down in Colorado."

She didn't speak. She just watched him, like a curious little cat, waiting.

He grimaced. "I was so crazy about her that I never suspected a thing. She'd go away for weekends with her girlfriend and I'd watch movies and do book work at home while she was away. One weekend I had nothing to do, so I drove over to Red Lodge, where she'd said she was checked into a motel so that she could go fly-fishing with her girlfriend." He sighed. "Red Lodge isn't so big that you can't find people in it, and it does a big business in tourism. Turned out, her friend was male, filthy rich, and they had a room together. She had the most surprised look on her face when they came downstairs and found me sitting in the lobby."

"What did she say?" she asked.

"Nothing. Not one thing. She bit her lip and pretended that she didn't know the man. He was furious, and I felt like a fool. I went back home. She called and tried to talk to me, but I hung up on her. Some things don't take a lot of explaining."

He didn't add that he'd also hired a private detective, much too late, to find out what he could about the woman. It hadn't been the first time she'd kept a string of wealthy admirers, and she'd taken one man for a quarter of a million dollars before he found her out. She'd been after John's money, all along; not himself. He wasn't as forthcoming as the millionaire she'd gone fly-fishing with, so she'd been working on the millionaire while she left John simmering on a back burner. As a result, she'd lost both men, which did serve her right. But the experience had made him bitter and suspicious of all women. He still thought they only wanted him for his money.

"The other guy, was he rich?" Sassy asked.

John's lips made a thin line. "Filthy rich."

She touched the front of his shirt with a shy, hesitant little hand. "I'm sorry about that," she told him. "But in a way, you're lucky that you aren't rich," she added.

"Why?"

"Well, you never have to worry if women like you for yourself or your wallet," she said innocently.

"There isn't much to like," he said absently, concentrating on the way she was touching him. She didn't even seem to be aware of it, but his body was rippling inside with the pleasure it gave him.

"You're kidding, right?" she asked. Her eyes laughed up into his. "You're very handsome. You stand up for people who can't take care of themselves. You like children. And dogs like you," she added mischievously, recalling one of his earlier quips. "Besides that, you must like animals, since you work around cattle."

While she was talking, the hand on his chest had been

joined by her other one, and they were flat on the broad, hard muscles, idly caressing. His body was beginning to respond to her touch in a profound way. His blue eyes became glittery with suppressed desire.

He caught her hands abruptly and moved them. "Don't do that," he said curtly, without thinking how it was going to affect her. He wanted to reach for her, slam her against him all the way up and down, and kiss that pretty mouth until he made it swell and moan under his lips.

She jerked back, appalled at her own boldness. "I'm sorry," she said at once, flushing. "I really am. I'm not used to men. I mean, I've never done that...excuse me!"

She turned and all but ran back down the aisle to the counter. When she got there, she jerked up the phone and called a customer to tell him his order was in. She'd already phoned him, and he hadn't answered, so she called again. It gave her something to do, so that John thought she was getting busy.

He muttered under his breath. Now he'd done it. He hadn't meant to make her feel brassy with that comment, but she was starting to get to him. He wanted her. She had warmth and compassion and an exciting little body, and she was getting under his skin. He needed a break.

He turned on his heel and walked out of the store. He should have gone back and apologized for being so abrupt, but he knew he'd never be able to explain himself without telling her the truth. He couldn't do that. She was years too young for him. He had to get out of town for a while.

HE LEFT BRADBURY'S former ranch foreman, Carl Baker, in charge of the place while he packed and went home to Medicine Ridge for the weekend.

It was a warm, happy homecoming. His big brother, Gil, met him at the door with a bear hug.

"Come on in," he said, chuckling. "We've missed you."

"Uncle John!"

Bess and Jenny, Gil's daughters by his first wife, came running down the hall to be picked up and cuddled and kissed.

"Oh, Uncle John, we missed you so much!" Bess, the eldest, cried, hugging him tightly around the neck.

"Yes, we did," Jenny seconded, kissing his bronzed cheek. "You can't stay away so long!"

"Did you bring us a present?" Bess asked.

He grinned. "Don't I always?" He laughed. "In the bag, next to my suitcase," he said, putting them down.

They ran to the bag, found the wrapped presents and literally tore the ribbons off to delve inside. There were two stuffed animals with bar codes that led children to websites where they could dress their pets and have adventures with them online in a safe environment.

"Web puppies!" Bess exclaimed, clutching a black Labrador.

Jenny had a Collie. She cuddled it close. "We seen these on TV!"

"Can we use the computer, Daddy?" Bess pleaded. "Please?"

"The computer?" Kasie, Gil's new wife, asked, grinning. "What are you babies up to, now?" she added, pausing to hug John before she pressed against Gil's side with warm affection.

"It's a web puppy, Kasie!" Bess exclaimed, showing hers. "Uncle John bought them for us."

"I got a Collie, just like Lassie." Jenny beamed.

"We got to use the computer," Bess insisted.

Kasie chuckled. "Come on, then. You staying for a while?" she asked John.

"For the weekend," John replied, smiling at the girls. "I needed a break."

"I guess you did," Gil replied. "You've taken on a big task up there. Sure you don't need more help? We could spare Green."

"I'm doing fine. Just a little complication."

Kasie led the girls off into Gil's office, where the computer lived. When they were out of earshot, Gil turned to John.

"What sort of complication?" he asked his younger brother.

John sighed. "There's a girl."

Gil's pale eyes sparkled. "It's about time."

John shook his head. "You don't understand. She's nineteen."

Gil only smiled. "Kasie was twenty-one. Barely. And I'm older than you are. Age doesn't have a lot to do with it."

John felt something of a load lift from his heart. "She's unworldly."

Gil chuckled. "Even better. Come have coffee and pie and tell me all about it!"

CHAPTER FIVE

SASSY PUT ON a cheerful face for the rest of the day, pretending for all she was worth that having John Taggert push her away didn't bother her at all. It was devastating, though. She was shy with most men, but John had drawn her out of her shell and made her feel feminine and charming. Then she'd gone all googly over him and edged closer as if she couldn't wait to have him put his arms around her and kiss her. Even the memory of her behavior made her blush. She'd never been so forward with anyone.

Of course, she knew she wasn't pretty or desirable. He was a good deal older than she was, too, and probably liked beautiful and sophisticated women who knew their way around. He might not be a ranch boss, but he drove a nice truck and obviously made a good salary. In addition to all that, he was very handsome and charming. He'd be a woman magnet in any big city.

He'd saved her from Bill Tarleton, gotten her a raise and a promotion, and generally been kinder to her than she deserved. He probably had the shock of his life when she moved close to him as if she had the right, as if he belonged to her. The shame of it wore on her until she was pale and almost in tears when she left the shop that afternoon.

"Something bothering you, Sassy?" Buck Mannheim asked as they were closing up.

She glanced at him and forced a smile. "No, sir. Nothing at all. It's just been a long day."

"It's that Tarleton thing, isn't it?" he asked quietly. "You're upset that you'll have to testify."

She was glad to have an excuse for the way she looked. The assault did wear on her, but it was John Taggert's behavior, not her former boss's, that had her upset. "I guess it is a little worrying," she confessed.

He sighed. "Sassy, it's a sad fact of life that there are men like him in the world. But if you don't testify, he could get away with it. The reason you had trouble with him is that some other poor girl didn't want to have to face him in front of a jury. If he'd been convicted of sexual harassment, instead of just charged with it, he'd probably be in jail now. It might have stopped him from coming on to you."

She had to agree. "I suppose that's true. It's just…well, you know, Mr. Mannheim, some men think a woman leads them on if she just looks at them."

"I know. But that isn't the case here. John… Taggert—" he caught himself in the nick of time from letting John's real surname out "—will certainly testify to what he saw. He'll be there to back you up."

Which didn't make her feel any better, because John would probably think she worked at leading men on, considering how he'd had to push her away from him for being forward. She couldn't say that to Mr. Mannheim. It was too embarrassing.

"You just go on home, have a nice dinner, and stop worrying," he said with a smile. "Everything is going to be all right."

She let out a breath and smiled. "You remind me of my grandfather. He always used to tell me that things worked out, if we just sat back and gave them a chance. He was the most patient person I ever knew."

"I'm not patient." Buck chuckled. "But I do agree with your grandfather. Time heals."

"Don't I wish," she mused. "Good night, Mr. Mannheim. See you in the morning."

"I'll be here."

She got into the battered old truck her grandfather had willed her on his death, and drove home with black smoke pouring out behind her. The vehicle was an embarrassment, but it was all she had. Just putting gas in it and keeping the engine from blowing up was exorbitant. She was grateful for the gas allowance that she'd gotten with her promotion. It would help financially.

She parked at the side of the rickety old house and studied it for a minute before she walked up onto the porch. It needed so much repair. The roof leaked, there was a missing board on the porch, the steps were starting to sag, at least two windows were rotting out...the list went on and on. She recalled what John had said about the improvements that were being made on the Bradbury place, and it wasn't in nearly as bad a shape as this place. She despaired about what she was going to do when winter came. Last winter, she'd barely been able to afford to fill one third of the propane tank they used to heat the house. There were small space heaters in both bedrooms and a stove with a blower in the living room. They'd had to ration carefully, so they'd used a lot of quilts during the coldest months, and tried their best to save on fuel costs. It looked as though this year the fuel price would be twice as much.

She didn't dare think about the obstacles that lay ahead, especially her mother's worsening health. If the doctor prescribed more medicine, they'd be over their heads in no time. She already owed the local pharmacy half her next week's paycheck, because she'd had to supplement the cost of her mother's extra pills.

Well, she had to stop thinking about that, she decided. People were more important than money. It was just that she was the only person making any money. Now she was going to be involved in a court case, and it was just possible that John's boss might hear about it and not want such a scandalous person working in his store. Worse, John might tell him about how forward she'd been in the feed store today. She couldn't forget how angry he'd been when he walked out.

Just as she started up the steps, the sky opened up and it began to rain buckets. There was no time to lose. There were three big holes in the ceiling. One was right over the television set. She couldn't afford to replace the enormous tube television, which was her mother's only source of pleasure. It was almost twenty years old, and the color wasn't good, but it had lasted them since Sassy was a baby.

"Hi!" she called on her way down the hall.

"It's raining, dear!" her mother called from the bedroom.

"I know! I'm on it!"

She made a dash for the little plastic tub under the sink, ran into the living room, and made it just in the nick of time to prevent drips from overwhelming the TV set. It was too big and heavy to move by herself. Her mother couldn't do any lifting at all, and Selene was too small. Sassy couldn't budge it, so the only alternative was to protect it. She put the tub on the flat top and breathed a sigh of relief.

"Don't forget the leak in the kitchen!" Mrs. Peale called again. Her voice was very hoarse and thin.

Sassy grimaced. She sounded as if she was getting a bad case of bronchitis, and she wondered how she'd ever get her mother willingly loaded into the truck if she had to take her to town to Dr. Bates. Maybe the dear old soul would make a house call, if he had to. He was a good man. He knew how stubborn Sassy's mother was, too.

She finished protecting the house with all sorts of buckets and pots. The drips on metal and plastic made a sort of soothing rhythm.

She peeked into her mother's bedroom. "Bad day?" she asked gently.

Her mother, pale and listless, nodded. "Hurts to cough."

Sassy felt even worse. "I'll call Dr. Bates…"

"No!" Her mother paused to cough again. "I've got antibiotic, Sassy, and I've used my breathing machine today already," she said gently. "I just need some cough syrup. It's on the kitchen counter." She managed a smile. "Try not to worry so much, darling," she coaxed. "Life just happens. We can't stop it."

Sassy bit her lower lip and nodded as tears threatened.

"Now, now." Mrs. Peale held out her thin arms. Sassy ran to the bed and into them, careful not to press on her mother's frail chest. She cried and cried.

"I'm not going to die yet," Mrs. Peale promised. "I have to see Selene through high school first!"

It was a standing joke. Usually they both laughed, but Sassy had been through the mill for the past week. Her life was growing more complicated by the hour.

"We had a visitor today," her mother said. "Guess who it was?"

Sassy wiped at her eyes and sat up, smiling through the tears. "Who?"

"Remember Brad Danner's son Caleb, that you had a crush on when you were fifteen?" she teased.

Memory produced a vague portrait of a tall, lanky boy

with black eyes and black hair who'd never seemed to notice her at all. "Yes."

"He came by to see you," Mrs. Peale told her. "He's been in the Army, serving overseas. He stopped by to visit and wanted to say hello to you." She grinned. "I told him to come to supper."

Sassy caught her breath. "Supper?" She sat very still. "But we've only got stew, and just barely enough for us," she began.

Mrs. Peale chuckled hoarsely. "He said we needed some take-out, so he's bringing a bucket of chicken with biscuits and honey and cottage fries all the way from Billings. We can heat it back up in the oven if it's cold when he gets here."

"Real chicken?" Sassy asked, her eyes betraying her hunger for protein. Mostly the Peales ate stews and casseroles, with very little meat because it was so expensive. "And biscuits with honey?"

"I guess I looked like I was starving," Mrs. Peale said wistfully. "I didn't have the heart to refuse. He was so persuasive." She smiled sheepishly.

"You wicked woman," Sassy teased. "What did you do?"

"Well, I was very hungry. He was talking about what he'd gotten himself and his aunt for supper last night, and I did mention that I'd forgotten what a chicken tasted like. He volunteered to come to dinner and bring it with him. What could I say?"

Sassy bent and hugged her mother warmly. "At least you'll get one good meal this week," she mused. "So will Selene." She sat up, frowning. "Where is Selene?"

"She's in her room, doing homework," Mrs. Peale replied. "She studies so hard. We have to find a way to let her go to college if she wants to."

"We'll work it out," Sassy promised. "Her grades will

probably be so high that she'll get scholarships all over the place. She's a good student."

"Just like you were."

"I goofed off more than Selene does."

"You should put on a nice pair of jeans and a clean shirt," she told her daughter. "You can borrow some of my makeup. Caleb is a handsome young man, and he isn't going with anybody."

"You didn't ask?" Sassy burst out, horrified.

"I asked in a very polite way."

"Mother!"

"You should never turn down a prospective suitor," she chuckled. The smile faded. "I know you like Mr. Taggert, Sassy, but there's something about him…"

Her heart sank. Her mother was oddly accurate with her "feelings."

"You don't think he's a criminal or something?"

"Silly girl. Of course not. I just mean that he seems out of place," Mrs. Peale continued. "He's intelligent and sophisticated, and he doesn't act like the cowboys who work around here, haven't you noticed? He's the sort of man who would look at home in elegant surroundings. He's immaculate and educated."

"He told me that he wanted to be a ranch manager one day," Sassy confided. "He probably works at building the right image, to impress people."

"That could be. But I think there's more to him than shows."

"You and your intuition," Sassy chided.

"You have it, too," the older woman reminded her. "It's that old Scotch-Irish second sight. My grandmother had it as well. She could see far ahead." She frowned. "She made a prediction that never made sense. It still doesn't."

"What sort?"

"She said I would be poor, but my daughter would live like royalty." She laughed. "I'm sorry, darling, but that doesn't seem likely."

"Everyone's entitled to a few misses," Sassy agreed.

"Anyway, go dress up. I told Caleb that we eat at six."

Sassy grinned at her. "I'll dress up, but it won't help. I'll still look like me, not some beauty queen."

"Looks fade. Character doesn't," her mother reminded her.

She sighed. "You don't find many young men in search of women with character."

"This may be the first. Hurry!"

CALEB WAS RUGGED-LOOKING, tall and muscular and very polite. He smiled at Sassy and his dark eyes were intent on her face while he sat at the table with the two women and the little girl. He was serving in an Army unit overseas, where he was a corporal, he told them. He was a communications specialist, although he was good at fixing motors as well. The Army hadn't needed a mechanic when he enlisted, but they did need communications people, so he'd trained for that.

"Is it very bad over there, where you were?" Mrs. Peale asked, having struggled to the table with Caleb's help over Sassy's objections.

"Yes, it has been," Caleb said. "But we're making progress."

"Do you have to shoot people?" Selene asked.

"Selene!" Sassy exclaimed.

Caleb chuckled. "We try very hard not to," he told her. "But sometimes the warlords shoot at us. We're stationed high up in the mountains, where terrorists like to camp. We come under fire from time to time."

"It must be frightening," Sassy said.

"It is," Caleb said honestly. "But we do the jobs we're given, and try not to think about the danger." He glanced at Selene and smiled. "There are lots of kids around our camp. We get packages from home and they beg for candy and cookies from us. They don't get many sweets."

"Is there lots of little girls?" Selene asked.

"Now, we don't see many little girls," he told her. "Their customs are very different from ours. The girls mostly stay with their mothers. The boys tag along after their fathers."

"I'd like to tag along with my father," Selene said sadly. "But he went away."

"Away?"

Sassy mouthed "he died," and Caleb nodded quickly.

"Do have some more coffee, Caleb," Mrs. Peale offered.

"Thank you. It's very good."

Sassy had rationed out enough for a pot of the delicious beverage. It was expensive, and they rarely drank it. But Mrs. Peale said that Caleb loved coffee and he had, after all, contributed the meal. Sassy felt that a cup of good coffee wasn't that much of a sacrifice, under the circumstances.

AFTER DINNER, THEY gathered around the television to watch the news. Caleb looked at his watch and said he had to get back to Billings, because his aunt wanted to go to a late movie, and he'd promised to take her.

"But I'd like to come back again before I return to duty, if I may," he told them. "I had a good time tonight."

"So did we," Sassy said at once. "Please do."

"We'll make you a nice macaroni and cheese casserole next time, our treat," Mrs. Peale offered.

He hesitated. "Would you mind if I contributed the cheese for it?" he asked. "I'm partial to a particular brand."

They saw right through him, but they pretended not to. It had to be obvious that they were managing at a subsistence level.

"That would be very kind of you," Mrs. Peale said with genuine gratitude.

He smiled. "It would be my pleasure. Sassy, would you walk me out?"

"Sure!"

She jumped up and walked out to his truck with him. He turned to her before he climbed up into the cab.

"My aunt has a cousin who lives here. She says your mother is in very bad shape," he said.

She nodded. "Lung cancer."

He grimaced. "If there's anything I can do, anything at all," he began. "Your mother was so good to my cousin when she lost her husband in the blizzard a few years ago. None of us have forgotten."

"You're very kind. But we're managing." She grinned. "Thanks for the chicken, I'd forgotten what they tasted like," she added, mimicking her mother's words.

He laughed at her honesty. "You always did have a great sense of humor."

"It's easier to laugh than to cry," she told him.

"So they say. I'll come by tomorrow afternoon, if I may, and tell you when I'm free. My aunt has committed me to no end of social obligations."

"You could phone me," she said.

He grinned. "I'd rather drive over. Humor me. I'll escape tea with one of aunt's friends who has an eligible daughter."

She chuckled. "Avoiding matrimony, are you?"

"Apparently," he agreed. He pursed his lips. "Are you attached?"

She sighed. "No. Sorry." Her eyes widened. "Are you?"

He grimaced. "I'm trying not to be." He shrugged. "She's my best friend's girl."

She relaxed. He wasn't hunting for a woman. "I have one of those situations, too. Except that he doesn't have a girlfriend, that I know of."

"And he doesn't like you?"

"Apparently not."

"Well, if that doesn't take the cake. Two fellow sufferers, and we meet by accident."

"That's life."

"It is." He studied her warmly. "You know, I was so shy in high school that I never got up the nerve to ask you out. I wanted to. You were always so cheerful, always smiling. You made me feel good inside."

That was surprising. She remembered him as a standoffish young man who seemed never to notice her.

"I was shy, too," she confessed. "I just learned to bluff."

"The Army taught me how to do that," he said, smiling. "This man you're interested in—somebody local?"

She sighed. "Actually, he's sort of the foreman of a ranch. The men he works for bought the old Bradbury place..."

"That wreck?" he exclaimed. "Whatever for?"

"They're going to run purebred calves out there, once they build a new barn and stable and remodel the house and run new fences. It's going to be quite a job."

"A very expensive job. Who are his bosses?"

"The Callister brothers. They live in Medicine Ridge."

He nodded. "Yes. I've heard of them. Hardworking men. One of their ranch hands was in my unit when I first shipped out. He said it was the best place he'd ever worked."

He laughed. "He said the brothers got right out in the pasture at branding time and helped. They weren't the sort to sit in parlors and sip expensive alcohol."

"Imagine, to be that rich and still go out to work cattle," she said with a wistful smile.

"I can't imagine it," he told her. "But I'd love to be able to. I'm getting my college degree in the military. When I come out, I'm going to apprentice at a mechanic's shop in Billings and, hopefully, work my way up to partnership one day. I love fixing motors."

She gave him a wry look. "I wish you'd love fixing mine," she said. "It's pouring black smoke."

"How old is it?" he asked curiously.

"About twenty years…"

"Rings and valves," he said at once. "It's probably going to need rebuilding. At today's prices, you'd come out better to sell it for scrap and buy a new one."

"Pipe dreams." She laughed. "We live up to the last penny I bring home. I could never make a car payment."

"Have you thought about moving to Billings, where you could get a better job?"

"I'd have to take Mama and Selene with me," she said simply, "and we'd have to rent a place to live. At least we still have the house, such as it is."

He frowned. "You landed in a fine mess," he said sympathetically.

"I did, indeed. But I love my family," she added. "I'd rather have what I have than be a millionaire."

His dark eyes met her green ones evenly. "You're a nice girl, Sassy. I wish I'd known you better before I met my best friend's girl."

"I wish I'd known you better before John Taggert came to town." She sighed. "As it is, I'll be very happy to have you for a friend." She grinned. "We can cry on each other's shoulders. I'll even write to you when you go back overseas if you'll give me your address."

His face lit up. "I'd like that. It will help throw my buddy off the trail. He caught me staring at his girlfriend's photo a little too long."

"I'll send you a picture of me," she volunteered. "You can tell him she reminded you of me."

His eyebrows lifted. "That won't be far-fetched. She's dark haired and has light eyes. You'd do that for me?"

"Of course I would," she said easily. "What are friends for?"

He smiled. "Maybe I can do you a good turn one day."

"Maybe you can."

He climbed into the truck. "Tell your family I said good-night. I'll drive over tomorrow."

She smiled up at him. "I'll look forward to it."

He threw up a hand and pulled out into the road. She watched him go, remembering that there were still a few pieces of chicken left. She'd have to rush inside and put them up quickly before Selene grew reckless and ate too much. If they stretched out that bucket of chicken, they could eat on it for most of the week. It was a godsend, considering their normal grocery budget. God bless Caleb, she thought warmly. He really did have a big heart.

JOHN CALLISTER HAD spent a pleasant weekend with his brother and Kasie and the girls. Mrs. Charters had made him his favorite foods, and even Miss Parsons, Gil's former governess who was now his bookkeeper, seemed to enjoy his visit. There was a new assistant since Gil had married Kasie. He was a male assistant, Arnold Sims, who seemed nice and was almost as efficient as Kasie had been.

He was an older man, and he and Miss Parsons spent their days off together.

It was nice to get away from the constant headache of construction and back to the bosom of his family. But he had to return to Hollister, and mend fences with Sassy. He should have found a kinder way to keep her at arm's length while he found his footing in their changing relationship. Her face had gone pale when he'd jerked back from her. She probably thought he found her offensive. He hated leaving her with that false impression, but his sudden desire for her had shocked and disturbed him. He hadn't been confident enough to go back and face her until he could hide his feelings.

There had to be some way to make it up to her. He'd think of a way when he got back to Hollister, he assured himself. He could explain it away without too much difficulty. Sassy had a kind heart. He knew she wouldn't hold grudges.

But when he walked into the store Monday afternoon, he got a shock. Sassy was leaning over the counter, smiling broadly at a very handsome young man in jeans and a chambray shirt. And if he wasn't mistaken, the young man was holding her hand.

He felt something inside him explode with pain and resentment. She'd put her hands on his chest and looked up at him with melting green eyes, and he'd wanted her to the point of madness. Now she was doing the same thing to another man, a younger man. Was she just a heartless flirt?

He walked up to the counter, noting idly that the younger man didn't seem to be disturbed by him, or even interested in him.

"Hi, Sassy," he said coolly. "Did you get in that special feed mix I asked you to order?"

"I'll check, Mr. Taggert," she said politely and with a quiet smile. She walked into the back to check the invoice of the latest shipment that had just come that morning, very proud that she'd been able to disguise her quick breathing and shaky legs. John Taggert had a shattering effect on her emotions. But he didn't want her, and she'd better remember it. What a blessing that Caleb had come to the store today. Perhaps John would believe that she had other interests and wasn't chasing after him.

"Nice day," John said to the young man. "I'm John Taggert. I'll be ramrodding the old Bradbury ranch."

The boy smiled and extended a hand. "I'm Caleb Danner. Sassy and I went to school together."

John shook the hand. "Nice to meet you."

"Same here."

John looked around at the shelves with seeming nonchalance. "You work around here?" he asked carelessly.

"No. I'm in the Army Rangers," the boy replied, surprising his companion. "I'm stationed overseas, but I've been home on leave for a couple of weeks. I'm staying with my aunt in Billings."

John's pale eyes met the boy's dark ones. "That's a substantial drive from here."

"Yes, I know," Caleb replied easily. "But I promised Sassy a movie and I'm free tonight. I came to see if she'd go with me."

CHAPTER SIX

THE BOY WAS an Army Ranger, he said, and he was dating Sassy. John felt uncomfortable trying to pump the younger man for information. He wondered if Caleb was seriously interested in Sassy, but he had no right to ask.

She was poring over bills of lading. He watched her with muted curiosity and a little jealousy. It disturbed him that this younger man had popped up right out of the ground, so to speak, under his own nose.

It took her a minute to find the order and calm her nerves. But she managed to do both. She looked up as John approached the counter. He looked very sexy in those well-fitting jeans and the blue-checked Western-cut shirt he was wearing with his black boots and wide-brimmed hat. She shouldn't notice that, she told herself firmly. He wouldn't like having her interested in him; he'd already made that clear. She had to be businesslike.

"The feed was backordered," she said politely. "But it should be here by Friday, if that's all right. If it isn't," she added quickly when he began to look irritated, "I can ask Mr. Mannheim to phone them..."

"No need," he said abruptly. "We can wait. We aren't moving livestock onto the place until we have the fences mended and the barn finished. I just want to have the feed on hand when they arrive."

"We'll have it by next week. No problem."

He nodded. He tried to avoid looking at her directly. She was wearing jeans with a neat little white peasant blouse that had embroidery on it, and she looked very pretty with her dark hair crisp and clean, and her green eyes shimmering with pleasure. Her face was flushed and she was obviously unsettled. The boy at the counter probably had something to do with that, he thought irritably. She seemed pretty wrapped up in him already.

"That's fine," he said abruptly. "I'll check back with you next week, or I'll have one of the boys come in."

"Yes, sir," she replied politely.

He nodded at Caleb and stalked out of the store without another glance at Sassy.

Caleb pursed his lips and noted Sassy's heightened color. "So that's him," he mused.

She drew in a steadying breath. "That's him."

"Talk about biting off more than you can chew," he murmured dryly.

"What do you mean?"

"Nothing," he returned, thinking privately that Taggert looked like a man who'd forgotten more about women than Sassy would ever learn about men. Taggert seemed sophisticated, for a cattleman, and was obviously used to giving orders. Sassy was too young for that fire-eater, too unsophisticated, too everything. Besides all that, the ranch foreman had spoken to her politely, but in a manner that was decidedly impersonal. Caleb didn't want to upset Sassy by putting all that into words. Still, he felt sympathy for her. She was as likely to land that big fish as he was to find himself out on the town with his best friend's girl.

"How about that movie?" he asked quickly, changing the subject. "The local theater has three new ones showing…"

THEY WENT TO Hollister's only in-town movie theater, a small building in town that did a pretty good business catering to families. There was a drive-in movie on the outskirts of town, in a cow pasture, but Caleb wasn't keen on that, so they went into town.

The movie they chose was a cartoon movie about a robot, and it was hilarious. Sassy had worried about leaving her mother and Selene alone, but Mrs. Peale refused to let her sacrifice a night out. Sassy did leave her prepaid cell phone with her mother, though, in case of an emergency. Caleb had one of his own, so they could use it if they were in any difficulties.

Caleb drove her back home. He had a nice truck; it wasn't new, but it was well-maintained. He was sending home the payments to his aunt, who was making them for him.

"I only have a year to go," he told her. "Yesterday, I got a firm offer of a partnership in Billings at a cousin's car dealership. He has a shop that does mechanical work. I'd be in charge of that, and do bodywork as well. I went by to see him on a whim, and he offered me the job, just like that." His dark eyes twinkled. "It's what I've wanted to do my whole life."

"I hope you make it," she told him with genuine feeling.

He bent and kissed her cheek. "You're a nice girl, Sassy," he said softly. "I wish…"

"Me, too," she said, reading the thought in his face. "But life makes other plans, sometimes."

"Doesn't it?" he chuckled.

"When do you report back to duty?" she asked.

"Not for a week, but my aunt has every minute scheduled. She had plans for tonight, too, but I outfoxed her," he said, grinning.

"I enjoyed the movie. And the chicken," she told him.

"I enjoyed the macaroni and cheese we had tonight," he replied. He was somber for a minute. "If you ever need help, I hope you'll ask me. I'd do what I can for you."

She smiled up at him. "I know that. Thanks, Caleb. I'd make the same offer. But—" she sighed "—I have no clue what I'd ever be able to help you with."

"I'll send you my address," he said, having already jotted hers down on a piece of paper. "You can send me that photo, to throw my buddy off the track."

She laughed. "Okay. I'll definitely do that."

"I'll phone you before I leave. Take care."

"You, too. So long."

He got into his truck and drove away.

Sassy walked slowly up the porch and into the house, her mind still on the funny movie.

She was halfway into the living room when she realized that one of the muffled voices she'd been hearing was male.

As she entered the room, John Taggert looked up from the sofa, where he was sitting with her mother. Her mother, she noted, was grinning like a Cheshire cat.

"Mr. Taggert came by to see how I was doing. Wasn't that sweet of him?" she asked her daughter.

"It really was," Sassy replied politely.

"Had a good time?" John asked her. He wasn't smiling.

"Yes," she said. "It was a cartoon movie."

"Just right for children," he replied, and there was something in his blue eyes that made her heart jump.

"We're all children at heart. I'm sure that's what you meant, wasn't it, Mr. Taggert?" Mrs. Peale asked sweetly.

He caught himself. "Of course," he replied, smiling at the older woman. "I enjoy them myself. We take the girls to movies all the time."

"Girls?" Mrs. Peale asked, frowning.

"My nieces," he explained. "They love cartoons. My brother and his wife take them mostly, but I fill in when I'm needed."

"You like children?"

He smiled. "I love them."

Mrs. Peale opened her mouth.

Sassy knew what was coming, so she jumped in. "Caleb's going to phone us before he goes back overseas," she told her mother.

"That's nice of him." Mrs. Peale beamed. "Such a kind young man."

"Kind." Sassy nodded.

"Would you like something to drink, Mr. Taggert?" Mrs. Peale asked politely. "Sassy could make some coffee…?"

John glanced at his watch. "I've got to go. Thanks anyway. I just wanted to make sure you were all right," he told Mrs. Peale, and he smiled at her. "Sassy's…boyfriend mentioned that he was taking her to a movie, and I thought about you out here all alone."

Sassy gave him a glare hot enough to scald. "I left Mama my cell phone in case anything happened," she said curtly.

"Yes, she did," Mrs. Peale added quickly. "She takes very good care of me. I insisted that she go with Caleb. Sassy hasn't had a night out in two or three years."

John shifted, as if that statement made him uneasy.

"She doesn't like to leave me at all," Mrs. Peale continued. "But it's not fair to her. So much responsibility, and at her age."

"I never mind it," Sassy interrupted. "I love you."

"I know that, sweetheart, but you should get to know nice young men," she added. "You'll marry one day and have children. You can't spend your whole life like this, with a sick old woman and a child..."

"Please," Sassy said, hurting. "I don't want to think about getting married for years yet."

Mrs. Peale's face mirrored her sorrow. "You should never have had to handle this all alone," she said regretfully. "If only your father had...well, that's not something we could help."

"I'll walk Mr. Taggert to the door," Sassy offered. She looked as if she'd like to drag him out it, before her mother could embarrass her even more.

"Am I leaving?" he asked Sassy.

"Apparently," she replied, standing aside and nodding toward the front door.

"In that case, I'll say good night." He smiled at Mrs. Peale. "I hope you know that you can call on me if you ever needed help. I'm not in the Army, but I do have skills that don't involve an intimate knowledge of guns—"

"This way, Mr. Taggert," Sassy interrupted emphatically, catching him firmly by the sleeve.

He grinned at Mrs. Peale, whose eyes were twinkling now. "Good night."

"Good night, Mr. Taggert. Thank you for stopping by."

"You're very welcome."

He followed Sassy out onto the front porch. She closed the door.

His eyebrows arched. "Why did you close the door?" he asked. His voice deepened with amusement. "Are you going to kiss me good night and you don't want your mother to see?"

She flushed. "I wouldn't kiss you for all the tea in China! There's no telling where you've been!"

"Actually," he said, twirling his wide-brimmed hat in

his big hands, "I've been in Medicine Ridge, reporting to my bosses."

"That's nice. Do drive safely on your way back to your ranch."

He stopped twirling the hat and studied her stiff posture. He felt between a rock and a hard place.

"The Army Ranger seems like a good sort of boy," he remarked. "Responsible. Not very mature yet, but he'll grow up."

She wanted to bite him. "He's in the Army Rangers," she reminded him. "He's been in combat overseas."

His eyebrows lifted. "Is that a requirement for your dates, that they've learned to dodge bullets?"

"I never said I wanted a man who could dodge bullets!" she threw at him.

"It might be a handy skill for a man—dodging things, I mean, if you're the sort of woman who likes to throw pots and pans at men."

"I have never thrown a pot at a man," she said emphatically. "However, if you'd like to step into our kitchen, I could make an exception for you!"

He grinned. He could have bet that she didn't talk like that to the soldier boy. She had spirit and she didn't take guff from anyone, but it took a lot to get under her skin. It delighted him that he could make her mad.

"What sort of pot did you have in mind throwing at me?" he taunted.

"Something made of cast iron," she muttered. "Although I expect you'd dent it."

"My head is not that hard," he retorted.

He stepped in, close to her, and watched her reaction with detached amusement. He made her nervous. It showed.

He put his hat back on, and pushed it to the back of his

head. One long arm went around Sassy's waist and drew
her to him. A big, lean hand spread on her cheek, coaxing
it back to his shoulder.

"You've got grit," he murmured deeply as his gaze fell
to her soft mouth. "You don't back away from trouble, or
responsibility. I like that."

"You...shouldn't hold me like this," she said.

"Why not? You're soft and sweet and I like the way you
smell." His head began to bend. "I think I'll like the way
you taste, too," he breathed.

He didn't need a program to know how innocent she was.
He loved the way her hands gripped him as his firm mouth
smoothed over the parted, shocked warmth of her lips.

"Nothing heavy," he whispered as his mouth played with
hers. "It's far too soon for that. Relax. Just relax, Sassy. It's
like dancing, slow and sweet..."

His mouth covered hers gently, brushing her lips apart,
teasing them to permit the slow invasion. Her hands relaxed on his arms as the slow rhythm began to increase her
heartbeat and make her breathing sound jerky and rough.
He was very good at this, she thought dizzily. He knew exactly how to make her shiver with anticipation as he drew
out the intimate torture of his mouth on her lips. He teased
them, playing with her lower lip, nibbling and rubbing, until
she went on tiptoe with a frustrated moan, seeking something far rougher and more passionate than this exquisite
whisper of motion.

He nipped her lower lip. "You want more, don't you,
honey?" he whispered roughly. "So do I. Hold tight."

Her hands slid up to his broad shoulders as his mouth
began to burrow hungrily into hers. She let her lips open
with a shiver, closing her eyes and reaching up to be swallowed whole by his arms.

It was so sweet that she moaned with the ardent passion he aroused in her. She'd never felt her body swell and shudder like this when a man held her. She'd never been kissed so thoroughly, so expertly. Her arms tightened convulsively around his neck as he riveted her to the length of his powerful body, as if he, too, had lost control of himself.

A minute later, he came to his senses. She was just nineteen. She worked for him, even though she didn't know it. They were worlds apart in every way. What the hell was he doing?

He pulled away from her abruptly, his blue eyes shimmering with emotion, his grasp a little bruising as he tried to get his breath back under control. His jealousy of the soldier had pushed him right into a situation he'd left town to avoid. Now, here he was, faced with the consequences.

She hung there, watching him with clouded, dreamy eyes in a face flushed with pleasure from the hungry exchange.

"That was a mistake," he said curtly, putting her firmly at arm's length and letting her go.

"Are you sure?" she asked, dazed.

"Yes, I'm sure," he said, his voice sharp with anger.

"Then why did you do it?" she asked reasonably.

He had to think about a suitable answer, and his brain wasn't working very well. He'd pushed her away at their last meeting and felt guilt. Now he'd compounded the error and he couldn't think of a good way to get out of it.

"God knows," he said heavily. "Maybe it's the full moon."

She gave him a wry look. "It's not a full moon. It's a crescent moon."

"A moon is a moon," he said doggedly.

"That's your story and you're sticking to it," she agreed.

He stared down at her with conflict eating him alive. "You're nineteen, Sassy," he said finally. "I'm thirty-one."

She blinked. "Is that supposed to mean something?"

"It means you're years too young for me. And not only in age."

She raised her eyebrows. "It isn't exactly easy to get experience when you're living in a tiny town and supporting a family."

He ground his teeth. "That isn't the point…"

She held up a hand. "You had too much coffee today and the caffeine caused you to leap on unsuspecting women."

He glowered. "I did not drink too much coffee."

"Then it must be either my exceptional beauty or my overwhelming charm," she decided. She waited, arms folded, for him to come up with an alternate theory.

He pulled his hat low over his eyes. "It's been a long, dry spell."

"Well, if that isn't the nicest compliment I ever had," she muttered. "You were lonely and I was the only eligible woman handy!"

"You were," he shot back.

"A likely story! There's Mrs. Harmon, who lives a mile down the road."

"Mrs. Harmon?"

"Yes. Her husband has been dead fifteen years. She's fifty, but she wears tight skirts and a lot of makeup and in dim light, she isn't half bad."

He glowered even more. "I am not that desperate."

"You just said you were."

"I did not!"

"Making passes at nineteen-year-old girls," she scoffed. "I never!"

He threw up his hands. "It wasn't a pass!"

She pursed her lips and gave him a sarcastic look.

He shrugged. "Maybe it was a small pass." He stuck his hands in his pockets. "I have a conscience. You'd wear on it."

So that was why he'd pushed her away in the store, before he left town. Her heart lifted. He didn't find her unattractive. He just thought she was too young.

"I'll be twenty next month," she told him.

It didn't help. "I'll be thirty-two in two months."

"Well, for a month we'll be almost the same age," she said pertly.

He laughed shortly. "Twelve years is a lot, at your age."

"In the great scheme of things, it isn't," she pointed out.

He didn't answer her.

"Thanks for stopping by to check on my mother," she said. "It was kind."

He lifted a shoulder. "I wanted to see if the soldier was hot for you."

"Excuse me?!"

"He didn't even kiss you good night," he said.

"That's because he's in love with his best friend's girl."

His expression brightened. "He is?"

"I'm somebody to talk about her with," she told him. "Which is why I don't get out much, unless a man wants to tell me about his love life and ask for advice." She studied him. "I don't guess you've got relationship problems?"

"In fact, I do. I'm trying not to have one with an inappropriate woman," he said, tongue-in-cheek.

That took a minute to register. She laughed. "Oh. I see."

He moved closer and toyed with a strand of her short hair. "I guess it wouldn't hurt to take you out once in a while. Nothing serious," he added firmly. "I am not in the market for a mistress."

"Good thing," she returned, "because I have no intention of becoming one."

He grinned. "Now, that's encouraging. I'm glad to know that you have enough willpower to keep us on the straight and narrow."

"I have my mother," she replied, "who would shoot you in the foot with a rusty gun if she even thought you were leading me into a life of sin. She's very religious. She raised me to be that way."

"In her condition," he said solemnly, "I'm not surprised that she's religious. She's a courageous soul."

"I love her a lot," she confessed. "I wish I could do more to help her."

"Loving her is probably what helps her the most," he said. He bent and brushed a soft kiss against her mouth. "I'll see you tomorrow."

She smiled. "Okay."

He started to walk down the steps, paused, and turned back to her. "You're sure it's not serious with the soldier?"

She smiled more broadly. "Very sure."

He cocked his hat at a jaunty angle and grinned at her. "Okay."

She watched him walk out to his vehicle, climb in, and drive away. She waved, but she noticed that he didn't look back. For some reason, that bothered her.

JOHN SPENT A rough night remembering how sweet Sassy was to kiss. He'd been fighting the attraction for weeks now, and he was losing. She was too young for him. He knew it. But on the other hand, she was independent. She was strong. She was used to responsibility. She'd had years of being the head of her family, the breadwinner. She might be young, but she was more mature than most women her age.

He could see how much care she took for her mother and her mother's little ward. She never shirked her duties, and she worked hard for her paycheck.

The bottom line was that he was far too attracted to her to walk away. He was taking a chance. But he'd taken chances before in his life, with women who were much inferior to this little firecracker. It wouldn't hurt to go slow and see where the path led. After all, he could walk away whenever he liked, he told himself.

The big problem was going to be the distance between them socially. Sassy didn't know that he came from great wealth, that his parents were related to most of the royal houses of Europe, that he and his brother had built a world-famous ranch that bred equally famous breeding bulls. He was used to five-star hotels and restaurants, stretch limousines in every city he visited. He traveled first-class. He was worldly and sophisticated. Sassy was much more used to small-town life. She wouldn't understand his world. Probably, she wouldn't be able to adjust to it.

But he was creating hurdles that didn't exist yet. It wasn't as if he was in love with her and aching to rush her to the altar, he told himself. He was going to take her out a few times. Maybe kiss her once in a while. It was nothing he couldn't handle. She'd just be companionship while he was getting this new ranching enterprise off the ground. When he had to leave, he'd tell her the truth.

It sounded simple. It was simple, he assured himself. She was just another girl, another casual relationship. He was going to enjoy it while it lasted.

He went to sleep, finally, having resolved all the problems in his mind.

The next day, he went back to the feed store with another list, this one of household goods that he was going to need. He was looking forward to seeing Sassy again. The memory of that kiss had prompted some unusually spicy dreams about her.

But when he got there, he found Buck Mannheim handling the counter and looking worried.

He waited while the older man finished a sale. The customer left and John approached the counter.

"Where's Sassy?" he asked.

Buck looked concerned. "She phoned me at home. Her mother had a bad turn. They had to send an ambulance for her and take her up to Billings to the nearest hospital. Sassy was crying…"

He was talking to thin air. John was already out the door.

HE FOUND SASSY and little Selene in the emergency waiting room, huddled together and upset.

He walked into the room and they both ran to him, to be scooped up and held close, comforted.

He felt odd. It was the first time he could remember being important to anyone outside his own family circle. He felt needed.

His arms contracted around them. "Tell me what happened," he asked at Sassy's ear.

She drew away a little, wiping at her eyes with the hem of her blouse. It was obvious that she hadn't slept. "She knocked over her water carafe, or I wouldn't even have known anything was wrong. I ran in to see what had happened and I found her gasping for breath. It was so bad that I just ran to the phone and called Dr. Bates. He sent for the ambulance and called the oncologist on staff here. They've been with her for two hours. Nobody's told me anything."

He eased them down into chairs. "Stay here," he said softly. "I'll find out what's going on."

She was doubtful that a cowboy, even a foreman, would be able to elicit more information than the patient's own family, but she smiled. "Thanks."

He turned and walked down the hall.

CHAPTER SEVEN

JOHN HAD MONEY and power, and he knew how to use both. Within two minutes, he'd been ushered into the office of the hospital administrator. He explained who he was, why he was there, and asked for information. Even in Billings, the Callister empire was known. Five minutes later, he was speaking to the physician in charge of Sassy's mother's case. He accepted responsibility for the bill and asked if anything more could be done than was being done.

"Sadly, yes," the physician said curtly. "We're bound by the family's financial constraints. Mrs. Peale does have insurance, but she told us that they simply could not afford anything other than symptomatic relief for her. If she would consent, Mrs. Peale could have surgery to remove the cancerous lung and then radiation and chemotherapy to insure her recovery. In fact, she'd have a very good prognosis…"

"If money's all that's holding things up, I'll gladly be responsible for the bill. I don't care how much it is. So what are you waiting for?" John asked.

The physician smiled. "You'll speak to the financial officer?"

"Immediately," he replied.

"Then I'll speak to the patient."

"They don't know who I am," John told him. "That's the only condition, that you don't tell them. They think I'm the foreman of a ranch."

The older man frowned. "Is there a reason?"

"Originally, it was to insure that costs didn't escalate locally because the name was known," he said. "But by then, it was too late to change things. They're my friends," he added. "I don't want them to look at me differently."

"You think they would?"

"People see fame and money and power. They don't see people. Not at first."

The other man nodded. "I think I understand. I'll get the process underway. It's a very kind thing you're doing," he added. "Mrs. Peale would have died. Very soon, too."

"I know that. She's a good person."

"And very important to her little family, from what I've seen."

"Yes."

He clapped John on the shoulder. "We'll do everything possible."

"Thanks."

WHEN HE WRAPPED up things in the financial office, he strolled back down to the emergency room. Sassy was pacing the floor. Selene had curled up into a chair with her cheek pillowed on her arm. She was sound asleep.

Sassy met him, her eyes wide and fascinated. "What did you *do*?" she exclaimed. "They're going to operate on Mama! The doctor says they can save her life, that she can have radiation and chemotherapy, that there's a grant for poor people…she can live!"

Her voice broke into tears. John pulled her close and rocked her in his strong, warm arms, his mouth against her temple. "It's all right, honey," he said softly. "Don't cry."

"I'm just so happy," she choked at his chest. "So happy! I never knew there were such things as grants for this sort

of thing, or I'd have done anything to find one! I thought…
I thought we'd have to watch her die…"

"Never while there was a breath in my body," he whispered. His arms contracted. A wave of feeling rippled through him. He'd helped people in various ways all his life, but it was the first time he'd been able to make this sort of difference for someone he cared about. He'd grown fond of Mrs. Peale. But he'd thought that her case was hopeless. He thanked God that the emergency had forced Sassy to bring her mother here. What a wonderful near-tragedy. A link in a chain that would lead to a better life for all three of them.

She drew back, wiping her eyes again and laughing. "Sorry. I seem to spend my life crying. I'm just so grateful. What did you do?" she asked again.

He grinned. "I just asked wasn't there something they could figure out to do to help her. The doctor said he'd check, and he came up with the grant."

She shook her head. "It happened so fast. They've got some crackerjack surgeon who's teaching new techniques in cancer intervention here, and he's the one they're getting to operate on Mama. What's more, they're going to do it tomorrow. They already asked her, and she just almost jumped out of the bed she was so excited." She wiped away more tears. "We brought her up here to die," she explained. "And it was the most wonderful, scary experience we ever had. She's going to live, maybe long enough to see Selene graduate from college!"

He smiled down at her. "You know, I wouldn't be surprised at all if that's not the case. Feel better?"

She nodded. Her eyes adored him. "Thank you."

He chuckled. "Glad I could help." He glanced down at

Selene, who was radiant. "Hear that? You'll have to go to college."

She grinned. "I want to be a doctor, now."

"There are scholarships that will help that dream come true, at the right time," he assured her.

Sassy pulled the young girl close. "We'll find lots," she promised.

"Thank you for helping save our mama," Selene told John solemnly. "We love her very much."

"She loves you very much," John replied. "That must be pretty nice, at your age."

He was saying something without saying it.

Sassy sent Selene to the vending machines for apple juice. While she was gone, Sassy turned to John. "What was your mother like when you were little?"

His face hardened. "I didn't have a mother when I was little," he replied curtly. "My brother and I were raised by our uncle."

She was shocked. "Were your parents still alive?"

"Yes. But they didn't want us."

"How horrible!"

He averted his eyes. "We had a rough upbringing. Until our uncle took us in, we were in—" he started to say boarding school, but that was a dead giveaway "—in a bad situation at home," he amended. "Our uncle took us with him and we grew up without a mother's influence."

"You still don't have anything to do with her? Or your father?"

"We started seeing them again last year," he said after a minute. "It's been hard. We built up resentments and barriers. But we're all working on it. Years too late," he added on a cold laugh.

"I'm sorry," she told him. "Mama's been there for me

all my life. She's kissed my cuts and bruises, loved me, fought battles for me... I don't know what I would have done without her."

He drew in a long breath and looked down into warm green eyes. "I would have loved having a mother like her," he said honestly. "She's the most optimistic person I ever knew. In her condition, that says a lot."

"I thought we'd be planning her funeral when we came in here," Sassy said, still shell-shocked.

He touched her soft cheek gently. "I can understand that."

"How did you know where we were?" she asked suddenly.

"I went into the feed store with a list and found Buck holding down the fort," he said. "He said you were up here."

"And you came right away," she said, amazed.

He put both big hands on her small waist and held her in front of him. His blue eyes were solemn. "I never planned to get mixed up with you," he told her honestly. "Or your family. But I seem to be part of it."

She smiled. "Yes. You are a part of our family."

His hands contracted. "I just want to make the point that my interest isn't brotherly," he added.

The look in his eyes made her heartbeat accelerate. "Really?"

He smiled. "Really."

She felt as if she could fly. The expression on her face made him wish that they were in a more private place. He looked down to her full mouth and contemplated something shocking and potentially embarrassing.

Before he could act on what was certainly a crazy impulse, the doctor who'd admitted Mrs. Peale came walking up to them with a taller, darker man. He introduced himself and his companion.

"Miss Peale, this is Dr. Barton Crowley," he told Sassy. "He's going to operate on your mother first thing in the morning."

Sassy shook his hand warmly. "I'm so glad to meet you. We're just overwhelmed. We thought we'd brought Mama up here to die. It's a miracle! We never even knew there were grants for surgery!"

John shot a warning look at the doctor and the surgeon, who nodded curtly. The hospital administrator had already told them about the financial arrangements.

"We can always find a way to handle critical situations here," the doctor said with a smile. He nodded toward Dr. Crowley. "He's been teaching us new surgical techniques. It really was a miracle that he was here when you arrived. He works at Johns Hopkins, you see," he added.

Sassy didn't know what that meant.

John leaned down. "It's one of the more famous hospitals back East," he told her.

She laughed nervously. "Sorry," she told Dr. Crowley, who smiled. "I don't get out much."

"She works at our local feed store," John told them, beaming down at her. "She's the family's only support. She takes care of her mother and their six-year-old ward as well. She's quite a girl."

"Stop that," Sassy muttered shyly. "I'm not some paragon of virtue. I love my family."

His eyebrows arched and his eyes twinkled. "All of it?" he asked amusedly.

She flushed when she recalled naming him part of the family. She forced her attention back to the surgeon. "You really think you can help Mama? Our local doctor said the cancer was very advanced."

"It is, but preliminary tests indicate that it's confined to one lobe of her lung. If we can excise it, then follow up with chemotherapy and radiation, there's a good chance that we can at least prolong her life. We might save it altogether."

"Please do whatever you can," Sassy pleaded gently. "She means so much to us."

"She was very excited when I spoke with her," Dr. Crowley said with a smile. "She was concerned about her daughters, she told me, much more than with her own condition. A most unique lady."

"Yes, she is," Sassy agreed. "She's always putting other people's needs in front of her own. She raised me with hardly any help at all, and it was rough."

"From what I see, young woman," the surgeon replied, "she did a very good job."

"Thanks," she said, a little embarrassed.

"Well, we'll get her into surgery first thing. When we see the extent of the cancerous tissue, we'll speak again. Try to get some rest."

"We will."

He and the doctor shook hands with John and walked back down the hall.

"I wish I'd packed a blanket or something," Sassy mused, eyeing the straight, lightly padded chairs in the distant waiting room. "I can sleep sitting up, but it gets cold in hospitals."

"Sitting up?" He didn't understand.

"Listen, you know how we're fixed," she said. "We can't afford a motel room. I always sleep in the waiting room when Mama's in the hospital." She nodded toward Selene, who was now asleep in the corner. "We both do it. Except

Selene fits in these chairs a little better, because she's so small."

He was shocked. It was a firsthand look at how the rest of the world had to live. He hadn't realized that Sassy would have to stay at the hospital.

"Don't look like that," she said. "You make me uncomfortable. I don't mind being poor. I've got so many blessings that it's hard to count them."

"Blessings." He frowned, as if he wondered what they could possibly be.

"I have a mother who sacrificed to raise me, who loves me with her whole heart. I have a little sort-of sister who thinks I'm Joan of Arc. I have a roof over my head, food to eat, and, thanks to you, a really good job with no harassment tied to it. I even have a vehicle that gets me to and from work most of the time."

"I wouldn't call that vehicle a blessing," he observed.

"Neither would I, if I could afford that fancy truck you drive," she chided, grinning. "The point is, I have things that a lot of other people don't. I'm happy," she added, curious about his expression.

She had nothing. Literally nothing. But she could count her blessings as if they made her richer than a princess. He had everything, but his life was empty. All the wealth and power he commanded hadn't made him happy. He was alone. He had Gil and his family, and his parents. But in a very personal sense, he was by himself.

"You're thinking that you don't really have a family of your own," Sassy guessed from his glum expression. "But you do. You have me, and Mama, and Selene. We're your family." She hesitated, because he looked hunted. She flushed. "I know we're not much to brag about..."

His arm shot out and pulled her to him. "Don't run yourself down. I've never counted my friends by their bank books. Character is far more important."

She relaxed. But only a little. He was very close, and her heart was racing.

"You suit me just the way you are," he said gently. He bent and kissed her, tenderly, before he let her go and walked toward Selene.

"What are you doing?" she exclaimed when he lifted the sleeping child in his arms and started toward the exit.

"I'm taking baby sister here to a modest guest room for the night. You can come, too."

She blinked. "John, I can't afford—"

"If I hear that one more time," he interrupted, "I'm going to say bad words. You don't want me to say bad words in front of the child. Do you?"

She was asleep and wouldn't hear them, but he was making a point and being noble. She gave in, smiling. "Okay. But you have to dock my wages for it or I'll stay here and Selene can just hear you spout bad words."

He smiled over Selene's head on his chest. "Okay, honey."

The word brought a soft blush into Sassy's cheeks and he chuckled softly. He led the way out the door to his truck.

JOHN'S IDEA OF a modest guest room was horrifying to Sassy when he stopped by the desk of Billings's best hotel to check in Sassy and Selene.

The child stirred sleepily in John's strong arms. She opened her eyes, yawning. "Mama?" she exclaimed, worried.

"She's fine," John assured her. "Go back to sleep, baby. Curl up in this chair until I get the formalities done, okay?" He placed her gently into a big, cushy armchair near the desk.

"Okay, John," Selene said, smiling as she closed her eyes and nodded off again.

"You'd better stay with her while I do this," John told Sassy, not wanting her to hear the clerk when he gave her his real name to pay for the room.

"Okay, John," she echoed her little sister, with a grin.

He winked at her and went back to the desk. The smile faded as he spoke to the male clerk.

"Their mother is in the hospital, about to have cancer surgery. They were going to sleep in the waiting room. I want a room for them, near mine, if it's possible."

The clerk, a kindly young man, smiled sympathetically. "There's one adjoining yours, Mr. Callister," he said politely. "It's a double. Would that do?"

"Yes."

The clerk made the arrangements, took John's credit card, processed the transaction, handed back the card, and then went to program the card-key for the new guests. He was back in no time, very efficient.

"I hope their mother does all right," he told John.

"So do I. But she's in very good hands."

He went back to Selene, lifted her gently, and motioned to Sassy, who was examining the glass coffee table beside the chairs.

She paused at a pillar as they walked into the elevator. "Gosh, this looks like real marble," she murmured, and then had to run to make it before the elevator doors closed. "John, this place looks expensive..."

"I'll make sure to tell Buck to dock your salary over several months, okay?" he asked gently, and he smiled.

She was apprehensive. It was going to be a big chunk of her income. But he'd already been so nice that she felt guilty for even making a fuss. "Sure, that's fine."

He led them down the hall and gave Sassy the card-key to insert in the lock. She stared at it.

"Why are you giving me a credit card?" she asked in all honesty.

He gaped at her. "It's the door key."

She cocked an eyebrow. "Right." She looked up at him as if she expected men with white nets to appear.

He laughed when he realized she hadn't a clue about modern technology. "Give it here."

He balanced Selene on one lifted knee, inserted the card, jerked it back out so the green light on the lock blinked, and then opened the door.

Sassy's jaw dropped.

"It's a card-key," he repeated, leading the way in.

Sassy closed the door behind them, turning on the lights as she went. The room was a revelation. There was a huge new double bed—two of them, in fact. There were paintings on the wall. There was a round table with two chairs. There was a telephone. There was a huge glass window, curtained, that looked out over Billings. There was even a huge television.

"This is a palace," Sassy murmured, spellbound as she looked around. She peered into the bathroom and actually gasped. "There's a hair dryer right here in the room!" she exclaimed.

John had put Selene down gently on one of the double beds. He felt two inches high. Sassy's life had been spent in a small rural town in abject poverty. She knew nothing of high living. Even this hotel, nice but not the five-star accommodation he'd frequented in his travels both in this country and overseas, was opulent to her. Considering where, and how, she and her family lived, this must have seemed like kingly extravagance.

He walked back to the bathroom and leaned against the door facing while she explored tiny wrapped packets of soap and little bottles of shampoo and soap.

"Wow," she whispered.

She touched the thick white towels, so plush that she wanted to wrap up in one. She compared them to her thin, tatty, worn towels at home and was shocked at the contrast. She glanced at John shyly.

"Sorry," she said. "I'm not used to this sort of place."

"It's just a hotel, Sassy," he said softly. "If you've never stayed in one, I imagine it's surprising at first."

"How did you know?" she asked.

"Know what?"

"That I'd never stayed in a hotel?"

He cleared his throat. "Well, it shows. Sort of."

She flushed. "You mean, I'm acting like an idiot."

"I mean nothing of the sort." He shouldered away from the door facing, caught her by the waist, pulled her close, and bent to kiss the breath out of her.

She held on tight, relieved about her mother, but worried about the surgery, and grateful for John's intervention.

"You've made miracles for us," she said when he let her go.

He searched her shimmering green eyes. "You've made one for me," he replied, and he wasn't kidding.

"I have? How?"

His hands contracted on her small waist. "Let's just say, you've taught me about the value of small blessings. I tend to take things for granted, I guess." His eyes narrowed. "You appreciate the most basic things in life. You're so... optimistic, Sassy," he added. "You make me feel humble."

"Oh, that's rich," she chuckled. "A backwoods hick like me making a sophisticated gentleman like you feel humble."

"I'm not kidding," he replied. "You don't have a lot of material things. But you're happy without them." He shrugged. "I've got a lot more than you have, and I'm..." He searched for the word, frowning. "I'm...empty," he said finally, meeting her quiet eyes.

"But you're the kindest man I've ever known," she argued. "You do things for people without even thinking twice what problems you may cause yourself in the process. You're a good person."

Her wide-eyed fascination made him tingle inside. In recent years, women had wanted him because he was rich and powerful. Here was one who wanted him because he was kind. It was an eye-opener.

"You look strange," she remarked.

"I was thinking," he said.

"About what?"

"About how late it is, and how much you're going to need some sleep. We'll get an early start tomorrow," he told her.

The horror came back, full force. The joy drained out of her face, to be replaced with fear and uncertainty.

He drew her close and rocked her in his arms, bending his head over hers. "That surgeon is rather famous," he said conversationally. "He's one of the best oncologists in the country, and it's a blessing that he ended up here just when your mother needed him. You have to believe that she's going to be all right."

"I'm trying to," she said. "It's just hard. We've had so many trips to the hospital," she confessed, and sounded weary.

John had never had to go through this with his family. Well, there was Gil's first wife who died in a riding accident. That had been traumatic. But since then, John had never worried about losing a relative to disease. He had, he decided, been very lucky.

"I'll be right there with you," he promised her. "All the time."

She drew back and looked up at him with fascinated eyes. "You will? You mean it? Won't you get in trouble with your boss?"

"I won't," he said. "But it wouldn't matter if I did. I'm not leaving you. Not for anything."

She colored and smiled at him.

"After all," he teased, "I'm a member of the family."

She smiled even more.

"Kissing kin," he added, and bent to brush a whisper of a kiss over her soft mouth. He forced himself to step away from her. "Go to bed."

"Okay. Thanks, John. Thanks for everything."

He didn't answer her. He just winked.

THE SURGERY TOOK several hours. Sassy bit her fingernails off into the quick. Selene sat very close to her, holding her hand.

"I don't want Mama to die," she said.

Sassy pulled her close. "She won't die," she promised. "She's going to get better. I promise." She prayed it wasn't going to be a lie.

John had gone to check with the surgical desk. He came back grinning.

"Tell me!" Sassy exclaimed.

"They were able to get all the cancerous tissue," he said. "It was confined to a lobe of her lung, as he suspected. They're cautiously optimistic that your mother will recover and begin to lead a full life again."

"Oh, my goodness!" Sassy exclaimed, hugging Selene close. "She'll get better!"

Selene hugged her back. "I'm so happy!"

"So am I."

Sassy let her go, got up, and went to hug John close, laying her cheek against his broad, warm chest. He enveloped her in his arms. She felt right at home there.

"Thank you," she murmured.

"For what?"

She looked up at him. "For everything."

He smiled at her, his eyes crinkling.

"What happens now?" she asked.

"Your mother recovers enough to go home, then we bring her back up here for the treatments. Dr. Crowley said that would take a few weeks, but except for some nausea and weakness, she should manage it very well."

"You'll come with us?" she asked, amazed.

He glowered at her. "Of course I will," he said indignantly. "I'm part of the family. You said so."

She drew in a long, contented breath. She was tired and worried but she felt newborn. "You're the nicest man I've ever known," she said.

He cocked an eyebrow. "Nicer than the Army guy?"

She smiled. "Even nicer than Caleb."

He looked over her head and glowered even more. "Speak of the devil!"

A tall, dark-haired man in an Army uniform was striding down the hall toward them.

CHAPTER EIGHT

SASSY TURNED AND, sure enough, Caleb was walking toward them in his Army uniform, complete with combat boots and beret. He looked very handsome.

"Caleb," Sassy said warmly, going to meet him. "How did you know we were here?"

He hugged her gently. "I have a cousin who works here. She remembered that I'd been down to see you in Hollister, and that your last name was Peale. How is your mother?"

"She just came out of surgery. Her prognosis is good. John found us a grant to pay for it all, isn't that incredible? I didn't know they had programs like that!"

Caleb knew they didn't. He looked at John and, despite the older man's foreboding expression, he smiled at him. He was quick enough to realize that John had intervened for Sassy's mother and didn't want anybody to know. "Yes, they do have grants, don't they? Nice of you to do that for them," he added, his dark eyes saying things to John that Sassy didn't see.

John relaxed a little. The boy might be competition, but his heart was in the right place. Sassy had said he was a friend, but Caleb here must care about her, to come right to the hospital when he knew about her mother. "They're a great bunch of people," he said simply.

"Yes, they are," Caleb agreed. He turned to smile down at Sassy while John fumed silently.

"Thank you for coming to see us," Sassy told the younger man.

"I wish I could stay," he told her, "but I'm on my way to the rimrocks right now. I'm due back at my assignment."

"The rimrocks?" Sassy asked, frowning.

"It's where the airport is," Caleb told her, grinning. "That's what we call it locally."

"I hope you have a safe flight back," she told him. "And a safe tour of duty."

"Now, that makes two of us," he agreed. "Don't forget to send me that photograph."

"I won't. So long, Caleb."

"So long." He bent and kissed her cheek, smiled ruefully at John, and walked back down the hall.

"What photograph?" John asked belligerently.

"It's not for him," she said, delighted that he looked jealous. "It's to throw his best friend off the track."

John was unconvinced. But just as he started to argue, the surgeon came into the waiting room, smiling wearily.

He shook hands with John and turned to Sassy. "Your mother is doing very well. She's in recovery right now, and then she'll go to the intensive care unit. Just for a couple of days," he added quickly when Sassy went pale and looked faint. "It's normal procedure. We want her watched day and night until she's stabilized."

"Can Selene and I see her?" Sassy asked. "And John?" she added, nodding to the man at her side.

The surgeon hesitated. "Have you ever seen anyone just out of surgery, young woman?" he asked gently.

"Well, there was Great-Uncle Jack, but I only got a glimpse of him...why?"

The surgeon looked apprehensive. "Post-surgical patients are flour-white. They have tubes running out of them, they're connected to machines...it can be alarming if you aren't prepared for it."

"Mama's going to live, thanks to you," Sassy said, smiling. "She'll look beautiful. I don't mind the machines. They're helping her live. Right?"

The surgeon smiled back. Her optimism was contagious. "Right. I'll let you in to see her for five minutes, no longer," he said, "as soon as we move her into intensive care. It will be a little while," he added.

"We're not going anywhere," she replied easily.

He chuckled. "I'll send a nurse for you, when it's time."

"Thank you," Sassy said. "From the bottom of my heart."

The surgeon shifted. "It's what I do," he replied. "The most rewarding job in the world."

"I've never saved anybody's life, but I expect it would be a great job," she told him.

After he left, John gave her a wry look.

"I saved a man's life, once," he told her.

"You did? How?" she asked, waiting.

"I threw a baseball bat at him, and missed."

"Oh, you," she teased. She went close to him, wrapped her arms around him, and laid her head on his broad chest. "You're just wonderful."

His hand smoothed over her dark hair. Over her head, Selene was smiling at him with the same kind of happy, affectionate expression that he imagined was on Sassy's face. Despite the fear and apprehension of the ordeal, it was one of the best days of his life. He'd never felt so necessary.

SASSY WAS ALLOWED into the intensive care unit just long enough to look at her mother and stand beside her. John was with her, the surgeon's whispered request getting him past the fiercely protective nurse in charge of the unit. Sassy was uneasy, despite her assurances, and she clung to John's hand as if she were afraid of falling without its warm support.

She stared at the still, white form in the hospital bed. Machines beeped. A breathing machine made odd noises as it pumped oxygen into Mrs. Peale's unconscious body. The shapeless, faded hospital gown was unfamiliar, like all the monitors and tubes that seemed to extrude from every inch of her mother's flesh. Mrs. Peale was white as a sheet. Her chest rose and fell very slowly. Her heartbeat was visible as the gown fluttered over her ample bosom.

"She's alive," John whispered. "She's going to get well and go home and be a different woman. You have to see the future, through the present."

Sassy looked up at him with tears in her eyes. "It's just… I love her so much."

He smiled tenderly and bent to kiss her forehead. "She loves you, too, honey. She's going to get well."

She drew in a shaky breath and got control of her emotions. She wiped at the tears. "Yes." She moved closer to the bed, bending over her mother. She remembered that when she was a little girl she'd had a debilitating virus that had almost dehydrated her. Mrs. Peale had perched on her bed, feeding her ice chips around the clock to keep fluids in her. She'd fetched wet cloths and whispered that she loved Sassy, that everything was going to be all right. That loving touch had chased the fear and misery and sickness right out of the room. Mrs. Peale seemed to glow with it.

"It's going to be all right, Mama," she whispered, kissing the pale, cool brow. "We love you very much. We're going home, very soon."

Mrs. Peale didn't answer her, but her hand on its confining board jumped, almost imperceptibly.

John squeezed Sassy's hand. "Did you see that?" he asked, smiling. "She heard you."

Sassy squeezed back. "Of course she did."

THREE DAYS LATER, Mrs. Peale was propped up in bed eating Jell-O. She was weak and sore and still in a lot of pain, but she was smiling gamely.

"Didn't I tell you?" John chided Sassy. "She's too tough to let a little thing like major surgery get her down."

Mrs. Peale smiled at him. "You've been so kind to us, John," she said. Her voice was still a little hoarse from the breathing tubes, but she sounded cheerful just the same. "Sassy told me all about the palace you're keeping her and Selene in."

"Some palace," he chuckled. "It's just a place to sleep." He stuck his hands into his jeans and his eyes twinkled. "But being kind goes with the job. I'm part of the family. She—" he pointed at Sassy "—said so."

"I did," Sassy confessed.

Mrs. Peale gave him a wry look. "But not too close a member…?"

"Definitely not," he agreed at once, chuckling. He looked at Sassy in a way that made her blush. Then he compounded the embarrassment by laughing.

IN THE WEEKS that followed, John divided his time between Mrs. Peale's treatments in Billings and the growing responsibility for the new ranch that was just beginning to shape up. The barn was up, shiny and attractive with bricked aisles and spotless stalls with metal gates. The corral had white fences interlaced with hidden electrical fencing that complemented the cosmetic look of the wood. The pastures had been sowed with old prairie grasses, with which John was experimenting. The price of corn had gone through the roof, with the biofuel revolution. Ranchers were scrambling for new means of sustaining their herds, so native grasses were being utilized, along with concentrated pelleted feeds and vitamin supplements. John had also hired a nearby farmer to plant grains for him and keep them during the growing season. His contractor was building a huge new concrete feed silo to house the grains when they were harvested at the end of summer. It was a monumental job, getting the place renovated. John had delegated as much authority as he could, but there were still management decisions that had to be made by him.

Meanwhile, Bill Tarleton's trial went on the docket and pretrial investigations were going on by both the county district attorney and the public defender's office for the judicial circuit where Hollister was located. Sassy was interviewed by both sides. The questions made her very nervous and uneasy. The public defender seemed to think she'd enticed Mr. Tarleton to approach her in a sexual manner. It hurt her feelings.

She told John about it when he stopped by after supper one Friday evening to check on Mrs. Peale. He hadn't been into the feed store the entire week because of obligations out at the ranch.

"He'll make me sound like some cheap tart in court," she moaned. "It will make my mother and Selene look bad, too."

"Telling the truth won't make anyone look bad, dear," Mrs. Peale protested. She was sitting up in the living room knitting. A knitted cap covered her head. Her hair had already started to fall out from the radiation therapy she was receiving, but she hadn't let it get her down. She'd made a dozen caps in different colors and styles and seemed to be enjoying the project.

"You should listen to your mother," John agreed, smiling. "You don't want him to get away with it, Sassy. It wasn't your fault."

"That lawyer made it sound like it was. The assistant district attorney who questioned me asked what sort of clothes I wore to work, and I told him jeans and T-shirts, and not any low-cut ones, either. He smiled and said that it shouldn't have mattered if I'd worn a bikini. He said Mr. Tarleton had no business making me uncomfortable in my workplace, regardless of my clothing."

"I like that assistant district attorney," John said. "He's a firecracker. One day he'll end up in the state attorney general's office. They say he's got a perfect record of convictions in the two years he's prosecuted cases for this judicial circuit."

"I hope he makes Mr. Tarleton as uncomfortable as that public defender made me," Sassy said with feeling. She rubbed her bare arms, as if it chilled her, thinking about the trial. "I don't know how I'll manage, sitting in front of a jury and telling what happened."

"You just remember that the people in that jury will most likely be people who've known you all your life," Mrs. Peale interrupted.

"That's the other thing." Sassy sighed. "The D.A.'s victim assistance person said the defending attorney is trying to get the trial moved to Billings, on account of Mr. Tarleton can't get a fair trial here."

John frowned. That did put another face on things. But he'd testify, as would Sassy. Hopefully Tarleton would get what he deserved. John knew for a fact that if he hadn't intervened, it would have been much more than a minor assault. Sassy knew it, too.

"It was a bad day for Hollister when that man came to town," Mrs. Peale said curtly. "Sassy came home every day upset and miserable."

"You should have called the owner and complained," John told Sassy.

She grimaced. "I didn't dare. He didn't know me that well. I was afraid he'd think I was telling tales on Mr. Tarleton because I wanted his job."

"It's been done," John had to admit. "But you're not like that, Sassy. He'd have investigated and found that out."

She sighed. "It's water under the bridge now," she replied sadly. "I know it's the right thing to do, taking him to court. But what if he gets off and comes after me, or Mama or Selene for revenge?" she added, worried.

"If he does," John said, and his blue eyes glittered dangerously, "it will be the worst decision of his life. I promise you. As for getting off, if by some miracle he does, you'll file a civil suit against him for damages and I'll bankroll you."

"I knew you were a nice man from the first time I laid eyes on you," Mrs. Peale chuckled.

Sassy was smiling at him with her whole face. She felt warm and protected and secure. She blushed when he looked back, with such an intent, piercing expression that her heart turned over.

"Why does life have to be so complicated?" Sassy asked after a minute.

John shrugged. "Beats me, honey," he said, getting to his feet and obviously unaware of the endearment that brought another soft blush to Sassy's face. "But it does seem to get more that way by the day." He checked his watch and grimaced. "I have to get back to the ranch. I've got an important call coming through. But I'll stop by tomorrow. We might take in a movie, if you're game."

Sassy grinned. "I'd love to." She looked at her mother and hesitated.

"I have a phone," her mother pointed out. "And Selene's here."

"You went out with the Army guy and didn't make a fuss," John muttered.

Mrs. Peale beamed. That was jealousy. Sassy seemed to realize it, too, because her eyes lit up.

"I'm not making a fuss," Sassy assured him. "And I love going to the movies."

John relented a little and grinned self-consciously. "Okay. I'll be along about six. That Chinese restaurant that just opened has good food—suppose I bring some along and we'll have supper before we go?"

They hesitated to accept. He'd done so much for them already...

"It's Chinese food, not precious jewels," he said. "Would you like to go out and look at my truck again? I make a handsome salary and I don't drink, smoke, gamble or run around with predatory women!"

Now Mrs. Peale and Sassy both looked sheepish and grinned.

"Okay," Sassy said. "But when I get rich and famous one day for my stock-clerking abilities, I'm paying you back for all of it."

He laughed. "That's a deal."

THE CHINESE FOOD was a huge assortment of dishes, many of which could be stored in the refrigerator and provide meals for the weekend for the women and the child. They knew what he'd done, but they didn't complain again. He was bighearted and he wanted to help them. It seemed petty to argue.

After they ate, he helped Sassy up into the cab of the big pickup truck, got in himself, and drove off down the road. It was still light outside, but the sun was setting in brilliant colors. It was like a symphony of reds and oranges and yellows, against the silhouetted mountains in the distance.

"It's so beautiful here," Sassy said, watching the sunset. "I'd never want to live anyplace else."

He glanced at her. He was homesick for Medicine Ridge from time to time, but he liked Hollister, too. It was a small, homey place with nice people and plenty of wide-open country. The elbow room was delightful. You could drive for miles and not meet another car or even see a house.

"Are we going to the theater in town?" she asked John.

He grinned like a boy. "We are not," he told her. "I found a drive-in theater just outside the city limits. The owner started it up about a month ago. He said he'd gone to them when he was young and thought it was time to bring them back. I don't know that he'll be able to stay open long, but I thought we'd check it out, anyway."

"Wow," she exclaimed. "I've read about them in novels."

"Me, too, but I've never been to one. Our uncle used to talk about them."

"Is it in a town?" she asked.

"No. It's in the middle of a cow pasture. Cattle graze nearby."

She laughed delightedly. "You're watching a movie with the windows open and a cow sticks its head into the car with you," she guessed.

"I wouldn't be surprised."

"I like cows," she said with a sigh. "I wouldn't mind."

"He runs beef cattle. Steers."

She looked at him. "Steers?"

"It's a bull with missing equipment," he told her, tongue-in-cheek.

"Then what's a cow?"

"It's a cow, if it's had calves. If it hasn't, it's a heifer."

"You know a lot about cattle."

"I've worked around them all my life," he said comfortably. "I love animals. We're going to have horses out at the ranch, too. You can come riding and bring Selene, any time you want."

"You'd have to teach Selene," she said. "She's never been on a horse and you'd have to coach me. It's been a long time since I've been riding."

He glanced at her with warm eyes. "I'd love that."

She laughed. "Me, too."

THE DRIVE-IN WAS in a cleared pasture about a quarter of a mile off the main highway. There was a marquee, which listed the movie playing, this time a science-fiction one about a space freighter and its courageous crew which was fighting a technological empire that ran the inner planets of the solar system where it operated. They drove through a tree-lined dirt road down to the cleared pasture. There was room for about twenty cars, and six were already occupying one of three slight inclines that faced a huge blank screen. Each space had a pole, which contained two speakers, one for cars on either side of it. At the ticket stand, which was a drive-through affair manned by a teenager who looked like the owner John had already met, most likely his son, John paid for their tickets.

He pulled the truck up into an unoccupied space and cut off the engine, looking around amusedly. "The only thing missing is a concession stand with drinks and pizza and a rest room," he mused. "Maybe he'll add that, later, if the drive-in catches on."

"It's nice out here, without all that," she mused, looking around.

"Yes, it is." He powered down both windows and brought the speaker in on his side of the truck. He turned up the volume just as the screen lit up with welcome messages and previews of coming attractions.

"This is great!" Sassy laughed.

"It is, isn't it?"

He tossed his hat into the small backseat of the double-cabbed truck, unfastened his seat belt, and stretched out. As an afterthought, he unfastened Sassy's belt and drew her into the space beside him, with his long arm behind her back and his cheek resting on her soft hair.

"Isn't that better?" he murmured, smiling.

One small hand went to press against his shirtfront as she curled closer with a sigh. "It's much better."

The first part of the movie was hilarious. But before it ended, they weren't watching anymore. John had looked down at Sassy's animated face in the flickering light from the movie screen and longing had grown in him like a hot tide. It had been a while since he'd felt Sassy's soft mouth under his lips and he was hungry for it. Since he'd known her, he hadn't had the slightest interest in other women. It was only Sassy.

He tugged on her hair so that she lifted her face to his. "Is this all you'll ever want, Sassy?" he asked gently. "Living in a small, rural town and working in a feed store? Will you miss knowing what it's like to go to college or work in a big city and meet sophisticated people?" he asked solemnly.

Her soft eyes searched his. "Why would I want to do that?" she asked with genuine interest.

"You're very young," he said grimly. "This is all you know."

"Mr. Barber, who runs the Ford dealership here, was born in Hollister and has never been outside the county in his whole life," she told him. "He's been married to Miss Jane since he was eighteen and she was sixteen. They have five sons."

He frowned. "Are you saying something?"

"I'm telling you that this is how people live here," she said simply. "We don't have extravagant tastes. We're country people. We're family. We get married. We have kids. We grow old watching our grandchildren grow up. Then we die. We're buried here. We have beautiful country where we can walk in the forest or ride through fields full of growing crops, or pass through pastures where cattle and horses graze. We have clear, unpolluted streams and blue skies. We sit on the porch after dark and listen to the crickets in the summer and watch lightning bugs flash green in the trees. If someone gets sick, neighbors come over to help. If someone dies, they bring food and comfort. Nobody in trouble is ever ignored. We have everything we need and want and love, right here in Hollister." She cocked her head. "What can a city offer us that would match that?"

He stared at her without speaking. He'd never heard it put exactly that way. He loved Medicine Ridge. But he'd been in college back East, and he'd traveled all over the world. He had choices. Sassy had never had the chance to make one. On the other hand, she sounded very mature as she recounted the reasons she was happy where she lived. There were people in John's acquaintance who'd never known who they were or where they belonged.

"What are you thinking?" she asked.

"That you're an old soul in a young body," he said.

She laughed. "My mother says that all the time."

"She's right. You have a profound grasp of life. So you're happy living here. What if you had a scholarship and you could go to college and study anything you liked?"

"Who'd take care of Mama and Selene?" she asked softly.

"Most women would be more focused on their career than family responsibilities at your age."

"Maybe, but my family is important to me, and I'm happy to put them first." She settled closer to John. "Everybody's so busy these days. When do parents have time to get to know their kids? I've read that some kids have to text-message their parents and make appointments to meet. And they wonder why kids are so screwed up."

He sighed. "I guess my brother and I were protected from a lot of that. Our uncle kept us close on the ranch. We played sports, but we were confined to one, and we had chores every day that had to be done. We didn't have cell phones or cars, and we mostly stayed at home until he thought we were old enough to drive. We always ate together and most nights we played board games or went outside with the telescopes to learn about the stars. He wasn't big on school activities, either. He said they were a corrupting influence, because we had city kids in our school with what he called outrageous ideas of morality."

She laughed. "That's what Mama called some of the kids at my school." She grimaced. "I guess I've been very sheltered. I do have a cell phone, but I don't know how to do half of what it's capable of."

"I'll teach you," he told her, smiling.

"I guess your phone does all kinds of stuff."

"The regular. Internet, movies, music, sports, email," he told her.

"Wow. I just use mine for calls and text."

He laughed. She was so out of touch. But he loved her that way. The smile faded as he looked down into her soft, melting eyes. He dropped his gaze to her mouth, faintly pink, barely parted.

"I suppose the future doesn't come with guarantees," he said to himself. He bent slowly. "I've been sitting here for five minutes remembering how your soft lips felt under my mouth, Sassy," he whispered as his parted lips met hers. "I ache like a boy for you."

As he spoke, he drew her across the seat, across his lap, and kissed her with slow, building hunger. His big hand deftly moved buttons out of buttonholes and slid right inside her bra with a mastery that left her breathless and excited.

He caressed the hard tip with slow, teasing movements while he fed on her mouth, teasing it, too, with slow, brief contacts that eventually made her moan and arch up toward him.

Her skin felt hot. She ached to have him take off her blouse and everything under it and look at her. She wanted to feel his lips swallowing that hard-tipped softness. It was madness. She could hear her own heartbeat, feel the growing desire that built inside her untried body. She'd never wanted a man before. Now she wanted him with a reckless abandon that blasted every sane reason for protest right out of her melting body.

John lifted his head, frustrated, and glanced around him in the darkness. The scene on the screen was subdued and so was the lighting. Nobody could see them. He bent his head again and, unobtrusively, suddenly stripped Sassy's blouse and bra up to her chin. His blazing eyes found her breasts, adored them. He shivered with need.

She arched faintly, encouraging him. He bent to her breasts and slowly drew one of them right inside his mouth, pulling at it gently as his tongue explored the hardness and drew a harsh moan from her lips.

The sound galvanized him. His mouth became rough. The arm behind her was like steel. His free hand slid down her bare belly and right into the opening of her jeans. He was so aroused that he didn't even realize where they were.

At least, he didn't realize it until something wet and rubbery slid over his bent head through the passenger window.

It took him a minute to realize it wasn't, couldn't be, Sassy's mouth. It was very wet. He forced his own head up and looked toward Sassy's window. A very large bovine head was inside the open window of the truck. It was licking him.

CHAPTER NINE

"Sassy?" he asked, his voice hoarse with lingering passion.

She opened her eyes. "What?"

"Look out your window."

She turned her head and met the steer's eyes. "Aaaah!" she exclaimed.

He burst out laughing. He smoothed down her blouse and bra and sat up, his hand going gingerly to his hair. "Good Lord! I wondered why my hair felt so wet."

She fumbled her bra back on, embarrassed and amused at the same time. The little steer had moved back from the window, but it was still curious. It let out a loud "MOOOO." Muffled laughter came from a nearby car.

"Well, so much for my great idea that this was a good place to make out," John chuckled, straightening his shirt with a sigh. "I guess it wasn't a bad thing to get interrupted," he added, with a rueful smile at Sassy's red face. "Things were getting a little intense."

He didn't seem to be embarrassed at all, but Sassy had never gone so far with a man before and she felt fragile. She was uneasy that she hadn't denied him such intimate access to her body. And she couldn't forget where his other hand had been moving when the steer came along.

"Don't," John said softly when he read her expression. His fingers caught hers and linked into them. "It was perfectly natural."

"I guess you...do that all the time," she stammered.

He shrugged. "I used to. But since I met you, I haven't wanted to do it with anyone else."

If it was a line, it sounded sincere. She looked at him with growing hope. "Really?"

His fingers tightened on hers. "We've been through a lot of intense situations together in a little bit of time. Tarleton's assault. Your mother's close call. The cancer treatments." He looked into her eyes. "You said that I was like part of your family and that's how I feel, too. I'm at home when I'm with you." He looked down at their linked hands. "I want it to go on," he said hesitantly. "I want us to be together. I want you in my life from now on." He drew in a long breath. "I ache to have you."

She was uncomfortable with the way he said it, not understanding that he'd never tried to make a commitment to another woman in his life; not even when he was intimate with other women.

"You want to sleep with me," she said bluntly.

He smoothed his thumb over her cold fingers. "I want to do everything with you," he replied. "You're too young," he added quietly. "But, then, my brother just married a woman ten years his junior and they're ecstatically happy. It can work. I guess it depends on the woman, and we've already agreed that you're mature for your age."

"You aren't exactly over the hill, John," she replied, still curious about what he was suggesting. "And you're very attractive." She gave him a gamine look. "Even small hoofed animals are drawn to you."

He glared at her.

"Don't look at me," she laughed. "It was you that the little steer was kissing."

He touched his wet hair and winced. "God knows where his mouth has been."

She laughed again. "Well, at least he has good taste."

"Thanks. I think." He pulled a red work rag from the console and dried his hair where the steer had licked it. He was watching Sassy. "You don't understand what I'm saying, do you?"

"Not really," she confessed.

"I suppose I'm making a hash of it," he muttered. "But I've never done this before."

"Asked someone to live with you, you mean," she said haltingly.

He met her eyes evenly. "Asked someone to marry me, Sassy."

She just stared. For a minute, she wasn't sure she wasn't dreaming. But his gaze was intent, intimate. He was waiting.

She let out the breath she'd been holding. She started to speak and then stopped, confused. "I..."

"If you've noticed any bad habits that disturb you, I'll try to change them," he mused, smiling, because she wasn't refusing.

"Oh, no, it's not that. I... I have a lot of baggage," she began nervously.

Then he remembered what she told him some time back, that her infrequent dates had said they didn't want to get involved with a woman who had so much responsibility for her family.

He grinned. "I love your baggage," he said. "Your mother and adopted sister are like part of my family already." He shrugged. "So I'll have more dependents." He gave her a wicked look. "Income tax time won't be so threatening."

She laughed out loud. He wasn't intimidated. He didn't

mind. She threw her arms around him and kissed him so fervently that he forgot what they'd been talking about and just kissed her back until they had to come up for air.

"But I'll still work," she promised breathlessly, her eyes sparkling like fireworks. "I'm not going to sit down and make you support all three of us. I'll carry my part of the load!" She laughed, unaware of his sudden stillness, of the guilty look on his face. "It will be fun, making our way together. Hard times are what bring people close, you know, even more than the good times."

"Sassy, there are some things we're going to have to talk about," he said slowly.

"A lot of things," she agreed dreamily, laying her cheek against his broad, warm chest. "I never dreamed you might want to marry me. I'll try to be the best wife in the world. I'll cook and clean and work my fingers to the bone. I like horses and cattle. I'll help you with chores on the ranch, too."

She was cutting his heart open and she didn't know it. He'd lied to her. He hadn't thought of the consequences. He should have been honest with her from the beginning. But he realized then that she'd never have come near him if he'd walked into that feed store in his real persona. The young woman who worshipped the lowly cattle foreman would draw back and stand in awe of the wealthy cattle baron who could walk into a store and buy anything he fancied without even looking at a price tag. It was a sickening thought. She was going to feel betrayed, at best. At worst, she might think he was playing some game with her.

He smoothed his hand over her soft hair. "Well, it can wait another day," he murmured as he kissed her forehead. "There's plenty of time for serious discussions." He tilted her mouth up to his. "Tonight, we're just engaged and cele-brating. Come here."

By the time they got back to her house, they were both disheveled and their mouths were swollen. Sassy had never been so happy in her life.

JOHN HAD CONSOLED himself that he still had time to tell Sassy the truth. He had no way of knowing that Bill Tarleton and his attorney had just gone before the district circuit judge in the courthouse in Billings for a hearing on a motion to dismiss all charges against him. The reason behind the motion, the attorney stated, was that the eyewitness who was to testify against Tarleton was romantically involved with the so-called victim and was, in fact, no common cowboy, but a wealthy cattleman from Medicine Ridge. The defense argued that this new information changed the nature of the accusation from a crime to an act of jealousy. It was a rich man victimizing a poor man because he was jealous of the man's attentions to his girlfriend.

The state attorney, who was also present at the hearing, argued that the new information made no difference to the primary charge, which was one of sexual assault and battery. A local doctor would testify to the young lady's physical condition after the assault. The public defender argued that he'd seen the doctor's report and it only mentioned reddish marks and bruising, on the young lady's arms, nothing more. That could not be construed as injury sustained in the course of a sexual assault, so only the alleged assault charge was even remotely applicable.

The judge took the case under advisement and promised a decision within the week. Meanwhile, the assistant district attorney handling the case in circuit court showed up at Sassy's home the following Monday evening, soon after Sassy had put Selene to bed, to discuss the case. His name was James Addy.

"Mr. Tarleton is alleging that Mr. Callister inflated the charges out of jealousy because of the attention Mr. Tarleton was paying you," Addy said in a businesslike tone, opening his briefcase on the dining room table while Sassy sat gaping at him.

"Mr. Callister? Who is that?" she asked, confused. "John Taggert rescued me. Mr. Tarleton kissed me and was trying to force me down on the floor. I screamed for help and Mr. Taggert, who came into the store at that moment, came to my assistance. I don't know any Mr. Callister."

The attorney stared at her. "You don't know who John Callister is?" he asked, aghast. "He and his brother Gil own the Medicine Ridge Ranch. It's world famous as a breeding bull enterprise. Aside from that, they have massive land holdings not only in Montana, but in adjoining states, including real estate and mining interests. Their parents own the Sportsman Enterprises chain of magazines. The family is one of the wealthiest in the country."

"Yes," Sassy said, trying to wrap her mind around the strange monolog, "I've heard of them. But what do they have to do with John Taggert, except that they're his bosses?" she asked innocently.

The attorney finally got it. She didn't know who her suitor actually was. A glance around the room was enough to tell him her financial status. It was unlikely that a millionaire would be seriously interested in such a poor woman. Apparently Callister had been playing some game with her. He frowned. It was a cruel game.

"The man's full name is John Taggert Callister," he said in a gentler tone. "He's Gil Callister's younger brother."

Sassy's face lost color. She'd been dreaming of a shared

life with John, of working to build something good together, along with her family. He was a millionaire. That sort of man moved in high society, had money to burn. He was up here overhauling a new ranch for the conglomerate. Sassy had been handy and she amused him, so he was playing with her. It hadn't been serious, not even when he asked her to marry him! She felt sick to her stomach. She didn't know what to do now. And how was she going to tell her mother and Selene the truth?

She folded her arms around her chest and sat like a stone, her green eyes staring at the attorney, pleading with him to tell her it was all a lie, a joke.

He couldn't. He grimaced. "I'm very sorry," he said genuinely. "I thought you knew the truth."

"Not until now," she said in a subdued tone. She closed her eyes. The pain was lancing, enveloping. Her life was falling apart around her.

He drew in a long breath, searching for the right words. "Miss Peale, I hate to have to ask you this. But was there an actual assault?"

She blinked. What had he asked? She met his eyes. "Mr. Tarleton kissed me and tried to handle me and I resisted him. He was angry. He got a hard grip on me and was trying to force me down on the floor when Mr. Taggert—" She stopped and swallowed, hard. "Mr. Callister, that is, came to help me. He pulled Mr. Tarleton off me. Then he called law enforcement."

The lawyer was looking worried. "You were taken to a doctor. What were his findings?"

"Well, I had some bruises and I was sore. He ripped my blouse. I guess there wasn't a lot of physical evidence. But it did scare me. I was upset and crying."

"Miss Peale, was there an actual *sexual* assault?"

She began to understand what he meant. "Oh! Well... no," she stammered. "He kissed me and he tried to fondle me, but he didn't try to take any of my other clothes off, if that's what you mean."

"That's what I mean." He sat back in his chair. "We can't prosecute for sexual assault and battery on the basis of an unwanted kiss. We can charge him with sexual assault for any sexual contact which is unwanted. However, the law provides that if he's convicted, the maximum sentence is six months in jail or a fine not to exceed $500. If in the course of sexual contact the perpetrator inflicts bodily injury, he can get from four years to life in prison. In this case, however, you would be required to show that injury resulted from the attempted kiss. Quite frankly," he added, "I don't think a jury, even under the circumstances, would consider unwanted touching and bruising to be worth giving a man a life sentence."

She sighed. "Yes. It does seem a bit drastic, even to me. Is it true that he doesn't have any prior convictions?" she asked curiously.

He shook his head. "We found out that he was arrested on a sexual harassment charge in another city, but he was cleared, so there was no conviction."

She was tired of the whole thing. Tired of remembering Tarleton's unwanted advances, tired of being tied to the memory as long as the court case dragged on. If she insisted on prosecuting him for an attack, she couldn't produce any real proof. His attorney would take her apart on the witness stand, and she'd be humiliated yet again.

But as bad as that thought was, it was worse to think about going into court and asking them to put a man, even Tarleton, in prison for the rest of his life because he'd tried to kiss her. The lawyer was right. Tarleton might have intended much worse, but he hadn't succeeded. It was hardly a major crime. Still, she hated letting him get off so lightly.

She almost protested. It had been a little more than bruising. The man had intended much more, and he'd done it to some other poor girl who'd been too ashamed to force him to go to trial. Sassy had guts. She could do this.

But then she had a sudden, frightening thought. If John Taggert Callister was called to appear for the prosecution, she realized suddenly, it would become a media event. He was famous. His presence at the trial would draw the media. There would be news crews, cameras, reporters. There might even be national exposure. Her mother would suffer for it. So would Selene. For herself, she would have taken the chance. For her mother, still undergoing cancer treatments and unsuited to stress of any kind right now, she could not.

Her shoulders lifted. "Mr. Addy, the trial will come with a media blitz if Mr.…. Mr. Callister is called to testify for me, won't it? My mother and Selene could be talked about on those horrible entertainment news programs if it came out that I was poor and John was rich and there was an attempted sexual assault in the mix. Think how twisted they could make it sound. It would be the sort of sordid subject some people in the news media love to get their hands on these days. Just John's name would guarantee that people would be interested in what happened. They could make a circus out of it."

He hesitated. "That shouldn't be a consideration…"

"My mother has lung cancer," she replied starkly. "She's just been through major surgery and is now undergoing radiation and chemo for it. She can't take any more stress than she's already got. If there's even a chance that this trial could bring that sort of publicity, I can't take it. So what can I do?"

Mr. Addy considered the question. "I think we can plea bargain him to a charge of sexual assault with the lighter sentence. I know, it's not perfect," he told her. "He'd likely get the fine and some jail time, even if he gets probation. And it would at least go on the record as a conviction and any future transgression on his part would land him in very hot water. He has a public defender, but he seems anxious to avoid spending a long time in jail waiting for the trial. I think he'll agree to the lesser charge. Especially considering who the witness is. When he has time to think about the consequences of trying to drag John Callister's good name through the mud, and consider what sort of attorneys the Callisters would produce for a trial, I believe he'll jump at the plea bargain."

She considered that, and then the trauma of a jury trial with all the media present. This way, at least Tarleton would now have a criminal record, and it might be enough to deter him from any future assaults on other women. "Okay," she said. "As long as he doesn't get away with it."

"Oh, he won't get away with it, Miss Peale," he said solemnly. "I promise you that." He pondered for a minute. "However, if you'd rather stand firm on the original charge, I'll prosecute him, despite the obstacles. Is this plea bargain what you really want?"

She sighed sadly. "Not really. I'd love to hang him out to dry. But I have to consider my mother. It's the only possible way to make him pay for what he tried to do without hurting my family. If it goes to a jury trial, even with the media all around, he might walk away a free man because of the publicity. You said they were already trying to twist it so that it looks like John was just jealous and making a fuss because he could, because he was rich and powerful. I know the Callisters can afford the best attorneys, but it wouldn't be right to put them in that situation, either. Mr. Callister has two little nieces..." She grimaced. "You know, the legal system isn't altogether fair sometimes."

He smiled. "I agree. But it's still the best system on earth," he replied.

"I hope I'm doing the right thing," she said on a sigh. "If he gets out and hurts some other woman because I backed down, I'll never get over it."

He gave her a long look. "You aren't backing down, Miss Peale. You're compromising. It may look as if he's getting away with it. But he isn't."

She liked him. She smiled. "Okay, then."

He closed his briefcase and got to his feet. He held out his hand and shook hers. "He'll have a criminal record," he promised her. "If he ever tries to do it again, in Montana, I can promise you that he'll spend a lot of time looking at the world through vertical bars." He meant every word.

"Thanks, Mr. Addy."

"I'll let you know how things work out. Good evening."

SASSY WATCHED HIM go with quiet, thoughtful eyes. She was compromising on the case, but on behalf of a good cause. She couldn't put her mother through the nightmare of a trial and the vicious publicity it would bring on them. Mrs. Peale had suffered enough.

She went back into the house. Mrs. Peale was coming out of the bedroom, wrapped in her chenille housecoat, pale and weak. "Could you get me some pineapple juice, sweetheart?" she asked, forcing a smile.

"Of course!" Sassy ran to get it. "Are you all right?" she asked worriedly.

"Just a little sick. That's nothing to worry about, it goes with the treatments. At least I'm through with them for a few weeks." She frowned. "What's wrong? And who was that man you were talking to?"

"Here, back to bed." Sassy went with her, helping her down on the bed and tucking her under the covers with her glass of cold juice. She sat down beside her. "That was the assistant district attorney—or one of them, anyway. A Mr. Addy. He came to talk to me about Mr. Tarleton. He wants to offer him a plea bargain so we don't end up in a messy court case."

Mrs. Peale frowned. "He's guilty of harassing you. He assaulted you. He should pay for it."

"He will. There's jail time and a fine for it," she replied, candy-coating her answer. "He'll have a criminal record. But I won't have to be grilled and humiliated by his attorney on the stand."

Mrs. Peale sipped her juice. She thought about what a trial would be like for Sassy. She'd seen such trials on her soap operas. She sighed. "All right, dear. If you're satisfied, I am, too." She smiled. "Have you heard from John? He was going to bring me some special chocolates when he came back."

Sassy hesitated. She couldn't tell her mother. Not yet. "I haven't heard from him," she said.

"You don't look well…"

"I'm just fine," Sassy said, grinning. "Now you go back to bed. I'm going to reconcile the bank statement and get Selene's clothes ready for school tomorrow."

"All right, dear." She settled back into the pillows. "You're too good to me, Sassy," she added. "Once I get back on my feet, I want you to go a lot of places with John. I'm going to be fine, thanks to him and those doctors in

Billings. I can take care of myself and Selene, finally, and you can have a life of your own."

"You stop that," Sassy chided. "I love you. Nothing I do for you, or Selene, is a chore."

"Yes, but you've had a ready-made family up until now," Mrs. Peale said softly. "It's limited your social life."

"My social life is just dandy, thanks."

The older woman grinned. "I'll say! Wait until John gets back. He's got a surprise waiting for you."

"Has he, really?" Sassy wondered if it was the surprise the attorney had just shared with her. She was too sick to care, but she couldn't let on. Her mother was so happy. It would be cruel to dash all her hopes and reveal the truth about the young man Mrs. Peale idolized.

"He has! Don't you stay up too late. You're looking peaked, dear."

"I'm just tired. We've been putting up tons of stock in the feed store," she lied. She smiled. "Good night, Mama."

"Good night, dear. Sleep well."

As if, Sassy thought as she closed the door. She gave up on paperwork a few minutes later and went to bed. She cried herself to sleep.

JOHN WALKED INTO the feed store a day later, back from an unwanted but urgent business trip to Colorado. He spotted Sassy at the counter and walked up to it with a beaming smile.

She looked up and saw him, and he knew it was all over by the expression on her face. She was apprehensive, uncomfortable. She fidgeted and could barely meet his intent gaze.

He didn't even bother with preliminary questions. His eyes narrowed angrily. "Who told you?" he asked tersely.

She drew in a breath. He looked scary like that. Now that she knew who he really was, knew the power and fame behind his name, she was intimidated. This man could write his own ticket. He could go anywhere, buy anything, do anything he liked. He was worlds away from Sassy, who lived in a house with a leaky roof. He was like a stranger. The smiling, easygoing cowboy she thought he was had become somebody totally different.

"It was the assistant district attorney," she said in a faint tone. "He came to see me. Mr. Tarleton was going to insinuate that you were jealous of him and forced me to file a complaint..."

He exploded. "I'll get attorneys in here who will put him away for the rest of his miserable life," he said tersely. He looked as if he could do that single-handed.

"No!" She swallowed. "No. Please. Think what it would do to Mama if a whole bunch of reporters came here to cover the story because of...because of who you are," she pleaded. "Stress makes everything so much worse for her."

He looked at her intently. "I hadn't thought about that," he said quietly. "I'm sorry."

"Mr. Addy says that Mr. Tarleton will probably agree to plead guilty or no contest to the sexual assault charge." She sighed. "There's a fine and jail time. He was willing to prosecute on the harder charge, but there would have to be proof that he did more than just kiss me and handle me..."

He frowned. He knew what she meant. A jury would be unlikely to convict for sexual assault and battery on an unwanted kiss and some groping, and how could they prove that Tarleton had intended much more? It made him angry. He wanted the man to go to prison. But Mrs. Peale would pay the price. In her delicate condition, it would probably kill her to have to watch Sassy go through the trial, even if she didn't get to court. John's name would guarantee news interest. Just the same, he was going to have a word with Mr. Addy. Sassy never had to know.

"How is your mother?" he asked.

"She's doing very well," she replied, her tone a little stilted. He did intimidate her now. "The treatments have left her a little anemic and weak, and there's some nausea, but they gave her medicine for that." She didn't add that it was bankrupting her to pay for it. She'd already had to pawn her grandfather's watch and pistol to manage a month's worth. She wasn't admitting that.

"I brought her some chocolates," he told her. He smiled gently. "She likes the Dutch ones."

She was staring at him with wide, curious eyes. "You'll spoil her," she replied.

He shrugged. "So? I'm rich. I can spoil people if I want to."

"Yes, I know, but…"

"If you were rich, and I wasn't," he replied solemnly, "would you hesitate to do anything you could for me, if I was in trouble?"

"Of course not," she assured him.

"Then why should it bother you if I spoil your mother a little? Especially, now, when she's had so much illness."

"It doesn't, really. It's just—" She stopped dead. The color went out of her face as she stared at him and suddenly realized how much he'd done for them.

"What's wrong?" he asked.

"There was no grant to pay for that surgery, and the treatments," she said in a choked tone. "You paid for it! You paid for it all!"

CHAPTER TEN

JOHN GRIMACED. "Sassy, there was no other way," he said, trying to reason with her. She looked anguished. "Your mother would have died. I checked your company insurance coverage when I had Buck put you on the payroll as assistant manager. It didn't have a major medical option. I told Buck to shop around for a better plan, but your mother's condition went critical before we could find one."

She knew her heart was going to beat her to death. She'd never be able to pay him back, not even the interest on the money he'd spent on her mother. She'd been poor all her life, but she'd never felt it like this. It had never hurt so much.

"You're part of my life now," he said softly. "You and your mother and Selene. Of course I was going to do all I could for you. For God's sake, don't try to reduce what we feel for each other to dollars and cents!"

"I can't pay you back." She groaned.

"Have I asked you to?" he returned.

"But..." she protested, ready for a long battle.

The door opened behind them and Theodore Graves, the police chief, walked in. His lean face was set in hard lines. He nodded at John and approached Sassy.

He pushed his Stetson back over jet-black hair. "That assistant district attorney, Addy, said you agreed to let Tarleton plea bargain to a lesser charge," he said. "He won't discuss the case with me and I can't intimidate him the way I intimidate most people. So I'd like to know why."

She sighed. He made her feel guilty. "It's Mama," she told him. "He—" she indicated John "—is very well-known. If it goes to court, reporters will show up to find out why he's mixed up in a sexual assault case. Mama will get stressed out, the cancer will come back, and we'll bury her."

Graves grimaced. "I hadn't thought about that. About the stress, I mean." He frowned. "What do you mean, he's well-known?" he added, indicating John. "He's a ranch foreman."

"He's not," Sassy said with a long sigh. "He's John Callister."

Graves lifted a thick, dark eyebrow. "Of the Callister ranching empire over in Medicine Ridge?"

John lifted a shoulder. "Afraid so."

"Oh, boy."

"Listen, at least he'll have a police record," Sassy said stubbornly. "Think about it. Do you really want a media circus right here in Hollister? Mr. Tarleton would probably love it," she added miserably.

"He probably would," Graves had to agree. He stuck his hands into his slacks pockets. "Seventy-five years ago, we'd have turned him out into the woods and sent men with guns after him."

"Civilized men don't do things like that," Sassy reminded him. "Especially policemen."

Graves shrugged. "So sue me. I never claimed to be civilized. I'm a throwback." He drew in a long breath. "All right, as long as the polecat gets some serious time in the slammer, I can be generous and put up the rope I just bought."

Sassy wondered how the chief thought Tarleton would

get a jail sentence when Mr. Addy had hinted that Tarleton would probably get probation.

"Good of you," John mused.

"Pity he didn't try to escape when we took him up to Billings for the motion hearing," Graves said thoughtfully. "I volunteered to go along with the deputy sheriff who transported him. I even wore my biggest caliber revolver, special, just in case." He pursed his lips and brightened. "Somebody might leave a door open, in the detention center..."

"Don't you dare," John said firmly. "You're not the only one who's disappointed. I was looking forward to the idea of having him spend the next fifteen years or so with one of the inmates who has the most cigarettes. But I'm not willing to see my future mother-in-law die over it."

"Mother-in-law?" Graves gave him a wry look from liquid black eyes in a lean, tanned face.

Sassy blushed. "Now, we have to talk about that," she protested.

"We already did," John said. "You promised to marry me."

"That was before I knew who you were," she shot back belligerently.

He grinned. "That's more like it," he mused. "The deference was wearing a little thin," he explained.

She flushed even more. She had been behaving like a working girl with the boss, instead of an equal. She shifted. She was still uncomfortable thinking about his background and comparing it to her own.

"I like weddings," Graves commented.

John glanced at him. "You do?"

He nodded. "I haven't been to one in years, of course, and I don't own a good suit anymore." He shrugged. "I guess I could buy one, if I got invited to a wedding."

John burst out laughing. "You can come to ours. I'll make sure you get an invitation."

Graves smiled. "That's a deal." He glanced at Sassy, who still looked undecided. "If I lived in a house that looked like yours, and drove a piece of scrap metal like that vehicle you ride around in, I'd say yes when a financially secure man asked me to marry him."

Sassy almost burst trying not to laugh. "Has any financially secure man asked you to marry him lately, Chief?"

He glared at her. "I was making a point."

"Several of them," Sassy returned. "But I do appreciate your interest. I wouldn't mind sending Mr. Tarleton to prison myself, if the cost wasn't so high."

He pursed his lips and his black eyes twinkled. "Now that's a coincidence. I've thought about nothing else except sending Mr. Tarleton to prison for the past few weeks. In fact, it never hurts to recommend a prison to the district attorney," he said pleasantly. "I know one where even the chaplain has to carry a Taser."

"Mr. Addy already said he isn't likely to get jail time, since he's a first offender," Sassy said sadly.

"Now isn't that odd," the chief replied with a wicked grin. "I spent some quality time on the computer yesterday and I turned up a prior conviction for sexual assault over in Wyoming, where Mr. Tarleton was working two years ago. He got probation for that one. Which makes him a repeat offender." He looked almost angelic. "I just told Addy. He was almost dancing in the street."

Sassy gasped. "Really?"

He chuckled. "I thought you'd like hearing that. I figured that a man with his attitude had to have a conviction somewhere. He didn't have one in Montana, so I started looking in surrounding states. I checked the criminal records in Wyoming, got a hit, and called the district attorney in the court circuit where it was filed. What a story I got from him! So I took it straight to Addy this morning." He gave her a wry look. "But I did want to know why you let him plead down, and Addy wouldn't tell me."

"Now I feel better, about agreeing to the plea bargain," Sassy said. "His record will affect the sentence, won't it?"

"It will, indeed," Graves assured her. "In another interesting bit of irony, the judge hearing his case had to step down on account of a family emergency. The new judge in his case is famous for her stance on sexual assault cases." He leaned forward. "She's a woman."

Sassy's eyes lit up. "Poor Mr. Tarleton."

"Right." John chuckled. "Good of you to bring us the latest news."

Graves smiled at him. "I thought it would be a nice surprise." He glanced at Sassy. "I understand now why you made the decision you did. Your mom's a sweet lady. It's like a miracle that the surgery saved her."

"Yes," Sassy agreed. Her eyes met John's. "It is a miracle."

Graves pulled his wide-brimmed hat low over his eyes. "Don't forget that wedding invitation," he reminded John. "I'll even polish my good boots."

"I won't forget," John assured him.

"Thanks again," she told the chief.

He smiled at her. "I like happy endings."

When he was gone, John turned back to Sassy with a searching glance. "I'm coming to get you after supper," he informed her. "We've got a lot to talk about."

"John, I'm poor," she began.

He leaned across the counter and kissed her warmly. "I'll be poor, if I don't have you," he said softly. He pulled a velvet-covered box out of his pocket and put it in her hands. "Open that after I leave."

"What is it?" she asked dimly.

"Something for us to talk about, of course." He winked at her and smiled broadly. He walked out the door and closed it gently behind him.

Sassy opened the box. It was a gold wedding band with an embossed vine running around it. There was a beautiful diamond ring that was its companion. She stared at them until tears burned her eyes. A man bought a set of rings like this when he meant them to be heirlooms, handed down from generation to generation. She clutched it close to her heart. Despite the differences, she knew what she was going to say.

It took Mrs. Peale several minutes to understand what Sassy was telling her.

"No, dear," she insisted. "John *works* for Mr. Callister. That's what he told us."

"Yes, he did, but he didn't mention that Taggert was his middle name, not his last name," Sassy replied patiently. "He and his brother, Gil, own one of the most famous ranches in the West. Their parents own that sports magazine Daddy always used to read before he left."

The older woman sat back with a rough sigh. "Then what was he doing coming around here?" she asked, and looked hurt.

"Well, that's the interesting part," Sassy replied, blushing. "It seems that he...well, he wants to...that is..." She jerked out the ring box, opened it, and put it in her mother's hands. "He brought that to me this morning."

Mrs. Peale eyed the rings with fascination. "How beautiful," she said softly. She touched the pattern on the wedding band. "He means these to be heirlooms, doesn't he? I had your grandmother's wedding band," she added sadly, "but I had to sell it when you were little and we didn't have the money for a doctor when you got sick." She looked up at her daughter with misty eyes. "He's really serious, isn't he?"

"Yes, I think he is." Sassy sighed. She sat down next to her mother. "I still can't believe it."

"That hospital bill," Mrs. Peale began slowly. "There was no grant, was there?"

Sassy shook her head. "John said that he couldn't stand by and let you die. He's fond of you."

"I'm fond of him, too," she replied. "And he wants to marry my daughter." Her eyes suddenly had a faraway look. "Isn't it funny? Remember what I told you my grandmother said to me, that I'd be poor but my daughter would live like royalty?" She laughed. "My goodness!"

"Maybe she really did know things." Sassy took the rings from her mother's hand and stared at them. It did seem that dreams came true.

JOHN CAME FOR her just at sunset. He took time to kiss Mrs. Peale and Selene and assure them that he wasn't taking Sassy out of the county when they married.

"I'm running this ranch myself," he assured her with a warm smile. "Sassy and I will live here. The house has plenty of room, so you two can move in with us."

Mrs. Peale looked worried. "John, it may not look like much, but I was born in this house. I've lived in it all my life, even after I married."

He bent and kissed her again. "Okay. If you want to stay here, we'll do some fixing up and get you a companion. You can choose her."

Her old eyes brightened. "You'd do that for me?" she exclaimed.

"Nothing is too good for my second mama," he assured her, and he wasn't joking. "Now Sassy and I are going out to talk about all the details. We'll be back later."

She kissed him back. "You're going to be the nicest son-in-law in the whole world."

"You'd better believe it," he replied.

JOHN TOOK HER over to the new ranch, where the barn was up, the stable almost finished, and the house completely remodeled. He walked her through the kitchen and smiled at her enthusiasm.

"We can have a cook, if you'd rather," he told her.

She looked back at him, running her hand lovingly over a brand-new stove with all sorts of functions. "Oh, I'd love to work in here myself." She hesitated. "John, about Mama and Selene…"

He moved away from the doorjamb he'd been leaning against and pulled her into his arms. His expression was very serious. "I know you're worried about her. But I was serious about the companion. It's just that she needs to be a nurse. We won't tell your mother that part of it just yet."

"She's not completely well yet. I know a nurse will look out for her, but…"

He smiled. "I like the way you care about people," he said softly. "I know she's not able to stay by herself and she won't admit it. But we're close enough that you can go over there every day and check on her."

She smiled. "Okay. I just worry."

"That's one of the things I most admire about you," he told her. "That big heart."

"You have to travel a lot, to show cattle, don't you?" she

asked, recalling something she'd read in a magazine about the Callisters, before she knew who John was.

"I used to," he said. "We have a cattle foreman at the headquarters ranch in Medicine Ridge who's showing Gil's bulls now. I'll put on one here to do the same for us. I don't want to be away from home unless I have to, now."

She beamed. "I don't want you away from home, unless I can go with you."

He chuckled. "Two minds running in the same direction." He shifted his weight a little. "I didn't tell your mother, but I've already interviewed several women who might want the live-in position. I had their backgrounds checked as well," he added, chuckling. "When I knew I was going to marry you, I started thinking about how your mother would cope without you."

"You're just full of surprises," she said, breathless.

He grinned. "Yes, I am. The prospective housemates will start knocking on the door about ten Friday morning. You can tell her when we get home." He sobered. "She'll be happier in her own home, Sassy. Uprooting her will be as traumatic as the chemo was. You can visit her every day and twice on Sundays. I'll come along, too."

"I think you're right." She looked up at him. "She loves you."

"It's mutual," he replied. He smiled down at her, loving the softness in her green eyes. "We can add some more creature comforts for her, and fix what's wrong with the house."

"There's a lot wrong with it," she said worriedly.

"I'm rich, as you reminded me," he replied easily. "I can afford whatever she, and Selene, need. After all, they're family."

She hugged him warmly and laid her cheek against his chest. "Do you want to have kids?" she asked.

His eyebrows arched and his blue eyes twinkled. "Of course. Do you want to start them right now?" He looked around. "The kitchen table's just a bit short...ouch!"

She withdrew her fist from his stomach. "You know what I mean! Honestly, what am I going to do with you?"

"Want me to coach you?" he offered, and chuckled wickedly when she blushed.

"Look out that window and tell me what you see," she said.

He glanced around. There were people going in and out of the unfinished stable, working on the interior by portable lighting. There were a lot of people going in and out.

"I guarantee if you so much as kiss me, we'll be on every social networking site in the world," she told him. "And not because of who you are."

He laughed out loud. "Okay. We'll wait." He glanced outside again and scowled. "But we are definitely not going to try to honeymoon here in this house!"

She didn't argue.

He tugged her along with him into a dark hallway and pulled her close. "They'll need night vision to see us here," he explained as he bent to kiss her with blatant urgency.

She kissed him back, feeling so explosively hot inside that she thought she might burst. She felt shivery when he kissed her like that, with his mouth and his whole body. His hands smoothed up under her blouse and over her breasts. He felt the hard tips and groaned, kissing her even harder.

She knew nothing about intimacy, but she wanted it suddenly, desperately. She lifted up to him, trying to get even closer. He backed her into the wall and lowered his body against hers, increasing the urgency of the kiss until she groaned out loud and shivered.

The frantic little sound got through his whirling mind. He pushed away from her and stepped back, dragging in deep breaths in an effort to regain the control he'd almost lost.

"You're stopping?" she asked breathlessly.

"Yes, I'm stopping," he replied. He took her hand and pulled her back into the lighted kitchen. There was a flush along his high cheekbones. "Until the wedding, no more time alone," he added huskily. His blue eyes met her green ones. "We're going to have it conventional, all the way. Okay?"

She smiled with her whole heart. "Okay!"

He laughed. "It's just as well," he sighed.

"Why?"

"We don't have a bed. Yet."

Her eyes twinkled. He was so much fun to be with, and when he kissed her, it was like fireworks. They were going to make a great marriage, she was sure of it. She stopped worrying about being poor. When they held each other, nothing mattered less than money.

BUT THE NEXT hurdle was the hardest. He announced a week later that his family was coming up to meet John's future bride. Sassy didn't sleep that night, worrying. What would they think, those fabulously wealthy people, when they saw where Sassy and her mother and Selene lived, how poor they were? Would they think she was only after John's wealth?

She was still worrying when they showed up at her front door late the next afternoon, with John. Sassy stood beside him in her best dress, as they walked up onto the front porch of the Peale homeplace. Her best dress wasn't saying much because it was off the rack and two years old. It was long, beige, and simply cut. Her shoes were older than the dress and scuffed.

But the tall blond man and the slender, dark-haired woman didn't seem to notice or care how she was dressed. The woman, who didn't look much older than Sassy, hugged her warmly.

"I'm Kasie," she introduced herself with a big smile. "He's Gil, my husband." Gil smiled and shook her hand warmly. "And these are our babies…" She motioned to two little blonde girls, one holding the other by the hand. "That's Bess," she said, smiling at the taller of the two, "and that's Jenny. Say hello! This is Uncle John's fiancée!"

Bess came forward and looked up at Sassy with wide, soft eyes. "You going to marry Uncle John? He's very nice."

"Yes, he is," Sassy said, sliding her hand into John's. "I promise I'll take very good care of him," she added with a smile.

"Okay," Bess said with a shy returning smile.

"Come on in," Sassy told them. "I'm sorry, it isn't much to look at…" she added, embarrassed.

"Sassy, we were raised by an uncle who hated material things," Gil told her gently. "We grew up in a place just like this, a rough country house. We like to think it gave us strength of character."

"What he means is, don't apologize," John said in a loud whisper.

She laughed when Gil and Kasie agreed. Later she would learn that Kasie had grown up in even rougher conditions, in a war zone in Africa with missionary parents who were killed there.

Mrs. Peale greeted them with Selene by her side, a little intimidated.

"Stop looking like that," John chided, and hugged her warmly. "This is my future little mother-in-law," he added with a grin, introducing her to his family. "She's the sweetest woman I've ever known, except for Kasie."

"You didn't say I was sweet, too," Sassy said with a mock pout.

"You're not sweet. You're precious," he told her with a warm, affectionate grin.

"Okay, I'll go with that," she laughed. She turned to the others. "Come in and sit down. I could make coffee…?"

"Please, no," Gil groaned. "She pumped me full of it all the way here. We were up last night very late trying to put fences back up after a storm. Kasie had to drive most of the way." He held his stomach. "I don't think I ever want another cup."

"You go out with your men to fix fences?" Mrs. Peale asked, surprised.

"Of course," he said simply. "We always have."

Mrs. Peale relaxed. So did Sassy. These people were nothing like they'd expected. Even Selene warmed to them at once, as shy as she usually was with strangers. It was a wonderful visit.

"Well, what do you think of them?" John asked Sassy much later, as he was getting ready to leave for the ranch.

"They're wonderful," she replied, pressed close against him on the dark porch. "They aren't snobs. I like them already."

"It's as Gil said," he replied. "We were raised by a rough and tumble uncle. He taught us that money wasn't the most important thing in life." He tilted her mouth up and kissed it. "They liked you, too," he added. He smiled. "So, no more hurdles. Now all we have to do is get married."

"But I don't know how to plan a big wedding," she said worriedly.

He grinned. "Not to worry. I know someone who does!"

THE WEDDING WAS arranged beautifully by a consultant hired by John, out of Colorado. She was young and pretty and sweet, and apparently she was very discreet. Sassy was fascinated by some of the weddings she'd planned for people all over the country. One was that of Sassy's favorite country western singing star.

"You did that wedding?" Sassy exclaimed.

"I did. And nobody knew a thing about it until they were on their honeymoon," she added smugly. "That's why your future husband hired me. I'm the soul of discretion. Now, tell me what colors you like and we'll get to work!"

They ended up with a color scheme of pink and yellow and white. Sassy had planned a simple white gown, until Mary Garnett showed her a couture gown with the three pastels embroidered in silk into the bodice and echoed in the lace over the skirt, and in the veil. It was the most beautiful gown Sassy had ever seen in her life. "But you could buy a house for that!" Sassy exclaimed when she heard the price.

John, walking through the living room at the Peale house, paused in the doorway. "We're only getting married once," he reminded Sassy.

"But it's so expensive," she wailed.

He walked to the sofa and peered over her shoulder at the color photograph of the gown. His breath caught. "Buy it," he told Mary.

Sassy opened her mouth. He bent and kissed it shut. He walked out again.

Mary just grinned.

He had another surprise for her as well, tied up in a small box, as an early wedding present. He'd discovered that she'd had to pawn her grandfather's watch and pistol to pay bills and he'd gotten them out of hock. She cried like a baby. Which meant that he got to kiss the tears away. He was, she thought as she hugged him, the most thoughtful man in the whole world.

Sassy insisted on keeping her job, regardless of John's protests. She wanted to help more with the wedding, and felt guilty that she hadn't, but Mary had everything organized. Invitations were going out, flower arrangements were being made. A minister was engaged. A small orchestra was hired to play at the reception.

The wedding was being held at the family ranch in Medicine Ridge, to ensure privacy. Gil had already said that he was putting on more security for the event than the president of the United States had. Nobody was crashing this wedding. They'd even outfoxed aerial surveillance by putting the entire reception inside and having blinds on every window.

Nobody, he told John and Sassy, was getting in without an invitation and a photo ID.

"Is that really necessary?" Sassy asked John when they were alone.

"You don't know how well-known our parents are." He sighed. "They'll be coming, too, and our father can't keep his mouth shut. He's heard about you from Gil and Kasie, and he's bragging to anybody who'll listen about his newest daughter-in-law."

"Me?" She was stunned. "But I don't have any special skills and I'm not even beautiful."

John smiled down at her. "You have the biggest heart of any woman I've ever known," he said softly. "It isn't what you do or what you have that makes you special, Sassy. It's what you are."

She flushed. "What about your mother?"

He kissed her on the tip of her nose. "She's so happy to have access to her grandchildren, that she never raises a fuss about anything. But she's happy to have somebody in the family who can knit."

"How did you know I can knit?"

"You think I hadn't noticed all the afghans and chair covers and doilies all over your house?"

"Mama could have made them."

"But she didn't. She said you can even knit sweaters. Our mother would love to learn how. She wants you to teach her."

She caught her breath. "But it's easy! Of course, I'll show her. She doesn't mind—neither of them mind—that I'm poor? They don't think I'm marrying you for your money?"

He laughed until his eyes teared up. "Sassy," he said, catching his breath, "you didn't know I had money until after I proposed."

"Oh."

"They know that, too."

She sighed. "Okay, then."

He bent and kissed her. "Only a few more days to go," he murmured. "I can hardly wait."

"Me, too," she said. "It's exciting. But it's a lot of work."

"Mary's doing the work so you don't have to. Well, except for getting the right dresses for your mother and Selene."

"That's not work," she laughed. "They love to shop. I'm so glad Mama's getting over the chemo. She's better every day. I was worried that she'd be too weak to come to the wedding, but she says she wouldn't miss it for anything."

"We'll have a nurse practitioner at the wedding," he assured her. "Just in case. Don't worry."

"I'll do my best," she promised.

"That's my girl."

FINALLY THERE WAS a wedding! Sassy had chewed her nails to the quick worrying about things going wrong. John assured her that it would be smooth as silk, but she couldn't relax. If only she didn't trip over her own train and go headfirst into the minister, or do something else equally clumsy! All those important people were going to be there, and she had stage fright.

But once she was at the door of the big ballroom at the Callister mansion in Medicine Ridge where the wedding was taking place, she was less nervous. The sight of John, in his tuxedo, standing at the altar, calmed her. She waited for the music and then, clutching her bouquet firmly, her veil in place over her face, she walked calmly down the aisle. Her heart raced like crazy as John turned and smiled down at her when she reached him. He was the most handsome man she'd ever seen in her life. And he was going to marry her!

The minister smiled at both of them and began the service. It was routine until he asked if John had the rings. John started fishing in his pockets and couldn't find them. He grimaced, stunned.

"Uncle John! Did you forget?" Jenny muttered at his side, shoving a silken pillow up toward him. "I got the rings, Uncle John!"

The audience chuckled. Sassy hid a smile.

John fumbled the rings loose from the pillow and bent and kissed his little niece on the forehead. "Thanks, squirt," he whispered.

She giggled and went to stand beside her sister, Bess, who was holding a basket full of fresh flower petals in shades of yellow, pink, and white.

The minister finished the ceremony and invited John to kiss his bride. John lifted the beautiful embroidered veil and pushed it back over Sassy's dark hair. His eyes searched hers. He framed her face in his big hands and bent and kissed her so tenderly that tears rolled down her cheeks, and he kissed every one away.

The music played again. Laughing, Sassy took the hand John held out and together they ran down the aisle and out the door. The reception was ready down the hall, in the big formal dining room that had been cleared of furniture for the occasion. As they ate cake and paused for photographs, to the strains of Debussy played by the orchestral ensemble, Sassy noticed movie stars, politicians, and at least two multimillionaires among the guests. She was rubbing elbows with people she'd only seen in magazines. It was fascinating.

"One more little hurdle, Mrs. Callister," John whispered to her, "and then we're going to Cancún for a week!"

"Sun and sand," she began breathlessly.

"And you and me. And a bed." He wiggled his eyebrows.

She laughed, pressing her face against him to hide her blushes.

"Well, it wasn't a bad wedding," came a familiar drawl from behind them.

Chief Graves was wearing a very nice suit, and nicely polished dress boots, holding a piece of cake on a plate.

"But I don't like chocolate cake," he pointed out. "And there's no coffee."

"There is so coffee," John chuckled, holding up a cup of it. "I don't go to weddings that don't furnish coffee."

"Where did you get that?" he asked.

John nodded toward the far corner, where a coffee urn was half-hidden behind a bouquet of flowers.

Graves grinned. "I hope you have a long and happy life together."

"Thanks, Chief," Sassy told him.

"Glad you could make it," John seconded.

"I brought you a present," he said unexpectedly. He reached into his pocket and drew out a small package. "Something you young folks might find old-fashioned, but useful."

"Thank you," Sassy said, touched, as she took it from his hand.

He gave John a worldly look, chuckled, and walked off to find coffee.

"What is it, I wonder?" Sassy mused, tearing the paper open.

"Well!" John exclaimed when he saw what was inside.

She peered over his arm and smiled warmly. It was a double set of CDs of romantic music and classical love themes.

They glanced toward the coffee urn. Graves lifted his cup and toasted them. They laughed and waved.

CHAPTER ELEVEN

THEY STAYED ON the beach in a hotel shaped like one of the traditional Maya pyramids. Sassy lay in John's strong arms still shivering with her first taste of intimacy, her face flushed, her eyes brilliant as they looked up into his.

"It gets better," he whispered as his mouth moved lightly over her soft lips. "First times are usually difficult."

"Difficult?" She propped up on one elbow. "Are we remembering the same first time? Gosh, I thought I was going to die!"

His blue eyes twinkled. "Forgive me. I naturally assumed from all the moaning and whimpering that you were...stop that!" He laughed when she pinched him.

An enthusiastic bout of wrestling followed.

He kissed her into limp submission. "We really must do this again, so that I can get my perspective back," he suggested. "I'll pay attention this time."

She laughed and kissed his broad shoulder. "See that you do," she replied. She pushed him back into the pillows and followed him down.

"Now don't be rough with me, I'm fragile," he protested. "See here, take your hand off that... I'm not that sort of man!"

"Yes, you are," she chuckled, and put her mouth squarely against his. He was obediently silent for a long time afterward. Except for various involuntary sounds.

THEY HELD HANDS and walked down the beach at sunrise, watching seagulls soar above the incredible shades of blue that were the Gulf of Mexico.

"I never dreamed there were places like this," Sassy said dreamily. "The sand looks just like sugar."

"We'll have to take some postcards back with us. I can't believe I forgot my cell phone in the hotel room." He sighed.

"We can get it later," she suggested. "I have to have at least one picture of you in a bathing suit to put up in our house."

"Turnabout is fair play," he teased.

She laughed. "Okay."

"While we're at it, we'll buy presents for everybody."

"We should get something for Chief Graves."

"What would you suggest?"

"Something musical."

He pursed his lips. "We'll get him one of those wooden kazoos."

"No! Musical."

He drew her close. "Musical it is."

AFTER THE HONEYMOON, they stopped for the weekend at the Callister ranch in Medicine Ridge, where Sassy had time to sit down and get acquainted with John's sister-in-law, Kasie.

"I was so worried about fitting in here," Sassy confessed as they walked around the house, where the flowers were blooming in abundance around the huge swimming pool. "I mean, this is a whole world away from anything I know."

"I know exactly how you feel," Kasie said. "I was born in Africa, where my parents were missionaries," she recalled, going quiet. "They were killed right in front of us, me and my brother, Kantor. We went to live with our aunt in Arizona. Kantor grew up and married and had a little girl. He was doing a courier service by air in Africa when an attack came. He and his family were shot down in his plane and died." She sat down on one of the benches, her eyes far away. "I never expected to end up like this," she said, meeting the other girl's sympathetic gaze. "Gil didn't even like me at first," she added, laughing. "He made my life miserable when I first came to work here."

"He doesn't look like that sort of man," Sassy said. "He seems very nice."

"He can be. But he'd lost his first wife to a riding accident and he didn't ever want to get married again. He said I came up on his blind side. Of course, he thought I was much too young for him."

"Just like John," Sassy sighed. "He thought I was too young for him." She glanced at Kasie and grinned. "And I was sure that he was much too rich for me."

Kasie laughed. "I felt that way, too. But you know, it doesn't have much to do with money. It has to do with feelings and things you have in common." Her eyes had a dreamy, faraway look. "Sometimes Gil and I just sit and talk, for hours at a time. He's my best friend, as well as my husband."

"I feel that way with John," Sassy said. "He just fits in with my family, as if he's always known them."

"Mama Luke took to Gil right away, too." She noted the curious stare. "Oh, she's my mother's sister. She's a nun."

"Heavens!"

"My mother was pregnant with me and Kantor and a mercenary soldier saved her life," she explained. "His name was K.C. Kantor. My twin and I were both named for him."

"I've heard of him," Sassy said hesitantly, not liking to repeat what she'd heard about the reclusive, crusty millionaire.

"Most of what you've heard is probably true," Kasie laughed, seeing the words in her expression. "But I owe my life to him. He's a kind man. He would probably have married Mama Luke, if she hadn't felt called to a religious life."

"Is he married?"

Kasie frowned. "You know, I heard once that he did get married, to some awful woman, and divorced her right afterward. I don't know if it's true. You don't ask him those sort of questions," she added.

"I can understand why."

"Gil's parents like you," Kasie said out of the blue.

"They do?" Sassy was astonished. "But I hardly had time to say ten words to them at the wedding!"

"John said considerably more than ten words." Kasie grinned. "He was singing your praises long before he went back to marry you. Magdalena saw that beautiful shawl you'd packed and John told her you knitted it yourself. She wants to learn how."

"Yes, John said that, but I thought he was kidding!"

"She's not. She'll be in touch, I guarantee. She'll turn up at your ranch one of these days with her knitting gear and you'll have to chase her out with a broom."

Sassy blushed. "I'd never do that. She's so beautiful."

"Yes. She and the boys didn't even speak before I married Gil. I convinced him to meet them on our honeymoon. He was shocked. You see, they were married very young and had children so early, long before they were ready for them. John and Gil's uncle took the boys to raise and sort of shut their parents out of their lives. It was a tragedy. They grew up thinking their parents didn't want them. It wasn't true. They just didn't know how to relate to their children, after all those years."

"I think parents and children need to be together those first few years," Sassy said.

"I agree wholeheartedly," Kasie said. She smiled. "Gil and I want children of our own, but we want the girls to feel secure with us first. There's no rush. We have years and years."

"The girls seem very happy."

Kasie nodded. "They're so much like my own children," she said softly. "I love them very much. I was heartbroken when Gil sent me home from Nassau and told me not to be here when they got home."

"What?"

Kasie laughed self-consciously. "We had a rocky romance. I'll have to tell you all about it one day. But for now, we'd better get back inside. Your husband will get all nervous and insecure if you're where he can't see you."

"He's a very nice husband."

"He's nice, period, like my Gil. We got lucky, for two penniless children, didn't we?" she asked.

Sassy linked her arm into Kasie's. "Yes, we did. But we'd both live in line cabins and sew clothes by hand if they asked us to."

"Isn't that the truth?" Kasie laughed.

"WHAT WERE YOU two talking about for so long?" John asked that night, as Sassy lay close in his arms in bed.

"About what wonderful men we married," she said drowsily, reaching up to kiss him. "We did, too."

"Did Kasie tell you about her background?"

"She did. What an amazing story. And she said Gil didn't like her!"

"He didn't," he laughed. "He even fired her. But he realized his mistake in time. She was mysterious and he was determined not to risk his heart again."

"Sort of like you?" she murmured.

He laughed. "Sort of like me." He drew her closer and closed his eyes. "We go home tomorrow. Ready to take on a full-time husband, Mrs. Callister?"

"Ready and willing, Mr. Callister," she murmured, and smiled as she drifted off to sleep.

SEVERAL WEEKS LATER, Sassy had settled in at the ranch and was making enough knitted and crocheted accessories to make a home of the place. Mrs. Peale had a new companion, a practical nurse named Helen who was middle-aged, sweet, and could cook as well as clean house. She had no family, so Mrs. Peale and Selene filled an empty place in her life. Her charges were very happy with her. Sassy and John found time to visit regularly. They were like lovebirds, though. People rarely saw one without the other. Sassy mused that it was like they were joined at the hip. John grinned and kissed her for that. It was, indeed, he said happily.

One afternoon, John walked in the back door with Chief Graves, who was grinning from ear to ear.

"We have company," John told her, pausing to kiss her warmly and pull her close at his side. "He has news."

"I thought you'd like to know that Mr. Tarleton got five years," he said pleasantly. "They took him away last Friday. He's appealing, of course, but it won't help. He was recorded agreeing to the terms of the plea bargain. I told you that judge hated sexual assault cases."

Sassy nodded. "I'm sorry for him," she said. "I wish he'd learned his lesson the last time, in Wyoming. I guess when you do bad things for a long time, you just keep doing them."

"Repeat offenders repeat, sometimes," Graves replied solemnly. "But he's off the street, where he won't be hurting other young women." He pursed his lips. "I also wanted to thank you for the gift you brought back from Mexico. But I'm curious."

"About what?" she asked.

"How did you know I could play a flute?"

Her eyebrows arched. "You can?" she asked, surprised.

He chuckled. "Maybe she reads minds," he told John. "Better take good care of her. A woman with that rare gift is worth rubies."

"You're telling me," John replied, smiling down at his wife.

"I'll get back to town. Take care."

"You, too," Sassy said.

He sauntered out to his truck. John turned to Sassy with pursed lips. "So you can read minds, can you?" He leaned his forehead down against hers and linked his hands behind her. "Think you can tell me what I'm thinking right now?" he teased.

She reached up and whispered in his ear, grinning.

He laughed, picked her up, and stalked down the hall carrying her. She held on tight. Some men's minds, she thought wickedly, weren't all that difficult to read after all!

* * * * *

WILL OF STEEL

To the readers, all of you,
many of whom are my friends on my Facebook page.
You make this job wonderful and worthwhile. Thank you
for your kindness and your support and your affection
through all the long years. I am still your biggest fan.

CHAPTER ONE

HE NEVER LIKED coming here. The stupid calf followed him around, everywhere he went. He couldn't get the animal to leave him alone. Once, he'd whacked the calf with a soft fir tree branch, but that had led to repercussions. Its owner had a lot to say about animal cruelty and quoted the law to him. He didn't need her to quote the law. He was, after all, the chief of police in the small Montana town where they both lived.

Technically, of course, this wasn't town. It was about two miles outside the Medicine Ridge city limits. A small ranch in Hollister, Montana, that included two clear, cold trout streams and half a mountain. Her uncle and his uncle had owned it jointly during their lifetimes. The two of them, best friends forever, had recently died, his uncle from a heart attack and hers, about a month later, in an airplane crash en route to a cattleman's convention. The property was set to go up on the auction block, and a California real estate developer was skulking in the wings, waiting to put in the winning bid. He was going to build a rich man's resort here, banking on those pure trout streams to bring in the business.

If Hollister Police Chief Theodore Graves had his way, the man would never set foot on the property. She felt that way, too. But the wily old men had placed a clause in both their wills pertaining to ownership of the land in question.

The clause in her uncle's will had been a source of shock to Graves and the girl when the amused attorney read it out to them. It had provoked a war of words every time he walked in the door.

"I'm not marrying you," Jillian Sanders told him firmly the minute he stepped on the porch. "I don't care if I have to live in the barn with Sammy."

Sammy was the calf.

He looked down at her from his far superior height with faint arrogance. "No problem. I don't think the grammar school would give you a hall pass to marry me anyway."

Her pert nose wrinkled. "Well, you'd have to get permission from the old folks' home, and I'll bet you wouldn't get it, either!"

It was a standing joke. He was thirty-one to her almost twenty-one. They were completely mismatched. She was small and blonde and blue-eyed, he was tall and dark and black-eyed. He liked guns and working on his old truck when he wasn't performing his duties as chief of police in the small Montana community where they lived. She liked making up recipes for new sweets and he couldn't stand anything sweet except pound cake. She also hated guns and noise.

"If you don't marry me, Sammy will be featured on the menu in the local café, and you'll have to live in the woods in a cave," he pointed out.

That didn't help her disposition. She glared at him. It wasn't her fault that she had no family left alive. Her parents had died not long after she was born of an influenza outbreak. Her uncle had taken her in and raised her, but he was not in good health and had heart problems. Jillian had taken care of him as long as he was alive, fussing over his diet and trying to concoct special dishes to make him comfortable. But he'd died not of ill health, but in a light airplane crash on his way to a cattle convention. He didn't keep many cattle anymore, but he'd loved seeing friends at the conferences, and he loved to attend them. She missed him. It was lonely on the ranch. Of course, if she had to marry Rambo, here, it would be less lonely.

She glared at him, as if everything bad in her life could be laid at his door. "I'd almost rather live in the cave. I hate guns!" she added vehemently, noting the one he wore, old-fashioned style, on his hip in a holster. "You could blow a hole through a concrete wall with that thing!"

"Probably," he agreed.

"Why can't you carry something small, like your officers do?"

"I like to make an impression," he returned, tongue-in-cheek.

It took her a minute to get the insinuation. She glared at him even more.

He sighed. "I haven't had lunch," he said, and managed to look as if he were starving.

"There's a good café right downtown."

"Which will be closing soon because they can't get a cook," he said with disgust. "Damnedest thing, we live in a town where every woman cooks, but nobody wants to do it for the public. I guess I'll starve. I burn water."

It was the truth. He lived on takeout from the local café and frozen dinners. He glowered at her. "I guess marrying you would save my life. At least you can cook."

She gave him a smug look. "Yes, I can. And the local café isn't closing. They hired a cook just this morning."

"They did?" he exclaimed. "Who did they get?"

She averted her eyes. "I didn't catch her name, but they say she's talented. So you won't starve, I guess."

"Yes, but that doesn't help our situation here," he pointed out. His sensual lips made a thin line. "I don't want to get married."

"Neither do I," she shot back. "I've hardly even dated anybody!"

His eyebrows went up. "You're twenty years old. Almost twenty-one."

"Yes, and my uncle was suspicious of every man who came near me," she returned. "He made it impossible for me to leave the house."

His black eyes twinkled. "As I recall, you did escape once."

She turned scarlet. Yes, she had, with an auditor who'd come to do the books for a local lawyer's office. The man, much older than her and more sophisticated, had charmed her. She'd trusted him, just as she'd trusted another man two years earlier. The auditor had taken her back to his motel room to get something he forgot. Or so he'd told her. Actually he'd locked the door and proceeded to try to remove her clothes. He was very nice about it, he was just insistent.

But he didn't know that Jillian had emotional scars already from a man trying to force her. She'd been so afraid. She'd really liked the man, trusted him. Uncle John hadn't. He always felt guilty about what she'd been through because of his hired man. She was underage, and he told her to stay away from the man.

But she'd had stars in her eyes because the man had flirted with her when she'd gone with Uncle John to see his attorney about a land deal. She'd thought he was different, nothing like Uncle John's hired man who had turned nasty.

He'd talked to her on the phone several times and persuaded her to go out with him. Infatuated, she sneaked out when Uncle John went to bed. But she landed herself in very hot water when the man got overly amorous. She'd managed to get her cell phone out and punched in 911. The result had been…unforgettable.

"They did get the door fixed, I believe…?" she said, letting her voice trail off.

He glared at her. "It was locked."

"There's such a thing as keys," she pointed out.

"While I was finding one, you'd have been…"

She flushed again. She moved uncomfortably. "Yes, well, I did thank you. At the time."

"And a traveling mathematician learned the dangers of trying to seduce teenagers in my town."

She couldn't really argue. She'd been sixteen at the time, and Theodore's quick reaction had saved her honor. The auditor hadn't known her real age. She knew he'd never have asked her out if he had any idea she was under legal age. He'd been the only man she had a real interest in, for her whole life. He'd quit the firm he worked for, so he never had to come back to Hollister. She felt bad about it. The whole fiasco was her own fault.

The sad thing was that it wasn't her first scary episode with an older man. The first, at fifteen, had scarred her. She'd thought that she could trust a man again because she was crazy about the auditor. But the auditor became the icing on the cake of her withdrawal from the world of dating for good. She'd really liked him, trusted him, had been infatuated with him. He wasn't even a bad man, not like that other one…

"The judge did let him go with a severe reprimand about making sure of a girl's age and not trying to persuade her into an illegal act. But he could have gone to prison, and it would have been my fault," she recalled. She didn't mention the man who had gone to prison for assaulting her. Ted didn't know about that and she wasn't going to tell him.

"Don't look to me to have any sympathy for him," he said tersely. "Even if you'd been of legal age, he had no right to try to coerce you."

"Point taken."

"Your uncle should have let you get out more," he said reluctantly.

"I never understood why he kept me so close to home," she replied thoughtfully. She knew it wasn't all because of her bad experience.

His black eyes twinkled. "Oh, that's easy. He was saving you for me."

She gaped at him.

He chuckled. "He didn't actually say so, but you must have realized from his will that he'd planned a future for us for some time."

A lot of things were just becoming clear. She was speechless, for once.

He grinned. "He grew you in a hothouse just for me, little orchid," he teased.

"Obviously your uncle never did the same for me," she said scathingly.

He shrugged, and his eyes twinkled even more. "One of us has to know what to do when the time comes," he pointed out.

She flushed. "I think we could work it out without diagrams."

He leaned closer. "Want me to look it up and see if I can find some for you?"

"I'm not marrying you!" she yelled.

He shrugged. "Suit yourself. Maybe you can put up some curtains and lay a few rugs and the cave will be more comfortable." He glanced out the window. "Poor Sammy," he added sadly. "His future is less, shall we say, palatable."

"For the last time, Sammy is not a bull, he's a cow. She's a cow," she faltered.

"Sammy is a bull's name."

"She looked like a Sammy," she said stubbornly. "When she's grown, she'll give milk."

"Only when she's calving."

"Like you know," she shot back.

"I belong to the cattleman's association," he reminded her. "They tell us stuff like that."

"I belong to it, too, and no, they don't, you learn it from raising cattle!"

He tugged his wide-brimmed hat over his eyes. "It's useless, arguing with a blond fence post. I'm going back to work."

"Don't shoot anybody."

"I've never shot anybody."

"Ha!" she burst out. "What about that bank robber?"

"Oh. Him. Well, he shot at me first."

"Stupid of him."

He grinned. "That's just what he said, when I visited him in the hospital. He missed. I didn't. And he got sentenced for assault on a police officer as well as the bank heist."

She frowned. "He swore he'd make you pay for that. What if he gets out?"

"Ten to twenty, and he's got priors," he told her. "I'll be in a nursing home for real by the time he gets out."

She glowered up at him. "People are always getting out of jail on technicalities. All he needs is a good lawyer."

"Good luck to him getting one on what he earns making license plates."

"The state provides attorneys for people who can't pay."

He gasped. "Thank you for telling me! I didn't know!"

"Why don't you go to work?" she asked, irritated.

"I've been trying to, but you won't stop flirting with me."

She gasped, but for real. "I am *not* flirting with you!"

He grinned. His black eyes were warm and sensuous as they met hers. "Yes, you are." He moved a step closer. "We could do an experiment. To see if we were chemically suited to each other."

She looked at him, puzzled, for a few seconds, until it dawned on her what he was suggesting. She moved back two steps, deliberately, and her high cheekbones flushed again. "I don't want to do any experiments with you!"

He sighed. "Okay. But it's going to be a very lonely marriage if you keep thinking that way, Jake."

"Don't call me Jake! My name is Jillian."

He shrugged. "You're a Jake." He gave her a long look, taking in her ragged jeans and bulky gray sweatshirt and boots with curled-up toes from use. Her long blond hair was pinned up firmly into a topknot, and she wore no makeup. "Tomboy," he added accusingly.

She averted her eyes. There were reasons she didn't accentuate her feminine attributes, and she didn't want to discuss the past with him. It wasn't the sort of thing she felt comfortable talking about with anyone. It made Uncle John look bad, and he was dead. He'd cried about his lack of judgment in hiring Davy Harris. But it was too late by then.

Ted was getting some sort of vibrations from her. She was keeping something from him. He didn't know what, but he was almost certain of it.

His teasing manner went into eclipse. He became a policeman again. "Is there something you want to talk to me about, Jake?" he asked in the soft tone he used with children.

She wouldn't meet his eyes. "It wouldn't help."

"It might."

She grimaced. "I don't know you well enough to tell you some things."

"If you marry me, you will."

"We've had this discussion," she pointed out.

"Poor Sammy."

"Stop that!" she muttered. "I'll find her a home. I could always ask John Callister if he and his wife, Sassy, would let her live with them."

"On their ranch where they raise purebred cattle."

"Sammy has purebred bloodlines on both sides," she muttered. "Her mother was a purebred Hereford cow and her father was a purebred Angus bull."

"And Sammy is a 'black baldy,'" he agreed, giving it the hybrid name. "But that doesn't make her a purebred cow."

"Semantics!" she shot back.

He grinned. "There you go, throwing those one-dollar words at me again."

"Don't pretend to be dumb, if you please. I happen to know that you got a degree in physics during your stint with the army."

He raised both thick black eyebrows. "Should I be flattered?"

"Why?"

"That you take an interest in my background."

"Everybody knows. It isn't just me."

He shrugged.

"Why are you a small-town police chief, with that sort of education?" she asked suddenly.

"Because I don't have the temperament for scientific research," he said simply. "Besides, you don't get to play with guns in a laboratory."

"I hate guns."

"You said."

"I really mean it." She shivered dramatically. "You could shoot somebody by accident. Didn't one of your patrolmen drop his pistol in a grocery store and it went off?"

He looked grim. "Yes, he did. He was off duty and carrying his little .32 wheel gun in his pants pocket. He reached for change and it fell out and discharged." He pursed his lips. "A mistake I can guarantee he will never make again."

"So his wife said. You are one mean man when you lose your temper, do you know that?"

"The pistol discharged into a display of cans, fortunately for him, and we only had to pay damages to the store. But it could have discharged into a child, or a grown-up, with tragic results. There are reasons why they make holsters for guns."

She looked at his pointedly. "That one sure is fancy," she noted, indicating the scrollwork on the soft tan leather. It also sported silver conchos and fringe.

"My cousin made it for me."

"Tanika?" she asked, because she knew his cousin, a full-blooded Cheyenne who lived down near Hardin.

"Yes." He smiled. "She thinks practical gear should have beauty."

"She's very gifted." She smiled. "She makes some gorgeous *parfleche* bags. I've seen them at the trading post in Hardin, near the Little Bighorn Battlefield." They were rawhide bags with beaded trim and fringe, incredibly beautiful and useful for transporting items in the old days for native people.

"Thank you," he said abruptly.

She lifted her eyebrows. "For what?"

"For not calling it the Custer Battlefield."

A lot of people did. He had nothing against Custer, but his ancestry was Cheyenne. He had relatives who had died in the Little Bighorn Battle and, later, at Wounded Knee. Custer was a sore spot with him. Some tourists didn't seem to realize that Native Americans considered that people other than Custer's troops were killed in the battle.

She smiled. "I think I had a Sioux ancestor."

"You look like it," he drawled, noting her fair coloring.

"My cousin Rabby is half and half, and he has blond hair and gray eyes," she reminded him.

"I guess so." He checked the big watch on his wrist. "I've got to be in court for a preliminary hearing. Better go."

"I'm baking a pound cake."

He hesitated. "Is that an invitation?"

"You did say you were starving."

"Yes, but you can't live on cake."

"So I'll fry a steak and some potatoes to go with it."

His lips pulled up into a smile. "Sounds nice. What time?"

"About six? Barring bank robberies and insurgent attacks, of course."

"I'm sure we won't have one today." He considered her invitation. "The Callisters brought me a flute back from Cancún when they went on their honeymoon. I could bring it and serenade you."

She flushed a little. The flute and its connection with courting in the Native American world was quite well-known. "That would be nice."

"It would?"

"I thought you were leaving." She didn't quite trust that smile.

"I guess I am. About six?"

"Yes."

"I'll see you then." He paused with his hand on the door-knob. "Should I wear my tuxedo?"

"It's just steak."

"No dancing afterward?" he asked, disappointed.

"Not unless you want to build a bonfire outside and dance around it." She frowned. "I think I know one or two steps from the women's dances."

He glared at her. "Ballroom dancing isn't done around campfires."

"You can do ballroom dances?" she asked, impressed.

"Of course I can."

"Waltz, polka…?"

"Tango," he said stiffly.

Her eyes twinkled. "Tango? Really?"

"Really. One of my friends in the service learned it down in Argentina. He taught me."

"What an image that brings to mind—" she began, tongue-in-cheek.

"He didn't teach me by dancing with me!" he shot back. "He danced with a girl."

"Well, I should hope so," she agreed.

"I'm leaving."

"You already said."

"This time, I mean it." He walked out.

"Six!" she called after him.

He threw up a hand. He didn't look back.

JILLIAN CLOSED THE door and leaned back against it. She was a little apprehensive, but after all, she had to marry some-body. She knew Theodore Graves better than she knew any other men. And, despite their quarreling, they got along fairly well.

The alternative was to let some corporation build a holiday resort here in Hollister, and it would be a disaster for local ranching. Resorts brought in all sorts of amusement, plus hotels and gas stations and businesses. It would be a boon for the economy, but Hollister would lose its rural, small-town appeal. It wasn't something Jillian would enjoy and she was certain that other people would feel the same. She loved the forests with their tall lodgepole pines, and the shallow, diamond-bright trout streams where she loved to fish when she had free time. Occasionally Theodore would bring over his spinning reel and join her. Then they'd work side by side, scaling and filleting fish and frying them, along with hush puppies, in a vat of hot oil. Her mouth watered, just thinking about it.

She wandered into the kitchen. She'd learned to cook from one of her uncle's rare girlfriends. It had delighted her. She might be a tomboy, but she had a natural affinity for flour and she could make bread from scratch. It amazed her how few people could. The feel of the dough, soft and smooth, was a gift to her fingertips when she kneaded and punched and worked it. The smell of fresh bread in the kitchen was a delight for the senses. She always had fresh homemade butter to go on it, which she purchased from an elderly widow just down the road. Theodore loved fresh bread. She was making a batch for tonight, to go with the pound cake.

She pulled out her bin of flour and got down some yeast from the shelf. It took a long time to make bread from scratch, but it was worth it.

She hadn't changed into anything fancy, although she did have on a new pair of blue jeans and a pink checked shirt that buttoned up. She also tucked a pink ribbon into her long blond hair, which she tidied into a bun on top of her head. She wasn't elegant, or beautiful, but she could at least look like a girl when she tried.

And he noticed the minute he walked in the door. He cocked his head and stared down at her with amusement.

"You're a girl," he said with mock surprise.

She glared up at him. "I'm a woman."

He pursed his lips. "Not yet."

She flushed. She tried for a comeback but she couldn't fumble one out of her flustered mind.

"Sorry," he said gently, and became serious when he noted her reaction to the teasing. "That wasn't fair. Especially since you went to all the trouble to make me fresh rolls." He lifted his head and sniffed appreciably.

"How did you know that?"

He tapped his nose. "I have a superlative sense of smell. Did I ever tell you about the time I tracked a wanted murderer by the way he smelled?" he added. "He was wearing some gosh-awful cheap cologne. I just followed the scent and walked up to him with my gun out. He'd spent a whole day covering his trail and stumbling over rocks to throw me off the track. He was so shocked when I walked into his camp that he just gave up without a fight."

"Did you tell him that his smell gave him away?" she asked, chuckling.

"No. I didn't want him to mention it to anybody when he went to jail. No need to give criminals a heads-up about something like that."

"Native Americans are great trackers," she commented.

He glowered down at her. "Anybody can be a good tracker. It comes from training, not ancestry."

"Well, aren't you touchy," she exclaimed.

He averted his eyes. He shrugged. "Banes has been at it again."

"You should assign him to school crossings. He hates that," she advised.

"No, he doesn't. His new girlfriend is a widow. She's got a little boy, and Banes has suddenly become his hero. He'd love to work the school crossing."

"Still, you could find some unpleasant duty to assign him. Didn't he say once that he hates being on traffic detail at ball games?"

He brightened. "You know, he did say that."

"See? An opportunity presents itself." She frowned. "Why are we looking for ways to punish him this time?"

"He brought in a new book on the Little Bighorn Battle and showed me where it said Crazy Horse wasn't in the fighting."

She gave him a droll look. "Oh, sure."

He grimaced. "Every so often, some writer who never saw a real Native American gets a bunch of hearsay evidence together and writes a book about how he's the only one who knows the true story of some famous battle. This guy also said that Custer was nuts and had a hand in the post trader scandal where traders were cheating the Sioux and Cheyenne."

"Nobody who reads extensively about Custer would believe he had a hand in something so dishonest," she scoffed. "He went to court and testified against President Ulysses S. Grant's own brother in that corruption trial, as I recall. Why would he take such a risk if he was personally involved in it?"

"My thoughts exactly," he said, "and I told Banes so."

"What did Banes say to that?"

"He quoted the author's extensive background in military history."

She gave him a suspicious look. "Yes? What sort of background?"

"He's an expert in the Napoleonic Wars."

"Great! What does that have to do with the campaign on the Greasy Grass?" she asked, which referred to the Lakota name for the battle.

"Not a damned thing," he muttered. "You can be brilliant in your own field of study, but it's another thing to do your research from a standing start and come to all the wrong conclusions. Banes said the guy used period newspapers and magazines for part of his research."

"The Lakota and Cheyenne, as I recall, didn't write about current events," she mused.

He chuckled. "No, they didn't have newspaper reporters back then. So it was all from the cavalry's point of view, or that of politicians. History is the story of mankind written by the victors."

"Truly."

He smiled. "You're pretty good on local history."

"That's because I'm related to people who helped make it."

"Me, too." He cocked his head. "I ought to take you down to Hardin and walk the battlefield with you sometime," he said.

Her eyes lit up. "I'd love that."

"So would I."

"There's a trading post," she recalled.

"They have some beautiful things there."

"Made by local talent," she agreed. She sighed. "I get so tired of so-called Native American art made in China. Nothing against the Chinese. I mean, they have aboriginal peoples, too. But if you're going to sell things that are supposed to be made by tribes in this country, why import them?"

"Beats me. Ask somebody better informed."

"You're a police chief," she pointed out. "There isn't supposed to be anybody better informed."

He grinned. "Thanks."

She curtsied.

He frowned. "Don't you own a dress?"

"Sure. It's in my closet." She pursed her lips. "I wore it to graduation."

"Spare me!"

"I guess I could buy a new one."

"I guess you could. I mean, if we're courting, it will look funny if you don't wear a dress."

"Why?"

He blinked. "You going to get married in blue jeans?"

"For the last time, I am not going to marry you."

He took off his wide-brimmed hat and laid it on the hall table. "We can argue about that later. Right now, we need to eat some of that nice, warm, fresh bread before it gets cold and butter won't melt on it. Shouldn't we?" he added with a grin.

She laughed. "I guess we should."

CHAPTER TWO

THE BREAD WAS as delicious as he'd imagined it would be. He closed his eyes, savoring the taste.

"You could cook, if you'd just try," she said.

"Not really. I can't measure stuff properly."

"I could teach you."

"Why do I need to learn how, when you do it so well already?" he asked reasonably.

"You live alone," she began.

He raised an eyebrow. "Not for long."

"For the tenth time today…"

"The California guy was in town today," he said grimly. "He came by the office to see me."

"He did?" She felt apprehensive.

He nodded as he bit into another slice of buttered bread with perfect white teeth. "He's already approached contractors for bids to build his housing project." He bit the words off as he was biting the bread.

"Oh."

Jet-black eyes pierced hers. "I told him about the clause in the will."

"What did he say?"

"That he'd heard you wouldn't marry me."

She grimaced.

"He was strutting around town like a tom turkey," he added. He finished the bread and sipped coffee. His eyes closed as he savored it. "You make great coffee, Jake!" he exclaimed. "Most people wave the coffee over water. You could stand up a spoon in this."

"I like it strong, too," she agreed. She studied his hard, lean face. "I guess you live on it when you have cases that keep you out all night tracking. There have been two or three of those this month alone."

He nodded. "Our winter festival brings in people from all over the country. Some of them see the mining company's bankroll as a prime target."

"Not to mention the skeet-and-trap-shooting regional championships," she said. "I've heard that thieves actually follow the shooters around and get license plate numbers of cars whose owners have the expensive guns."

"They're targets, all right."

"Why would somebody pay five figures for a gun?" she wondered out loud.

He laughed. "You don't shoot in competition, so it's no use trying to explain it to you."

"You compete," she pointed out. "You don't have a gun that expensive and you're a triple-A shooter."

He shrugged. "It isn't that I wouldn't like to have one. But unless I take up bank robbing, I'm not likely to be able to afford one, either. The best I can do is borrow one for the big competitions."

Her eyes popped. "You know somebody who'll loan you a fifty-thousand-dollar shotgun?"

He laughed. "Well, actually, yes, I do. He's police chief of a small town down in Texas. He used to do shotgun competitions when he was younger, and he still has the hardware."

"And he loans you the gun."

"He isn't attached to it, like some owners are. Although, you'd never get him to loan his sniper kit," he chuckled.

"Excuse me?"

He leaned toward her. "He was a covert assassin in his shady past."

"Really?" She was excited by the news.

He frowned. "What do women find so fascinating about men who shoot people?"

She blinked. "It's not that."

"Then what is it?"

She hesitated, trying to put it into words. "Men who have been in battles have tested themselves in a way most people never have to," she began slowly. "They learn their own natures. They... I can't exactly express it..."

"They learn what they're made of, right where they live and breathe," he commented. "Under fire, you're always afraid. But you harness the fear and use it, attack when you'd rather run. You learn the meaning of courage. It isn't the absence of fear. It's fear management, at its best. You do your duty."

"Nicely said, Chief Graves," she said admiringly, and grinned.

"Well, I know a thing or two about being shot at," he reminded her. "I was in the first wave in the second incursion in the Middle East. Then I became a police officer and then a police chief."

"You met the other police chief at one of those conventions, I'll bet," she commented.

"Actually I met him at the FBI academy during a training session on hostage negotiation," he corrected. "He was teaching it."

"My goodness. He can negotiate?"

"He did most of his negotiations with a gun before he was a Texas Ranger," he laughed.

"He was a Ranger, too?"

"Yes. And a cyber-crime expert for a Texas D.A., and a merc, and half a dozen other interesting things. He can also dance. He won a tango contest in Argentina, and that's saying something. Tango and Argentina go together like coffee and cream."

She propped her chin in her hands. "A man who can do the tango. It boggles the mind. I've only ever seen a couple of men do it in movies." She smiled. "Al Pacino in *Scent of a Woman* was my favorite."

He grinned. "Not the 'governator' in *True Lies?*"

She glared at him. "I'm sure he was doing his best."

He shook his head. "I watched Rudolph Valentino do it in an old silent film," he sighed. "Real style."

"It's a beautiful dance."

He gave her a long look. "There's a new Latin dance club in Billings."

"What?" she exclaimed with pure surprise.

"No kidding. A guy from New York moved out here to retire. He'd been in ballroom competition most of his life and he got bored. So he organized a dance band and opened up a dance club. People come up from Wyoming and across from the Dakotas just to hear the band and do the dances." He toyed with his coffee cup. "Suppose you and I go up there and try it out? I can teach you the tango."

Her heart skipped. It was the first time, despite all the banter, that he'd ever suggested taking her on a date.

He scowled when she hesitated.

"I'd love to," she blurted out.

His face relaxed. He smiled again. "Okay. Saturday?"

She nodded. Her heart was racing. She felt breathless.

She was so young, he thought, looking at her. He hesitated.

"They don't have grammar school on Saturdays," she quipped, "so I won't need an excuse from the principal to skip class."

He burst out laughing. "Is that how I looked? Sorry."

"I'm almost twenty-one," she pointed out. "I know that seems young to you, but I've had a lot of responsibility. Uncle John could be a handful, and I was the only person taking care of him for most of my life."

"That's true. Responsibility matures people pretty quick."

"You'd know," she said softly, because he'd taken wonderful care of his grandmother and then the uncle who'd owned half this ranch.

He shrugged. "I don't think there's a choice about looking after people you love."

"Neither do I."

He gave her an appraising look. "You going to the club in blue jeans and a shirt?" he asked. "Because if you are, I plan to wear my uniform."

She raised both eyebrows.

"Or have you forgotten what happened the last time I wore my uniform to a social event?" he added.

She glowered at him.

"Is it my fault if people think of me as a target the minute they realize what I do for a living?" he asked.

"You didn't have to anoint him with punch."

"Sure I did. He was so hot under the collar about a speeding ticket my officer gave him that he needed instant cooling off."

She laughed. "Your patrolman is still telling that story."

"With some exaggerations he added to it," Theodore chuckled.

"It cured the guy of complaining to you."

"Yes, it did. But if I wear my uniform to a dance club where people drink, there's bound to be at least one guy who thinks I'm a target."

She sighed.

"And since you're with me, you'd be right in the thick of it." He pursed his lips. "You wouldn't like to be featured in a riot, would you?"

"Not in Billings, no," she agreed.

"Then you could wear a skirt, couldn't you?"

"I guess it wouldn't kill me," she said, but reluctantly.

He narrowed his eyes as he looked at her. There was some reason she didn't like dressing like a woman. He wished he could ask her about it, but she was obviously uncomfortable discussing personal issues with him. Maybe it was too soon. He did wonder if she still had scars from her encounter with the auditor.

He smiled gently. "Something demure," he added. "I won't expect you to look like a pole dancer, okay?"

She laughed. "Okay."

He loved the way she looked when she smiled. Her whole face took on a radiance that made her pretty. She didn't smile often. Well, neither did he. His job was a somber one, most of the time.

"I'll see you about six, then."

She nodded. She was wondering how she was going to afford something new to wear to a fancy nightclub, but she would never have admitted it to him.

SHE RAN INTO Sassy Callister in town while she was trying to find something presentable on the bargain table at the single women's clothing store.

"You're looking for a dress?" Sassy exclaimed. She'd known Jillian all her life, and she'd never seen her in anything except jeans and shirts. She even wore a pantsuit to church when she went.

Jillian glared at her. "I do have legs."

"That wasn't what I meant." She chuckled. "I gather Ted's taking you out on a real date, huh?"

Jillian went scarlet. "I never said…!"

"Oh, we all know about the will," Sassy replied easily. "It's sensible, for the two of you to get married and keep the ranch in the family. Nobody wants to see some fancy resort being set up here," she added, "with outsiders meddling in our local politics and throwing money around to get things the way they think they should be."

Jillian's eyes twinkled. "Imagine you complaining about the rich, when you just married one of the richest men in Montana."

"You know what I mean," Sassy laughed. "And I'll remind you that I didn't know he was rich when I accepted his proposal."

"A multimillionaire pretending to be a ranch foreman." Jillian shook her head. "It came as a shock to a lot of us when we found out who he really was."

"I assure you that it was more of a shock to me," came the amused reply. "I tried to back out of it, but he wouldn't let me. He said that money was an accessory, not a character trait. You should meet his brother and sister-in-law," she added with a grin. "Her parents were missionaries and her aunt is a nun. Oh, and her godfather is one of the most notorious ex-mercenaries who ever used a gun."

"My goodness!"

"But they're all very down-to-earth. They don't strut, is what I mean."

Jillian giggled. "I get it."

Sassy gave her a wise look. "You want something nice for that date, but you're strained to the gills trying to manage on what your uncle left you."

Jillian started to deny it, but she gave up. Sassy was too sweet to lie to. "Yes," she confessed. "I was working for old Mrs. Rogers at the florist shop. Then she died and the shop closed." She sighed. "Not many jobs going in a town this small. You'd know all about that," she added, because Sassy had worked for a feed store and was assaulted by her boss. Fortunately she was rescued by her soon-to-be husband and the perpetrator had been sent to jail. But it was the only job Sassy could get. Hollister was very small.

Sassy nodded. "I wouldn't want to live anyplace else, though. Even if I had to commute back and forth to Billings to get a job." She laughed. "I considered that, but I didn't think my old truck would get me that far." Her eyes twinkled. "Chief Graves said that if he owned a piece of junk like I was driving, he'd be the first to agree to marry a man who could afford to replace it for me."

Jillian burst out laughing. "I can imagine what you said to that."

She laughed, too. "I just expressed the thought that he wouldn't marry John Callister for a truck." She cocked her head. "He really is a catch, you know. Theodore Graves is the stuff of legends around here. He's honest and kind-hearted and a very mean man to make an enemy of. He'd take care of you."

"Well, he needs more taking care of than I do," came the droll reply. "At least I can cook."

"Didn't you apply for the cook's job at the restaurant?"

"I did. I got it, too, but you can't tell Theodore."

"I won't. But why can't I?"

Jillian sighed. "In case things don't work out, I want to have a means of supporting myself. He'll take it personally if he thinks I got a job before he even proposed."

"He's old-fashioned."

"Nothing wrong with that," Jillian replied with a smile.

"Of course not. It's just that some men have to be hit over the head so they'll accept that modern women can have outside interests without giving up family. Come over here."

She took Jillian's arm and pulled her to one side. "Everything in here is a three-hundred-percent markup," she said under her breath. "I love Jessie, but she's overpriced. You're coming home with me. We're the same size and I've got a closet full of stuff you can wear. You can borrow anything you like. Heck, you can have what you like. I'll never wear all of it anyway."

Jillian flushed red and stammered, "No, I couldn't...!"

"You could and you're going to. Now come on!"

JILLIAN WAS TRANSPORTED to the Callister ranch in a Jaguar. She was so fascinated with it that she didn't hear half of what her friend was saying.

"Look at all these gadgets!" she exclaimed. "And this is real wood on the dash!"

"Yes," Sassy laughed. "I acted the same as you, the first time I rode in it. My old battered truck seemed so pitiful afterward."

"I like my old car. But this is amazing," she replied, touching the silky wood.

"I know."

"It's so nice of you to do this," Jillian replied. "Theodore wanted me to wear a skirt. I don't even own one."

Sassy looked at her briefly. "You should tell him, Jilly."

She flushed and averted her eyes. "Nobody knows but you and your mother. And I know you won't say anything."

"Not unless you said I could," Sassy replied. "But it could cause you some problems later on. Especially after you're married."

Jillian clenched her teeth. "I'll cross that bridge if I come to it. I may not marry Theodore. We may be able to find a way to break the will."

"One, maybe. Two, never."

That was true. Both old men had left ironclad wills with clauses about the disposition of the property if Theodore and Jillian refused to get married.

"The old buzzards!" Jillian burst out. "Why did they have to complicate things like that? Theodore and I could have found a way to deal with the problem on our own!"

"I don't know. Neither of you is well-off, and that California developer has tons of money. I'll bet he's already trying to find a way to get to one of you about buying the ranch outright once you inherit."

"He'll never get it," she said stubbornly.

Sassy was going to comment that rich people with intent sometimes knew shady ways to make people do what they wanted them to. But the developer wasn't local and he didn't have any information he could use to blackmail either Theodore or Jillian, so he probably couldn't force them to sell to him. He'd just sit and wait and hope they couldn't afford to keep it. Fat chance, Sassy thought solemnly. She and John would bail them out if they had to. No way was some out-of-state fat cat taking over Jillian's land. Not after all she'd gone through in her young life.

Maybe it was a good thing Theodore didn't know everything about his future potential wife. But Jillian was setting herself up for some real heartbreak if she didn't level with him. After all, he was in law enforcement. He could dig into court records and find things that most people didn't have access to. He hadn't been in town when Jillian faced her problems, he'd been away at the FBI Academy on a training mission. And since only Sassy and her mother, Mrs. Peale, had been involved, nobody else except the prosecuting attorney and the judge and the public defender had knowledge about the case. Not that any of them would disclose it.

She was probably worrying unnecessarily. She smiled at Jillian. "You are right. He'll never get the ranch," she agreed.

THEY PULLED UP at the house. It had been given a makeover and it looked glorious.

"You've done a lot of work on this place," Jillian commented. "I remember what it looked like before."

"So do I. John wanted to go totally green here, so we have solar power and wind generators. And the electricity in the barn runs on methane from the cattle refuse."

"It's just fantastic," Jillian commented. "Expensive, too, I'll bet."

"That's true, but the initial capital outlay was the highest. It will pay for itself over the years."

"And you'll have lower utility bills than the rest of us," Jillian sighed, thinking about her upcoming one. It had been a colder than usual winter. Heating oil was expensive.

"Stop worrying," Sassy told her. "Things work out."

"You think?"

They walked down the hall toward the master bedroom. "How's your mother?" Jillian asked.

"Doing great. She got glowing reports from her last checkup," Sassy said. The cancer had been contained and her mother hadn't had a recurrence, thanks to John's interference at a critical time. "She always asks about you."

"Your mother is the nicest person I know, next to you. How about Selene?"

The little girl was one Mrs. Peale had adopted. She was in grammar school, very intelligent and with definite goals. "She's reading books about the Air Force," Sassy laughed. "She wants to be a fighter pilot."

"Wow!"

"That's what we said, but she's very focused. She's good at math and science, too. We think she may end up being an engineer."

"She's smart."

"Very."

Sassy opened the closet and started pulling out dresses and skirts and blouses in every color under the sun.

Jillian just stared at them, stunned. "I've never seen so many clothes outside a department store," she stammered.

Sassy chuckled. "Neither did I before I married John. He spoils me rotten. Every birthday and holiday I get presents from him. Pick something out."

"You must have favorites that you don't want to loan," Jillian began.

"I do. That's why they're still in the closet," she said with a grin.

"Oh."

Sassy was eyeing her and then the clothes on the bed. "How about this?" She picked up a patterned blue skirt, very long and silky, with a pale blue silk blouse that had puffy sleeves and a rounded neckline. It looked demure, but it was a witchy ensemble. "Try that on. Let's see how it looks."

Jillian's hands fumbled. She'd never put on something so expensive. It fit her like a glove, and it felt good to move in, as so many clothes didn't. She remarked on that.

"Most clothes on the rack aren't constructed to fit exactly, and the less expensive they are, the worse the fit," Sassy said. "I know, because I bought clothes off the sales rack all my life before I married. I was shocked to find that expensive clothes actually fit. And when they do, they make you look better. You can see for yourself."

Jillian did. Glancing in the mirror, she was shocked to find that the skirt put less emphasis on her full hips and more on her narrow waist. The blouse, on the other hand, made her small breasts look just a little bigger.

"Now, with your hair actually down and curled, instead of screwed up into that bun," Sassy continued, pulling out hairpins as she went and reaching for a brush, "you'll look so different that Ted may not even recognize you. What a difference!"

It was. With her long blond hair curling around her shoulders, she looked really pretty.

"Is that me?" she asked, shocked.

Sassy grinned. "Sure is."

She turned to her friend, fighting tears. "It's so nice of you," she began.

Sassy hugged her. "Friends look out for each other."

They hadn't been close friends, because Sassy's home problems had made that impossible before her marriage. But they were growing closer now. It was nice to have someone she could talk to.

She drew away and wiped at her eyes. "Sorry. Didn't mean to do that."

"You're a nice person, Jilly," Sassy told her gently. "You'd do the same for me in a heartbeat, if our situations were reversed, and you know it."

"I certainly would."

"I've got some curlers. Let's put up your hair in them and then we can snap beans."

"You've got beans in the middle of winter?" Jillian exclaimed.

"From the organic food market," she laughed. "I have them shipped in. You can take some home and plant up. Ted might like beans and ham hocks."

"Even if he didn't, I sure would. I'll bet it's your own pork."

"It is. We like organic all the way. Put your jeans back on and we'll wash your hair and set it. It's thin enough that it can dry while we work."

AND IT DID. They took the curlers out a couple of hours later. Jillian was surprised at the difference a few curls made in her appearance.

"Makeup next," Sassy told her, grinning. "This is fun!"

"Fun and educational," Jillian said, still reeling. "How did you learn all this?"

"From my mother-in-law. She goes to spas and beauty parlors all the time. She's still gorgeous, even though she's gaining in years. Sit down."

Sassy put her in front of a fluorescent-lit mirror and proceeded to experiment with different shades of lipstick and eye shadow. Jillian felt as spoiled as if she'd been to an exclusive department store, and she said so.

"I'm still learning," Sassy assured her. "But it's fun, isn't it?"

"The most fun I've had in a long time, and thank you. Theodore is going to be shocked when he shows up Saturday!" she predicted.

SHOCKED WAS AN UNDERSTATEMENT. Jillian in a blue ensemble, with her long hair soft and curling around her shoulders, with demure makeup, was a revelation to a man who'd only ever seen her without makeup in ragged jeans and sweatshirts or, worse, baggy T-shirts. Dressed up, in clothes that fit her perfectly, she was actually pretty.

"You can close your mouth, Theodore," she teased, delighted at his response.

He did. He shook his head. "You look nice," he said. It was an understatement, compared to what he was thinking. Jillian was a knockout. He frowned as he thought how her new look might go down in town. There were a couple of younger men, nice-looking ones with wealthy backgrounds, who might also find the new Jillian a hot item. He might have competition for her that he couldn't handle.

Jillian, watching his expressions change, was suddenly insecure. He was scowling as if he didn't actually approve of how she looked.

"It isn't too revealing, is it?" she worried.

He cleared his throat. "Jake, you're covered from stem to stern, except for the hollow of your throat, and your arms," he said. "What do you think is revealing?"

"You looked…well, you looked…"

"I looked like a man who's considering the fight ahead."

"Excuse me?"

He moved a step closer and looked down at her with pure

appreciation. "You really don't know what a knockout you are, all dressed up?"

Her breath caught in her throat. "Me?"

His big hands framed her face and brought it up to his dancing black eyes. "You." He rubbed his nose against hers. "You know, I really wonder if you taste as good as you look. This is as good a time as any to find out."

He bent his head as he spoke and, for the first time in their relationship, he kissed her, right on the mouth. Hard.

Whatever he expected her reaction to be, the reality of it came as a shock…

CHAPTER THREE

JILLIAN JERKED BACK away from him as if he'd offended her, flushing to the roots of her hair. She stared at him with helpless misery, waiting for the explosion. The auditor had cursed a blue streak, called her names, swore that he'd tell every boy he knew that she was a hopeless little icicle.

But Theodore didn't do that. In fact, he smiled, very gently.

She bit her lower lip. She wanted to tell him. She couldn't. The pain was almost physical.

He took her flushed face in his big hands and bent and kissed her gently on the forehead, then on her eyelids, closing them.

"We all have our own secret pain, Jake," he whispered. "One day you'll want to tell me, and I'll listen." He lifted his head. "For the time being, we'll be best buddies, except that you're wearing a skirt," he added, tongue-in-cheek. "I have to confess that very few of my buddies have used a women's restroom."

It took her a minute, then she burst out laughing.

"That's better," he said, and grinned. He cocked his head and gave her a very male appraisal. "You really do look nice." He pursed his lips as he contemplated the ensemble and its probable cost.

"They're loaners," she blurted out.

His black eyes sparkled with unholy glee. "Loaners?"

She nodded. "Sassy Callister."

"I see."

She grinned. "She said that she had a whole closet of stuff she never wore. I didn't want to, but she sort of bulldozed me into it. She's a lot like her new husband."

"He wears petticoats?" he asked outrageously.

She glared at him. "Women don't wear petticoats or hoop skirts these days, Theodore."

"Sorry. Wrong era."

She grinned. "Talk about living in the dark ages!"

He shrugged. "I was raised by my grandmother and my uncle. They weren't forthcoming about women's intimate apparel."

"Well, I guess not!"

"Your uncle John was the same sort of throwback," he remarked.

"So we both come by it honestly, I suppose." She noted his immaculate dark suit and the spotless white shirt and blue patterned tie he was wearing with it. "You look nice, too."

"I bought the suit to wear to John Callister's wedding," he replied. "I don't often have the occasion to dress up."

"Me, neither," she sighed.

"I guess we could go to a few places together," he commented. "I like to hunt and fish."

"I do not like guns," she said flatly.

"Well, in my profession, they're sort of a necessity, Jake," he commented.

"I suppose so. Sorry."

"No problem. You used to like fishing."

"It's been a while since I dipped a poor, helpless worm into the water."

He chuckled. "Everything in life has a purpose. A worm's is to help people catch delicious fish."

"The worm might not share your point of view."

"I'll ask, the next time I see one."

She laughed, and her whole face changed. She felt better than she had in ages. Theodore didn't think she was a lost cause. He wasn't even angry that she'd gone cold at his kiss. Maybe, she thought, just maybe, there was still hope for her.

His black eyes were kind. "I'm glad you aren't wearing high heels," he commented.

"Why?"

He glanced down at his big feet in soft black leather boots. "Well, these aren't as tough as the boots I wear on the job. I'd hate to have holes in them from spiked heels, when you step on my feet on the dance floor."

"I will not step on your feet," she said with mock indignation. She grinned. "I might trip over them and land in a flowerpot, of course."

"I heard about that," he replied, chuckling. "Poor old Harris Twain. I'll bet he'll never stick his legs out into the walkway of a restaurant again. He said you were pretty liberally covered with potting soil. You went in headfirst, I believe...?"

She sighed. "Most people have talents. Mine is lack of coordination. I can trip over my own feet, much less someone else's."

He wondered about that clumsiness. She was very capable, in her own way, but she often fell. He frowned.

"Now, see, you're thinking that I'm a klutz, and you're absolutely right."

"I was wondering more about your balance," he said. "Do you have inner ear problems?"

She blinked. "What do my ears have to do with that?"

DIANA PALMER   215

"A lot. If you have an inner ear disturbance, it can affect balance."

"And where did you get your medical training?" she queried.

"I spend some time in emergency rooms, with victims and perps alike. I learn a lot about medical problems that way."

"I forgot."

He shrugged. "It goes with the job."

"I don't have earaches," she said, and averted her eyes. "Shouldn't we get going?"

She was hiding something. A lot, maybe. He let it go. "I guess we should."

"A Latin dance club in Billings." She grinned. "How exotic!"

"The owner's even more exotic. You'll like him." He leaned closer. "He was a gun runner in his wild youth."

"Wow!"

"I thought you'd be impressed. So was I."

"You have an interesting collection of strange people in your life," she commented on the way to his truck.

"Goes with the—"

"Job. I guess." She grinned when she saw the truck. "Washed and waxed it, huh?" she teased.

"Well, you can't take a nice woman to a dance in a dirty truck," he stated.

"I wouldn't have minded."

He turned to her at the passenger side of the truck and looked down at her solemnly in the light from the security lamp on a pole nearby. His face was somber. "No, you wouldn't. You don't look at bank accounts to judge friendships. It's one of a lot of things I like about you. I dated a woman attorney once, who came here to try a case for a client in district court. When she saw the truck, the old one I had several years ago, she actually backed out of the date. She said she didn't want any important people in the community to see her riding around in a piece of junk."

She gasped. "No! How awful for you!"

His high cheekbones had a faint flush. Her indignation made him feel warm inside. "Something you'd never have said to me, as blunt as you are. It turned me off women for a while. Not that I even liked her. But it hurt my pride."

"As if a vehicle was any standard to base a character assessment on," she huffed.

He smiled tenderly. "Small-town police chiefs don't usually drive Jaguars. Although this guy I know in Texas does. But he made his money as a merc, not in law enforcement."

"I like you just the way you are," she told him quietly. "And it wouldn't matter to me if we had to walk to Billings to go dancing."

He ground his teeth together. She made him feel taller, more masculine, when she looked at him like that. He was struggling with more intense emotions than he'd felt in years. He wanted to grab her and eat her alive. But she needed careful handling. He couldn't be forward with her. Not until he could teach her to trust him. That would take time.

She felt uneasy when he scowled like that. "Sorry," she said. "I didn't mean to blurt that out and upset you…"

"You make me feel good, Jake," he interrupted. "I'm not upset. Well, not for the reasons you're thinking, anyway."

"What reasons upset you?"

He sighed. "To be blunt, I'd like to back you into the truck and kiss you half to death." He smiled wryly at her shocked expression. "Won't do it," he promised. "Just telling you what I really feel. Honesty is a sideline with most people. It's first on my list of necessities."

"Mine, too. It's okay. I like it when you're up-front."

"You're the same way," he pointed out.

"I guess so. Maybe I'm too blunt, sometimes."

He smiled. "I'd call it being forthright. I like it."

She beamed. "Thanks."

He checked his watch. "Got to go." He opened the door for her and waited until she jumped up into the cab and fastened her seat belt before he closed it.

"It impresses me that I didn't have to tell you to put that on," he said as he started the engine, nodding toward her seat belt. "I don't ride with people who refuse to wear them. I work wrecks. Some of them are horrific, and the worst fatalities are when people don't have on seat belts."

"I've heard that."

He pulled out onto the highway. "Here we go, Jake. Our first date." He grinned. "Our uncles are probably laughing their ghostly heads off."

"I wouldn't doubt it." She sighed. "Still, it wasn't nice of either of them to rig the wills like that."

"I guess they didn't expect to die for years and years," he commented. "Maybe it was a joke. They expected the lawyer to tell us long before they died. Except he died first and his partner had no sense of humor."

"I don't know. Our uncles did like to manipulate people."

"Too much," he murmured. "They browbeat poor old Dan Harper into marrying Daisy Kane, and he was miserable. They thought she was a sweet, kind girl who'd never want anything more than to go on living in Hollister for the rest of her life."

"Then she discovered a fascination for microscopes, got a science degree and moved to New York City to work in a research lab. Dan wouldn't leave Hollister, so they got a divorce. Good thing they didn't have kids, I guess."

"I guess. Especially with Dan living in a whiskey bottle these days."

She glanced at him. "Maybe some women mature late."

He glanced back. "You going to develop a fascination with microscopes and move to New York?" he asked suspiciously.

She laughed out loud. "I hope not. I hate cities."

He grinned again. "Me, too. Just checking."

"Besides, how could I leave Sammy? I'm sure there isn't an apartment in a big city that would let you keep a calf in it."

He laughed. "Well, they would. But only in the fridge. Or the freezer."

"You bite your tongue!" she exclaimed. "Nobody's eating my cow!"

He frowned thoughtfully. "Good point. I'm not exactly sure I know how to field dress a cow. A steer, sure. But cows are, well, different."

She glared at him. "You are not field dressing Sammy, so forget it."

He sighed. "There go my dreams of a nice steak."

"You can get one at the restaurant in town anytime you like. Sammy is for petting, not eating."

"If you say so."

"I do!"

He loved to wind her up and watch the explosion. She was so full of life, so enthusiastic about everything new. He enjoyed being with her. There were all sorts of places he could take her. He was thinking ahead. Far ahead.

"You're smirking," she accused. "What are you thinking about?"

"I was just remembering how excited you get about new things," he confessed. "I was thinking of places we could go together."

"You were?" she asked, surprised. And flattered.

He smiled at her. "I've never dated anybody regularly," he said. "I mean, I've had dates. But this is different." He searched for a way to put into words what he was thinking.

"You mean, because we're sort of being forced into it by the wills."

He frowned. "No. That's not what I mean." He stopped at an intersection and glanced her way. "I haven't had regular dates with a woman I've known well for years and years," he said after a minute. "Somebody I like."

She beamed. "Oh."

He chuckled as he pulled out onto the long highway that led to Billings. "We've had our verbal cut-and-thrust encounters, but despite that sharp tongue, I enjoy being with you."

She laughed. "It's not that sharp."

"Not to me. I understand there's a former customer of the florist shop where you worked who could write a testimonial for you about your use of words in a free-for-all."

She flushed and fiddled with her purse. "He was obnoxious."

"Actually they said he was just trying to ask you out."

"It was the way he went about it," she said curtly. "I don't think I've ever had a man talk to me like that in my whole life."

"I don't think he'll ever use the same language to any other woman, if it's a consolation." He teased. "So much for his inflated ego."

"He thought he was irresistible," she muttered. "Bragging about his fast new car and his dad's bank balance, and how he could get any woman he wanted." Her lips set. "Well, he couldn't get this one."

"Teenage boys have insecurities," he said. "I can speak with confidence on that issue, because I used to be one myself." He glanced at her with twinkling black eyes. "They're puff adders."

She blinked. "Excuse me?"

"I've never seen one myself, but I had a buddy in the service who was from Georgia. He told me about them. They're these snakes with insecurities."

She burst out laughing. "Snakes with insecurities?"

He nodded. "They're terrified of people. So if humans come too close to them, they rise up on their tails and weave back and forth and blow out their throats and start hissing. You know, imitating a cobra. Most of the time, people take them at face value and run away."

"What if people stand their ground and don't run?"

He laughed. "They faint."

"They faint?"

He nodded. "Dead away, my buddy said. He took a friend home with him. They were walking through the fields when a puff adder rose up and did his act for the friend. The guy was about to run for it when my buddy walked right up to the snake and it fainted dead away. I hear his family is still telling the story with accompanying sound effects and hilarity."

"A fainting snake." She sighed. "What I've missed, by spending my whole life in Montana. I wouldn't have known any better, either, though. I've never seen a cobra."

"They have them in zoos," he pointed out.

"I've never been to a zoo."

"What?"

"Well, Billings is a long way from Hollister and I've

never had a vehicle I felt comfortable about getting there in." She grimaced. "This is a very deserted road, most of the time. If I broke down, I'd worry about who might stop to help me."

He gave her a covert appraisal. She was such a private person. She kept things to herself. Remembering her uncle and his weak heart, he wasn't surprised that she'd learned to do that.

"You couldn't talk to your uncle about most things, could you, Jake?" he wondered out loud.

"Not really," she agreed. "I was afraid of upsetting him, especially after his first heart attack."

"So you learned to keep things to yourself."

"I pretty much had to. I've never had close girlfriends, either."

"Most of the girls your age are married and have kids, except the ones who went into the military or moved to cities."

She nodded. "I'm a throwback to another era, when women lived at home until they married. Gosh, the world has changed," she commented.

"It sure has," he agreed. "When I was a boy, television sets were big and bulky and in cabinets. Now they're so thin and light that people can hang them on walls. And my iPod does everything a television can do, right down to playing movies and giving me news and weather."

She frowned. "That wasn't what I meant, exactly."

He raised his eyebrows.

"I mean, that women seem to want careers and men in volume."

He cleared his throat.

"That didn't come out right." She laughed self-consciously. "It just seems to me that women are more like the way men used to be. They don't want commitment. They have careers and they live with men. I heard a newscaster say that marriage is too retro a concept for modern people."

"There have always been people who lived out of the mainstream, Jake," he said easily. "It's a choice."

"It wouldn't be mine," she said curtly. "I think people should get married and stay married and raise children together."

"Now that's a point of view I like."

She studied him curiously. "Do you want kids?"

He smiled. "Of course. Don't you?"

She averted her eyes. "Well, yes. Someday."

He sighed. "I keep forgetting how young you are. You haven't really had time to live yet."

"You mean, get fascinated with microscopes and move to New York City," she said with a grin.

He laughed. "Something like that, maybe."

"I could never see stuff in microscopes in high school," she recalled. "I was so excited when I finally found what I thought was an organism and the teacher said it was an air bubble. That's all I ever managed to find." She grimaced. "I came within two grade points of failing biology. As it was, I had the lowest passing grade in my whole class."

"But you can cook like an angel," he pointed out.

She frowned. "What does that have to do with microscopes?"

"I'm making an observation," he replied. "We all have skills. Yours is cooking. Somebody else's might be science. It would be a pretty boring world if we all were good at the same things."

"I see."

He smiled. "You can crochet, too. My grandmother loved

her crafts, like you do. She could make quilts and knit sweaters and crochet afghans. A woman of many talents."

"They don't seem to count for much in the modern world," she replied.

"Have you ever really looked at the magazine rack, Jake?" he asked, surprised. "There are more magazines on handicrafts than there are on rock stars, and that's saying something."

"I hadn't noticed." She looked around. They were just coming into Billings. Ahead, she could see the awesome outline of the Rimrocks, where the airport was located, in the distance. "We're here?" she exclaimed.

"It's not so far from home," he said lazily.

"Not at the speed you go, no," she said impudently.

He laughed. "There wasn't any traffic and we aren't overly blessed with highway patrols at this hour of the night."

"You catch speeders, and you're local law enforcement," she pointed out.

"I don't catch them on the interstate unless they're driving on it through my town," he replied. "And it's not so much the speed that gets them caught, either. It's the way they're driving. You can be safe at high speeds and dangerous at low ones. Weaving in and out of traffic, riding people's bumpers, running stop signs, that sort of thing."

"I saw this television program where an experienced traffic officer said that what scared him most was to see a driver with both hands white-knuckled and close together on the steering wheel."

He nodded. "There are exceptions, but it usually means someone who's insecure and afraid of the vehicle."

"You aren't."

He shrugged. "I've been driving since I was twelve. Kids

grow up early when they live on ranches. Have to learn how to operate machinery, like tractors and harvesters."

"Our ranch doesn't have a harvester."

"That's because our ranch can't afford one," he said, smiling. "But we can always borrow one from neighbors."

"Small towns are such nice places," she said dreamily. "I love it that people will loan you a piece of equipment that expensive just because they like you."

"I imagine there are people in cities who would do the same, Jake, but there's not much use for them there."

She laughed. "No, I guess not."

He turned the corner and pulled into a parking lot next to a long, low building. There was a neon sign that said Red's Tavern.

"It's a bar?" she asked.

"It's a dance club. They do serve alcohol, but not on the dance floor."

"Theodore, I don't think I've ever been in a bar in my life."

"Not to worry, they won't force you to drink anything alcoholic," he told her, tongue-in-cheek. "And if they tried, I'd have to call local law and have them arrested. You're underage."

"Local law?"

"I'm not sanctioned to arrest people outside my own jurisdiction," he reminded her. "But you could make a citizen's arrest. Anybody can if they see a crime being committed. It's just that we don't advise it. Could get you killed, depending on the circumstances."

"I see what you mean."

He got out and opened her door, lifting her gently down from the truck by the waist. He held her just in front of him for a minute, smiling into her soft eyes. "You're as light as a feather," he commented softly. "And you smell pretty."

A shocked little laugh left her throat. "I smell pretty?"

"Yes. I remember my grandmother by her scent. She wore a light, flowery cologne. I recognize it if I smell it anywhere. She always smelled so good."

Her hands rested lightly on his broad shoulders. He was very strong. She loved his strength, his size. She smiled into his dark eyes. "You smell good, too. Spicy."

He nuzzled her nose with his. "Thanks."

She sighed and slid her arms around his neck. She tucked her face into his throat. "I feel so safe with you," she said softly. "Like nothing could ever hurt me."

"Now, Jake, that's not the sort of thing a man likes to hear."

She lifted her head, surprised. "Why?"

He pursed his lips. "We want to hear that we're dangerous and exciting, that we stir you up and make you nervous."

"You do?"

"It's a figure of speech."

She searched his eyes. "You don't want me to feel comfortable with you?" she faltered.

"You don't understand what I'm talking about, do you?" he wondered gently.

"No…not really. I'm sorry."

It was early days yet, he reminded himself. It was disappointing that she wasn't shaky when he touched her. But, then, she kept secrets. There must be a reason why she was so icy inside herself.

He set her down but he didn't let her go. "Some things have to be learned," he said.

"Learned."

He framed her face with his big, warm hands. "Passion, for instance."

She blinked.

It was like describing ice to a desert nomad. He smiled wistfully. "You haven't ever been kissed in such a way that you'd die to have it happen again?"

She shook her head. Her eyes were wide and innocent, unknowing. She flushed a little and shifted restlessly.

"But you have been kissed in such a way that you'd rather undergo torture than have it happen again," he said suddenly.

She caught her breath. He couldn't know! He couldn't!

His black eyes narrowed on her face. "Something happened to you, Jake. Something bad. It made you lock yourself away from the world. And it wasn't your experience with the traveling auditor."

"You can't know…!"

"Of course not," he interrupted impatiently. "You know I don't pry. But I've been in law enforcement a long time, and I've learned to read people pretty good. You're afraid of me when I get too close to you."

She bit down hard on her lower lip. She drew blood.

"Stop that," he said in a tender tone, touching her lower lip where her teeth had savaged it. "I'm not going to try to browbeat you into telling me something you don't want to. But I wish you trusted me enough to talk to me about it. You know I'm not judgmental."

"It doesn't have anything to do with that."

He cocked his head. "Can't you tell me?"

She hesitated noticeably. She wanted to. She really wanted to. But…

He bent and kissed her eyelids shut. "Don't. We have all the time in the world. When you're ready to talk, I'll listen."

She drew in a long, labored breath and laid her forehead against his suit coat. "You're the nicest man I've ever known."

He smiled over her head. "Well, that's a start, I guess."

She smiled, too. "It's a start."

CHAPTER FOUR

IT WAS THE liveliest place Jillian had ever been to. The dance band was on a platform at the end of a long, wide hall with a polished wooden floor. Around the floor were booths, not tables, and there was a bar in the next room with three bartenders, two of whom were female.

The music was incredible. It was Latin with a capital L, pulsing and narcotic. On the dance floor, people were moving to the rhythm. Some had on jeans and boots, others were wearing ensembles that would have done justice to a club in New York City. Still others, apparently too intimidated by the talent being displayed on the dance floor, were standing on the perimeter of the room, clapping and smiling.

"Wow," Jillian said, watching a particularly talented couple, a silver-haired lean and muscular man with a willowy blonde woman somewhat younger than he was. They whirled and pivoted, laughing, with such easy grace and elegance that she couldn't take her eyes off them.

"That's Red Jernigan," he told her, indicating the silver-haired man, whose thick, long hair was in a ponytail down his back.

"He isn't redheaded," she pointed out.

He gave her an amused look. "It doesn't refer to his coloring," he told her. "They called him that because in any battle, he was the one most likely to come out bloody."

She gasped. "Oh."

"I have some odd friends." He shrugged, then smiled. "You'll get used to them."

He was saying something profound about their future. She was confused, but she returned his smile anyway.

The dance ended and Theodore tugged her along with him to the dance floor, where the silver-haired man and the blonde woman were catching their breath.

"Hey, Red," he greeted the other man, who grinned and gripped his hand. "Good to see you."

"About time you came up for a visit." Red's dark eyes slid to the small blonde woman beside the police chief. His eyebrows arched.

"This is Jillian," Theodore said gently. "And this is Red Jernigan."

"I'm Melody," the pretty blonde woman said, introducing herself. "Nice to meet you."

Red slid his arm around the woman and pulled her close. "Nice to see Ted going around with somebody," he observed. "It's painful to see a man come alone to a dance club and refuse to dance with anyone except the owner's wife."

"Well, I don't like most modern women." Theodore excused himself. He smiled down at a grinning Jillian. "I like Jake, here."

"Jake?" Red asked, blinking.

"He's always called me that," Jillian sighed. "I've known him a long time."

"She has," Theodore drawled, smiling. "She likes cattle."

"I don't," Melody laughed. "Smelly things."

"Oh, but they're not smelly if they're kept clean," Jillian protested at once. "Sammy is always neat."

"Her calf," Theodore explained.

"Is he a bull?" Red asked.

"She's a heifer," Jillian inserted. "A little black baldy."

Red and Melody were giving her odd looks.

"As an acquaintance of mine in Jacobsville, Texas, would say," Red told them, "if Johnny Cash could sing about a girl named Sue, a person can have a girl animal with a boy's name." He leaned closer. "He has a female border collie named Bob."

They burst out laughing.

"Well, don't stand over here with us old folks," Red told them. "Get out there with the younger generation and show them how to tango."

"You aren't old, Bud," Theodore told his friend with twinkling eyes. "You're just a hair slower than you used to be, but with the same skills."

"Which I hope I'm never called to use again," Red replied solemnly. "I'm still on reserve status."

"I know."

"Red was a bird colonel in spec ops," Theodore explained to Jillian later when they were sitting at a table sampling the club's exquisitely cooked seasoned steak and fancy baked sweet potatoes, which it was as famous as for its dance band.

"And he still is?" she asked.

He nodded. "He can do more with recruits than any man I ever knew, and without browbeating them. He just encourages. Of course, there are times when he has to get a little more creative, with the wilder sort."

"Creative?"

He grinned. "There was this giant of a kid from Milwaukee who was assigned to his unit in the field. Kid played video games and thought he knew more about strategy and tactics than Red did. So Red turns him loose on the enemy, but with covert backup."

"What happened?" she asked, all eyes.

"The kid walked right into an enemy squad and froze in his tracks. It's one thing to do that on a computer screen. Quite another to confront armed men in real life. They were aiming their weapons at him when Red led a squad in to recover him. Took about two minutes for them to eliminate the threat and get Commando Carl back to his own lines." He shook his head. "In the excitement, the kid had, shall we say, needed access to a restroom and didn't have one. So they hung a nickname on him that stuck."

"Tell me!"

He chuckled. "Let's just say that it suited him. He took it in his stride, sucked up his pride, learned to follow orders and became a real credit to the unit. He later became mayor of a small town somewhere up north, where he's still known, to a favored few, as 'Stinky.'"

She laughed out loud.

"Actually, he was in good company. I read in a book on World War II that one of our better known generals did the same thing when his convoy ran into a German attack. Poor guy. I'll bet Stinky cringed every time he saw that other general's book on a rack."

"I don't doubt it."

She sipped her iced tea and smiled. "This is really good food," she said. "I've never had a steak that was so tender, not even from beef my uncle raised."

"This is Kobe beef," he pointed out. "Red gets it from Japan. God knows how," he added.

"I read about those. Don't they actually massage the beef cattle?"

"Pamper them," he agreed. "You should try that sweet

potato," he advised. "It's really a unique combination of spices they use."

She frowned, picking at it with her fork. "I've only ever had a couple of sweet potatoes, and they were mostly taste-less."

"Just try it."

She put the fork into it, lifted it dubiously to her lips and suddenly caught her breath when the taste hit her tongue like dynamite. "Wow!" she exclaimed. "What do they call this?"

"Red calls it 'the ultimate jalapeño-brown-sugar-sweet-potato delight.'"

"It's heavenly!"

He chuckled. "It is, isn't it? The jalapeño gives it a kick like a mule, but it's not so hot that even tenderfeet wouldn't eat it."

"I would never have thought of such a combination. And I thought I was a good cook."

"You are a good cook, Jake," he said. "The best I ever knew."

She blushed. "Thanks, Theodore."

He cocked his head. "I guess it would kill you to shorten that."

"Shorten what?"

"My name. Most people call me Ted."

She hesitated with the fork in midair. She searched his black eyes for a long time. "Ted," she said softly.

His jaw tautened. He hadn't expected it to have that ef-fect on him. She had a soft, sweet, sexy voice when she let herself relax with him. She made his name sound differ-ent; special. New.

"I like the way you say it," he said, when she gave him a

worried look. "It's—" he searched for a word that wouldn't intimidate her "—it's stimulating."

"Stimulating." She didn't understand.

He put down his fork with a long sigh. "Something happened to you," he said quietly. "You don't know me well enough to talk to me about it. Or maybe you're afraid that I might go after the man who did it."

She was astounded. She couldn't even manage words. She just stared at him, shocked.

"I'm in law enforcement," he reminded her. "After a few years, you read body language in a different way than most people do. Abused children have a look, a way of dressing and acting, one that's obvious to a cop."

She went white. She bit her lower lip and her fingers toyed with her fork as she stared at it, fighting tears.

His big hand curled around hers, gently. "I wish you could tell me. I think it would help you."

She looked up into quiet, patient eyes. "You wouldn't... think badly of me?"

"For God's sake," he groaned. "Are you nuts?"

She blinked.

He grimaced. "Sorry. I didn't mean to put it that way. Nothing I found out about you would change the way I feel. If that's why you're reluctant."

"You're sure?"

He glared at her.

She lowered her eyes and curled her small hand into his big one, a trusting gesture that touched him in a new and different way.

"When I was fifteen, Uncle John had this young man he got to do odd jobs around here. He was a drifter, very intelligent. He seemed like a nice, trustworthy person to have around the house. Then one day Uncle John felt bad and went to bed, left me with the hired man in the kitchen."

Her jaw clenched. "At first, he was real helpful. Wanted to put out the trash for me and sweep the floor. I thought it was so nice of him. Then all of a sudden, he asked what was my bra size and if I wore nylon panties."

Theodore's eyes began to flash.

She swallowed. "I was so shocked I didn't know what to do or say. I thought it was some sick joke. Until he tried to take my clothes off, mumbling all the time that I needed somebody to teach me about men and he was the perfect person, because he'd had so many virgins."

"Good God!"

"Uncle John was asleep. There was nobody to help me. But the Peales lived right down the road, and I knew a back way through the woods to their house. I hit him in a bad place and ran out the door as fast as my legs could carry me. I was almost naked by then." She closed her eyes, shivering with the memory of the terror she'd felt, running and hearing him curse behind her as he crashed through the undergrowth in pursuit.

"I didn't think what danger I might be placing Sassy Peale and her mother and stepsister in, I just knew they'd help me and I was terrified. I banged on the door and Sassy came to it. When she saw how I looked, she ran for the shotgun they kept in the hall closet. By the time the hired man got on the porch, Sassy had the shotgun loaded and aimed at his stomach. She told him if he moved she'd blow him up."

She sipped tea while she calmed a little from the remembered fear. Her hand was shaking, but just a little. Her free hand was still clasped gently in Theodore's.

"He tried to blame it on me, to say I'd flirted and tried to seduce him, but Sassy knew better. She held him at bay

until her mother called the police. They took him away."
She drew in a breath. "There was a trial. It was horrible,
but at least it was in closed session, in the judge's chambers. The hired man plea-bargained. You see, he had priors, many of them. He drew a long jail sentence, but it did
at least spare me a public trial." She sipped tea again. "His
sister lived over in Wyoming. She came to see me, after
the trial." Her eyes closed. "She said I was a slut who had
no business putting a sweet, nice guy like him behind bars
for years." She managed a smile. "Sassy was in the kitchen
when the woman came to the door. She marched into the
living room and gave that woman hell. She told her about
her innocent brother's priors and how many young girls
had suffered because of his inability to control his own de-
sires. She was eloquent. The woman shut up and went away.
I never heard from her again." She looked over at him.
"Sassy's been my friend ever since. Not a close one, I'm
sorry to say. I was so embarrassed at having her know about
it that it inhibited me with her and everyone else. Everyone
would believe the man's sister, and that I'd asked for it."

His fingers curled closer into hers. "No young woman
asks for such abuse," he said softly. "But abusers use that
argument to defend themselves. It's a lie, like all their other
lies."

"Sometimes, innocent people go to jail," she said, to
be fair.

"Sure," he agreed. "But more often than not, such lies
are found out."

"I guess so."

"I wasn't here when that happened."

"No. You were doing that workshop at the FBI Academy.
And I begged the judge not to tell you or anybody else. She
was very kind to me."

He looked over her head, his eyes flashing cold and black as he thought what he might have done to the man if he'd been in town. He wasn't interested in Jillian as a woman back then, because she was still almost a child, but he'd always been fond of her. He would have wiped the floor with the man.

His expression made her feel warm inside. "You'd have knocked him up and down main street," she ventured.

He laughed, surprised, and met her eyes. "Worse than that, probably." He frowned. "First the hired man, then the accountant."

"The accountant was my fault," she confessed. "I never told him how old I was, and I was infatuated with him. He was drinking when he tried to persuade me." She shook her head. "I can't believe I even did that."

He stared at her. "You were a kid, Jake. Kids aren't known for deep thought."

She smiled. "Thanks for not being judgmental."

He shrugged. "I'm such a nice man that I'm never judgmental."

Her eyebrows arched.

He grinned. "And I really can do the tango. Suppose I teach you?"

She studied his lean, handsome face. "It's a very, well, sensual sort of dance, they say."

"Very." He pursed his lips. "But I'm not an aggressive man. Not in any way that should frighten you."

She colored a little. "Really?"

"Really."

She drew in a long breath. "I guess every woman should dance the tango at least once."

"My thoughts exactly."

He wiped his mouth on the linen napkin, took a last sip of the excellent but cooling coffee and got to his feet.

"You have to watch your back on the dance floor, though," he told her as he led her toward it.

"Why is that?"

"When the other women see what a great dancer I am, they'll probably mob you and take me away from you," he teased.

She laughed. "Okay." She leaned toward him. "Are you packing?"

"Are you kidding?" he asked, indicating the automatic nestled at his waist on his belt. "I'm a cop. I'm always packing. And you keep your little hands off my gun," he added sternly. "I don't let women play with it, even if they ask nicely."

"Theodore, I'm scared of guns," she reminded him. "And you know it. That's why *you* come over and sit on the front porch and shoot bottles on stumps, just to irritate me."

"I'll try to reform," he promised.

"Lies."

He put his hand over his heart. "I only lie when I'm salving someone's feelings," he pointed out. "There are times when telling the truth is cruel."

"Oh, yeah? Name one."

He nodded covertly toward a woman against the wall. "Well, if I told that nice lady that her dress looks like she had it painted on at a carnival, she'd probably feel bad."

She bit her lip trying not to laugh. "She probably thinks it looks sexy."

"Oh, no. Sexy is a dress that covers almost everything, but leaves one little tantalizing place bare," he said. "That's why Japanese kimonos have that dip on the back of the neck, that just reveals the nape, when the rest of the woman is covered from head to toe. The Japanese think the nape of the neck is sexy."

"My goodness!" She stared up at him, impressed. "You've been so many places. I've only ever been out of Montana once, when I drove to Wyoming with Uncle John to a cattle convention. I've never been out of the country at all. You learn a lot about other people when you travel, don't you?"

He nodded. He smiled. "Other countries have different customs. But people are mostly the same everywhere. I've enjoyed the travel most of all, even when I had to do it on business."

"Like the time you flew to London with that detective from Scotland Yard. Imagine a British case that involved a small town like Hollister!" she exclaimed.

"The perpetrator was a murderer who came over here fishing to provide himself with an alibi while his wife committed the crime and blamed it on her absent husband. In the end, they both drew life sentences."

"Who did they kill?" she asked.

"Her cousin who was set to inherit the family estate and about ten million pounds," he said, shaking his head. "The things sensible people will do for money never ceases to amaze me. I mean, it isn't like you can take it with you when you die. And how many houses can you live in? How many cars can you drive?" He frowned. "I think of money the way the Crow and Cheyenne people do. The way most Native Americans do. The man in the tribe who is the most honored is always the poorest, because he gives away everything he has to people who need it more. They're not capitalists. They don't respect societies that equate prestige with money."

"And they share absolutely everything," she agreed. "They don't respect private property."

He laughed. "Neither do I. The woods and the rivers and the mountains are ageless. You can't own them."

"See? That's the Cheyenne in you talking."

He touched her blond hair. "Probably it is. We going to dance, or talk?"

"You're leading, aren't you?"

He tugged her onto the dance floor. "Apparently." He drew her gently to him and then hesitated. After what she'd told him, he didn't want to do anything that would make her uncomfortable. He said so.

"I don't...well, I don't feel uncomfortable, like that, with you," she faltered, looking up into his black eyes. She managed a shaky little smile. "I like being close to you." She flushed, afraid she'd been too bold. Or that he'd think she was being forward. Her expression was troubled.

He just smiled. "You can say anything to me," he said gently. "I won't think you're being shallow or vampish. Okay?"

She relaxed. "Okay. Is this going to be hard to learn?"

"Very."

She drew in a long breath. "Then I guess we should get started."

His eyes smiled down at her. "I guess we should."

He walked her around the dance floor, to her amusement, teaching her how the basic steps were done. It wasn't like those exotic tangos she'd seen in movies at first. It was like kindergarten was to education.

She followed his steps, hesitantly at first, then a little more confidently, until she was moving with some elegance.

"Now, this is where we get into the more exotic parts,"

he said. "It involves little kicks that go between the legs." He leaned to her ear. "I think we should have kids one day, so it's very important that you don't get overenthusiastic with the kicks. And you should also be very careful where you place them."

It took her a minute to understand what he meant, and then she burst out laughing instead of being embarrassed.

He grinned. "Just playing it safe," he told her. "Ready? This is how you do it."

It was fascinating, the complexity of the movements and the fluid flow of the steps as he paced the dance to the music.

"It doesn't look like this in most movies," she said as she followed his steps.

"That's because it's a stylized version of the tango," he told her. "Most people have no idea how it's supposed to be done. But there are a few movies that go into it in depth. One was made in black and white by a British woman. It's my favorite. Very comprehensive. Even about the danger of the kicks." He chuckled.

"It's Argentinian, isn't it? The dance, I mean."

"You'd have to ask my buddy about that, I'm not sure. I know there are plenty of dance clubs down there that specialize in tango. The thing is, you're supposed to do these dances with strangers. It's as much a social expression as it is a dance."

"Really?"

He nodded. He smiled. "Maybe we should get a bucket and put all our spare change into it. Then, when we're Red's age, we might have enough to buy tickets to Buenos Aires and go dancing."

She giggled. "Oh, I'm sure we'd have the ticket price in twenty or thirty years."

He sighed as he led, "Or forty." He shook his head. "I've always wanted to travel. I did a good bit of it in the service, but there are plenty of places I'd love to see. Like those ruins in Peru and the pyramids, and the Sonoran desert."

She frowned. "The Sonoran desert isn't exotic."

He smiled. "Sure it is. Do you know, those Saguaro cacti can live for hundreds of years? And that if a limb falls on you, it can kill you because of the weight? You don't think about them being that heavy, but they have a woody spine and limbs to support the weight of the water they store."

"Gosh. How do you know all that?"

He grinned. "The *Science Channel*, the *Discovery Channel*, the *National Geographic Channel*..."

She laughed. "I like to watch those, too."

"I don't think I've missed a single nature special," he told her. He gave her a droll look. "Now that should tell you all you need to know about my social life." He grinned.

She laughed, too. "Well, my social life isn't much better. This is the first time I've been on a real date."

His black eyebrows arched.

She flushed. She shrugged. She averted her eyes.

He tilted her face up to his and smiled with a tenderness that made her knees weak. "I heartily approve," he said, "of the fact that you've been saving yourself for me, just like your uncle did," he added outrageously.

She almost bent over double laughing. "No fair."

"Just making the point." He slid his arm around her and pulled her against him. She caught her breath.

He hesitated, his dark eyes searching hers to see if he'd upset her.

"My...goodness," she said breathlessly.

He raised his eyebrows.

She averted her eyes and her cheeks took on a glow. She

didn't know how to tell him that the sensations she was feeling were unsettling. She could feel the muscles of his chest pressed against her breasts, and it was stimulating, exciting. It was a whole new experience to be held close to a man's body, to feel its warm strength, to smell the elusive, spicy cologne he was wearing.

"You've danced with men before."

"Yes, of course," she confessed. She looked up at him with fascination. "But it didn't, well, it didn't...feel like this."

That made him arrogant. His chin lifted and he looked down at her with possession kindling in his eyes.

"Sorry," she said quickly, embarrassed. "I just blurt things out."

He bent his head, so that his mouth was right beside her ear as he eased her into the dance. "It's okay," he said softly.

She bit her lip and laughed nervously.

"Well, it's okay to feel like that with me," he corrected. "But you should know that it's very wrong for you to feel that way with any other man. So you should never dance with anybody but me for the rest of your life."

She burst out laughing again.

He chuckled. "You're a quick study, Jake," he noted as she followed his steps easily. "I think we may become famous locally for this dance once you get used to it."

"You think?" she teased.

He turned her back over his arm, pulled her up, and spun her around with skill. She laughed breathlessly. It was really fun.

"I haven't danced in years," he sighed. "I love to do it, but I'm not much of a party person."

"I'm not, either. I'm much more at home in a kitchen than I am in a club." She grimaced. "That's not very modern, either, for a woman. I always feel that I should be working my way up a corporate ladder somewhere or immersing myself in higher education."

"Would you like to be a corporate leader?"

She made a face. "Not really. Jobs like that are demanding, and you have to want them more than anything. I'm just not ambitious, I guess. Although," she mused, "I think I might like to take a college course."

"What sort?" he asked.

"Anthropology."

He stopped dancing and looked down at her, fascinated. "Why?"

"I like reading about ancient humans, and how archaeologists can learn so much from skeletal material. I go crazy over those National Geographic specials on Egypt."

He laughed. "So do I."

"I'd love to see the pyramids. All of them, even those in Mexico and Asia."

"There are pyramids here in the States," he reminded her. "Those huge earthen mounds that ancient people built were the equivalent of pyramids."

She stopped dancing. "Why do you think they built them?"

"I don't know. It's just a guess. But most of the earthen mounds are near rivers. I've always thought maybe they were where the village went to get out of the water when it flooded."

"It's as good a theory as any other," she agreed. "But what about in Egypt? I don't think they had a problem with flooding," she added, tongue-in-cheek.

"Now, see, there's another theory about that. Thousands of years ago, Egypt was green and almost tropical, with abundant sources of water. So who knows?"

"It was green?" she exclaimed.

He nodded. "There were forests."

"Where did you learn that?"

"I read, too. I think it was in Herodotus. They called him the father of history. He wrote about Egypt. He admitted that the information might not all be factual, but he wrote down exactly what the Egyptian priests told him about their country."

"I'd like to read what he said."

"You can borrow one of my books," he offered. "I have several copies of his Histories."

"Why?"

He grimaced. "Because I keep losing them."

She frowned. "How in the world do you lose a book?"

"You'll have to come home with me sometime and see why."

Her eyes sparkled. "Is that an invitation? You know, 'come up and see my books'?"

He chuckled. "No, it's not a pickup line. I really mean it."

"I'd like to."

"You would?" His arm contracted. "When? How about next Saturday? I'll show you my collection of maps, too."

"Maps?" she exclaimed.

He nodded. "I like topo maps, and relief maps, best of all. It helps me to understand where places are located."

She smiled secretively. "We could compare maps."

"What?"

She sighed. "I guess we do have a lot in common. I think I've got half the maps Rand McNally ever published!"

CHAPTER FIVE

"WELL, WHAT DO you know?" He laughed. "We're both closet map fanatics."

"And we love ancient history."

"And we love shooting targets from the front porch."

She glowered up at him.

He sighed. "I'll try to reform."

"You might miss and shoot Sammy," she replied.

"I'm a dead shot."

"Anybody can miss once," she pointed out.

"I guess so."

They'd stopped on the dance floor while the band got ready to start the next number. When they did, he whirled her around and they started all over again. Jillian thought she'd never enjoyed anything in her life so much.

TED WALKED HER to the front door, smiling. "It was a nice first date."

"Yes, it was," she agreed, smiling back. "I've never had so much fun!"

He laughed. She made him feel warm inside. She was such an honest person. She wasn't coy or flirtatious. She just said what she felt. It wasn't a trait he was familiar with.

"What are you thinking?" she asked curiously.

"That I'm not used to people who tell the truth."

She blinked. "Why not?"

"Almost all the people I arrest are innocent," he ticked off. "They were set up by a friend, or it was a case of mistaken identity even when there were eyewitnesses. Oh, and, the police have it in for them and arrest them just to be mean. That's my personal favorite," he added facetiously.

She chuckled. "I guess they wish they were innocent."

"I guess."

She frowned. "There's been some talk about that man you arrested for the bank robbery getting paroled because of a technicality. Is it true?"

His face set in hard lines. "It might be. His attorney said that the judge made an error in his instructions to the jury that prejudiced the case. I've seen men get off in similar situations."

"Ted, he swore he'd kill you if he ever got out," she said worriedly.

He pursed his lips and his dark eyes twinkled. "Frightened for me?"

"Of course I am."

He sighed and pulled her close. "Now, that's exactly the sort of thing that makes a man feel good about himself, when some sweet little woman worries about him."

"I'm not little, I'm not sweet and I don't usually worry," she pointed out.

"It's okay if you worry about me," he teased. "As long as you don't do it excessively."

She toyed with the top button of his unbuttoned jacket. "There are lots of safer professions than being a police chief."

He frowned. "You're kidding, right?"

She grimaced. "Ted, Joe Brown's wife was one of my uncle's friends. She was married to that deputy sheriff who was shot to death a few years ago. She said that she spent their whole married lives sitting by the phone at night, almost shaking with worry every time he had to go out on a case, hoping and praying that he'd come home alive."

His hands on her slender waist had tightened unconsciously. "Anyone who marries someone in law enforcement has to live with that possibility," he said slowly.

She bit her lower lip. She was seeing herself sitting by the phone at night, pacing the floor. She was prone to worry anyway. She was very fond of Ted. She didn't want him to die. But right now, she wasn't in love. She had time to think about what she wanted to do with her life. She was sure she should give this a lot of thought before she dived headfirst into a relationship with him that might lead very quickly to marriage. She'd heard people talk about how it was when people became very physical with each other, that it was so addictive that they couldn't bear to be apart at all. Once that happened, she wouldn't have a chance to see things rationally.

Ted could almost see the thoughts in her mind. Slowly he released her and stepped back.

She felt the distance, and it was more than physical. He was drawing away in every sense.

She looked up at him. She drew in a long breath. "I'm not sure I'm ready, Ted."

"Ready for what?"

That stiffness in him was disturbing, but she had to be honest. "I'm not sure I'm ready to think about marriage."

His black eyes narrowed. "Jillian, if we don't get married, there's a California developer who's going to make this place into hot real estate with tourist impact, and Sammy could end up on a platter."

She felt those words like a body blow. Her eyes, tormented, met his. "But it's not fair, to rush into something without having time to think about it!" she exclaimed. "The wills didn't say we have to get married tomorrow! There's no real time limit!"

There was, but he wasn't going to push her. She had cold feet. She didn't know him that well, despite the years they'd been acquainted, and she wasn't ready for the physical side of marriage. She had hang-ups, and good reasons to have them.

"Okay," he said after a minute. "Suppose we just get to know each other and let the rest ride for a while?"

"You mean, go on dates and stuff?"

He pursed his lips. "Yes. Dates and stuff."

She noticed how handsome he was. In a crowd, he always stood out. He was a vivid sort of person, not like she was at all. But they did enjoy the same sorts of things and they got along, most of the time.

"I would like to see your place," she said.

"I'll come and get you Saturday morning," he said quietly.

He waited for her answer with bridled impatience. She could see that. He wasn't sure of her at all. She hated being so hesitant, but it was a rushed business. She would have to make a decision in the near future or watch Uncle John's ranch become a resort. It didn't bear thinking about. On the other hand, if she said yes to Ted, it would mean a relationship that she was certain she wasn't ready for.

"Stop gnawing your lip off and say yes," Ted told her. "We'll work out the details as we go along."

She sighed. "Okay, Ted," she said after a minute.

He hadn't realized that he'd been holding his breath. He smiled slowly. She was going to take the chance. It was a start.

"Okay." He frowned. "You don't have any low-cut blouses

and jeans that look like you've been poured into them, do you?"

"Ted!"

"Well, I was just wondering," he said. "Because if you do, you can't wear them over at my place. We have a dress code."

"A dress code." She nodded. "So your cowboys have to wear dresses." She nodded again.

He burst out laughing. He bent and kissed her, hard, but impersonally, and walked down the steps. "I'll see you Saturday."

"You call that a kiss?" she yelled after him, and shocked herself with the impertinent remark that had jumped out of her so impulsively.

But he didn't react to it the way she expected. He just threw up his hand and kept walking.

THEY WORKED SIDE by side in his kitchen making lunch. He was preparing an omelet while she made cinnamon toast and fried bacon.

"Breakfast for lunch," she scoffed.

"Hey, I very often have breakfast for supper, if I've been out on a case," he said indignantly. "There's no rule that says you have to have breakfast in the morning."

"I suppose not."

"See, you don't know how to break rules."

She gasped. "You're a police chief! You shouldn't be encouraging anybody to break rules."

"It's okay as long as it's only related to food," he replied.

She laughed, shaking her head.

"You going to turn that bacon anytime soon?" he asked, nodding toward it. "Or do you really like it raw on one side and black on the other?"

"If you don't like it that way, you could fry it yourself."

"I do omelets," he pointed out. "I don't even eat bacon."

"What?"

"Pig meat," he muttered.

"I like bacon!"

"Good. Then you can eat it. I've got a nice country ham all carved up and cooked in the fridge. I'll have that with mine."

"Ham is pig meat, too!"

"I think of it as steak with a curly tail," he replied.

She burst out laughing. He was so different off the job. She'd seen him walking down the sidewalk in town, somber and dignified, almost unapproachable. Here, at home, he was a changed person.

"What are you brooding about?" he wondered.

"Was I? I was just thinking how different you are at home than at work."

"I should hope so," he sighed, as he took the omelet up onto a platter. "I mean, think of the damage to my image if I cooked omelets for the prisoners."

"Chief Barnes used to," she said. "I remember Uncle John talking about what a sweet man he was. He'd take the prisoners himself to funerals when they had family members die, and in those days, when the jail was down the hall from the police department, he'd cook for them, too."

"He was a kind man," Ted agreed solemnly.

"To think that it was one of the prisoners who killed him," she added quietly as she turned the bacon. "Of all the ironies."

"The man was drunk at the time," Ted said. "And, if you recall, he killed himself just a few weeks later while he was waiting for trial. He left a note saying he didn't want to put the chief's family through any more pain."

"Everybody thought that was so odd," she said. "But people forget that murderers are just like everybody else. They aren't born planning to kill people."

"That's true. Sometimes it's alcohol or drugs that make them do it. Other times it's an impulse they can't control. Although," he added, "there are people born without a conscience. They don't mind killing. I've seen them in the military. Not too many, thank goodness, but they come along occasionally."

"Your friend who was a sniper, was he like that?"

"Not at all," he said. "He was trained to think of it as just a skill. It was only later, when it started to kill his soul, that he realized what was happening to him. That was when he got out."

"How in the world did he get into law enforcement, with such a background?" she wondered.

He chuckled. "Uncle Sam often doesn't know when his left hand is doing something different than his right one," he commented. "Government agencies have closed files."

"Oh. I get it. But those files aren't closed to everyone, are they?"

"They're only accessible to people with top-secret military clearance." He glanced at her amusedly. "Never knew a civilian, outside the executive branch, who even had one."

"That makes sense."

He pulled out her chair for her.

"Thank you," she said, with surprise in her tone.

"I'm impressing you with my good manners," he pointed out as he sat down across from her and put a napkin in his lap.

"I'm very impressed." She tasted the omelet, closed her eyes and sighed. "And not only with your manners. Ted, this is delicious!"

He grinned. "Thanks."

"What did you put in it?" she asked, trying to decide what combination of spices he'd used to produce such a taste.

"Trade secret."

"You can tell me," she coaxed. "After all, we're almost engaged."

"The 'almost' is why I'm not telling," he retorted. "If things don't work out, you'll be using my secret spices in your own omelets for some other man."

"I could promise."

"You could, but I'm not telling."

She sighed. "Well, it's delicious, anyway."

He chuckled. "The bacon's not bad, either," he conceded, having forgone the country ham that would need warming. He was hungry.

"Thanks." She lifted a piece of toast and gave it a cold look. "Shame we can't say the same for the toast. Sorry. I was busy trying not to burn the bacon, so I burned the toast instead."

"I don't eat toast."

"I do, but I don't think I will this time." She pushed the toast aside.

After they ate, he walked her around the property. He only had a few beef steers in the pasture. He'd bought quite a few Angus cattle with his own uncle, and they were at the ranch that Jillian had shared with her uncle John. She was pensive as she strolled beside him, absently stripping a dead branch of leaves, thinking about the fate of Uncle John's prize beef if she didn't marry Ted sometime soon.

"Deep thoughts?" he asked, hands in the pockets of his jeans under his shepherd's coat.

She frowned. She was wearing her buckskin jacket. One

of the pieces of fringe caught on a limb and she had to stop to disentangle it. "I was thinking about that resort," she confessed.

"Here. Let me." He stopped and removed the branch from the fringe. "Do you know why these jackets always had fringe?"

She looked up at him, aware of his height and strength so close to her. He smelled of tobacco and coffee and fir trees. "Not really."

He smiled. "When the old-timers needed something to tie up a sack with, they just pulled off a piece of fringe and used that. Also, the fringe collects water and drips it away from the body."

"My goodness!"

"My grandmother was full of stories like that. Her grandfather was a fur trapper. He lived in the Canadian wilderness. He was French. He married a Blackfoot woman."

She smiled, surprised. "But you always talk about your Cheyenne heritage."

"That's because my other grandmother was Cheyenne. I have interesting bloodlines."

Her eyes sketched his high-cheekboned face, his black eyes and hair and olive complexion. "They combined to make a very handsome man."

"Me?" he asked, surprised.

She grinned. "And not a conceited bone in your body, either, Ted."

He smiled down at her. "Not much to be conceited about."

"Modest, too."

He shrugged. He touched her cheek with his fingertips. "You have beautiful skin."

Her eyebrows arched. "Thank you."

"You get that from your mother," he said gently. "I remember her very well. I was only a boy when she died, but she was well-known locally. She was the best cook in two counties. She was always the first to sit with anyone sick, or to take food when there was a funeral."

"I only know about her through my uncle," she replied. "My uncle loved her. She was his only sister, much older than he was. She and my father had me unexpectedly, late in life."

Which, he thought, had been something of a tragedy.

"And then they both died of the flu, when I was barely crawling," she sighed. "I never knew either of them." She looked up. "You did at least know your parents, didn't you?"

He nodded. "My mother died of a stroke in her early thirties," he said. "My father was overseas, working for an oil corporation as a roughneck, when there was a bombing at the installation and he died. My grandmother took me in, and my uncle moved in to help support us."

"Neither of us had much of a childhood," she said. "Not that our relatives didn't do all they could for us," she added quickly. "They loved us. Lots of orphaned kids have it a lot worse."

"Yes, they do," he agreed solemnly. "That's why we have organizations that provide for orphaned kids."

"If I ever get rich," she commented, "I'm going to donate to those."

He grinned. "I already do. To a couple, at least."

She leaned back against a tree and closed her eyes, drinking in the sights and sounds and smells of the woods. "I love winter. I know it isn't a popular season," she added. "It's cold and there's a lot of snow. But I enjoy it. I can smell the smoke from fireplaces and woodstoves. If I close my eyes, it reminds me of campfires. Uncle John used to take me camping with him when I was little, to hunt deer."

"Which you never shot."

She opened her eyes and made a face. "I'm not shooting Bambi."

"Bull."

"People shouldn't shoot animals."

"That attitude back in colonial times would have seen you starve to death," he pointed out. "It's not like those old-timers could go to a grocery store and buy meat and vegetables. They had to hunt and garden or die."

She frowned. "I didn't think about that."

"In fact," he added, "people who refused to work were turned out of the forts into the wilderness. Some stole food from the Indians and were killed for it. Others starved or froze to death. It was a hard life."

"Why did they do it?" she wondered aloud. "Why leave their families and their homes and get on rickety old ships and go to a country they'd never even seen?"

"A lot of them did it to escape debtor's prison," he said. "They had debts they couldn't pay. A few years over here working as an indentured servant and they could be free and have money to buy their own land. Or the people they worked for might give them an acre or two, if they were generous."

"What about when the weather took their crops and they had nothing to eat?"

"There are strings of graves over the eastern seaboard of pilgrims who starved," he replied. "A sad end to a hopeful beginning. This is a hostile land when it's stripped of supermarkets and shopping centers."

A silence fell between them, during which he stared at

the small rapids in the stream nearby. "That freezes over in winter," he said. "It looks pretty."

"I'd like to see it then."

He turned. "I'll bring you over here."

She smiled. "Okay."

His black eyes looked long and deep into hers across the distance, until she felt as if something snapped inside her. She caught her breath and forced her eyes away.

Ted didn't say anything. He just smiled. And started walking again.

SHE LOVED IT that he didn't pressure her into a more physical relationship. It gave her a breathing space that she desperately needed.

He took her to a play in Billings the following weekend, a modern parody of an old play about two murderous old women and their assorted crazy relatives.

She laughed until her sides ached. Later, as they were driving home, she realized that it had been a long time since she'd been so amused by anything.

"I'm so glad I never had relatives like that," she ventured.

He laughed. "Me, too. The murderous cousin with the spooky face was a real pain, wasn't he?"

"His associate was even crazier."

She sat back against the seat, her eyes closed, still smiling. "It was a great play. Thanks for asking me."

"I was at a loose end," he commented. "We have busy weekends and slow weekends. This was a very slow one, nothing my officers couldn't handle on their own."

That was a reminder, and not a very pleasant one, of what he did for a living. She frowned in the darkness of the cab, broken only by the blue light of the instrument panel. "Ted, haven't you ever thought about doing something else for a living?"

"Like what?" he asked. "Teaching chemistry to high school students?"

He made a joke of it, but she didn't laugh. "You're not likely to be killed doing that."

"I guess you don't keep up with current events," he remarked solemnly, and proceeded to remind her of several terrible school shootings.

She grimaced. "Yes, but those are rare incidents. You make enemies in your work. What if somebody you locked up gets out and tries to kill you?"

"It goes with the job," he said laconically. "So far, I've been lucky."

Lucky. But it might not last forever. Could she see herself sitting by the phone every night of her life, waiting for that horrible call?

"You're dwelling on anticipation of the worst," he said, glancing her way. "How in the world do you think people get by who have loved ones with chronic illness or life-threatening conditions?"

She looked at him in the darkness. "I've never thought about it."

"My grandmother had cancer," he reminded her. "Had it for years. If I'd spent that time sitting in a chair, brooding on it, what sort of life would it have been for her?"

She frowned. "Lonely."

"Exactly. I knew it could happen, anytime. But I lived from day to day, just like she did. After a while, I got used to the idea, like she did, and we went on with our lives. It was always there, in the background, but it was something we just—" he searched for the word "—lived with. That's how husbands and wives of people in law enforcement and the military deal with it."

It was a new concept for her, living with a terrifying reality and getting used to it.

"You're very young," he said heavily. "It would be harder for you."

It probably would. She didn't answer him. It was something new to think about.

He walked her up the steps to her front door. He looked good in a suit, she thought, smiling.

"What are you thinking?" he teased.

"That you look very elegant in a suit."

He shrugged. "It's a nice suit."

"It's a nice man wearing it."

"Thanks. I like your dress."

She grinned. "It's old, but I like the color. It's called Rose Dust."

He fingered the lacy collar. He wouldn't have told her, because it would hurt her feelings, but it looked like the sort of dress a high school girl would wear. It wasn't sophisticated, or even old enough for her now. But he just smiled.

"Nice color," he agreed.

She cocked her head, feeling reckless. "Going to kiss me?" she asked.

"I was thinking about it."

"And what did you decide?"

He stuck his hands in his pockets and just smiled down at her. "That would be rushing things a little too much," he said gently. "You want to date and get to know each other. I think that's a good idea. Plenty of time for the other, later."

"Well, my goodness!"

"Shocked by my patience, are you?" he asked with a grin. "Me, too."

"Very."

His eyes were old and wise. "When things get physical, there's a difference in the way two people are, together. There's no time to step back and look at how things really are."

She nodded. "You mean, like Sassy and her husband, John Callister, when they first got married. They couldn't stand to be apart, even for an hour or two. They still pretty much go everywhere together. And they're always standing close, or touching."

"That's what I mean."

She frowned. "I haven't ever felt like that," she said.

He smiled. "I noticed."

She flushed. "I'm sorry, I just blurt things out..."

"I don't mind that you're honest," he said. "It helps. A lot."

She bit her lower lip. "I'd give anything if Uncle John hadn't hired that man to come work for him."

"I'm sure your uncle felt the same way. I'm surprised that he never told me about it," he added curtly.

"I imagine he thought you'd hold him responsible for it. He blamed himself," she added softly. "He never stopped apologizing." She sighed. "It didn't help very much."

"Of course it didn't." He stepped closer and tilted her chin up. "You'll deal with it. If you don't think you can, there are some good psychologists. Our department works with two, who live in Billings."

She made a face. "I don't think I could talk about something like that to a total stranger."

He stared at her for a long time. "How about me?" he asked suddenly. "Could you talk about it to me?"

CHAPTER SIX

JILLIAN STARED UP at him with conflicting emotions. But after a minute she nodded. "I think I could," she replied finally.

He beamed. His black eyes were twinkling. "That's a major step forward."

"Think so?"

"I know so."

She moved a step closer. "I enjoyed tonight. Thank you."

He gave her a teasing look and moved a step away. "I did, too, and I'll thank you to keep your distance. I don't want to be an object of lust to a single woman who lives alone."

She gasped theatrically. "You do so!"

"I do?"

"Absolutely!" she agreed. She grinned. "But not right now. Right?"

He laughed. "Not right now." He bent and brushed a lazy kiss against her forehead. "Get some sleep. I'll call you Monday."

"You do that. Not early," she added, without telling him why. She had a secret, and she wasn't sharing it.

"Not early," he agreed. "Good night."

"Good night, Ted."

He bounded down the steps, jumped in his truck and sat there deliberately until she got the message. She went inside, locked the door and turned off the porch light. Only then did he drive away. It made her feel safe, that attitude of his. Probably it was instinctive, since he was in law enforcement, but she liked it. She liked it very much.

Snow came the next morning. Jillian loved it. She drove slowly, so that she didn't slip off the road. But there wasn't much traffic, and she lived close to town. It was easier than she expected to get in on the country roads.

When she left again, at noon, it was a different story. The snow had come fast and furiously, and she could barely crawl along the white highway. The road crews had been busy, spreading sand and gravel, but there were icy spots just the same.

She hesitated to go all the way back to the ranch when she couldn't see the road ahead for the blinding snow, so she pulled into the town's only restaurant and cut off the engine.

"Well," she said to herself, "I guess if worse comes to worst, they might let me sleep in a booth in the restaurant." She laughed at the imagery.

She grabbed her purse and got out, grateful for her high-heeled cowboy boots that made it easier to get a foothold in the thick, wet snow. This was the kind that made good snowmen. She thought she might make one when she finally got home. A calf, perhaps, to look like Sammy. She laughed. Ted would howl at that, if she did it.

She opened the door of the restaurant and walked right into a nightmare. Davy Harris, the man who had almost raped her, was standing by the counter, paying his bill. He was still thin and nervous-looking, with straggly brown hair and pale eyes. He looked at her with mingled distaste and hatred.

"Well, well, I hoped I might run into you again," he said in a voice dripping with venom. "I don't guess you expected to see me, did you, Jillian? Not the man you put in prison for trying to kiss you!"

The owner of the restaurant knew Jillian, and liked her, but he was suddenly giving her a very odd look. There was another customer behind him, one who'd known Jillian's uncle. He gave her an odd look, too.

"There was more to it than that," Jillian said unsteadily.

"Yes, I wanted to marry you, I can't imagine why, you little prude," he said with contempt. "Put a man in prison for trying to teach you about life."

She flushed. She had a good comeback for that, but it was too embarrassing to talk about it in public, especially around men she didn't really know. She felt sick all over.

He came up to her, right up to her, and looked down at her flushed face. "I'm going to be in town for a while, Jillian," he said. "And don't get any ideas about having your boyfriend try to boot me out, or I'll tell him a few things he doesn't know about you."

With that shocking statement, he smiled at the owner, praised the food and walked out the door.

JILLIAN SAT DRINKING coffee with cold, trembling hands. She felt the owner's eyes on her, and it wasn't in a way she liked. He seemed to be sizing her up with the new information his customer had given him about her.

People who didn't know you tended to accept even unsavory details with openhandedness, she thought miserably. After all, how well did you really know somebody who worked for you a few days a week? Jillian lived outside town and kept to herself. She wasn't a social person.

There would be gossip, she was afraid, started by the man who'd just gotten out of prison. And how had he gotten out? she wondered. He'd been sentenced to ten years.

When she finished her coffee, she paid for it and left a tip, and paused to speak to the owner. She didn't really know what to say. Her enemy had made an accusation about her, but how did she refute it?

"What he said," she stammered, "there's a lot more to it than it sounds like. I was...fifteen."

The owner wasn't a stupid man. He'd known Jillian since she was a child. "Listen," he said gently, "I don't pay any mind to gossip. I know Jack Haynes, the assistant circuit D.A. He'd never prosecute a man unless he was sure he could get a conviction."

She felt a little relieved. "Thanks, Mr. Chaney."

He smiled. "Don't worry about it. You might talk to Jack, though."

"Yes, I might." She hesitated. "You won't, well, fire me?"

"Don't be ridiculous. And you be careful out there in the snow. If it gets worse, stay home. I can get old Mrs. Barry to sub for you in the morning, okay?"

"Okay," she said. "Thanks."

"We don't want to lose you in an accident," he replied.

She smiled back.

JACK HAYNES HAD his office in the county courthouse, in Hollister. She walked in, hesitantly, and asked the clerk if he was there and could she see him.

"Sure," he said. "He's just going over case files." He grimaced. "Not a fun thing to do. Court's next week."

"I can imagine."

He announced her and she walked in. Jack Haynes smiled, shook hands with her and offered her a chair.

"Davy Harris is out of prison," she blurted out. "I walked right into him at the restaurant this morning."

He scowled. "Who's out?"

She repeated the man's name.

He pushed the intercom button. "Did we receive notification that they'd released Davy Harris in that attempted rape case?"

"Just a minute, sir, I'll check."

The prosecutor cursed under his breath. "I had no idea! You saw him?"

She nodded. "He told everybody in earshot that I had him put in prison for trying to kiss me." She flushed.

"What a whitewash job!"

"Tell me about it."

The intercom blared. "Sir, they sent a notification, but it wasn't on the server. I'm sorry. I don't know how it got lost."

"Electronic mail," Haynes scoffed. "In my day, we went to the post office to get mail!"

"And even there it gets lost sometimes, sir," his clerk said soothingly. "Sorry."

"So am I. How did Harris get out?"

"On a technicality, pertaining to the judge's instructions to the jury being prejudicial to his case," came the reply. "He's only out until the retrial."

"Yes, well, that could take a year or two," Haynes said coldly.

"Yes," his clerk said quietly.

"Thanks, Chet," he replied, and closed the circuit.

He turned his attention back to Jillian. "That's the second piece of unsettling news I've had from the court system this week," he said curtly. "They've released Smitty Jones, the bank robber, who threatened our police chief, also on a technicality. He's out pending retrial, too." His face hardened. "It shouldn't come as a surprise that they have the same lawyer, some hotshot from Denver."

Jillian clenched her teeth. "He said he'd kill Ted."

Haynes smiled reassuringly. "Better men than him have
tried to kill Ted," he pointed out. "He's got good instincts
and he's a veteran law enforcement officer. He can take
care of himself, believe me."

"I know that, but anybody can be ambushed. Look at
Chief Barnes. He was a cautious, capable law enforcement
officer, too."

He grimaced. "I knew him. He was such a good man.
Shame, what happened."

"Yes."

He gave her a long look. "Jillian, we can't do anything
about Harris while he's out on bond," he told her. "But
you can take precautions, and you should. Don't go anywhere alone."

"I live alone," she pointed out, worriedly.

He drew in a sharp breath. He'd seen cases like this before, where stalkers had vowed revenge and killed or raped
their accusers when they were released from prison. He
hated the thought of having something bad happen to this
poor woman, who'd seen more than her share of the dark
side of men.

"I'll tell Ted," she said after a minute.

His eyebrows arched.

She averted her eyes. "We're sort of in a situation, about
the ranch. Our uncles left a clause that if we don't get married, the ranch has to be sold at public auction. Ted thinks
we should get married very soon. But I've been hesitant,"
she said, and bit off the reason.

He knew, without being told by her. "You need to be in
therapy," he said bluntly.

She grimaced. "I know. But I can't, I just can't talk about
things like that to a stranger."

He had a daughter about her age. He thought how it would be for her in a similar circumstance. It made him sad.

"They're used to all sorts of terrible stories," he began.

"I can't talk about personal things to a stranger," she repeated.

He sighed. "It could ruin your whole life, lock you up in ways you don't even realize yet," he said gently. "I've seen cases where women were never able to marry because of it."

She nodded.

"Don't you want a husband and a family?"

"Very much," she said. She ground her teeth together. "But it seems just hopeless right now." She looked up. "That California developer is licking his lips over my ranch already. But I don't know if I can be a good wife. Ted thinks so, but it's a terrible gamble. I know I have hang-ups."

"They'll get worse," he said bluntly. "I speak from experience. I've tried many cases like yours over the years. I've seen the victims. I know the prognosis. It isn't pretty."

Her eyes were haunted and sad. "I don't understand why he did it," she began.

"It's a compulsion," he explained. "They know it's wrong, but they can't stop. It isn't a matter of will." He leaned forward. "It's like addiction. You know, when men try to give up alcohol, but there's something inside them that pushes them to start drinking again. It doesn't excuse it," he said immediately. "But I'm told that even when they try to live a normal life, it's very difficult. It's one day at a time."

He shook his head. "I see the results of addiction all the time. Alcohol, sex, cards, you name it. People destroy not only their own lives, but the lives of their families because they have a compulsion they can't control."

"It's a shame there isn't a drug you can give people to keep them from getting addicted," she said absently.

He burst out laughing. "Listen to you. A drug. Drugs are our biggest headache."

She flushed. "Sorry. Wasn't thinking."

He gave her a compassionate smile. "Talk to Ted," he said. "He'll look out for you until our unwanted visitor leaves. In fact, there's a vagrancy law on the books that could give him a reason to make the man leave. Tell him I said so."

She smiled. "I will. Thanks so much, Mr. Haynes."

She stood up. He did, too, and shook her hand.

"If you need help, and you can't find Ted, you can call me," he said unexpectedly. He pulled out a business card and handed it to her. "My Jessica is just your age," he added quietly. "Nothing like that ever happened to her. But if it had, I'd have a hard time remembering that my job is to uphold the law."

"Jessica is very nice."

"Why, thank you," he chuckled. "I think so, too."

They didn't discuss why he'd raised Jessica alone. Her mother had run off with a visiting public-relations man from Nevada and divorced Mr. Haynes. He'd been left with an infant daughter that his wife had no room for in her new and exciting life of travel and adventure. But he'd done very well raising her. Jessica was in medical school, studying to be a doctor. He was very proud of her.

"Don't forget," he told Jillian on the way out. "If you need me, you call."

She was very touched. "Thanks, Mr. Haynes."

He shrugged. "When I'm not working, which isn't often even after hours, my social life is playing World of Warcraft online." He smiled. "I don't get out much. You won't bother me if you call."

"I'll remember."

She went out and closed the door, smiling at the young clerk on her way outside.

She ran headlong into Ted, who had bounded up the steps, wearing an expression that would have stopped a charging bull.

"What did he say to you?" he demanded hotly. His black eyes were sparking with temper.

"What... Mr. Haynes?" she stammered, nodding toward the office she'd just left.

"Not him. That..." He used some language that lifted both her eyebrows. "Sorry," he said abruptly. "I heard what happened."

She let out a breath. "He announced in the diner that he got put in prison because he wanted to marry me and I didn't want him to kiss me," she said coldly. "He's out on bond because of a technicality, Mr. Haynes said."

"I know. I phoned the prison board."

She tried to smile. "Mr. Haynes says you can arrest him for vagrancy if he stays in town long enough."

He didn't smile back. "He got a job," he said angrily.

She had to lean against the wall for support. "What?"

"He got a damned job in town!" he snapped. "Old Harrington at the feed store hired him on as a day laborer, delivering supplies to ranchers."

She felt sick to her stomach. It meant that Davy Harris had no plans to leave soon. He was going to stay. He was going to live in her town, be around all the time, gossip about her to anybody who would listen. She felt hunted.

Ted saw that and grimaced. He drew her into his arms

and held her gently, without passion. "I'll find a way to get him out of here," he said into her hair.

"You can't break the law," she said miserably. She closed her eyes and felt the strong beat of his heart under her ear. "It gets worse. Smitty Jones, that man you arrested for bank robbery, got out, too, didn't he?"

He hesitated. "Yes."

"I guess it's our day for bad news, Ted," she groaned.

He hugged her, hard, and then let her go. "I don't like the idea of your living alone out at the ranch," he said curtly. "It makes you a better target if he came here with plans for revenge. Which he might have."

She bit her lower lip. "I don't want to get married yet."

He let out an exasperated sigh. "I don't have funds that I could use to get you police protection," he said angrily. "And even if I did, the man hasn't made any threats. He's just here."

"I know," she said. "And he's got a job, you said."

He nodded. "I could have a word with the owner of the feed store, but that would be crossing the line, big time. I can't tell a merchant who to hire, as much as I'd like to," he added.

"I know that. He'd just find another job, anyway, if he's determined to stay here." She closed her eyes on a grimace. "He'll talk to everybody he meets, he'll say I had him put away for some frivolous reason." She opened her eyes. "Ted, he makes it all sound like I was just a prude that he shocked with a marriage proposal. He can tell a lie and make it believeable."

"Some people will believe anything they hear," he agreed. His black eyes were turbulent. "I don't like it."

"I don't, either." She felt sick all over. She'd thought

things were bad before. Now, they were worse. "I could leave town."

"That would make it worse," he said flatly. "If you run, it will give him credibility."

"I guess so." She looked up at him worriedly. "Don't you let him convince you that I had him put away for trying to kiss me. It was a lot more than that."

He only smiled. "I'm not easy to sway. Besides, I've known you most of your life."

That was true. She didn't add that Ted hadn't known her really well until just recent times.

"There are other people he won't convince, including the prosecutor."

"Mr. Haynes said I could call him if I got in trouble and you weren't available," she said.

He smiled. "He'd come, too. He's a good guy."

"I can't understand why a woman would run away from her husband and a little baby," she said. "He's such a nice person."

"Some women don't want nice, they want dangerous or reckless or vagabond."

"Not me," she said. "I want to stay in Hollister my whole life."

"And have kids?"

She looked up at Ted worriedly. "I want kids a lot," she told him. "It's just…"

"It's just what you have to do to make them," he replied. She blushed.

"Sorry," he said gently. "I didn't mean for it to come out like that."

"I'm a prude. I really am."

"You're not."

She was beginning to wonder. She didn't like recalling what had happened with the man in her past, but his accusations had disturbed her. Was she really so clueless that she'd sent him to prison for something that wasn't his fault? Had she overreacted? She had been at fault with the auditor; she'd gone with him to the motel and at first she'd let him kiss her. Then things got out of hand and she panicked, largely because of what Davy Harris had done to her.

Ted was looking at his watch. "Damn! I've got a meeting with a defense attorney in my office to take a deposition in a theft case. I'll have to go." He bent and kissed her cheek. "You stay clear of that coyote, and if he gives you any trouble, any at all, you tell me. I'll throw his butt in jail."

She smiled. "I will. Thanks, Ted."

"What are friends for?" he asked, and smiled back.

She watched him walk away with misgivings. She wanted to tell him that she wasn't confident about her actions in the past, tell him that maybe the man she'd accused wasn't as guilty as she thought. She wished she had somebody to talk to about it.

She sighed and got in her truck and drove to the ranch. It was going to be the biggest problem of her life, and she didn't know how she was going to solve it.

THINGS WENT FROM bad to worse very quickly. She went in to work the next morning and Davy Harris was sitting in a booth the minute the doors opened. She had to come out to arrange pies and cakes in the display case for the lunch crowd. She didn't work lunch, but she did much of the baking after she'd finished making breakfast for the customers.

Every time she came out to arrange the confections, the man was watching her. He sat as close to the counter as he could get, sipping coffee and giving her malicious looks. He made her very nervous.

"Sir, can I get you anything else?" the waitress, aware of Jillian's discomfort, asked the man in a polite but firm tone.

He lifted his eyebrows. "I'm finishing my coffee."

"Breakfast is no longer being served, sir. We're getting ready for the lunch crowd."

"I know. I'll be back for lunch," he assured her. "I'm almost done."

"Yes, sir." She produced the check and put it next to his plate, and went back to her other customer, the only other one left in the room.

"You always did cook sweets so well, Jilly," Harris told her with a long visual appraisal. "I loved the lemon cake you used to make for your uncle."

"Thanks," she muttered under her breath.

"You live all alone in that big ranch house, now, don't you?" he asked in a pleasant tone that was only surface. His eyes were full of hate. "Don't you get scared at night?"

"I have a shotgun," she blurted out.

He looked shocked. "Really!"

"Really," she replied with a cold glare. "It would be so unwise for anybody to try to break in at night."

He laughed coldly. "Why, Jilly, was that a threat?" he asked, raising his voice when the waitress came back to that side of the restaurant. "Were you threatening to shoot me?"

"I was saying that if anybody broke into my house, I would use my shotgun," she faltered.

"Are you accusing me of trying to break in on you?" he asked loudly.

She flushed. "I didn't say that."

"Are you sure? I mean, accusing people of crimes they haven't committed, isn't that a felony?" he persisted.

The waitress marched back to his table. "Are you finished, sir?" she asked with a bite in her voice, because she was fond of Jillian. "We have to clear the tables now."

He sighed. "I guess I'm finished." He looked at the bill, pulled out his wallet, left the amount plus a ten-cent tip. He gave the waitress an amused smile. "Now, don't you spend that whole tip all in one place," he said with dripping sarcasm.

"I'll buy feed for my polo ponies with it," she quipped back.

He glared at her. He didn't like people one-upping him, and it showed. "I'll see you again, soon, Jilly," he purred, with a last glance.

He left. Jillian felt her muscles unlocking. But tears stung her eyes.

"Oh, Jill," the waitress, Sandra, groaned. She put her arms around Jillian and hugged her tight. "He'll go away," she said. "He'll have to, eventually. You mustn't cry!"

Jillian bawled. She hadn't known the waitress well at all, until now.

"There, there," Sandra said softly. "I know how it is. I was living with this guy, Carl, and he knocked me around every time he got drunk. Once, he hit me with a glass and it shattered and cut my face real bad. I loved him so much," she groaned. "But that woke me up, when that happened. I moved out. He made threats and even tried to set fire to my house. But when he finally realized I meant it, he gave up and found another girlfriend. Last I heard, she was making weekly trips to the emergency room up in Billings."

Jillian pulled back, wiping her eyes. "It wasn't like that," she whispered. "I was fifteen, and he tried to…"

"Fifteen?"

Jillian bit her lower lip. "My uncle hired him as a handy man."

"Good Lord! You should have had him arrested!"

"I did," Jillian said miserably. "But he got out, and now he's going to make my life hell."

"You poor kid! You tell Chief Graves," she said firmly. "He'll take care of it."

Jillian's eyes were misty. "You can't have somebody thrown out of town without good reason," she said. "He hasn't threatened me or done anything except show up here to eat all the time. And it's the only restaurant in town, Sandra," she added.

"Yes, but he was making some pretty thick accusations," she reminded the other girl.

"Words. Just words."

"They can hurt as bad as fists," Sandra said curtly. "I ought to know. My father never hesitated to tell me how ugly and stupid I was."

Jillian gasped. Nobody in her family had ever said such things to her.

"I guess you had nice people to live with, huh?" Sandra asked with a worldly smile. "That wasn't the case with me. My father hated me, because I wasn't his. My mother had an affair. People do it all the time these days. She came back, but he could never get over the fact that she had me by somebody else. She died and he made me pay for it."

"I'm so sorry."

"You're a nice kid," Sandra told her quietly. "That guy makes any trouble for you in here, he'll have to deal with me."

Jillian chuckled. "I've seen you handle unruly customers. You're good at it."

"I ought to be. I was in the army until two years ago," she added. "I worked as military police. Not much I don't know about hand-to-hand combat."

Jillian beamed. "My heroine!"

Sandra just laughed. "Anyway, you get those cakes arranged and go home. I'll deal with the visiting problem while you're away."

"Thanks. For everything."

"Always wished I had a kid sister," Sandra scoffed. She grinned. "So now I do. You tell people I'm your sister and we'll have some laughs."

That would have been funny, because Sandra's skin was a very dark copper, compared to Jillian's very pale skin. Sandra was, after all, full-blooded Lakota.

"Chief Graves is Cheyenne," she said aloud.

"Nothing wrong with the Cheyenne, now that we're not bashing each other's brains out like we did a century ago," came the amused reply. Sandra winked. "Better get cracking. The boss is giving us dark looks."

Jillian grinned. "Can't have that!" she laughed.

JILLIAN DID FEEL BETTER, and now she had an ally at work. But she was still worried. That man had obviously come to Hollister to pay her back for his jail sentence, and now she was doubting her own story that had cost him his freedom.

CHAPTER SEVEN

JILLIAN HAD NEVER considered that she might become a victim of a stalker. And she wondered if it could even be called stalking. Davy Harris came into the restaurant every morning to eat. But it was the only diner in town. So was that stalking?

Ted thought so, but the law wasn't on the victim's side in this case. A man couldn't be arrested for stalking by eating in the only restaurant in town.

But he made Jillian uptight. She fumbled a cake onto the floor two mornings later, one that had taken a lot of trouble to bake, with cream filling. Harris laughed coldly.

"Why, Jilly, do I make you nervous?" he chided. "I'm only having breakfast here. I haven't tried to touch you or anything."

She cleaned the floor, flushed and unsettled. Sandra had called in sick that morning, so they had a substitute waitress, one who just did her job and didn't waste time on getting to know the other employees. She had no one to back her up, now.

"I only wanted to marry you," Harris said in a soft, quiet tone. "You were real young, but I thought you were mature enough to handle it. And you liked me. Remember when the little white kittens were born and they were going to have to be put down because you couldn't keep them all?

I went around to almost every house in town until I found places for them to live."

She bit her lip. That was true. He'd been kind.

"And when your uncle John had that virus and was so sick that he couldn't keep the medicine down? I drove both of you to the hospital."

"Yes," she said reluctantly.

He laughed. "And you repaid my kindness by having me put in prison with murderers."

Her face was stricken as she stared at him.

He got to his feet, still smiling, but his eyes were like a cobra's. "Did you think I'd just go away and you'd never have to see me again?"

She got up, a little wobbly. "I didn't realize…"

"What, that I really would go to prison because you exaggerated what happened?" he interrupted. "What kind of woman does that to a man?"

She felt really sick. She knew her face was white.

"I just wanted to marry you and take care of you, and your uncle," he said. "I wouldn't have hurt you. Did I ever hurt you, Jilly?"

She was growing less confident by the second. Had she misjudged him? Was he in prison because she'd blown things out of proportion?

He put a five-dollar bill down beside his plate. "Why don't you think about that?" he continued. "Think about what you did to me. You don't know what it's like in prison, Jilly. You don't know what men can do to other men, especially if they aren't strong and powerful." His face was taut with distaste. "You stupid little prude," he said harshly. "You landed me in hell!"

"I'm… I'm sorry," she stammered.

"Are you really?" he asked sarcastically. "Well, not sorry

enough, not yet." He leaned toward her. "But you're going to be," he said in a voice that didn't carry. "You're going to wish you never heard my name when I'm through with you."

He stood back up again, smiling like a used car salesman. "It was a really good breakfast, Jilly," he said out loud. "You're still a great little cook. Have a nice day, now."

He walked out, while the owner of the restaurant and the cashier gave him a thoughtful look. Jillian could imagine how it would sound. Here was the poor, falsely accused man trying to be nice to the woman who'd put him away. Jillian wasn't going to come out smelling like roses, no matter what she said or did. And now she had her own doubts about the past. She didn't know what she was going to do.

TED CAME BY the next day. She heard his car at the front door of the ranch house and she went to the steps with a feeling of unease. She didn't think Ted would take the side of the other man, but Davy could be very convincing.

Ted came up the steps, looking somber. He paused when he saw her expression.

"What's happened?" he asked.

She blinked. "What do you mean?"

"You look like death warmed over."

"Do I? It must be the flour," she lied, and forced a laugh. "I've been making a cherry pie."

Once, he would have made a joke, because it was his favorite. But he was quiet and preoccupied as he followed her into the kitchen.

"Any coffee going?" he asked as he sailed his hat onto the counter.

"I can make some."

"Please."

She started a pot, aware of his keen and penetrating gaze, following her as she worked.

"What's going on with you and Harris?" he asked suddenly.

The question startled her so much that she dropped a pan she'd been putting under the counter. Her hands were shaking.

She turned back to him. "No...nothing," she stammered, but her cheeks had flushed.

His face hardened. "Nothing."

"He comes in the restaurant to have breakfast every day," she said.

"And you'd know this, how?"

She put the pan down gently on the counter and drew in a breath. "Because I've got a job there, cooking for the breakfast crowd."

He looked angry. "Since when?"

She hesitated. She hadn't realized how difficult it was going to be, telling him about her job, and explaining why she'd decided to keep it secret from him. It would look bad, as if she didn't trust him.

The guilt made him angrier.

She poured coffee into a mug and put it in front of him on the table. Her hands were unsteady. "I realize it must seem like I'm keeping secrets," she began.

"It sounds a lot like that."

"I was going to tell you," she protested.

"When?"

She hesitated.

"You said you didn't want to get married yet. Is that why?" he persisted. "You got a job so you could take care of your bills here, so that you could refuse to honor the terms of our uncles' wills?"

It was sounding worse than it was. He was mad. He couldn't even hide it.

He hadn't touched his coffee. He got to his feet. "You back away every time I come close to you. When I take you out, you dress like a teenager going to a dance in the gym. You get a job and don't tell me. You're being overheard flirting with the man who supposedly assaulted you years ago." His eyes narrowed as she searched for ways to explain her behavior. "What other secrets are you keeping from me, Jillian?"

She didn't know what to say that wouldn't make things worse. Her face was a study in misery.

"I'm not flirting with him," she said.

"That isn't what one of the diners said," he returned.

She bit her lower lip. "I've been wondering," she began.

"Wondering what?"

She lifted one shoulder. "Maybe I made a mistake," she blurted out. "Maybe I did exaggerate what happened, because I was so naive." She swallowed hard. "Like with the auditor, when I went out with him and didn't tell him my age, and he got in trouble."

Ted's expression wasn't easily explained. He just stared at her with black eyes that didn't give any quarter at all.

"Davy Harris was kind to Uncle John," she had to admit. "And he was always doing things for him, and for me." She lowered her eyes to the floor, so miserable that she almost choked on her own words. "He said the other men did things to him in prison."

He still hadn't spoken.

She looked up, wincing at his expression. "He wasn't a mean sort of person. He never hurt me…"

He picked up his hat, slammed it over his eyes, and walked out the door.

She ran after him. "Ted!"

He kept walking. He went down the steps, got into his truck and drove off without a single word.

Jillian stared after him with a feeling of disaster.

SANDRA GAPED AT her the next morning at work. "You told Ted Graves that you made a mistake?" she asked. "What in the world is the matter with you? You were so young, Jillian! What sort of man tries to get it on with a kid barely in high school?"

"He was just twenty-one," she protested.

"He should have known better. No jury in the world would have turned him loose for making advances to you."

"Yes, but he, well, while he was in prison, some of the men…" She hesitated, searching for the words to explain.

"I know what you mean," Sandra replied shortly. "But you're missing the whole point. A grown man tried to make you go to bed with him when you were young then. Isn't that what happened?"

Jillian drew in a long breath. "Yes. I guess so."

"Then why are you trying to take the blame for it? Did you lead him on? Did you wear suggestive clothing, flirt with him, try to get him to come into your room when your uncle wasn't around?"

"Good heavens, no!" Jillian protested.

Sandra's black eyes narrowed. "Then why is it your fault?"

"He went to prison on my testimony."

"Sounds to me like he deserved to," Sandra replied curtly.

"But he was a kind man," she said. "He was always doing things for other people. One week when Uncle John was real sick, he even did the grocery shopping for us."

"A few years back in a murder trial, a witness testified that the accused murderer helped her take her groceries into the house. Another told the jury that he tuned up her old car when it wouldn't start. What does that have to do with a man's guilt or innocence?"

Jillian blinked. "Excuse me?"

"Don't you think that a man can do kind things and still kill someone, given the motive?" she asked.

"I never thought of it like that."

"Even kind people can kill, Jillian," Sandra said bluntly. "I knew this guy on the reservation, Harry. He'd give you the shirt off his back. He drove old Mr. Hotchkiss to the doctor every month to get his checkup. But he killed another man in an argument and got sent to prison for it. Do you think they should have acquitted him because he did a couple of kind things for other people?"

"Well, no," she had to admit.

"We all have good and evil in us," the older woman replied. "Just because we're capable of good doesn't mean we can't do something evil."

"I guess I understand."

"You think about that. And stop trying to assume responsibility for something that wasn't your fault. You were just out of grade school when it happened. You weren't old enough or mature enough to permit any man liberties like that, at the time. You weren't old enough to know better, Jillian, but he was."

She felt a little better.

"Besides that, did you like it?"

"Are you kidding?" Jillian exclaimed. "No, I hated it!"

"Then that should tell you who's at fault, shouldn't it?"

Jillian began to relax. "You have a way with words."

"I should have been a writer," Sandra agreed. She

grinned, showing perfect white teeth. "Now you stop spouting nonsense and start working on that bacon. We'll have customers ranting because breakfast isn't ready!"

Jillian laughed. "I guess we will. Thanks."

Sandra grinned. "You're welcome."

JILLIAN DIDN'T GO out front when the doors opened, not even to put out the cakes and pies. Sandra did that for her.

"Curious," she said when she came back into the kitchen.

"What is?"

"Your old friend Davy wasn't out there."

"Maybe he decided to leave," Jillian said hopefully.

"It would take somebody more gullible than me to believe that," the older woman replied.

"Yes, but I can hope."

JILLIAN DID HOPE for the best, anyway, and not only about Davy Harris leaving town. She hoped that Ted might come by to talk, or just smooth things over with her. But he didn't come to the restaurant, or to the ranch. And the next morning, Davy Harris was right back in the same booth, waiting for his breakfast.

"Did you miss me?" he teased Jillian, having surprised her as she was putting a pound cake in the display case.

"I didn't notice you were gone," she lied, flushing.

"We both know better than that, don't we?" He leaned back in the booth, his pale eyes so smug that it made her curious. "I've been talking to people about you."

She felt uneasy. "What people?"

"Just people."

She didn't know what to say. She got to her feet and went back into the kitchen. Her stomach was cutting somersaults all the way.

THAT AFTERNOON, AS she went out to get into her old vehicle to go home, she walked right into Davy.

She gasped and jumped back. He laughed.

"Do I make you nervous?" he chided. "I can't imagine why. You know, I never tried to hurt you. I never did. Did I?"

"N-no," she blurted out, embarrassed, because a few people standing outside the bank were listening, and watching them.

"I told your uncle I wanted to marry you," he said, without lowering his voice. He even smiled. "He said that he hoped I would, because he liked me and he knew I'd take care of you. But that was before you told those lies about me, wasn't it, Jilly? That was before you got me put in jail for trying to kiss you."

She was embarrassed because they were talking about something private in a very public location, and several people were listening.

"It wasn't...wasn't like that," she stammered, flushing.

"Yes, it was, you just don't like admitting that you made a mistake," he said, his voice a little louder now. "Isn't that the truth?"

She was fumbling for words. She couldn't get her mind to work at all.

"You lied about me," he continued, raising his voice. "You lied."

She should have disputed that. She should have said that it was no lie, that he'd tried to assault her in her own home. But she was too embarrassed. She turned and almost ran to her truck. Once inside, she locked the door with cold, trembling fingers.

Davy stood on the sidewalk, smiling. Just smiling. A man and woman came up to him and he turned and started talking to them as Jillian drove away. She wondered what they were saying. She hoped it wasn't about her.

BUT IN THE next few days, she noticed a change in attitude, especially in customers who came to the restaurants. Her pretty cakes had been quickly bought before, but now they stayed in the case. Jill took most of them back home. When she went to the bank, the teller was polite, but not chatty and friendly as she usually was.

Even at the local convenience store where she bought gas, the clerk was reserved, all business, when she paid at the counter.

The next morning, at work, she began to understand why she was being treated to a cold shoulder from people she'd known most of her life.

"Everybody thinks you did a job on me, Jilly," Davy said under his breath when she was putting a cake on the counter—only one cake today, instead of the variety she usually produced, since they weren't selling.

She glared at him over the cake. "It wouldn't do to tell them the truth."

"What is the truth?" He leaned back in the booth, his eyes cold and accusing. "You had me sent to jail."

She stood up, tired of being harassed, tired of his unspoken accusations, tired of the way local people were treating her because of him.

"I was a freshman in high school and you tried to force me to have sex with you," she said shortly, aware of a shocked look from a male customer. "How hard is that to understand? It's called statutory rape, I believe…?"

Davy flushed. He got to his feet and towered over her. "I never raped you!"

"You had my clothes off and the only reason you stopped

was because I slugged you and ran. If Sassy Peale hadn't had a shotgun, you never would have stopped! You ran after me all the way to her house!"

He clenched his fists by his side. "I went to jail," he snapped. "You're going to pay for that. I'll make sure you pay for that!"

She took the cake, aimed it and threw it right in his face.

"I could have you arrested for assault!" he sputtered.

"Go ahead," she said, glaring at him. "I'll call the police for you, if you like!"

He took a quick step toward her, but the male customer stood up all at once and moved toward him. He backed away.

"You'll be sorry," he told Jillian. He glared at the other customer, and walked out, wiping away cake with a handkerchief.

Jillian was shaking, but she hadn't backed down. She took a shaky breath, fighting tears, and started picking up cake.

"You think he'll go away," the customer, a tall blond man with a patch over one eye, said quietly, in an accented tone, like a British accent, but with a hard accent on the consonants. She recalled hearing accents like that in one of the *Lethal Weapon* movies. "He won't."

She stopped picking up cake and got to her feet, staring at him.

He was tall and well built. His blond hair was in a ponytail. His face was lean, with faint scars, and he had one light brown eye visible. He looked like the sort of man who smiled a lot, but he wasn't smiling now. He had a dangerous look.

"You should talk to a lawyer," he said quietly.

She bit her lip. "And say what? He eats here every day, but this is the only restaurant in town."

"It's still harassment."

She sighed. "Yes. It is. But I can't make him leave."

"Talk to Ted Graves. He'll make him leave."

"Ted isn't speaking to me."

He lifted an eyebrow expressively.

"I ticked him off, too, by saying I might have made a mistake and overreacted to what Davy did to me," she said miserably. "Davy made it sound as if I did. And then he reminded me about all the kind things he did for my uncle and me..."

"Adolph Hitler had a dog. He petted it and took it for walks and threw sticks for it to chase," he said blandly.

She grimaced. She went back down and picked up more cake.

"If you were so young and it took a shotgun to deter him," the man continued, "it wasn't an innocent act."

"I'm just beginning to get that through my thick skull," she sighed.

"This sort of man doesn't quit," he continued, sticking his hands deep in the pockets of his jeans. His eye was narrow and thoughtful. "He's here for more than breakfast, if you get my drift. He wants revenge."

"I guess so."

"I hope you keep a gun."

She laughed. "I hate guns."

"So do I," he mused. "I much prefer knives."

He indicated a huge Bowie knife on one hip, in a fringed leather sheath.

She stared at it. "I don't guess you'd have to do much more than show that to somebody to make them back off."

"That's usually the case."

She finished cleaning up the cake. "They aren't selling well lately, but I thought this one might. Davy seems to have been spending all his spare time telling people what an evil woman I am. There's a distinct chill in the air wherever I go now."

"That's because he's telling his side of the story to anybody who'll listen," he replied. "And that's harassment, as well."

"I can see Ted arresting him for talking to someone," she said sarcastically.

"It depends on what he's saying. I heard what he said in here. If you need a witness, I'm available."

She frowned. "He didn't say much."

"He said enough," he replied.

She shrugged. "I like to handle my own problems."

"Ordinarily I'd say that's admirable. Not in this case. You're up against a man who's done hard time and came out with a grudge. He wants blood. If you're not very careful, he'll get it. He's doing a number on your character already. People tend to believe what they want to believe, and it isn't always the truth. Especially when a likeable young man who's apparently been railroaded by a nasty young girl tells the right kind of story."

She blinked. "I'd be the nasty young girl in this story?"

He nodded.

She put the remnants of her cake into the trash can behind the counter. She shrugged. "I never thought of myself as a bad person."

"It's his thoughts that you have to worry about. If he's mad enough, and I think he is if he came here expressly to torment you, he won't stop with gossip."

That thought had occurred to her, too. She looked up at

the customer with wide, worried eyes. "Maybe I should get a job over in Billings."

"And run for it?" he asked. "Fat chance. He'd follow you."

She gasped. "No...!"

His face hardened. "I've seen this happen before, in a similar case," he said tersely. "In fact, I was acting as an unpaid bodyguard as a favor to a friend. The perp not only got out of jail, he went after the girl who testified against him and beat her up."

She glared. "I hope you hurt him."

"Several of us," he replied, "wanted to, but her boyfriend got to him first. He's back in jail. But if she'd been alone, there might not have been anybody to testify."

She felt sick to her stomach. "You're saying something, aren't you?"

"I'm saying that such men are unpredictable," he replied. "It's better to watch your back than to assume that everything will work itself out. In my experience, situations like this don't get better."

She put down the rag she'd been cleaning with, and looked up with worried eyes. "I wish Ted wasn't mad at me," she said quietly.

"Go make up with him," he advised. "And do it soon." He didn't add that he'd seen the expression on her assailant's face and he was certain the man would soon resort to violence to pay her back.

"I suppose I should," she said. She managed a smile. "Thanks, Mr....?"

"Just call me Rourke," he said, and grinned. "Most people do."

"Are you visiting somebody local?"

His eyebrows arched. "Don't I look like a local?"

She shook her head, softening the noncomment with a smile.

He laughed. "Actually," he said, "I came by to see the police chief. And not on a case. Ted and I were in the military together. I brought a message from an old friend who works as a police chief down in Texas."

She cocked her head. "That wouldn't be the one who taught him to tango?"

He blinked his single eye. "He taught Ted to dance?"

She nodded. "He's pretty good, too."

Rourke chuckled. "Wonders never cease."

"That's what I say."

He smiled down at her. "Talk to Ted," he advised. "You're going to need somebody who can back you up, if that man gets violent."

"I'll do that," she said after a minute. "And thanks."

"You're welcome, but for what?"

"For making me see the light," she replied flatly. "I've been blaming myself for sending Davy to prison."

"You mark my words," he replied. "Very soon, Davy is going to prove to you that it was where he belonged."

She didn't reply. She just hoped it wasn't a prophecy. But she was going to see Ted, the minute she got off work.

CHAPTER EIGHT

BEFORE JILLIAN COULD finish her chores and get out of the restaurant, Sassy Peale Callister came into the restaurant and dragged her to one side.

"I can't believe what I just heard," she said shortly. "Did you actually say that you might have been wrong to have Davy Harris put in jail?"

Jillian flushed to the roots of her hair. "How did you hear about that?" she stammered.

"Hollister is a very small town. You tell one person and everybody else knows," the other woman replied. "Come on, is it true?"

Jillian felt even more uncomfortable. "He was reminding me how much he helped me and Uncle John around the ranch. He was always kind to us. Once, when we were sick, he went to the store and pharmacy for us, and then nursed us until we were well again."

Sassy wasn't buying it. Her face was stony. "That means he's capable of doing good deeds. It doesn't mean he can't do bad things."

"I know," Jillian said miserably. "It's just...well, he's been in here every day. He makes it sound like I overreacted..."

"You listen to me, he's no heartsick would-be suitor," Sassy said firmly. "He's a card-carrying coyote with delusions of grandeur! I wasn't sure that he wasn't going to try to take the shotgun away from me, even if I'd pulled the trigger. He was furious! Don't you remember what he said?"

Jillian glanced around her. The restaurant was empty, but the owner was nearby, at least within earshot.

"He said that he'd get both of us," Sassy replied. "John thinks he meant it and that he's here for revenge. He hired me a bodyguard, if you can believe that." She indicated the tall man with a long blond ponytail and a patch over one eye.

"That's Rourke," Jilly exclaimed.

Sassy blinked. "Excuse me?"

"That's Rourke. He was in here this morning, when I threw a cake at Davy." She ignored Sassy's gasp and kept going. "He said that I was nuts trying to make excuses for the man, and that I should make up with Ted. He thinks Davy is dangerous."

"So do I," Sassy said quietly. "You should come and stay with us until this is over, one way or the other."

Jillian was tempted. But she thought of little Sammy and a means of revenge that might occur to a mind as twisted as Davy's. He might even burn the house down. She didn't dare leave it unattended.

"Thanks," she said gently, "but I can't do that. Anyway, I've got my uncle's shotgun."

"Which you've never touched," Sassy muttered. "I doubt it's been cleaned since he died."

Jillian stared at the floor. "Ted would clean it for me if I asked him to."

"Why don't you ask him to?" came the short reply. "And then tell him why you need it cleaned. I dare you."

"I don't think Davy would hurt me, really," she said slowly.

"He assaulted you."

"Maybe he just got, well, overstimulated, and..."

"He assaulted you," Sassy replied firmly.

Jillian sighed. "I hate unpleasantness."

"Who doesn't? But this isn't just a man who let a kiss go too far. This is a man who deliberately came to Hollister, got a job and devils you every day at your place of work," Sassy said quietly. "It's harassment. It's stalking. Maybe you can't prove it, but you should certainly talk to Ted about it."

"He'll think I'm overreacting."

"He's a policeman," Sassy reminded her. "He won't."

Jillian was weakening. She was beginning to feel even more afraid of Davy. If Sassy's husband thought there was a threat, and went so far as to hire his wife a bodyguard, he must be taking it seriously.

"John tried to have him arrested, but Ted reminded him that you can't put somebody behind bars for something he said years ago. He has to have concrete evidence."

That made things somehow even worse. Jillian's worried eyes met her friend's. "Davy does scare me."

Sassy moved closer. "I'm going to have Rourke keep an eye on you, too, when I'm safely home with John. We've got enough cowboys at the ranch who have federal backgrounds to keep me safe," she added with a chuckle. "One of them used to work for the godfather of John's sister-in-law. He was a mercenary with mob connections. He's got millions and he still comes to see her." She leaned forward, so that Rourke couldn't hear. "There was gossip once that Rourke was his son. Nobody knows and Rourke never talks about him."

"Wow," Jillian exclaimed. "That would be K.C. Kantor, wouldn't it?"

Sassy was impressed. "How did you know?"

"I wouldn't have, but your husband was talking about him at the restaurant one morning when you were on that shopping trip to Los Angeles and he had to eat in town."

"Eavesdropping, were you?" Sassy teased.

Jillian smiled. "Sorry. Sometimes a waitress can't help it."

"I don't mind." She drew in a breath. "I have to go. But if you need anything, you call. I'll lend Rourke to you."

"My ears work, even if I'm missing one eye," the tall blond man drawled.

Both women turned, surprised.

"And K.C. Kantor is not my father." He bit off every word. "That's malicious gossip, aimed at my dad, who was a military man in South Africa and made enemies because of his job."

"Sorry," Sassy said at once, and looked uneasy. Rourke rarely did anything except smile pleasantly and crack jokes, but his pale brown eye was glittering and he looked dangerous.

He saw the consternation his words had produced, and fell back into his easygoing persona with no visible effort. He grinned. "I eavesdrop shamelessly, too," he added. "I never know when some pretty young woman might be making nice remarks about me. Wouldn't want to miss it."

They both relaxed.

"Sorry," Sassy said again. "I wasn't saying it to be unkind."

He shrugged. "I know that. Kantor took me in when I was orphaned, because he and my dad were friends. It's a common misconception." He frowned. "You're right about Jillian. Living alone is dangerous when you've got an enemy with unknown intentions. Mrs. Callister is safe at night, unless she's going out without her husband. I could come over and sleep on your sofa, if you like."

"Yes, he could," Sassy seconded at once.

That made Jillian visibly uncomfortable. She averted her eyes. "That's very kind of you, thanks, but I'll manage."

Rourke lifted an eyebrow. "Is it my shaving lotion? I mean, it does sometimes put women off," he said blandly.

Sassy laughed. "No. It's convention."

"Excuse me?"

"She won't stay alone at night with a man in the house," Sassy said. "And before you say anything—" she stopped him when he opened his mouth to reply "—I would have felt exactly the same way when I was single. Women in small towns, brought up with certain attitudes, don't entertain single men at night."

He looked perplexed.

"You've never lived in a small town," Jillian ventured.

"I was born in Africa," he said, surprisingly. "I've lived in small villages all my life. But I don't know much about small American towns. I suppose there are similarities. Well, except for the bride price that still exists in some places."

"Bride price?" Jillian stared at him, waiting.

"A man who wants to marry a woman has to give her father a certain number of cattle."

She gaped at him.

"It's a centuries-old tradition," he explained. He pursed his lips and smiled at Jillian. "I'll bet your father would have asked a thousand head for you."

She glared at him. "My father would never have offered to sell me to you!" she exclaimed.

"Different places, different customs," he said easily.

"I've lived in places, in ways, that you might never imagine."

"John said you were a gunrunner," Sassy mused.

He glared at her. "I was not," he said indignantly. Then he grinned. "I was an arms dealer."

"Semantics!" she shot back.

He shrugged again. "A man has to make a living when he's between jobs. At the time, there wasn't much action going on in my part of Africa for mercenaries."

"And now you work as a bodyguard?" Jillian asked.

He hesitated. "At times, when I'm on vacation. I actually work as an independent contractor these days. Legit," he added when they looked at him with open suspicion. "I don't do mercenary work anymore."

"So that case in Oklahoma where you helped free a kidnapping victim was legit, too?" Sassy asked.

"I was helping out a friend," he replied, chuckling. "He works for the same federal agency I work for these days."

"But you're an African citizen, aren't you?" Jillian asked. "I mean, if you were born there...?"

"I have American citizenship now," he said, and looked uncomfortable.

"When he went to work for Mr. Kantor, he had to have it," Sassy murmured. "I imagine he pulled some strings at the state department?"

Rourke just looked at her, without speaking.

She held out her hands, palms up. "Okay, I'm sorry, I won't pry. I'm just grateful you're around to look out for me." She glanced at Jillian. "But you still have a problem. What if Harris decides he wants to get even one dark night, and you can't get to that shotgun in time? The one that hasn't been cleaned since your uncle died?"

"I said I'd get Ted to clean it for me," the other woman protested.

"You and Ted aren't speaking."

"I'll come over and clean it for you," Rourke said quietly. "And teach you to shoot it."

Jillian looked hunted. "I hate guns," she burst out. "I hated it when Ted would come over and shoot targets from the front porch. I'll never get used to the sound of them. It's like dynamite going off in my ears!"

Rourke looked at her with shocked disdain. "Didn't anybody ever tell you about earplugs?"

"Earplugs?"

"Yes. You always wear them on the gun range," he explained, "unless you want to go deaf at an early age. Ear protectors are fine on the range, but earplugs can be inserted quickly if you're on a job and expecting trouble."

"How do you hear?"

"They let in sound. They just deaden certain frequencies of sound," he explained. He glanced at Sassy. "You won't need me tonight. I heard your husband say he's lined up a new werewolf movie to watch with you on pay-per-view."

She laughed. "Yes. It's the second in a vampire trilogy, actually. I love it!"

He didn't react. He glanced toward Jillian. "So I'll be free about six. I can come over and clean the shotgun and do a security sweep. If you need locks and silent sentries, I can install them."

She bit her lip, hard. She couldn't afford such things. She could barely pay the bills on what she made as a cook.

The owner of the restaurant, who had been blatantly eavesdropping, joined them. "You can have an advance on your salary anytime you need it," he told Jillian gently. "I'd bar Harris from coming on the premises, if I could, but he's the sort who'd file a lawsuit. I can't afford that," he added heavily.

"Thanks, Mr. Chaney," Jillian said quietly. "I thought you might fire me, because of all that's going on right now."

"Fat chance," he said amusedly. "You're the best cook I've ever had."

"He shouldn't be allowed to harass her while she's doing her job," Sassy said curtly.

"I agree," the restaurant owner said gently. "But this is a business and I can't bar people I dislike without proof they're causing problems. I've never heard him threaten Jillian or even be disrespectful to her."

"That's because he whispers things to me that he doesn't want anybody to overhear," she said miserably. "He made me believe that I had him locked up for no reason at all."

"I live in Hollister," he said quietly. "Even if it's not in blaring headlines, most of us know what's going on here. I remember the case. My sister, if you recall, was the assistant prosecutor in the case. She helped Jack Haynes with the precedents."

"I do remember," Jillian said. She folded her arms over her slight breasts. "It's so scary. I never thought he'd get out."

"People get out all the time on technicalities," Rourke said. "A case in point is the bank robber your police chief put away. And a friend of mine in the FBI in Texas has a similar problem. A man he sent away for life just got out and is after him. My friend can't do much more than you're doing. The stalker doesn't do anything he could even be charged with."

"Life is hard," Sassy said.

"Then you die," Rourke quipped, and grinned. "Did you watch that British cop show, too? You're pretty young."

"Everything's on disc now, even those old shows. It's one of John's favorites," Sassy chuckled.

"Mine, too," Chaney added, laughing. "They were an odd mix, the female British cop and the American one, in a team."

"Pity it ended before we knew how things worked out between them," Rourke sighed. "I would have loved a big, romantic finale."

Both women and the restaurant owner stared at him.

"I'm a romantic," he said defensively.

The women stared pointedly at the pistol in the shoulder holster under his loose jacket.

"I can shoot people and still be romantic," he said belligerently. "Out there somewhere is a woman who can't wait to marry me and have my children!"

They stared more.

He moved uncomfortably. "Well, my profession isn't conducive to child-raising, I guess, but I could still get married to some nice lady who wanted to cook and darn my socks and take my clothes to the dry cleaner when I was home between jobs."

"That's not romantic, that's delusional," Sassy told him.

"And you're living in the wrong century," Jillian added.

He glared. "I'm not shacking up with some corporate raider in a pin-striped business suit."

"It's not called shacking up, it's called cohabiting," Sassy said drolly. "And I really can't see you with a corporate raider. I should think a Dallas Cowboy linebacker would be... Don't hit me, I'll tell John!" she said in mock fear when he glowered and took a step forward.

"A woman in a pin-striped suit," he qualified.

Sassy nodded. "A female mob hit-person."

He threw up his hands. "I can't talk to you."

"You could if you'd stop mixing metaphors and looking for women who lived in the dark ages." She frowned. "You don't get out much, do you?"

He looked out the window of the restaurant. "In this burg, it wouldn't matter if I did. I think there are two un-married ladies who live in this town, and they're both in their sixties!"

"We could ask if anybody has pretty cousins or nieces who live out of town," Jillian offered.

He gave her a pursed-lip scrutiny. "You're not bad. You have your own ranch and you can cook."

"I don't want to get married," Jillian said curtly.

"That's true," Sassy said sadly. "I think Harris has put her off men for life. She won't even marry Ted, and that means she'll lose the ranch to a developer."

"Good grief," Rourke exclaimed. "Why?"

"It's in my uncle's will and his uncle's will that we have to marry each other or the ranch gets sold at public auc-tion," Jillian said miserably. "There's a California devel-oper licking his lips in the background, just waiting to turn my ranch into a resort."

Rourke was outraged. "Not that beautiful hunk of land!"

She nodded. "It will look like the West Coast when he gets through. He'll cut down all the trees, pave the land, and build expensive condominiums. I hear he even has plans for a strip mall in the middle. Oh, and an amusement park."

Rourke was unusually thoughtful. "Nice piece of land, that," he remarked.

"Very nice."

"But that doesn't solve your problem," Sassy replied.

"I can be over about six, if that's okay?" he told Jillian, with a questioning glance at Sassy.

"That will be fine with us," Sassy assured him. She

glared at Jillian, who was hesitating. "If Ted won't talk to you, somebody has to clean the shotgun."

"I suppose so."

"Enthusiasm like that has launched colonies," Rourke drawled.

Jillian laughed self-consciously. "Sorry. I don't mean to sound reluctant. I just don't know what Ted will think. He's already mad because I said I might have overreacted to Davy Harris when I had him arrested."

"It wasn't overreaction," the restaurant owner, Mr. Chaney, inserted indignantly. "The man deserved what he got. I'm just sorry I can't keep him out of here. If he ever insults you or makes a threat, you tell me. I'll bar him even if I do get sued."

"Thanks, boss. Really," Jillian said.

"Least I could do." He glanced at the front door. "Excuse me. Customers." He left with a smile.

"He always greets people when they come in," Jillian explained with a smile, "and then he comes around to the tables and checks to make sure the service and the food are okay with them. He's a great boss."

"It's a good restaurant," Rourke agreed. "Good food." He grinned at Jillian.

"So. Six?" he added.

Jillian smiled. "Six. I'll even feed you."

"I'll bring the raw materials, shall I?" he asked with a twinkle in his eyes. "Steaks and salad?"

"Lovely!" Jillian exclaimed. "I haven't had a steak in a long time!"

"You've got all that beef over there and you don't eat steak?" he exclaimed. "What about that prime young calf, the little steer…?"

"Sammy?" Jillian gasped. "She's not eating beef!"

"She?" he asked.

"She's a cow. Or she will be one day."

"A cow named Sammy." He laughed. "Sounds like Cy Parks, down in Jacobsville, Texas. He's got a girl dog named Bob."

Everyone laughed.

"See?" Jillian said indignantly. "I'm not the only person who comes up with odd names for animals."

Sassy hugged her. "No, you aren't. I'm going home. You let Rourke clean that shotgun."

"Okay. Thanks," she added.

"My pleasure," Rourke said.

Sassy grinned. "And don't let him talk you into marrying him," she added firmly. "Ted will never speak to us again."

"No danger of that," Jillian sighed. "Sorry," she added to Rourke.

"Don't be so hasty, now," Rourke said. "I have many good qualities. I'll elaborate on them tonight. See you at six."

He left with Sassy. Jillian stared after them, grateful but uneasy. What was Ted going to think?

ROURKE SHOWED UP promptly at six with a bag of groceries.

He put his purchases out on the table. Expensive steaks, lettuce, all the ingredients for salad plus a variety of dressings, and a cherry pie and a pint of vanilla ice cream.

"I know you cook pies and cakes very well," he explained, "but I thought you might like a taste of someone else's cooking. Mrs. Callister's new cook produced that. It's famous where she comes from, up in Billings, Montana."

"I'll love it. Cherry pie is one of my favorites."

"Mine, too."

He started the steaks and then used her gourmet knives to do a fantastic chopping of vegetables for the salad.

Jillian watched his mastery of knives with pure fascination. "It must have taken you a long time to learn to do that so effortlessly."

"It did. I practiced on many people."

She stared at him, uncertain how to react.

He saw that and burst out laughing. "I was joking," he explained. "Not that I've never used knives on people, when the occasion called for it."

"I suppose violence is a way of life to someone in your position."

He nodded. "I learned to handle an AK-47 when I was ten years old."

She gasped.

"Where I grew up, in Africa, there were always regional wars," he told her. "The musclemen tried to move in and take over what belonged to the local tribes. I didn't have family at that time, was living in an orphanage, so I went to fight with them." He laughed. "It was an introduction to mean living that I've never been able to get past. Violence is familiar."

"I suppose it would have to be."

"I learned tactics and strategy from a succession of local warlords," he told her. "Some of them were handed down from the time of Shaka Zulu himself."

"Who was that?"

"Shaka Zulu? The most famous of the Zulu warriors, a strategist of the finest kind. He revolutionized weaponry and fighting styles among his people and became a great warlord. He defeated the British, with their advanced weapons."

"Good grief! I never heard of him."

"There was a miniseries on television about his exploits," he said while he chopped celery and cucumbers into strips. "I have it. I watch it a lot."

"I saw *Out of Africa*."

He smiled. "That's a beaut."

"It is. I loved the scenery." She laughed. "Imagine, playing Mozart for the local apes."

"Inventive." He stopped chopping, and his eye became dreamy. "I think Africa is the most beautiful place on earth. It's sad that the animals are losing habitat so quickly. Many of the larger ones will go extinct in my lifetime."

"There are lots of people trying to save them. They raise the little ones and then turn them back out onto the land."

"Where poachers are waiting to kill them," he said laconically. "You can still find ivory, and elephant feet used for footstools, and rhinoceros horn in clandestine shops all over the world. They do catch some of the perps, but not all of them. It's tragic to see a way of life going dead. Like the little Bushmen," he added quietly. "Their culture was totally destroyed, denigrated, ridiculed as worthless by European invaders. The end result is that they became displaced people, living in cities, in slums."

"I could tell you the same is true here, where Native Americans received similar treatment," she told him.

He smiled. "It seems that the old cultures are so primitive that they're considered without value. Our greatest modern civilizations are less than two thousand years old, yet those of ancient peoples can measure in the hundreds of thousands. Did you know that the mighty civilizations of Middle America were based on agriculture? Ours are based on industry."

"Agriculture. Farming."

He nodded. "Cities grew up around irrigated lands where

crops were planted and grew even in conditions of great drought. The Hohokam in Arizona had canals. The Mayan civilization had astronomy." He glanced at her. "The medical practitioners among the Incas knew how to do trepanning on skulls to relieve pressure in the brain. They used obsidian scalpels. It isn't well-known, but they're still in use today in scalpels for surgery."

"How did you learn all that?" she wondered.

"Traveling. It's one of the perks of my job. I get to see things and mix with people who are out in the vanguard of research and exploration. I once acted as bodyguard to one of the foremost archaeologists on earth in Egypt."

"Gosh!"

"Have you ever traveled?" he asked.

She thought about that. "Well, I did go to Oklahoma City, once," she said. "It was a long drive."

He was holding the knife in midair. "To Oklahoma City."

She flushed. "It's the only place outside Montana that I've ever been," she explained.

He was shocked. "Never to another country?"

"Oh, no," she replied. "There was never enough money for..." She stopped and glanced out the window. A pickup truck pulled up in the yard, very fast. The engine stopped, the door opened and was slammed with some fury.

Rourke's hand went involuntarily to the pistol under his arm.

"Oh, dear," Jillian said, biting her lip.

"Harris?" he asked curtly.

She sighed. "Worse. It's Ted."

CHAPTER NINE

THERE WERE QUICK, heavy footsteps coming up onto the porch. Jillian didn't have to ask if Ted was mad. When he wasn't, his tread was hardly audible at all, even in boots. Now, he was walking with a purpose, and she could hear it.

He knocked on the door. She opened it and stepped back.

His black eyes glittered at her. "I hear you have company," he said shortly.

Rourke came out of the kitchen. His jacket was off, so the .45 automatic he carried was plainly visible in its holster. "She does, indeed," he replied. He moved forward with easy grace and extended a hand. "Rourke," he introduced himself. "I'm on loan from the Callisters."

Ted shook the hand. "Theodore Graves. Chief of police," he added.

Rourke grinned. "I knew that. I came to town to try to see you the other day, but you were out on a case. Cash Grier said to tell you hello."

Ted seemed surprised. "You know him?"

"We used to work together under, shall we say, unusual conditions, in Africa," came the reply.

Ted relaxed a little. "Rourke. I think he mentioned you."

He shrugged. "I get around. I really came over to clean her shotgun for her, but I'm cooking, too." He gave Ted an appraisal that didn't miss much, including the other man's jealousy. "I'm impressing her with my culinary skills, in hopes that she might want to marry me after supper."

Ted gaped at him. "What?"

"He's just kidding," Jillian said, flushing.

"I am?" Rourke asked, and raised both eyebrows.

Ted glared at the other man. "She's engaged to me."

"I am not!" Jillian told him emphatically.

Rourke backed up a step and held up a hand. "I think I'll go back into the kitchen. I don't like to get mixed up in family squabbles," he added with a grin.

"We are not a family, and we're not squabbling!" Jillian raged.

"We're going to be a family, and yes, we are," Ted said angrily.

Rourke discreetly moved into the kitchen.

"I could have cleaned the shotgun, if you'd just asked me," he said angrily.

"You stormed out of here in a snit and never said a word," she returned. "How was I supposed to ask you, mail a letter?"

"Email is quicker," came a droll voice from the kitchen.

"You can shut up, this is a private argument," Ted called back.

"Sorry," Rourke murmured. "Don't be too long now, cold steak is unappetizing."

"You're feeding him steak?" Ted exclaimed. "What did he do, carve up Sammy?"

"I don't eat ugly calves!" Rourke quipped.

"Sammy is not ugly, she's beautiful!" Jillian retorted.

"If you say so," Rourke said under his breath.

"There's nothing wrong with black baldies," she persisted.

"Unless you've never seen a Brahma calf," Rourke sighed. "Gorgeous little creatures."

"Brahmas are the ugliest cattle on earth," Ted muttered.

"They are not!" Rourke retorted. "I own some of them!"

Ted stopped. "You run cattle around here?" he asked.

Rourke came back into the room, holding a fork. "In Africa. My home is in Kenya."

Ted's eyes narrowed. "So that's how Cash met you."

"Yes. I was, shall we say, gainfully employed in helping oust a local warlord who was slaughtering children in his rush to power."

"Good for you," Ted replied.

"Now you're teaming up?" Jillian said, fuming.

"Only as far as cattle are concerned," Rourke assured her with a flash of white teeth. "I'm still a contender in the matrimonial sweepstakes," he added. "I can cook and clean and make apple strudel." He gave Ted a musing appraisal, as if to say, top that.

Ted was outdone. It was well-known that he couldn't boil water. He glared at the blond man. "I can knock pennies off bottles with my pistol," he said, searching for a skill to compare.

"I can do it with an Uzi," Rourke replied.

"Not in my town, you won't—that's an illegal weapon."

"Okay, but that's a sad way to cop out of a competition." He blinked. "I made a pun!"

"I'm not a cop, I'm a police chief."

"Semantics," Rourke said haughtily, borrowing Jillian's favorite word, and walked back to the kitchen.

Ted looked down at Jillian, who was struggling not to laugh. He was more worried than he wanted to admit about her assailant, who kept adding fuel to the fire in town with gossip about Jillian's past. He knew better, but some people wouldn't. He'd been irritable because he couldn't find a way to make the little weasel leave town. Jillian was pale and nervous. He hadn't helped by avoiding her. It was self-defense. She meant more to him than he'd realized. He didn't want her hurt, even if she couldn't deal with marrying him.

He rested his hand on the butt of the automatic holstered on his belt. "I heard about what happened in the restaurant. You should listen to Sassy. It's possible that Harris may try to get revenge on you here, where you're alone."

"She's not alone," Rourke chimed in. "I'm here."

"Not usually, and he'll know that," Ted said irritably. He didn't like the other man assuming what he thought of as his own responsibility.

"Mrs. Callister already asked her to come stay at the ranch, but she won't," came the reply.

Ted didn't like the idea of Jillian being closer to Rourke, either. But he had to admit that it was the safest thing for her, if she wouldn't marry him.

"We could get married," he told her, lowering his voice.

"Can you cook?" Rourke asked. "Besides, I have all my own teeth."

Ted ignored him. He was worried, and it showed. He searched her eyes. "Harris bought a big Bowie at the hard-ward store yesterday."

"It's not illegal to own a knife," Rourke said.

"Technically it's not, although a Bowie certainly falls under the heading of an illegal weapon if he wears it in town. It has a blade longer than three-and-a-quarter inches. It's the implication of the purchase that concerns me," he added.

Rourke quickly became more somber. "He's making a statement of his intentions," he said.

"That's what I thought," Ted agreed. "And he knows

there's not a damned thing I can do about it, unless he carries the weapon blatantly. He's not likely to do that."

Rourke didn't mention that he'd been wearing his own Bowie knife in town. "You could turn your back and I could have a talk with him," Rourke suggested, not completely facetiously.

"He'd have me arrest you, and he'd call his lawyer," was the reply.

"I suppose so."

"Maybe I could visit somebody out of state," Jillian said on a sigh.

"He'd just follow you, and pose a threat to anybody you stayed with," Ted said. "Besides that, you don't know anybody out of state."

"I was only joking," Jillian replied. "I'm not running," she added firmly.

The men looked at her with smiling admiration.

"Foolhardy," Rourke commented.

"Sensible," Ted replied. "Nobody's getting past me in my own town to do her harm."

"I'm not needed at the ranch at night," Rourke said. "I could stay over here."

Ted and Jillian both glared at him.

He threw up his hands. "You people have some incredible hang-ups for twenty-first century human beings!"

"We live in a small town," Jillian pointed out. "I don't want to be talked about. Any more than I already am, I mean," she said miserably. "I guess Harris has convinced half the people here that I'm a heartless flirt who had him arrested because he wanted to marry me."

"Good luck to anybody brain-damaged enough to believe a story like that," Rourke said. "Especially anybody who knows you at all."

"Thanks, Rourke," Jillian replied.

Ted shook his head. "There are people who will believe anything. I'd give real money if I could find a law on the books that I could use to make him leave town."

"Vagrancy would have been a good one until he got that job."

"I agree," Ted said.

"It's not right," Jillian blurted out. "I mean, that somebody can come here, harass me, make my life miserable and just get away with it."

Ted's expression was eloquent. His high cheekbones flushed with impotent bad temper.

"I'm not blaming you," Jillian said at once. "I'm not, Ted. I know there's nothing you can do about it."

"Oh, for the wild old days in Africa," Rourke sighed. "Where we made up the laws as we went along."

"Law is the foundation of any civilization," Ted said firmly.

"True. But law, like anything else, can be abused." Rourke pursed his lips. "Are you staying for supper? I actually brought three steaks."

Jillian frowned. "Three?"

He chuckled. "Let's say I anticipated that we might have company," he said with a wry glance at Ted.

Ted seemed to relax. He gave Jillian an appraising look. "After supper, we might sit on the front porch and do a little target shooting."

She glared at him.

"We could practice with her shotgun," Rourke agreed, adding fuel to the fire.

"I only have two shells," Jillian said curtly.

Rourke reached into a bag he'd placed on a nearby shelf.

"I anticipated that, too." He handed the shells to Ted with a grin.

"Double ought buckshot," Ted mused. "We use that in our riot shotguns."

"I know."

"What does that mean?" Jillian wanted to know.

"It's a heavy load, used by law enforcement officers to ensure that criminals who fire on them pay dearly for the privilege," Ted said enigmatically.

"Tears big holes in things, love," Rourke translated.

Ted didn't like the endearment, and his black eyes glittered.

Rourke laughed. "I'll just go turn those steaks."

"Might be safer," Ted agreed.

Rourke left and Ted took Jillian's hand and led her into the living room. He closed the door.

"I don't like him being over here with you alone," he said flatly.

She gave him a hunted look. "Well, I wasn't exactly overflowing with people trying to protect me from Davy!"

He averted his eyes. "Sorry."

"Why did you get so angry?"

"You were making excuses for him," he said, his voice curt. "Letting him convince you that it was all a mistake. I got access to the court records, Jillian."

She realized what he was saying, and flushed to her hairline.

"Hey," he said softly. "It's not your fault."

"He said I wore suggestive things…"

"You never wore suggestive things in your life, and you were fifteen," he muttered. "How would you feel, at your age now, if a fifteen-year-old boy actually flirted with you?"

"I'd tell his mama," she returned.

"Exactly." He waited for that to register.

Her eyes narrowed. "You mean, I didn't have the judgment to involve myself with a man, even one just six years older than me."

"You didn't. And you never wore suggestive things."

"I wasn't allowed, even if I'd wanted to. My uncle was very conservative."

"Harris was a predator. He still is. But in his own mind, he didn't do anything wrong. That's why he's giving you the business. He really feels that he had every right to pursue you. He can't understand why he was arrested for it."

"But that's crazy!"

"No crazier than you second-guessing your own reactions, when you actually had to run to a neighbor's house to save yourself from assault," he pointed out.

She gnawed her lower lip. "I was scared to death." She looked up at him. "Men are so strong," she said. "Even thin men like Davy. I almost didn't get away. And when I did, he went nuts. He was yelling threats all the way to the Peales' house. I really think he would have killed me if Sassy hadn't pulled that shotgun. He might have killed her, too, and it would have been my fault, for running over there for help. But it was the only house close enough."

"I'm sure Sassy never blamed you for that. She's a good person."

"So are you," she commented quietly. "I'm sorry I've been such a trial to you."

His face softened. His black eyes searched hers. "I should have been more understanding." He grimaced. "You don't get how it is, Jake, to go out with a woman you want and be apprehensive about even touching her."

She had a blank look on her face.

"You don't know what I'm talking about, do you?" he asked in a frustrated tone. He moved closer. "Maybe it's time you did."

He curled her into his body with a long, powerful arm and bent his head. He kissed her with soft persuasion at first, then, when she relaxed, his mouth probed further. He teased her lips apart and nibbled them. He felt her stiffen at first, but after a few seconds, she became more flexible. She stopped resisting and stood very still.

She hadn't known that she could feel such things. Up until now, Ted had been almost teasing when he kissed her. But this time, he wasn't holding anything back. His arm, at her back, arched her up against him. His big hand smoothed up from her waist and brushed lightly at the edges of her small, firm breast.

As the kisses grew longer and hungrier, her body began to feel swollen and hot. She ached for more than she was getting, but she didn't understand what she wanted.

Ted felt those vague longings in her and knew how to satisfy them. His mouth ground down onto hers as his fingers began to smooth over the soft mound of flesh, barely touching, kindling hungers that Jillian had never known before.

She gasped when his fingers rubbed over the nipple and it became hard and incredibly sensitive. She tried to draw back, but not with any real enthusiasm.

"Scared?" he whispered against her mouth. "No need. We have a chaperone."

"The door...it's closed."

"Yes, thank goodness," he groaned, "because if it wasn't, I wouldn't dare do this."

"This" involved the sudden rise of her shirt and the bra

up under her chin and the shocking, delicious, invasion of Ted's warm mouth over her breast.

She shuddered. It was the most intense pleasure she'd ever felt. Her short nails dug into his broad shoulders as she closed her eyes and arched backward to give him even better access to the soft, warm flesh that ached for his tender caress.

She felt his hand cupping her, lifting her, as his mouth opened over the nipple and he took it between his lips and tongue.

Her soft gasp was followed by a harsh, shivering little moan that cost him his control. Not only had it been a long, dry spell, but this woman was the most important person in his life and he wanted her with an obsessive hunger. He hadn't been able to sleep for thinking about how sweet it would be to make love to her. And now she was, despite her hang-ups, not only welcoming his touch, but enjoying it.

"You said you didn't want to marry me," he whispered roughly as his mouth became more demanding.

Her nails dug into his back. "I said a lot of things," she agreed. Her eyes closed as she savored the spicy smell of his cologne, the tenderness of his mouth on forbidden flesh. "I might have even…believed them, at the time."

He lifted his head and looked down at her. His expression tautened at the sight of her pretty, firm breasts, and his body clenched. "I took it personally. Like you thought there was something wrong with me."

"Ted, no!" she exclaimed.

He pulled back the hand that was tracing around her nipple.

She bit her lip. "I wasn't saying no to that," she said with hopeless shyness, averting her eyes. "I meant, I don't think there's anything wrong with you...!"

She gasped as he responded to the blatant invitation in her voice and teased the hard rise of flesh with his thumb and forefinger.

"You don't?" he whispered, and smiled at her in a way that he never had before.

"Of course not! I was just scared," she managed, because what he was doing was creating sensations in some very private places. "Scared of marriage, I mean."

"Marriage is supposed to be a feast of pleasure for two people who care about each other," he pointed out, watching with delight her fascination with what he was doing to her willing body. He drew in a long breath and bent his head. "I'm beginning to believe it."

He opened his mouth over her soft breast and drew it inside, suckling it with his lips and his tongue in a slow, easy caress that caused her whole body to clench and shiver. As his ardor increased, he felt with wonder the searching fingers on the buttons of his shirt. They hesitated.

"Men like to be touched, too," he whispered into her ear. "Oh."

She finished opening the button, a little clumsily, and spread her hands over the thick, curling mass of hair that covered his chest. "Wow," she whispered when sensations rippled through her body and seemed to be echoed coming from his. "You like that?" she asked hesitantly.

"I love it," he gritted.

She smiled with the joy of discovery as she looked up at him, at his mussed hair, his sensuous mouth, his sparkling black eyes. It was new, this shared pleasure. And she'd been so certain that she'd never be able to feel it with him, with anyone.

He bent to her mouth and crushed his lips down over it as his body eased onto hers. She felt the press of his bare chest against her breasts and arched up to increase the contact. Her arms went around him tightly, holding on as the current of passion swept her along.

He eased one long, powerful leg between both of hers and moved against her in a rhythm that drew shudders and soft moans from her throat. She buried her teeth in his shoulder as the sensations began to rise and become obsessive. He must have felt something comparable, because he suddenly pushed down against her with a harsh groan as his control began to slip.

The soft knock on the door came again and again, until it was finally a hammering.

Ted lifted his head, his shocked eyes on Jillian's pretty pink breasts with visible passion marks, her face flushed and rigid with desire, her eyes turbulent as they met his.

"What?" Ted said aloud.

"Steak's ready! Don't let it get cold!" Rourke called, and there were audible footsteps going back down the hall.

With the passion slowly receding, Jillian was disturbed at letting Ted see her like this. Flushed, she fumbled her blouse and bra back on, wincing as the sensitive nipple was brushed by the fabric.

"Sorry," he whispered huskily. "I lost my head."

She managed a shaky smile. "It's okay. I lost mine, too." She looked at him with absolute wonder. "I didn't know it could feel like that," she stammered. "I mean, I never felt like that with anybody. Not that I ever let any man do that…!"

He put a long finger over her lips and smiled at her in a way he never had before. "It's okay, Jake."

She was still trying to catch her breath, and not doing a good job of it.

"I think you could say that we're compatible, in that way," he mused, enjoying her reaction to him more than he could find a way to express.

She laughed softly. "Yes, I think you could."

He smiled. "So, suppose we get married. And you can live with me, here on the ranch, and you'll never have to worry about Harris again."

She hesitated, but not for very long. She nodded, slowly. "Okay."

His high cheekbones went a ruddy color. It flattered him that she'd agree after a torrid passionate interlude, when he hadn't been able to persuade her with words.

"Don't get conceited," she said firmly, figuring out his thoughts.

His eyes twinkled. "Not possible."

She laughed. It was as if the world had changed completely in those few minutes. All her hang-ups had gone into eclipse the minute Ted turned the heat up.

"I wondered," he confessed, "if you'd be able to respond to a man after what happened to you."

"I did, too." She moved close to him and put her hands on his chest. "It was one reason I was afraid to let things go, well, very far. I didn't want to lead you on in any way and then pull away and run. I almost did that once."

"Yes," he said.

"If we get married, you'll give me a little time, won't you?" she asked worriedly. "I mean, I think I can do what you want me to. But it's just getting used to the idea."

Ted, who knew more than she did about women's reactions when passion got really hot, only smiled. "No problem."

She grinned. "Okay, then. Do we get married in the justice of the peace's office…?"

"In a church," he interrupted. "And you have to have a white gown and carry a bouquet. I'll even wear my good suit." He smiled. "I'm only getting married once, you know. We have to do it right."

She loved that attitude. It was what she'd wanted, but she was sensitive about being pushy. "Okay," she said.

"You'll be beautiful in a wedding gown," he murmured, bending to kiss her tenderly. "Not that you aren't beautiful in blue jeans. You are."

"I'm not," she faltered.

"You are to me," he corrected. His black eyes searched hers and he thought about the future, about living with her, about loving her… He bent and kissed her hungrily, delighting when she returned the embrace fervently.

"The steak's going to be room temperature in about thirty seconds!" Rourke shouted down the hall.

Ted pulled back, laughing self-consciously. "I guess we could eat steak, since he's been nice enough to cook it," he told her. His eyes glittered. "We can tell him we're engaged before we even start eating."

"Rourke's not interested in me that way," she said easily, smiling. "He's a nice man, but he's just protective of women. It isn't even personal."

Ted had his doubts about that. Jillian underestimated her appeal to men.

"Come on," she said, and slid her little hand into his big one.

That knocked the argument right out of him. It was the first physical move she'd made toward him. Well, not the first, but a big one, just the same. He slid his fingers between hers sensually, and smiled at her.

She smiled back. Her heart was hammering, her senses were alive and tumultuous. It was the beginning of a whole new life. She could hardly wait to marry Ted.

ROURKE GAVE THEM a knowing smile when he noticed the telltale signs of what they'd been doing. He served up supper.

"This is really good," Ted exclaimed when he took the first bite of his steak.

"I'm a gourmet chef," Rourke replied, surprisingly. "In between dangerous jobs, I used to work in one of the better restaurants in Jo'burg," he said, giving Johannesburg its affectionate abbreviation.

"Wonders will never cease," Jillian said with a grin. "From steaks to combat."

"Oh, it was always combat first," Rourke said easily, "since I was born in Africa."

"Africa was always a rough venue, from what Cash told me," Ted said.

Rourke nodded. "We have plenty of factions, all trying to gain control of the disputed African states, although each is a sovereign nation in the Organization of African Unity, which contains fifty-four nations. The wars are always bloody. And there are millions upon millions of displaced persons, trying to survive with their children. A mercenary doesn't even have to look for work, it's all around him." His face hardened. "What's hardest is what they do to the kids."

"They must die very young there," Jillian commented sadly.

"No. They put automatic weapons in their hands when they're grammar school age, teach them to fire rocket launchers and set explosive charges. They have no sense of what childhood should actually be."

"Good heavens!" she exclaimed.

"You've never traveled, Jake," Ted said gently. "The world is a lot bigger than Hollister."

"I guess it is. But I never had the money, even if I'd had the inclination," she said.

"That's why I joined the army." Ted chuckled. "I knew it was the only way I'd get to travel."

"I wanted to see the world, too." Rourke nodded. "But most of what I've seen of it wouldn't be appropriate for any travel magazine."

"You have a ranch?" Ted asked.

He smiled. "Yes, I do. Luckily it's not in any of the contested areas, so I don't have to worry about politicians seizing power and taking over private land."

"And you run Brahmas," Ted said, shaking his head. "Ugly cattle."

"They're bred to endure the heat and sometimes drought conditions that we have in Africa," Rourke explained. "Our cattle have to be hearty. And some of your American ranchers use them as breeding stock for that very reason."

"I know. I've seen a lot of them down in Texas."

"They don't mind heat and drought, something you can't say for several other breed of cattle," Rourke added.

"I guess," Jillian said.

Rourke finished his steak and took a sip of the strong coffee he'd brewed. "Harris has been frustrated because Jillian got one of the waitresses to start putting cakes out for her in the display case."

"They haven't been selling," Jillian said sadly. "They used to be very popular, and now hardly anybody wants slices of them. I guess Davy has convinced people that they shouldn't eat my cooking because I'm such a bad person."

"Oh, that's not true," Ted said at once. "Don't you know about the contest?"

She frowned. "What contest?"

"You don't read the local paper, do you?" Rourke chided her.

She shook her head. "We already know what's going on, we only read a paper to know who got caught. But I have him," she pointed at Ted, "to tell me that, so why do I need to spend money for a newspaper?"

They both laughed.

"The mayor challenged everyone in Hollister to give up sweets for two weeks. It's a competition between businesses and people who work for them. At the end of the two weeks, everybody gets weighed, and the business with the employees who lost the most weight gets a cash prize, put up by the businesses themselves. The employees get to decide how the money's spent, too, so they can use it for workplace improvements or cash bonuses."

Jillian perked up. "Then it isn't about me!"

"Of course not," Ted chuckled. "I've heard at least two men who eat in that restaurant complain because they couldn't eat those delicious cakes until the contest ended."

"I feel so much better," she said.

"I'm glad," Rourke told her. "But that still doesn't solve your problem. Harris bought a Bowie knife and he doesn't hunt." He let the implication sink in. "He's facing at least ten to fifteen on the charges if he goes back to trial and is convicted again. He's been heard saying that he'll never go back to that hellhole voluntarily. So basically he's got nothing to lose." He glanced at Ted. "You know that already."

Ted nodded. "Yes, I do," he replied. He smiled at Jillian. "Which is why we're getting married Saturday."

She gasped. "Saturday? But there's not enough time…!"

"There is. We'll manage. Meanwhile," Ted said, "you're going to take Sassy's invitation seriously and stay out at her ranch until the ceremony. Right?"

She wanted to argue, but both males had set faces and determined expressions. So she sighed and said, "Right."

CHAPTER TEN

NOT ONLY DID John and Sassy Callister welcome Jillian as a houseguest, Sassy threw herself into wedding preparations and refused to listen to Jillian's protests.

"I've never gotten to plan a wedding, not even my own," Sassy laughed. "John hired a professional to do it for us because so many important people came to the ceremony. So now I'm taking over preparations for yours."

"But I can't afford this store," the younger woman tried to complain. "They don't even put price tags on this stuff!"

Sassy gave her a smile. "John and I agreed that our wedding present to you is going to be the gown and accessories," she said. "So you can hand it down through your family. You might have a daughter who'd love to wear it at her own wedding."

Jillian hadn't thought about that. She became dreamy. A child. A little girl that she could take on walks, cuddle and rock, read stories to. That was a part of marriage she'd never dwelled on before. Now, it was a delightful thought.

"So stop arguing," Sassy said gently, "and start making choices."

Jillian hugged her. "Thanks. For the gown and for letting me stay with you until the wedding."

"This is what friends are for. You'd do it for me in a heartbeat if our situations were reversed."

"Yes, but I could have gotten you killed that night by running to you for help," Jillian said. "It torments me."

"I was perfectly capable of handling Davy Harris. And now I've got John, who can handle anything."

"You're very lucky. He's a good man."

"Yes, he is," Sassy agreed with a smile.

"I've never seen anything as beautiful as these dresses," Jillian began.

"I hear you're getting married Saturday, Jilly," came a cold, taunting voice from behind her.

Both women turned. Davy Harris was watching them, a nasty look on his face.

"Yes, I'm getting married," Jillian told him.

"There was a time when I thought you'd marry me," he said. "I had it all planned, right down to what sort of dress you'd wear and where we'd live. I'd lined up a full-time job with a local rancher. Everything was set." His lips twisted. "Then you had to go and get outraged when I tried to show you how I felt."

"I'll show you how I feel," Sassy said pertly. "Where's my shotgun?"

"Terroristic threats and acts, Mrs. Callister," he shot back. "Suppose I call the news media and tell them that you're threatening me?"

Jillian was horrified.

Sassy just smiled. "Well, wouldn't it be a shame if that same news media suddenly got access to the trial transcripts?" she asked pleasantly.

His face hardened. "You think you're so smart. Women are idiots. My father always said so. My mother was utterly worthless. She couldn't even cook without burning something!"

Jillian stared at him. "That doesn't make a woman worthless."

"She was always nervous," he went on, as if she hadn't spoken. "She called the police once, but my father made sure she never did it again. They put him in prison. I never understood why. She had him locked up. He was right to make her pay for it."

Sassy and Jillian exchanged disturbed looks.

Harris gave Jillian a chilling smile. "He died in prison. But I won't. I'm never going back." He shrugged. "You enjoy thinking about that wedding, Jilly. Because all you're going to get to do is think about it. Have a nice day, now."

He walked out.

The shopping trip was ruined for Jillian. Sassy insisted that they get the gown and the things that went with it, but Jillian was certain that Davy had meant what he said. He was going to try to kill her. Maybe he'd even kill himself, afterward. In his own mind, he was justified. There was no way to reason with such a person, a man who thought that his own mother deserved to die because she'd had his father arrested for apparently greatly abusing her.

"You know, there are scary people in the world," Jillian told Sassy in a subdued tone. "I'll bet if Uncle John had ever really talked to Davy, he'd never have let him in the front door in the first place. He's mentally disturbed, and it isn't apparent until he starts talking about himself."

"I noticed that," Sassy replied. She drew in a long breath. "I'm glad we have Rourke."

Jillian frowned. "Where is he?"

"Watching us. If Harris had made a threatening move, he'd already be in jail, probably after a trip to the emergency room. I've never seen Rourke mad, but John says it's something you don't want to experience."

"I got that impression." She laughed. "He cooked steaks for Ted and me."

"I heard about that," the other woman said in an amused tone. "Ted was jealous, was he?"

"Very. But after he realized that Rourke was just being friendly and protective, his attitude changed. Apparently he knows a police chief in Texas that Ted met at a workshop back east."

"Rourke does get around." She glanced at Jillian. "He acts like a perpetual clown, but if you see him when he thinks he's alone, it's all an act. He's a very somber, sad person. I think he's had some rough knocks."

"He doesn't talk about them much. Just about his ranch."

"He doesn't talk about K.C. Kantor, either," Sassy replied. "But there's some sound gossip about the fact that Rourke's mother was once very close to the man."

"From what everybody says about that Kantor man, he isn't the sort to have kids."

"That's what I thought. But a man can get into a situation where he doesn't think with his mind," Sassy chuckled. "And when people get careless, they have kids."

"I'd be proud of Rourke, if I was his father."

"You're the wrong age and gender," Sassy said, tongue-in-cheek.

"Oh, you know what I mean. He's a good person."

"He is," Sassy said as she pulled up in front of the ranch house. "I'm glad John hired him. At least we don't have to worry about being assassinated on the way to town!"

"Amen," Jillian sighed.

JOHN CALLISTER WAS an easygoing, friendly man. He didn't seem at all like a millionaire, or at least, Jillian's vision of one. He treated her as he would a little sister, and was happy to have her around.

Jillian also liked Sassy's mother, who was in poor health, and her adopted sister, Selene, who was a whiz at math and science in grammar school. John took care of them, just as he took care of Sassy.

But the easygoing personality went into eclipse when he heard that Davy Harris had followed them into the dress shop in Billings.

"The man is dangerous," he said as they ate an early supper with Rourke.

"He is," Rourke agreed. "He shouldn't be walking around loose in the first place. What the hell is wrong with the criminal justice system in this country?"

John gave him a droll look. "It's better than the old vigilante system of the distant past," he pointed out. "And it usually works."

"Not with Harris," Rourke replied, his jaw set as he munched on a chef's salad. "He can put on a good act for a while, but he can't keep it up. He starts talking, and you see the lunacy underneath the appearance of sanity."

"Disturbed people often don't know they're disturbed," Sassy said.

"That's usually the case, I'm sad to say," Rourke added. "People like Harris always think they're being persecuted."

"I knew a guy once who was sure the government sent invisible spies to watch him," John mused. "He could see them, but nobody else could. He worked for us one summer on the ranch back home. Gil and I put up with him because he was the best horse wrangler we'd ever had. But that was a mistake."

"How so?" Rourke asked.

"Well, he had this dog. It was vicious and he refused

to get rid of it. One day it came right up on the porch and threatened Gil's little girls. Gil punched him and fired him. Then he started cutting fences and killing cattle. At the last, he tried to kill us. He ended up in prison, too."

"Good heavens!" Jillian said. "No wonder you hired a bodyguard for Sassy."

"Exactly," John replied tersely. He didn't mention that Sassy had been the victim of a predator herself, in the feed store where she was working when they met. That man was serving time now.

His eyes lingered on Sassy with warm affection. "Nobody's hurting my best girl. Or her best friend," he declared with a grin at Jillian.

"Not while I'm on the job," Rourke added, chuckling. "You could marry me, you know," he told Jillian. "I really do have most of my own teeth left, and I can cook. Your fiancé can't boil water, I hear."

"That's true," Jillian said, smiling. "But I've known him most of my life, and we think the same way about most things. We'll have a good marriage." She was sure of that. Ted would be gentle, and patient, and he'd rid her of the distaste Davy had left in her about physical relationships. She'd never been more certain of anything.

"Well, it's a great shame," Rourke said with a theatrical sigh. "I'll have to go back home to my ugly cattle and live in squalor because nobody wants to take care of me."

"You'll find some lovely girl who will be happy living on a small farm in Africa," Jillian assured him.

John almost choked on his coffee.

Rourke gave him a cold glare.

"What is wrong with you?" Sassy asked her husband.

He wiped his mouth, still stifling laughter. "Private

joke," he said, sharing a look with Rourke, who sighed and shrugged.

"But it had better be somebody who can dress bullet wounds," John added with a twinkle in his eyes as he glanced at the other man.

"I only get shot occasionally," Rourke assured him. "And I usually duck in time."

"That's true," John agreed, forking another piece of steak into his mouth. "He only has one head wound, and it doesn't seem to have affected his thinking processes." He didn't mention the lost eye, because Rourke was sensitive about it.

"That was a scalp wound," Rourke replied, touching a faint scar above his temple. He glared at the other man from a pale brown eye. "And not from a bullet. It was from a knife."

"Poor thing," Jillian murmured.

John choked on his steak.

"Will you stop?" Rourke muttered.

"Sorry." John coughed. He sipped coffee.

Jillian wished she knew what they were talking about. But it was really none of her business, and she had other worries.

THE WEDDING GOWN was exquisite. She couldn't stop looking at it. She hung it on the door in the guest bedroom and sighed over it at every opportunity.

Ted came by to visit frequently and they took long walks in the woods, to talk and to indulge in a favorite of dating couples, the hot physical interludes that grew in intensity by the day.

He held her hand and walked with her down a long path through the snow, his fingers warm and strong in hers.

"I can't stand it if I go a whole day without seeing you," he said out of the blue.

She stopped walking and looked up at him with pure wonder. "Really?"

He pulled her into his arms. "Really." He bent and kissed her slowly, feeling her respond, feeling her warm lips open and move tenderly. She reached her arms up around his neck as if it was the most natural thing in the world. He smiled against her lips. It was a delightful surprise, her easy response to him.

"Maybe I can get used to Sammy following me around, and you can get used to me shooting targets off the front porch," he teased.

She grinned. "Maybe you can teach me to shoot, too."

He looked shocked. "I can?"

"We should share some interests," she said wisely. "You always go to that shooting range and practice. I could go with you sometimes."

He was surprised and couldn't hide it.

She toyed with a shirt button. "I don't like being away from you, either, Ted," she confessed and flushed a little. "It's so sweet..."

He pulled her close. One lean hand swept down her back, riveting her to his powerful body. "Sweeter than honey," he managed before he kissed her.

His hand pushed her hips against the sudden hardness of his own, eliciting a tiny sound from her throat. But it wasn't protest. If anything, she moved closer.

He groaned out loud and ground her hips into his.

"I can't wait until Saturday," he said in a husky tone, easing his hands under Jillian's blouse, under the bra to caress her soft breasts. "I'm dying!"

"So am I," she whispered shakily. "Oh, Ted!" she gasped

when he pulled the garments out of his way and covered her breast with his mouth. It was so sweet. Too sweet for words!

He didn't realize what he was doing until they were lying on the cold ground, in the snow, while he kissed her until she was breathless.

She was shaking when he lifted his head, but not from cold or fear. Her eyes held the same frustrated desire that his held.

"I want to, so much!" she whispered.

"So do I," he replied.

For one long instant, they clung together on the hard ground, with snow making damp splotches all down Jillian's back and legs, while they both fought for control.

Ted clenched his hands beside her head and closed his eyes as he rested his forehead against hers. He was rigid, helplessly aroused and unable to hide it.

She smoothed back his black hair and pressed soft, undemanding little kisses all over his taut face, finally against the closed eyelids and short thick black lashes.

"It's all right," she whispered. "It's all right."

He was amazed at the effect those words, and the caresses, had on him. They eased the torment. They calmed him, in the sweetest way he'd ever imagined. He smiled against her soft throat.

"Learning how to tame the beast, aren't you?" he whispered in a teasing tone.

She looked up at him with soft, loving eyes. "How to calm him down, anyway," she said with a little laugh. "I think marriage is going to be an adventure."

"So do I."

He stood and tugged her up, too, helping to rearrange her disheveled clothing. He grinned at her. "We both love maps and the tango. We'll go dancing every week."

Her eyes brightened. "I'd like that."

He enveloped her against him and stood holding her, quietly, in the silence of the snow-covered woods. "Heaven," he whispered, "must be very like this."

She smiled, hugging him. "I could die of happiness."

His heart jumped. "So could I, sweetheart."

The endearment made her own heart jump. She'd never been so happy in her life.

"Saturday can't come soon enough for me," he murmured.

"Or for me. Ted, Sassy bought me the most beautiful wedding gown. I know you aren't supposed to see it before the ceremony, but I just have to show it to you."

He drew back, smiling. "I'd like that."

They walked hand in hand back to the ranch house, easy and content with each other in a way they'd never been before. They looked as if they'd always been together, and always would be.

Sassy, busy in the kitchen with the cook, grinned at them. "Staying for lunch, Ted? We're having chili and Mexican corn bread."

"I'd love to, if you have enough to share."

"Plenty."

"Then, thanks, I will. Jillian wants me to see the wedding gown."

"Bad luck," Sassy teased.

"We make our own luck, don't we, honey?" he asked Jillian in a husky, loving tone.

She blushed at the second endearment in very few minutes and squeezed his hand. "Yes, we do."

She opened her bedroom door and gasped, turning pale. There, on the floor, were the remains of her wedding gown, her beautiful dress. It had been slashed to pieces.

"Stop right there," Ted said curtly, his arm preventing Jillian from entering the room. "This is now a crime scene. I'll get the sheriff's department's investigator out here right now, and the state crime-lab techs. I know who did this. I only want enough proof to have him arrested!"

Jillian wrapped her arms around her chest and shivered. Davy had come right into the house and nobody knew. Not even Rourke. It was chilling. Sassy, arriving late, took in the scene with a quick glance and hugged Jillian.

"It will be all right," she promised. But her own eyes were troubled. It was scary that he'd come into the house without being seen.

Rourke, when he realized what had happened, was livid. "That polecat!" he snarled. "Right under my bloody nose, and me like a raw recruit with no clue he was on the place! That won't happen again! I'm calling in markers. I'll have this place like a fortress before Saturday!"

Nobody argued with him. The situation had become a tragedy in the making. They'd all underestimated Davy Harris's wilderness skills, which were apparently quite formidable.

"He was a hunter," Jillian recalled. "He showed me how to track deer when he first started working with Uncle John, before he got to be a problem. He could walk so nobody heard a step. I'd forgotten that."

"I can ghost-walk myself," Rourke assured her.

"He used to set bear traps," Jillian blurted out, and reddened when everybody looked at her. "He said it was to catch a wolf that had been preying on the calves, but Uncle John said there was a dog caught in it..." She felt sick. "I'd forgotten that."

The men looked at each other. A bear trap could be used for many things, including catching unsuspecting people.

Jillian stared at Ted with horror. "Ted, he wouldn't use that on Sammy, would he?" she asked fearfully. Davy knew how much she loved her calf.

"No," he assured her with a comforting arm around her shoulders as he lied. "He wouldn't."

Rourke left the room for a few minutes. He came back, grim-faced. "We're going to have a lot of company very soon. All we need is proof that he was here, and he won't be a problem again."

WHICH WOULD HAVE been wonderful. Except that there wasn't a footprint in the dirt, a fingerprint, or any trace evidence whatsoever that Davy Harris had been near the Callister home. The technicians with all their tools couldn't find one speck of proof.

"So much for Locard's Exchange Principle," Ted said grimly, and then had to explain what it meant to Jillian. "A French criminalist named Edmond Locard noted that when a crime is committed, the perpetrator both carries away and leaves behind trace evidence."

"But Davy didn't," she said sadly.

"He's either very good or very lucky," Ted muttered. He slid a protective arm around Jillian. "And it won't save him. He's the only person in town who had a motive for doing this. It's just a matter of proving it."

She laughed hollowly. "Maybe you could check his new Bowie knife to see if it's got pieces of white lace sticking to it," she said, trying to make the best of a bad situation.

But he didn't laugh. He was thoughtful. "That might not be such a bad idea," he murmured. "All I'd need is probable cause, if I can convince a judge to issue a search warrant on the basis of it." He pursed his lips and narrowed his eyes, nodding to himself. "And that's just what I'm going to do. Stick close to the house today, okay?"

"Okay."

He kissed her and left.

But Ted came back a few hours later and stuck to her like glue. She noticed that he was suddenly visible near her, everywhere she went around the house and the barn. It was just after he'd received a phone call, to which nobody was privy.

"What's going on?" Jillian asked him bluntly.

He smiled, his usual easygoing self, as he walked beside her with his hands deep in the pockets of his khaki slacks. "What would be going on?"

"You're usually at work during the day, Ted," she murmured dryly.

He grinned at her. "Maybe I can't stay away from you, even on a workday," he teased.

She stopped and turned to him, frowning. "That's not an answer and you know…!"

She gasped as he suddenly whirled, pushing her to the ground as he drew his pistol and fired into a clump of snow-covered undergrowth near the house. Even as he fired, she felt a sting in her arm and then heard a sound like a high-pitched crack of thunder.

That sound was followed by the equally loud rapid fire of a .45 automatic above her. She heard the bullets as they connected with tree trunks in the distance.

"You okay?" he asked urgently.

"I think so."

He stopped firing, and eased up to his feet, standing very still with his head cocked, listening. Far in the distance was the sound of a vehicle door closing, then an engine starting. He whipped out his cell phone and made a call. He gave a quick explanation, a quicker description of the direction of travel of the vehicle and assurances that the intended victim was all right. He put up the cell phone and knelt beside a shaken Jillian.

There was blood on her arm. The sleeve of her gray sweatshirt was ripped. She looked at it with growing sensation. It stung.

"What in the world?" she stammered.

"You've been hit, sweetheart," he said curtly. "That's a gunshot wound. I didn't want to tell you, but one of my investigators learned that Harris bought a high-powered rifle with a telescopic sight this morning, after I had his rented room tossed for evidence."

"He's a convicted felon, nobody could have sold him a gun at all...!" she burst out.

"There are places in any town, even small ones, where people can buy weapons under the table." His face was hard as stone. "I don't know who sold it to him, but you'd better believe that I'm going to find out. And God help whoever did, when I catch up to him!"

She was still trying to wrap her mind around the fact that she'd been shot. Rourke, who'd been at the other end of the property, came screeching up in a ranch Jeep and jumped out, wincing when he saw the blood on Jillian's arm.

"I spotted him, I was tracking him, when I heard the gunshot. God, I'm sorry!" he exclaimed. "I should have been quicker. Do you think you hit him?" he asked Ted.

"I'm not sure. Maybe." He helped Jillian up. "I'll get you to a doctor." He glanced at Rourke. "I called the sheriff to bring his dogs and his best investigator out here," he added. "They may need some help. I told the sheriff you'd been on the case, working for the Callisters."

Rourke's pale brown eye narrowed. He looked far different from the man Jillian had come to know as her easygoing friend. "I let him get onto the property, and I'm sorry. But I can damned sure track him."

"None of us could have expected what happened here," Ted said reassuringly, and put a kindly hand on the other man's shoulder. "She'll be okay. Sheriff's department investigator is on his way out here. I gave the sheriff's investigator your cell phone number," Ted added.

Rourke nodded. He winced at Jillian's face. "I'm sorry," he said curtly.

She smiled, holding her arm. "It's okay, Rourke."

"I didn't realize he was on the place, either, until I heard the gunshots," Ted said.

"Not the first time you've been shot at, I gather?" she asked with black humor.

"Not at all. You usually feel the bullet before you hear the sound," he added solemnly.

"And that's a fact," Rourke added with faint humor.

"Let's go," Ted said gently.

She let him put her into the patrol car. She was feeling sick, and she was in some pain. "It didn't hurt at first," she said. "I didn't even realize I was shot. Oh, Ted, I'm sorry, you have to wait...!" She opened the door and threw up, then she cried with embarrassment.

He handed her a clean white handkerchief, put her back in the car, and broke speed limits getting her to the emergency room.

"IT'S NEVER LIKE that on television," she said drowsily, when she'd been treated and was in a semi-private room for the night. They'd given her something for pain, as well. It was making her sleepy.

"What isn't, sweetheart?"

She smiled at the endearment as he leaned over her, gently touching her face. "People getting shot. They don't throw up."

"That's not real life, either," he reminded her.

She was worried, but not only for herself.

"What is it?" he asked gently.

"Sammy," she murmured. "I know, it's stupid to be worried about a calf, but if he can't get to me, he might try to hurt something I love." She searched his eyes. "You watch out, too."

His dark eyes twinkled. "Because you love me?" he drawled.

She only nodded, her face solemn. "More than anyone in the world."

There was a flush on his high cheekbones. He cupped her head in his big hands and kissed her with blatant possession. "That goes double for me," he whispered against her lips.

She searched his eyes with fascination. "It does?"

"Why in the world do you think I'd want to marry you if I didn't love you?" he asked reasonably. "No parcel of land is worth that sort of sacrifice."

"You never said," she stammered.

"Neither did you," he pointed out, chuckling.

She laid her hand against his shoulder. "I didn't want to say it first."

He kissed her nose. "But you did."

She sighed and smiled. "Yes. I did."

For one long moment, they were silent together, savoring the newness of an emotion neither had realized was so intense.

Finally he lifted his head. "I don't want to leave you, but we've got a lot of work to do and not a lot of time to do it."

She nodded. "You be careful."

"I will."

"Ted, could you check on Sammy?" she asked worriedly.

"Yes. I'll make sure she's okay."

She smiled. "Thanks."

"No problem."

SASSY CAME AND took her back to the Callister ranch as soon as the doctor released her.

"I still think they should have kept you overnight," Sassy muttered.

"They tried to, but I refused," Jillian said drowsily. "I don't like being in hospitals. Have you heard anything more?"

"About Harris?" Sassy shook her head. "I know they've got dogs in the woods, hunting him. But if he's a good woodsman, he'll know how to cover his trail."

"He talked about that once," Jillian recalled. "He said there were ways to cover up a scent trail so a dog couldn't track people. Funny, I never wondered why he'd know such a thing."

"I'm sorry he does," Sassy replied. "If he didn't have those skills, he'd be a lot easier to find."

"I guess so."

"I'VE GOT A surprise for you," Sassy said when they walked into the house. She smiled mysteriously as she led Jillian down the hall to the guest bedroom she'd been occupying.

"What is it?" Jillian asked.

Sassy opened the door. There, hanging on the closet door, was a duplicate of the beautiful wedding gown that Sassy had chosen, right down to the embroidery.

"They only had two of that model. The other was in a store in Los Angeles. I had them overnight it," Sassy chuckled. "Nothing is going to stop this wedding!"

Jillian burst into tears. She hugged Sassy, as close as her wounded arm would permit. "Thank you!"

"It's little enough to do. I'm sorry the other one was ruined. We're just lucky that there was a second one in your size."

Jillian fingered the exquisite lace. "It is the most beautiful gown I'd ever seen. I'll never be able to thank you enough, Sassy."

The other woman was solemn. "We don't talk about it, but I'm sure you know that I had a similar experience, with my former boss at the feed store where I worked just before I married John. It wasn't quite as traumatic as yours, but I know how it feels to be assaulted." She sighed. "Funny thing, I had no idea when you came running up to the door with Harris a step behind you that I'd ever face the same situation in my own life."

"I'm sorry."

"Yes, so am I. There are bad men in the world. But there are good ones, too," Sassy reminded her. "I'm married to one of them, and you're about to marry another one."

"If Davy doesn't find some horrible new way to stop it," Jillian said with real concern in her voice.

"He won't," Sassy said firmly. "There are too many people in uniforms running around here for him to take that sort of a chance."

She bit her lower lip. "Ted was going to see about

Sammy. I don't know if Harris might try to hurt her, to get back at me."

"He won't have the chance," Sassy said. "John and two of our hands took a cattle trailer over to your house a few minutes before I left to pick you up at the hospital. They're bringing her over here, and she'll stay in our barn. We have a man full-time who does nothing but look after our prize bulls who live in it."

"You've done so much for me," Jillian said, fighting tears.

"You'd do it for me," was the other woman's warm reply. "Now stop worrying. You have two days to get well enough to walk down the aisle."

"Maybe we should postpone it," she began.

"Not a chance," Sassy replied. "We'll have you back on your feet by then if we have to fly in specialists!" And she meant it.

CHAPTER ELEVEN

Jillian carried a small bouquet of white and pale pink roses as she walked down the aisle of the small country church toward Ted, who was waiting at the altar. Her arm was sore and throbbing a little, and she was still worried about whether or not Davy Harris might try to shoot one of them through the window. But none of her concerns showed in her radiant expression as she took her place beside Ted.

The minister read the marriage ceremony. Jillian repeated the words. Ted repeated them. He slid a plain gold band onto her finger. She slid one onto his. They looked at each other with wonder and finally shared a kiss so tender that she knew she'd remember it all her life.

They held hands walking back down the aisle, laughing, as they were showered with rose petals by two little girls who were the daughters of one of Ted's police officers.

"Okay, now, stand right here while we get the photos," Sassy said, stage-managing them in the reception hall where food and punch were spread out on pristine white linen tablecloths with crystal and china to contain the feast. She'd hired a professional photographer to record the event, over Jillian's protests, as part of the Callisters' wedding gift to them.

Jillian felt regal in her beautiful gown. The night before, she'd gone out to the barn with Ted to make sure little Sammy was settled in a stall. It was silly to be worried about an animal, but she'd been a big part of Jillian's life since she was first born, to a cow that was killed by a freak lightning strike the next day. Jillian had taken the tiny calf to the house and kept her on old blankets on the back porch and fed her around the clock to keep her alive.

That closeness had amused Ted, especially since the calf followed Jillian everywhere she went and even, on occasion, tried to go in the house with her. He supposed he was lucky that they didn't make calf diapers, he'd teased, or Jillian would give the animal a bedroom.

"Did anybody check to see if I left my jacket down that trail where I took Sammy for her walks?" Jillian asked suddenly. "The buckskin one, with the embroidery. It hasn't rained, but if it does, it will be soaked. I forgot all about it when I came to stay with Sassy."

"I'll look for it later," Ted told her, nuzzling her nose with his. "When we go home."

"Home." She sighed and closed her eyes. "I forgot. We'll live together now."

"Yes, we will." He touched her face. "Maybe not as closely as I'd like for a few more days," he teased deeply and chuckled when she flushed. "That arm is going to take some healing."

"I never realized that a flesh wound could cause so much trouble," she told him.

"At least it was just a flesh wound," he said grimly. "Damned if I can figure out why we can't find that polecat," he muttered, borrowing Rourke's favorite term. "We've had men scouring the countryside for him."

"Maybe he got scared and left town," she said hopefully.

"We found his truck deserted, about halfway between the Callisters' ranch and ours," he said. "Dogs lost his trail when it went off the road." He frowned. "One of our trackers said that his footprints changed from one side of the truck to the other, as if he was carrying something."

"Maybe a suitcase?" she wondered.

He shook his head. "We checked the bus station and we had the sheriff's department send cars all over the back roads. He just vanished into thin air."

"I'm not sorry," she said heavily. "But I'd like to know that he wasn't coming back."

"So would I." He bent and kissed her. "We'll manage," he added. "Whatever happens, we'll manage."

She smiled up at him warmly. "Yes. We will."

THEY SETTLED DOWN into married life. Ted had honestly hoped to wait a day or so until her arm was a little less sore.

But that night while they were watching a movie on television, he kissed her and she kissed him back. Then they got into a more comfortable position on the sofa. Very soon, pieces of clothing came off and were discarded on the floor. And then, skin against skin, they learned each other in ways they never had before.

Just for a minute, it was uncomfortable. He felt her stiffen and his mouth brushed tenderly over her closed eyelids. "Easy," he whispered. "Try to relax. Move with me. Move with me, sweetheart...yes!"

And then it was all heat and urgency and explosions of sensation like nothing she'd ever felt in her life. She dug her nails into his hips and moaned harshly as the hard, fierce thrust of his body lifted her to elevations of pleasure that built on each other until she was afraid that she might die trying to survive them.

"Yes," he groaned, and he bruised her thighs with his fingers as he strained to get even closer to her when the pleasure burst and shuddered into ecstacy.

She cried out. Her whole body felt on fire. She moved with him, her own hips arching up in one last surge of strength before the world dissolved into sweet madness.

She was throbbing all over, like her sore arm that she hadn't even noticed until now. She shivered under the weight of Ted's body.

"I was going to wait," he managed in a husky whisper.

"What in the world for?" she laughed. "It's just a sore arm." Her eyes met his with shy delight.

He lifted an eyebrow rakishly. "Is anything else sore?" he asked.

She grinned. "No."

He pursed his lips. "Well, in that case," he whispered, and began to move.

She clutched at him and gasped with pure delight.

He only laughed.

MUCH LATER, THEY curled up together in bed, exhausted and happy. They slept until late the next morning, missing church and a telephone call from the sheriff, Larry Kane.

"Better call me as soon as you get this," Larry said grimly on the message. "It's urgent."

Ted exchanged a concerned glance with Jillian as he picked up his cell phone and returned the call.

"Graves," he said into the phone. "What's up?"

There was a pause while he listened. He scowled. "What?" he exclaimed.

"What is it?" Jillian was mouthing at him.

He held up a hand and sighed heavily. "How long ago?"

He nodded. "Well, it's a pity, in a way. But it's ironic, you have to admit. Yes. Yes. I'll tell her. Thanks, Larry."

He snapped the phone shut. "They found Davy Harris this morning."

"Where is he?" she asked, gnawing her lip.

"They've taken him to the state crime lab."

She blinked. "I thought they only took dead people... Oh, dear. He's dead?"

He nodded. "They found him with his leg caught in a bear trap. He'd apparently been trying to set it on the ranch, down that trail where you always walk with Sammy, through the trees where it's hard to see the ground."

"Good Lord!" she exclaimed, and the possibilities created nightmares in her mind.

"He'd locked the trap into place with a log chain, around a tree, and padlocked it in place. Sheriff thinks he lost the key somewhere. He couldn't get the chain loose or free himself from the trap. He bled to death."

She felt sick all over. She pressed into Ted's arms and held on tight. "What a horrible way to go."

"Yes, well, just remember that it was how he planned for Sammy to go," he said, without mentioning that Harris may well have planned to catch Jillian in it.

"His sister will sue us all for wrongful death and say we killed him," Jillian said miserably, remembering the woman's fury when her brother was first arrested.

"His sister died two years ago," he replied. "Of a drug overdose. A truly troubled family."

"When did you find that out?" she wondered.

"Yesterday," he said. "I didn't want to spend our wedding day talking about Harris, but I did wonder if he might run to his sister for protection. So I had an investigator try to find her."

"A sad end," she said.

"Yes. But fortunately, not yours," he replied. He held her close, glad that it was over, finally.

She sighed. "Not mine," she agreed.

Rourke left three days later to go back to Africa. He'd meant to leave sooner, but Sassy and John wanted to show him around Montana first, despite the thick snow that was falling in abundance now.

"I've taken movies of the snow to show back home," he mentioned as he said his farewells to Jillian and Ted while a ranch hand waited in the truck to drive him to the airport in Billings. "We don't get a lot of snow in Kenya," he added, tongue-in-cheek.

"Thanks for helping keep me alive," Jillian told him.

"My pleasure," he replied, and smiled.

Ted shook hands with him. "If you want to learn how to fish for trout, come back in the spring when the snows melt and we'll spend the day on the river."

"I might take you up on that," Rourke said.

They watched him drive away.

Jillian slid her arm around Ted's waist. "You coming home for lunch?" she asked as they walked to his patrol car.

"Thought I might." He gave her a wicked grin. "You going to fix food or are we going to spend my lunch hour in the usual way?"

She pursed her lips. "Oh, I could make sandwiches."

"You could pack them in a plastic bag," he added, "and I could take them back to work with me."

She flushed and laughed. "Of course. We wouldn't want to waste your lunch hour by eating."

He bent and kissed her with barely restrained hunger. "Absolutely not! See you about noon."

She kissed him back. "I'll be here."

He drove off, throwing up a hand as he went down the driveway. She watched him go and thought how far she'd come from the scared teenager that Davy Harris had intimidated so many years before. She had a good marriage and her life was happier than ever before. She still had her morning job at the local restaurant. She liked the little bit of independence it gave her, and they could use the extra money. Ted wasn't likely to get rich working as a police chief.

On the other hand, their lack of material wealth only brought them closer together and made their shared lives better.

She sighed as she turned back toward the house, her eyes full of dreams. Snow was just beginning to fall again, like a burst of glorious white feathers around her head. Winter was beautiful. Like her life.

* * * * *